Isaac A. Bingham

 VOLUME 36

If found unattended,
please return
to Pottery Niederbipp

Discovering Isaac
The Beloved Potter of Niederbipp

First printing, November 2009

Published by
Abendmahl Press
P.O. Box 581083
Salt Lake City, Utah 84158-1083

ISBN -978-0-615-33313-7

Artwork by Ben Behunin and of historical origins
Photography of pottery sequence by Al Thelin
Designed by Ben Behunin and Bert Compton
Layout by Bert Compton- Compton Design Studio
All scriptural references are from the King James
Translation of the Bible.

DISCOVERING ISAAC

THE BELOVED POTTER OF NIEDERBIPP

VOLUME TWO IN A SERIES
BY
BEN BEHUNIN

REMEMBER, DISCOVER BECOME

TO LYNNETTE-
FOR LOVING ME
AND
BELIEVING
IN
NIEDERBIPP.

But now,
oh Lord,
thou art our
FATHER,
we are the clay,
and thou our
POTTER
and we are all
the work of thy
HANDS.

ISAIAH 64:8

DISCLAIMER

YOU MAY THINK YOU KNOW THE PEOPLE IN THIS BOOK, BUT UNLESS YOU'VE BEEN TO NIEDERBIPP, ANY SIMILARITIES TO THE PEOPLE YOU KNOW ARE MERELY COINCIDENTAL.

P:RELUDE

I never set out to become a writer. I am a potter. For the past thirteen years I have made my living exclusively as a slinger of slime, a maker of mud pies. But I've learned that life rarely happens exactly as we plan.

I began my work with clay at age fourteen as part of a high school art requirement, thinking it would be an easy "A." I was awful. I nearly failed, trying to keep myself from getting dirty. I made a lot of dog bowls that first year, but clay has a way of getting under your fingernails and absorbing into your skin. By the time I graduated from high school, I was dreaming of my future as a potter.

After a few years of studying pottery and business in college and an apprenticeship in Germany, I decided it was time to put my dreaming aside and get to work. Many who were closest to me tried to dissuade me, but I was stubborn and passionate. Those things propelled me forward onto my chosen path.

The universe has a way of opening doorways and windows to those who follow their passions. Thirteen years later, I often find myself asking how I got here. When I look back on those years, I realize my path has been cut by an unseen hand, leading me in ways I did not design. There have been many times when I wanted so badly to see the big picture that I have lost sight of the present. Most of the time, however, I have chosen to walk by faith, and my life has been blessed because of it.

Eleven years ago, I began receiving visits from Isaac. He came to me as I sat at my wheel and whispered these things in my ear as I worked. I began to write them down at night. The lessons were beautiful. They often left me weak and emotional, but always desiring to become a better man, a better husband, a better father. I knew I needed to share them. I knew the people of Niederbipp had things to share that our world needs desperately.

And so, I began. I wrote when I could. Sometimes it came quickly. Sometimes I didn't write for months at a time; pulled away by doubt and fear and the need to provide for my growing family.

But things changed as they always do. Over five years ago, I was diagnosed with arthritis in my hands, of all places—not a great place for a potter to be afflicted. For many years, I fought against it, praying to be healed and seeking out answers from all kinds of sources. Instead of getting better, it got worse. And through it all, Isaac continued to visit me, telling me his stories and bringing others to tell theirs.

This book, the one before it and the one that will follow are the stories the people of Niederbipp told me as I sat at my wheel and turned mud into vessels. In part, it is my story. A story of remembering. A story of discovering. A story of becoming. But this story is much more than me, or you, or any one person. As I have read this book and the one that preceded it, I am humbled with the realization that these are not my words, but have come from a source exponentially wiser than I.

I never planned to write a book, let alone two. I have learned life is never as you expect it will be, but if we will listen, it can be infinitely better.

Ben Behunin
Christmas 2009

TABLE OF CONTENTS

① A NEW DAY

THERE IS NO REMEDY FOR LOVE
BUT TO LOVE MORE.
—HENRY DAVID THOREAU

The magic of a kiss can change the whole world. Jake Kimball, the newest potter of Niederbipp, experienced his first kiss at the age of twenty-two. Jake was shy, a late bloomer, and a self-proclaimed social imbecile. Any outsider looking into the budding relationship between him and Amy might have thought the kiss was a long time coming. Maybe too long. Inexperienced in matters of the heart, Jake had been slow to move. He didn't want to do anything stupid, or that he would later regret. The town of Niederbipp was already keeping him humble and honest. People were watching him and he didn't want to give the townsfolk anything more to talk about.

Jake lay in bed Sunday morning, relishing a quiet moment after weeks of hard work and excitement. Good weeks, he reflected. The Mayor had offered Jake a ticket to anywhere in the world if he would change

11

his plans and give Niederbipp a chance through the end of the summer. Jake's first weeks in Niederbipp were lonely and discouraging—much less than what he had envisioned the life of a village potter would be. Some days he wished he had taken the bus back to New York and flown to Greece. But things were different now. Things were somehow.... better.

As he mused over all that had changed in his life, Jake's thoughts returned continually to Amy. She had awakened something within him that he didn't even know was there. The time they had spent together was invigorating, wonderful, amazing. He had been in love before, but both times it had ended badly. As a result, he had sworn off love and girls in general, hoping to spare himself any further pain. And yet, here he was again, knocking on the door of love and asking to be let in.

If a kiss can change one's world, then falling in love—really falling in love—can change the entire universe. And Jake had fallen hard. Love was the furthest thing from his mind when he arrived just a month before. The world that had seemed so big, waiting for him to explore, suddenly seemed smaller, brighter, and gentler. Even the dumpy little shop was becoming more tolerable. It was still too small, but now that it was organized, there was a charm to it that he could not deny. Neiderbipp was beginning to feel more like home. The insatiable wanderlust that in previous summers had sent him on adventures around the world was being tamed by the seed of pure joy taking root in his heart.

The church bells began their Sabbath morning peal and Jake rose from his bed, anxious to see Amy. He quickly showered, shaved and made his way to the church yard.

The church was filling quickly when he arrived. He broke through the bottleneck at the front door and made his way into the bright chapel. Amy and Aunt Bev were already on the front row, their backs toward him and their heads together in a furtive whispered conversation. He looked around for Jerry, Amy's uncle, and found him on the third row far against the wall, working on a crossword puzzle that he had inserted into the middle of a hymnal. Jake sat down quietly on the row behind Amy and Bev, wondering if they would notice him. Their quiet conversation seemed to consume them and by the time the organ music started and Father Thomas had taken his place at the pulpit to begin the worship services, they were still oblivious to Jake sitting behind them.

When the congregation stood to sing the opening hymn, Jake sang as loud as he could, hoping Amy would turn around and see him. But it was as if Amy and Aunt Bev were alone in the world and Jake began to worry he was being ignored.

After the hymn and invocation, Thomas announced that the Symbology and History Tour of the church that he normally led on Memorial Day Weekend would have to be postponed until the following Sunday because of the expected storm that afternoon. The word "symbols" pulled Jake's attention away from Amy and he looked up at Thomas who winked at him before welcoming Susan Rosenthal to the pulpit. Thomas thanked her for accepting the invitation to present the sermon. After mentioning that she would be spending the summer in Niederbipp, he expressed hope that with her extensive teaching experience, she "would be willing to enlighten us frequently  with her knowledge and understanding of the world and the place of religion in it." Thomas then turned the pulpit over to her without any further introduction or fanfare, as if everyone knew who she was.

Susan stood at the pulpit, opening her books. She was a smart looking woman with red plastic rim glasses that glowed magically in the light of the morning. Her short, jet black hair was gelled to stand up in subtle tufts. She was dressed in a black pleated skirt and a white collared blouse that was pressed and neat. Jake guessed she was in her mid-thirties.

"Good Morning" she said, looking up from her books with a kind and disarming smile. "Today, I would like to talk about the parable of the ten virgins as outlined in the 25th chapter of Matthew."

Jake watched as many of the people in the congregation fumbled with their Bibles and he cursed himself for once again forgetting to bring the Bible from his apartment.

Susan looked up from her notes and books when the rustling of pages had quieted. "I have asked a virtuous woman to help me today with some of my visual aids." She reached out her hand and pointed to Amy. "She will also provide a shield for me to hide behind."

Her words met with several snickers from the congregation.

"I'm used to teaching and presenting to large groups, but teaching things of a spiritual nature is somehow much more difficult for me. Teaching things that the Lord himself taught is even more daunting."

She read the first four verses of Matthew 25 before looking up again. Reaching out to Amy, she smiled, "I would like to invite my lovely assistant, Amy, to come forward."

Amy walked toward Susan who handed her a small ceramic vase, a vessel with a stopper on the top. Amy took this in her right hand and with her left, cradled another object, handed to her by Susan—a small orange something that looked like a scone. Amy turned around and faced the congregation, holding out the strange objects in her hands.

"I would like each of you to handle these items, but I know from sad experience that pottery is quite fragile and so I have asked Amy to walk down the center aisle and give you all an opportunity to look at them."

Amy moved forward slowly, looking quite embarrassed. As she approached the bench where Jake was sitting, he smiled at her. When she saw him, she turned a dark shade of red and smiled back, looking confused. She continued to walk and display her objects like a hostess on a home shopping network channel.

"These items were a gift from one of my students," Susan continued.

"You'll notice that the orange, earthenware lamp in Amy's hand is quite small. I think when I first heard this story several years ago, I imagined in my mind something big and ornate, like a genie lamp. But as my student told me, the lamps used at the time of Christ were much like the one Amy is holding: small, simple, and handmade of native clay.

"Most of us have probably heard this story before, but I'd like to share with you some of my own insights that I hope might be useful to all of us. I'm quite sure there are as many ways to interpret this story as there are people, but these are some of my thoughts. Perhaps I should read the rest of the verses and then go back to some of these ideas."

She read through verse thirteen, giving Amy time to walk to the door and back, allowing all who cared an opportunity to look at the items. Amy returned the items to Susan and quickly ducked into her seat, obviously uncomfortable. She smiled again at Jake as she sat down.

"How long have you been there?" she whispered.

Beverly turned to smile at Jake.

"I'll talk to you later," he said under his breath, and the two women turned back to Susan.

"It has been said that the Bridegroom in this story represents Christ," she began again. "As we learn in the twelfth and thirteenth verses, we will never know the day or the hour when Christ will come again, but we are told to watch and to be ready for the time of His return.

"As I have thought about this parable over the last few years, I think I've learned some important lessons. First of all, I don't know about you, but I think I've had occasion to be both a wise and a foolish person at different times in my life. I'm not ready to meet my maker today, but I feel like I'm in a much better place now than I have been over the years. It's quite humbling to stand before you today and talk about these things—you who know my past, you who have been there to help me over the bumps and potholes I have met along my path in life. Perhaps you too have been in a place when your oil has run dry, when your faith has waned or your life seems to be traveling down a rocky road."

Jake smiled. He liked the humility of this woman. She seemed real to him.

"I'm afraid that there were times in my life when the faith I discovered in my youth seemed to evaporate into thin air, when not only the oil in my lamp failed, but also the oil in my vessel. There was a time when I tried to fill my lamp and my vessel with something else… the philosophies of men. When I first left Niederbipp for the university, I'm afraid I turned far away from the things I knew, believing I was trading my naiveté for sophistication, experience and a higher level of understanding.

"A few years ago, I came back to where my lamp and my vessel had been filled with my faith-oil and realized that the substance I had substituted in my vessel was a weak counterfeit. It looked a bit like oil, but to my surprise, it was only water, completely incapable of producing a flame or a light of any kind.

"Unfortunately, at first I thought I had just grown too big for my britches, that this town and its people were too ignorant to understand me. For the most part, I kept my mouth shut and believed it was just because you were all unaware of the world beyond the river and the hills. I think I may have gone on believing this for some time if it had not been for the love and understanding of one of you, a humble man who taught me with kindness the differences between oil and water.

"It's not an easy thing to realize you're a foolish virgin, especially after you've spent the better part of a decade gaining the best education money can buy. It's difficult to realize that your life is void of the things that matter most, filled instead with an imitation. Pride is a difficult thing to swallow; and it's even more difficult to digest! But once it's gone and you can see clearly, the world is a much better place. I'm afraid that in my efforts to open my mind to the wisdom of the world, I closed my mind to the eternal truths of God and denied myself the resuscitative influence of His love and truth…His oil.

"The thirteen short verses of this parable have spawned dozens of pictures in my head over the last few years. In my efforts to understand the Bible, I often try to apply or translate these ideas into events in my own life. This parable has been easy for me to apply because of my assignment as an advisor for the Alpha Phi sorority on campus."

Jake smiled to himself as he imagined Greek Row, the neighborhood filled with sorority and fraternity houses not far from campus in Albany.

"As you all know, things have changed a bit in the past two thousand years. Few of us would even know what to do with a lamp like the one Amy displayed. During my second year of teaching, we had a scare on campus when a female student was attacked while walking home from class one night after dark. Many of the sororities responded by issuing their girls large, heavy flashlights like this one."

She held up a long black flashlight for the congregation to see. "When fully loaded with batteries, this flashlight weighs about six pounds. Its bulb boasts 25,000 candle power. The thought was that such a bright light would dissuade any would-be attacker, but if it didn't, the flashlight could also be used for self protection. A flashlight like this could leave quite a goose egg." She smiled when the congregation giggled a little.

"When I became the advisor for the Alpha Phi house, I noticed most of the girls kept their flashlights on a shelf above the coat racks near the back door. Even though I encouraged their use, only a few of the girls regularly used the flashlights, most complaining that they were too big and heavy to fit into purses.

"Now, if you will permit me a few creative liberties, I would like to explain what I have learned from this parable. I invite you to imagine with me a tired looking mailman, knocking on the sorority house door early one evening, apologizing that the letter he holds in his hand was lost in his jeep for a couple of weeks. The letter, it turns out, is a wedding invitation. Ten beautiful girls have been invited to attend the wedding party. All of the most eligible bachelors from campus will be in attendance. The hitch is, because the mailman lost the invitation, there is no time to prepare. In order to arrive on time, they have to leave immediately.

"Because it is nearly dark and the road to the reception hall leads through a shady part of town, all of the girls grab their flashlights before setting off. Not long into their walk, they are all happy they brought their flashlights, as the light fades to a starless night that is dark and shadowy.

"I have imagined five of these young ladies pressing forward a little faster than the rest, eager to reach the party on time. The other five fall behind, perhaps believing the party really won't get going before they get there. But soon after losing sight of their more punctual companions, the batteries in their flashlights begin to fail. One fades out, then another and before long, they find themselves in total darkness. This is definitely not part of the agenda. Anxious to be on their way, they retrace their steps until they come to a convenience store. The store is ill-equipped to handle all their needs. Only one package of six batteries is available. While they take turns preening themselves in the bathroom, the helpful clerk teaches them how to cheat the flashlights by removing one dead battery from each flashlight and replacing it with a new one. The light each produces is not as bright as it once was, but bright enough for the girls to continue on their journey.

"The lights work for a while, but long before the ladies reach their destination, the batteries have failed again. They try a variety of combinations, finally removing the newer batteries and putting them all into one flashlight. This too works for a while, but eventually fails. There is simply not enough power. They take turns leading the way, stumbling along the path with the dim light of their cell phones. But when even the last of these lights goes out, they are left groping for the path in total darkness.

"In my mind's eye, I can imagine these ladies reaching the party hours after it started—dirty, tired, scraped and bruised. They pound wildly at the doors, begging to be let in. I can imagine the bridegroom looking out on these ladies and not being able to recognize them. He suspects them of being party crashers and turns them away into the dark of the night.

"My friends of Niederbipp, I don't know about you, but I love a happy ending. This ending was only happy for fifty percent of the participants—not very good odds if you ask me."

The congregation laughed softly together.

Susan shook her head before continuing. "I don't believe in a God who would be satisfied if only half of his children succeeded. Therefore, I have to believe that this parable is less about numbers than it is about substance…the stuff we carry with us. A wise friend once told me that there is a light within us all: a gift from the God who gave us life. I believe we all know people whose light burns brighter than all the rest. Perhaps we have also known some whose light seems to have been snuffed out. I humbly stand before you today as one who had to depend on borrowed light until I could rekindle my own.  Despite my years of learning and all my degrees, I believe I am just beginning to understand what that oil is…what those batteries contain to make the light burn bright."

She scratched her chin and removed her glasses before looking back to the congregation. "To be honest, I feel I've been preaching to the choir. As I stand before you, looking out on the collective light burning bright within you, my mouth begins to water. I am hungry to learn from you, to learn what you know. Within the light of your eyes, I see truth. I see love. I see faith and understanding. It makes me want to embrace you, to rub elbows and shoulders with you, hoping some of that light will rub off on me.

"Coming home is always a bittersweet experience for me. I spent ten years of my life obtaining my education. But when I am here, I see how much my pursuit of learning has gotten in the way of my education of the things that are most important. We all do foolish things. Some of us, like myself, tend to do foolish things for multiple years in a row. But the beauty is, we can change. We can repent, begin again, and move forward with hope and new understanding.

God has invited all of us to the wedding—the wise and the foolish alike—and we can honor his invitation best by accepting his oil: the wisdom, the truth and the love he so freely offers us. I have learned that His well is always full, but we must decide if we will drink, if we will fill our lamps and our vessels with the goodness He offers us. In recent years I have recognized that our world is filled with counterfeits that offer some semblance of truth, but in reality, lead many of us down dark and crooked paths. The light of God's love beckons us all to return. There is hope in the light of His love. There is safety. There is peace. The oil He offers us will burn bright, giving light to our path until the perfect day."

She took a deep breath, tilting her head way back as if examining the ceiling. After a long moment of silence, she focused again on the congregation. "I want to thank you all for your patience, not only today, but for the majority of my life. I'm afraid I'm quite scattered. I keep looking down the aisle to the back row where an old friend used to sit and I'm sad to see his seat empty."

Jake looked up into Susan's eyes and saw that she was about to cry.

"In my heart," she said, putting her fist to her chest, "I know what I'm trying to say is true. It was told to me in a much more eloquent way than I have just explained it, by a simple potter with a heart bigger than his chest. My one wish in sharing this lesson with you today was that I might share some of that love with you."

She pursed her lips and nodded. Then, obviously holding back emotion, she began folding up her books. Father Thomas came forward to thank Susan for her heartfelt lesson and announce the closing hymn.

Jake noticed many in the congregation wiping their eyes. He wondered if they were emotional about the words they had just heard or because of their own memories of the old potter. Either way, Susan's words were powerful and thought provoking.

Following the hymn and benediction, the congregation left the chapel more slowly than usual, hampered in part by those surging forward to speak to Susan. Jake stood, but finding himself penned in by people, stayed where he was and listened as the crowd thanked Susan for her words. Many mentioned Isaac's name and pointed to Jake. He smiled at Susan when their eyes met, offering a little nod. Gloria and Joseph took a place in line. Gloria smiled and waved. Jake grinned at her before turning his attention to Amy.

"It seems everywhere we go, we hear something about Isaac."

Jake nodded. He knew it was still new for Amy, but he had been hearing about Isaac since he'd arrived in Niederbipp.

"It might be interesting to talk to her, don't you think?" she asked, turning to look at Susan interacting with her friends.

"What do you know about her?" Jake asked.

"Next to nothing. I just got conned into making a fool of myself by showing everyone her stuff."

Jake smiled. "You did a great job. I was thinking, if you're up for it, maybe you could walk up and down Hauptstrasse carrying my wares and sending people to the shop."

She laughed. "How much do you pay?"

"I'll match whatever you're getting now."

She smiled, shaking her head. "Forget it! I'm an artist, not a billboard."

Beverly returned to the pew to retrieve her purse and Bible. "Hello Jake!" she said.

"Hello," he said back, unsure of how he should address her.

"I hope you're still planning on dinner with us this evening."

"Sure," he said. "Thanks for the invitation. I've been looking forward to it."

"So has Amy," Bev said without hesitation. She winked at her niece.

Jake tried to subdue a laugh as Amy reached across the bench to take his hand. It was the first time she had displayed affection toward Jake in front of her aunt. He caught his breath, surprised by the swell of emotion the simple gesture set loose inside of him. Holding her hand in his, he turned to the aisle to see a dark-haired fellow approaching.

21

Jake had seen this guy before, but he couldn't remember where. Amy squeezed his hand tighter as the boy walked past Jake, rounding the corner to approach her. Amy squeezed Jake's hand twice until he met her gaze. He couldn't read whatever it was she was trying to communicate with him, but she held onto his hand even tighter.

"Hello, Amy." The guy had moved through the crowd at the front of the chapel and squeezed in between Amy and her aunt.

Amy moved her eyes to meet the man's gaze, but her face stayed focused on Jake. "Hello." Just one word, cool and sharp, certainly distant if not unfriendly.

The man didn't seem to notice her tone before continuing. "Hey, I was just thinking that it would be fun to hang out tonight. My buddies and I were going to go to the drive-in up in Warren. Do you think you'd like to come?"

She remained rigid and aloof, her knuckles turning white as she continued to squeeze Jake's hand. "It's Matt, isn't it?"

"No... Michael."

"Oh yes, Michael. Well, I'm sorry but I have to decline your invitation. I'm busy this evening."

Amy squeezed Jake's hand again, turning back to wink at him.

Jake looked closer at the man, recognizing him as the snooty clerk from the housewares store where he had purchased the peeler on the first day he had gone looking for Amy.

"Well, what about next week sometime?" Michael asked.

Amy smiled softly at Jake, shaking her head before turning back to Michael. "I'm sorry. I think I'm going to be busy for the rest of the summer."

Michael looked down at Amy's hand, as if noticing for the first time that Jake held it in his own hand. He grimaced and nodded before falling back into the crowd. Jake struggled to wipe the smirk off his face— the most beautiful girl in town had just proclaimed herself his for the summer!

"Wow, Amy... really!...the whole summer?" It was Aunt Bev. She moved to the space just vacated by Michael and looked at her niece with wide eyes.

Amy looked away from Jake. "Yeah. I came here to paint and after Tuesday, I plan to spend my time doing just that. If there's any time left over, I hope to spend it with Jake."

Jake smiled broadly as he turned from Amy to Aunt Bev.

Beverly raised her right hand to her mouth, placing her left hand on Jake's shoulder. "Oh, I hoped something would work out for you two. I've always considered myself a bit of a matchmaker. I guess I still have what it takes to know when two people are suited for each other."

Amy smiled again at Jake, rolling her eyes playfully and loosening her grip on his hand.

"Excuse me, Beverly, Amy." It was Gloria with Susan in tow. "Susan asked me to make some introductions. This is Jake," said Gloria warmly. "And I guess you already met his friend, Amy."

Susan smiled at both of them as she took Jake's hand in hers. Her hand was warm and firm and as Jake looked into her eyes, he noticed they were a brilliant, emerald green.

"Well," she said turning to Amy. "Your aunt told me you were seeing someone, but she didn't mention how handsome he was."

Jake immediately felt his face blush. He glanced up at Gloria and Joseph behind her, who were beaming as if they were his own proud parents.

"I understand you've taken over the pottery shop," said Susan, still holding Jake's hand.

He nodded, at a loss for words.

She looked at him intensely for a moment before a warm smile spread across her lips. She knelt on the pew that stood between them and pulled him closer to her, wrapping her arms around him.

Jake looked at Beverly who was nodding slightly as she watched the embrace. Amy had a surprised look on her face. Jake scanned the rest of the crowd, looking for a clue as to how he should respond. His eyes fell on Gloria and Joseph who were smiling with teary eyes.

"I'm sorry to be so forward," Susan said, pulling back from Jake, but resting her hands on his upper arms. She started laughing, but tears were falling from her eyes. "I don't usually hug strangers. I promise I'm not crazy, just missing a very dear friend. Not seeing Isaac on the back row today was more traumatic than I expected." She removed her glasses and wiped her eyes. "I was in the middle of mid-terms and couldn't get away for his funeral. I know you're not him, but...." She shook her head. "Would you mind if I came and visited you sometime? I just need to sit in the Pottery and smell the scent of clay."

The crowd around Susan had fallen silent and Jake was suddenly aware of a hundred eyes on him. He felt his face grow hot again as he wondered how to respond.

"It's ok," he finally uttered, speaking softly to Susan, but saying it loud enough for everyone who stood nearby to hear. "I know the Pottery is more yours than it is mine." He raised his head, looking out at the crowd. "I want you all to feel welcome at the Pottery. From all I've learned, it's as much a part of Niederbipp as this church." He looked back at Susan. "I'm out of tea right now, but if you give me a couple of days, I might be able to have some for you when you come."

"Are you trying to duplicate Isaac's tea?" asked Beverly with a devious grin.

"I'm trying. I have to do something to keep the customers coming." He looked at Amy and winked.

Beverly shook her head. "Good luck with that," she said, sounding sarcastic. "I've tried it a dozen times myself. I even planted a whole garden full of peppermint, but it never tastes quite the same as Isaac's. Those of us who knew him best and had regular occasion to stop by for a cup of tea believe he must have a secret ingredient."

Jake smiled to himself, recalling their discovery of the secret ingredient just a few days before. A part of him wanted to announce that he already knew what that secret ingredient was, but before he declared victory, he had to make some tea and see if he was right...

"Isaac told me it was just because it comes from the plants of a hundred different gardens," offered a woman who Jake had never met before.

"Oh, Lucy, you've always been gullible," retorted another woman.

"And how do you know. Did you ever try it yourself?" said the woman now known as Lucy.

"As a matter of fact, I did. It took me the better part of a week but I gathered peppermint from a hundred different gardens and it didn't taste any better than the stuff I made from my own garden. Bev's right. There has to be a secret ingredient. I just wish I had access to that sketchbook Isaac carried around with him all the time. He must have written his secret down somewhere."

Jake tried to hide his look of surprise from the others. He wondered if Isaac's sketchbook really did hold such secrets. The woman's words piqued his curiosity.

"I need to run some taste tests," he said, "but I think I should have something for you all to sample by the end of the week."

Susan pursed her lips, smiling thinly. "I'm sorry to cry all over you," she said again.

Jake nodded, looking down at her still kneeling on the pew in front of him. "It's ok. I'm starting to get used to it," he said softly, stealing a glance at Gloria. "You're welcome at the Pottery anytime."

"Does this mean you're staying in Niederbipp?" a male voice came from the back of the crowd, from beyond where Jake could see.

"Only for the summer. I'll be leaving after Labor Day to get back to the university," said Susan.

"I was asking about the potter," said the same male voice.

Jake looked pointedly at Amy. "I'll be here until at least the end of summer."

"And then what?"

Jake was flustered. He couldn't see the heckler who was asking questions he didn't have answers to. But the crowd seemed anxious to hear the answer, as if this was their question.

Jake looked at Amy again who raised her eyebrows. The wordless action seemed flirty, but also challenging, making him smile despite his awkward situation. "I haven't made up my mind yet. I will tell you, though, that I won't leave until I've finished Sam's floor and Isaac's bench."

His response seemed to satisfy the answer-hungry crowd whose chatter began again. The heckler, whoever he was, asked no more questions.

ONE STONE

THE ONLY GIFT IS A PORTION OF THYSELF.

—RALPH WALDO EMERSON

h Jake, I'm glad I caught you." It was Thomas.

Jake and Amy were standing on the church's front terrace, looking out on the congregants milling about in the courtyard. Amy was holding the hem of her dress to keep it from blowing wildly in the wind. A storm was rolling in quickly, clouds racing across the graying sky.

Thomas retreated momentarily back into the church, reemerging with an older man dressed in a pea green, three piece suit. He was stooped over and freckles dotted the top of his head. "Mr. Allan, here, asked me to point you out and take care of introductions. Jake Kimball, meet Mr. William Allan." Thomas nodded to Amy. "I think you already know Mr. Allan, don't you Amy?"

Amy nodded, pulling her windswept hair away from her face as Jake extended his hand to the older man. Mr. Allan looked up into Jake's eyes, awkwardly pumping his hand as if he was trying to catch his balance.

"Hello there, young man. And hello to you too, Miss Amy," he said, finally dropping Jake's hand to take hers.

"Hello, Mr. Allen," she said with a gentle smile.

He turned his attention back to Jake. "I've wanted to come see you for a couple of weeks now, but I don't make it into town as often as I used to. It seems like Sundays are the only days I can count on for sure."

Jake nodded, glancing quickly up at Thomas who winked at him.

"I wanted to give you something." Mr. Allan fumbled in his pocket for a moment before pulling out something held tightly in his hand. He reached out and extended his closed fist to Jake.

Jake opened his hand to receive whatever it was.

Mr. Allan opened his fist and dropped something warm and smooth into Jake's hand. For a long moment, the older man didn't move his hand, resting it lightly on top of Jake's, hiding whatever it was he put there.

"I wanted to share my treasure with you."

Jake studied the old man as he returned his hand to his pocket, then extended it again, this time to Amy.

Jake looked down at his own, still-open palm. It was a rock—a single black rock about the size of a walnut. He turned to look at Amy run her fingers over her own rock, a soft tan color.

Jake looked back at Mr. Allan who, with the wide eyes of a child, awaited their reactions.

Amy nudged Jake in the ribs with her elbow.

"Wow...this is really... nice," Jake said, confused, but wanting to be polite.

Mr. Allan rocked back on his heels looking quite pleased with himself. "It's one of my favorites. I've had that one for more than ten years," he said, pointing at Jake's new treasure.

"And what about mine?" asked Amy, holding her rock in her finger tips like it was a small fruit.

"I found that one last week, but it's a good one." The old man winked at her, forcing a smile to spread across her face.

"Mr. Allan likes to share his treasures," Thomas interjected. He nodded approvingly at Jake who turned to examine his rock more closely.

"Thank you," Jake uttered after an awkward silence.

"Oh, it's nothing really. If you like this treasure, I'll have to bring you another one next week."

"Wow, I don't know what to say." He looked at Amy and Thomas, hoping for a hint.

"Thank you, Mr. Allan," Amy responded.

Thomas patted the older man on the shoulder and the two of them turned back to the church doors.

Jake and Amy watched them go in silence. When they were gone, Jake started laughing. "He's not related to the Mancinis, is he?"

Amy laughed out loud before poking Jake in the ribs again. "No, he's just a cute, crazy old man. He's probably given me a dozen of his treasures over the years."

"Treasure, huh?" Jake looked closer at his new rock, rolling it around in his fingertips. It was smooth and rather pretty, as far as rocks go, but it was just a rock. "I don't get it. There has to be millions of rocks just like this one down by the river."

"Yeah, I guess it is pretty strange to go around handing out rocks."

"Yeah it is! This town has a higher percentage of strange people than most places I've been."

"Maybe people just aren't afraid of showing it here."

"What do you mean?" asked Jake.

Amy looked thoughtful. "Oh, I don't know. Doesn't it seem like people are more honest here? You've probably met more of the strange ones than I have, but I don't see a lot of folks faking it."

Jake smirked. "Go on."

"Maybe because it's such a small town, and everyone seems connected or related. They know they can't very well hide their quirks so they might as well let it all hang out."

Jake laughed again, thinking of the Mancinis.

Amy continued, "What is normal anyway? Maybe those who seem normal are just better at faking it than others. Aren't we all at least a little bit strange?"

Her words surprised Jake. They were candid and honest and rather profound. He looked again at the rock in his hand, wondering about the old man and his treasure. "What is normal, anyway?" he repeated softly to himself.

"So, what are we going to do?"

"With our rocks?" Jake asked.

"No," Amy said, laughing. "I don't have to be home to help Aunt Bev until three. Do you want some help with the tea?"

"I'd like that."

Without another word, she locked her arm through Jake's and they headed out through the crowded courtyard toward his apartment.

GATHER YE ROSEBUDS
WHILE YE MAY...
— ROBERT HERRICK —

③
THE STORM

TO LOVE AND BE LOVED IS TO FEEL THE SUN FROM BOTH SIDES.
—DAVID VISCOTT

my's ginger hair blew across Jake's face, filling him with the memory of their first afternoon together on the banks of the river. Oh, how things had changed! She saw his smile as they rounded the corner of Hinterstasse and entered the courtyard behind the Pottery.

"What are you thinking about?" she asked.

"That day down on the swing," he said without hesitation. "The scent of your hair triggered a memory, I guess."

Amy returned his smile. "That was the first day I began to wonder if swearing off guys was such a good idea."

Jake looked surprised. "And now?"

"And now I wish we hadn't wasted the whole week after that, trying to figure out what the other person was thinking."

Jake stopped under the chestnut tree in the middle of the courtyard and turned Amy around to face him. "I can't tell you how many times I've thought about that day down by the river. I think it was while I was pushing you on that swing that I really saw you for the first time. I first felt something for you."

"That was the first day for me too," she admitted.

Jake looked at her inquisitively.

"It was when you stopped to look at the rocks on the river bank."

Jake smiled a goofy smile. "What do you mean? I was just looking at rocks."

She nodded. "I think it was that you noticed them at all. Most of the guys I've dated wouldn't have even noticed all the pretty rocks. I know it's a small thing, but that's what started it all. I was probably most impressed that day by your humility."

Jake tried hard to remember, unsure of what she was talking about.

She took a deep breath. "You weren't bragging or boastful about how good you are at this or that. You even conceded that I was better at drawing than you and I felt like you were sincere when you complimented me. It probably sounds small and silly, but that really impressed me. I'm embarrassed to admit that I played it cool because I was afraid I'd be interested in you."

"Is that so bad?" he asked, raising his eyebrows.

"Yes! I didn't come here to fall in love. I came here to paint and figure my life out and, so far, I've painted five paintings and my life has taken a tangent I never would have considered."

"I'm sorry to get in your way," Jake said, feigning offense.

"That's just it," she said. "You are totally in my way and I've loved every minute of it. When we didn't see each other for a whole week after that picnic at the river, I drove myself crazy, fighting with myself about what I thought I wanted and what my heart knew I wanted. I'm really glad my heart won."

Jake looked at her for a long moment before pulling her close. She rested her chin on his shoulder as she had so many times before. "What's happening?" he asked.

"I don't know, but I hope it never stops."

The wind blew harder and the branches of the chestnut tree whipped wildly as the rain began to fall from the sky. By the time  they reached the stairs, they were both wet and laughing. The stairs were sheltered by the roof overhead and they turned to look out on the deserted cobblestone streets as the rain began to pile up in puddles in the low spots. The ping of the raindrops was peaceful, but the loud and distant sound of thunder rumbled off the surrounding hills.

Jake pointed up the hill. A soft glow of yellow light illuminated the church and the horizon as darker, grayer light encircled the rest of the town.

"It's beautiful light," he said.

"Do potters look at light like that, too?"

"Do you think only painters recognize beauty?"

"No, I've just never been with a guy who recognizes stuff like that."

"It's kind of hard to miss."

"I know, but you just seem to see it more than most. And the other night, on our bike ride, you pointed out the stars. I guess I'm just glad to have a friend who sees that kind of stuff rather than rushing through it to get to the game on TV."

Jake raised his eyebrows. "How do you know that it's just because I don't have a TV?"

She shook her head, taking a step backwards until her back rested against his chest. They stood watching the light change in the heavens as it poured down its offering on the town.

There was silence between them for several minutes as they watched and listened to the rain. Suddenly, there was a flash of light followed immediately by a crash of thunder. The racket vibrated off the walls, and reverberated through the stairs on which they stood, causing them both to jump.

"I love this!" Jake said.

She turned her head to look at him.

"My mom used to call thunderstorms 'natures fireworks.' When everyone else headed inside to get out of the weather, my mom would grab me and a couple of big umbrellas. We'd take off our shoes and walk around the neighborhood in our bare feet, listening to the rain fall on our umbrellas as we jumped in the puddles."

"I think I would have liked your mom," she said, flashing a devious smile.

"What are you thinking?"

"I was just wondering if you have an umbrella."

He smiled and turned toward the door, pulling her by the hand. Just inside the door, Jake pointed to a tall, brown vase with four umbrella handles poking above the rim like an arrangement of flowers. He turned to see Amy slipping out of her shoes. Without another word, Jake slipped off his own shoes and socks and then rolled his pants halfway up his calves. Amy handed him an umbrella and they ran out into the rain like children with wild abandon, giddy and playful.

Amy led the way as they ran down the deserted back streets and finally out onto Hauptstrasse. The wind that had pushed the storm into town was gone now and the rain fell straight down in huge drops, filling the gutter that ran down the middle of the street. Amy stopped at the gutter's edge for a moment before stepping into the flow, the water spraying up onto her calves. As Jake followed her, he was struck with a flash of memory and suddenly he was ten years old again. He kicked his feet forward, splashing water onto the back of Amy's legs. She turned around, laughing. She jumped, splashing water all over his pants. When she realized what she had done, she squealed, then turned and ran several paces ahead of him.

But Jake was not far behind. He caught up with her, laughing, and careened her off the street and under the awning of the shoe store where they had window shopped just a week before. They smiled as they saw their reflection in the window, looking like happy, water logged cats. The street was still and quiet except for the sound of the rain.

"I'm really glad we did this," she said with a smile that seemed to fill her whole face. She dropped her umbrella on the stones and wrapped her arms around him, squeezing him tightly like she had the first time she hugged him.

"What's that for?" he asked when he had caught his breath.

"I'm cold, she said.

He laughed as he pulled her closer. "I'm glad I could be of service."

She squeezed him tighter as they stood looking out on the wet, abandoned street.

"Thank you for this," she said.

He was thinking the same thing, but instead of sharing his thoughts with words, he lifted her chin with his hand and softly kissed her lips. She smiled and then shivered in the cold. "I need some of that tea," she said. Jake nodded, letting her go.

Grabbing their umbrellas, they zigzagged back down the street in search of puddles, only making it as far as the fountain where they stopped to listen to the sounds of laughter. The rain and the echo of the old buildings made it difficult to know where the sound was coming from, but as they rounded the corner of Zubergasse, they discovered the source of the laughter. With their backs towards them, Kai was dancing an Irish jig under a broken red umbrella as Molly laughed, bouncing and swaying the best she could to the music that seemed audible only to them.

Jake and Amy watched for a full minute before the dancers

discovered they were being watched. As they did, the four friends broke into laughter.

"This is crazy," said Kai. "We were just talking about you. I was thinking about tomorrow. Are you still good to help me with the cabinets?"

"Sure," said Jake. He dropped his arm from Amy's shoulder and walked towards Kai, leaving the two women to talk together.

"I was thinking it would be good to get started early if you're ok with that. The cabinet shop is open at eight and Molly's dad said he'd help out in the store until I can get back. I know it's your day off, but would you mind if I stopped by around 7:30?"

"That's fine," said Jake. "My day is getting a little busier than I had originally planned, so early would be better anyway."

They were interrupted by laughter from the women and they turned to look at them. "Dude, you gotta know they're totally talking about you."

Jake looked at him incredulously. "And how would you know that?"

"Because Molly hasn't talked about anything else since she woke me up this morning at six. She kept me awake, wondering if you and Amy snogged last night."

"Snogged?"

"Yeah, you know, kissed, made out, watched the submarine races...snogged." Jake smiled, looking at Amy and Molly whispering together, stopping often to laugh. "What'd you tell her?"

"I told her you'd be stupid if you didn't. It's not hard to tell you two are whooped over each other."

Jake looked at Kai and smiled.

"I'm just calling it like I see it. We're both really happy for you and hope we'll be hanging out with you guys more. It's been a while since we've had friends our own age to hang with."

Jake nodded. "It's been fun."

The women's hushed tones erupted again in laughter and Jake

wondered if he should be embarrassed at whatever information was being shared. They looked on in silence as the girls continued their quiet but animated commentary.

"What do you think they're talking about now?" asked Jake.

Kai shook his head. "I gave up guessing a year after we got married. It seems to make perfect sense to them, but I guarantee that if you stood in the middle of it and listened to every word they were saying, it would fry your brains."

Jake laughed out loud, but he knew Kai was probably right.

"It's better just to let them get it out of their systems," Kai added. "Women need this kind of talk. I think it must be in their genes."

"How do you figure?"

Kai turned to him, smiling. "I've been working out this theory for a long time and the way I figure it, we all used to be Neanderthals, right? And the guys used to go off hunting while the chicks were hanging out around camp, looking for berries."

Jake listened, trying to subdue a smile.

"Guys had to learn how to be very quiet so they could sneak up on the unsuspecting mammoths and dinosaurs and stuff."

Jake gave in to the urge to smile.

"And the whole time the guys were out quietly hunting, the women were back having a grand ol' time around the berry bushes, talking, singing, laughing, swapping tales and bragging about their men folk. Over the years, men just naturally evolved into quiet creatures while women learned to chatter all day long with the other women. I'm not sure how scientific my theory is, but I could see it happening that way."

"You're probably right," agreed Jake, turning again to watch the girls.

After another minute, the women finished their conversation and rejoined the men. Jake and Kai had been intently straining to catch what they were saying, but had gathered little.

"So what are you guys doing today?" asked Kai.

"They're going to work on the tea recipe and then they're having dinner at Jerry and Beverly's place," reported Molly.

Jake raised his eyebrows when Kai looked at him. "It seems the berry bush speaks."

Kai laughed out loud.

A gust of wind blew through the street, jostling their umbrellas and raising visible goose bumps on the girls' arms.

"I'm freezing!" Molly cried. "And the baby is kicking my bladder again."

Kai shook his head.

"Maybe we'll see you guys tomorrow," said Molly, putting an end to the conversation as she began her retreat. "Good luck with the tea."

Kai followed. "I'll see you in the morning," he said, nodding to Jake.

"So how was your talk with Molly?" Jake asked as they watched them go.

Amy turned and looked up at Jake. "Just girl talk," she said.

"What does that mean?"

"She knew we kissed before I could say a word, just like I told you."

"So what did you talk about then?"

"Oh, just the usual stuff girls talk about, I guess."

"Like what?"

"Oh, details, I suppose," she said with another broad smile.

"So she knows everything?" he asked.

She raised her shoulders with a shrug. "All the important stuff. Did you tell Kai?"

"No, we just talked about cabinets and his theory about how men's and women's communication evolved from the time of Neanderthals and dinosaurs."

She laughed. "So what's the theory?"

Jake recited it the best he could to Amy's unmistakable amusement.

"It sounds like you have us all figured out," she said.

"If only that were true, I'd be a happy man."

She stopped him and looked up into his eyes. "Aren't you?"

"I guess I am. Maybe there's happiness in ambiguity."

She wove her fingers through his as they entered the courtyard. They walked toward the stairs, oblivious to those who watched the quiet streets from the windows above.

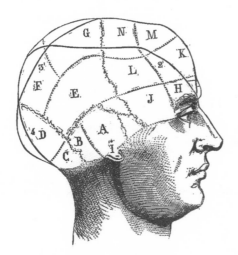

④

ISAAC'S SKETCHBOOK

PRIDE IS A SPIRITUAL CANCER: IT EATS UP THE VERY POSSIBILITY OF LOVE, OR CONTENTMENT, OR EVEN COMMON SENSE.

—C.S. LEWIS

What's this?" Amy sat at the table, wrapped in the old patchwork quilt.

"That's Isaac's sketchbook," Jake replied, turning away from the sink where he was filling the kettle with water.

She slid it across the table. The book was sealed with a wide rubber band.

"It looks really old. Where did you find it?"

"Sam gave it to me yesterday. He said he hoped to find a sketch Isaac might have made for the bakery floor mosaic."

"Have you looked at it yet?"

"No. I was kind of occupied with other things yesterday." He winked at her but then grew serious. "And I guess I also wonder if I should."

She turned to look at him. "Why?"

"It's kind of silly, but I know how I feel about my sketchbook. I don't know how I'd feel about strangers pawing through it, even if I was dead."

Amy nodded thoughtfully. "But what if there's something in here for you or whoever it was who was going to take over for him?"

Jake pulled a chair next to Amy and sat down. "Maybe I'm worried that there is."

She cast him a surprised look. "But aren't you trying to learn all you can about him?"

"Yeah. It's just that the more I learn, the more I feel like I'm getting sucked into this place. Until I started hanging around with you, I couldn't wait until September, to be done with my commitment to the Mayor and be on my way to Greece or wherever the wind blew me. I know I have some promises to keep, but I'm still not sold on spending the rest of my life here. I guess I feel like the more I learn…the more invested I become in this place… the more I realize how much there is to learn. Part of me wants to commit to this, but part of me wants to run. I always wanted to see the rest of the world before tying myself down."

Amy paused before her next question, as if she was not sure she should ask. "What are you afraid of?"

Jake squirmed. "I'm afraid of lots of things. Like I told you that night up at Taufer's Pond, I'm afraid that there's a better place for me out there somewhere. I'm happy today, but I wasn't happy two weeks ago and I'm not sure what tomorrow will bring."

"Wouldn't that be the same anywhere you went?"

Jake shook his head. "Yes and no. I don't know. I guess I just like only being able to see a little way down the road. I've never been really big on planning out my future. I mean I know what I want, or at least I used to, but this kind of commitment is new for me. Change has always been an integral part of my life."

"And now?"

"And now I wonder if I'm ready to settle into a life with little change."

"Do you think you won't be able to see the world if you stay here?"

He shook his head. "I don't know. I heard that Isaac rarely left town after he came here. He just sort of settled in and put down roots. My mom was the only root I ever knew and now that she's gone..." He looked away, trying to hide his emotion.

Amy put her hand on Jake's knee. After a moment of silence, she spoke. "Is that what you're afraid of? Roots?"

"I don't know, Amy. My rootless life has been pretty great. I don't feel like I owe anyone anything. Until I came here I was free to go wherever I wanted and do whatever I wanted to do. But it's different here. And the more I learn about Isaac, the more I fear that he is speaking to me. It's spooky—the stories people have told me. Kai and Albert were both wanderers and now they both have their roots buried deep here. I just don't know if I'm ready to exchange my freedom for commitment."

Amy looked disappointed.

"What are you thinking?"

There was silence for a long time before she spoke. "I know what you mean about freedom, but I guess my experience here in the last month has been a little different from yours. I feel like I've found more freedom than I've lost. I've wanted to be an artist for as long as I can remember and I feel like I am closer to that than I've ever been before. When my job is finally done on Tuesday, I'm sure that feeling will be even better." She looked away as tears formed in her eyes. "Jake, thank you for inspiring me to do what I want to do. It's what my heart is telling me I have to do, but I haven't had the faith to begin." She paused and then added, smiling, "I can't imagine where I would be without your friendship but I'm quite sure I'd be miserable— wanting to paint but stuck selling cosmetics."

The kettle whistled, stirring them from their thoughts. Jake stood and poured the water into a teapot. He lifted a dried bundle of peppermint from the hook above the sink and grabbed a couple of gooseberry leaves from the baking sheet. He placed them on another baking sheet along with a few sprigs of forget-me-nots.

Few words broke the silence as they crumbled the leaves and mixed them together on the baking sheet. When the mix looked like Jake remembered it, he filled a spoon with the dried leaves and dumped them into the teapot. The rest of the mix he slid off the tray into a lidded canister from the shelf.

The silence between them unsettled Jake and he wondered why. There had been silence before, but it had been comfortable. He poured the tea and returned to the table where Amy sat looking sad or somehow disappointed.

Jake's discomfort-level rose. He'd never been good with girls' emotions. But he sat down beside her and placed his hand on top of hers. "What's wrong?"

She tried to smile. "I'm having a hard time dealing with the fact that our friendship is only temporary."

"This is crazy," Jake replied. "We've known each other for exactly two weeks and we're already talking like this. We've got the whole summer ahead of us! Who knows what that time will bring? I'm anticipating that you're going to come to your senses any day now and realize what I dud I am. You might not even like me in a week."

She laughed, shaking her head. "I love you, Jake. I know we're still just getting to know each other, but I don't want to lose you."

Jake smirked and shook his head. "So what are we going to do?" he asked, passing her the sugar bowl.

"I think we've done pretty well so far. I want to spend as much time with you as I can. I want to learn more about Isaac and the history of this town. My family has been here since the beginning and I don't know anything about them. Something tells me I'll connect to them in the same way I've connected to Isaac and Lily. I need to paint and I need you to continue to push me, if you're willing."

"What's in it for me?" he asked, smiling at her.

"I am."

⑤
A HISTORY LESSON

THOUGH WE TRAVEL THE WORLD OVER TO FIND
THE BEAUTIFUL,
WE MUST CARRY IT WITH US, OR WE FIND IT NOT.
—RALPH WALDO EMERSON

he tea turned out just as they had hoped, even though the recipe and measurements of each ingredient were less than scientific: a handful of gooseberry leaves, lots of handfuls of peppermint, and a few pinches of forget-me-not petals. After Jake made an omelet with the wild mushrooms Thomas had dropped by the day before, he spent the afternoon running taste tests while Amy rendered a painting of a bunch of pots she pulled down from the shelves and situated on the table. When they were satisfied that they had duplicated Isaac's tea, Jake busied himself reading to Amy from a leather bound

copy of Thoreau's *Walden* that he found in Isaac's collection. And so Isaac's sketchbook was put off for another day. If Jake had been honest with himself, he would have admitted to avoiding the sketchbook. It had too many unknowns, and Jake was not yet ready to face his fears.

When it came time for Amy to leave, Jake insisted on walking her home. They left just before three, walking out again into the rain with their umbrellas. The temperature had dropped substantially since their morning fling and the coolness dissuaded them from engaging in any water play. Jake had planned to return to his apartment for a couple of hours until the appointed hour of his invitation, but was invited in and put to work peeling potatoes in the kitchen while Jerry read to them the headlines from the Sunday paper.

Just before six, Jake remembered the bread Sam had given him to take to dinner and excused himself, running most of the way back to his apartment. When he returned, the table had been set and dinner was ready. Jerry offered a prayer on the food and the four hungry diners heartily enjoyed the Sunday meal of roast beef and mashed potatoes, along with friendly conversation. Jake and Amy's reports of success with the tea were met with words of doubt from Beverly, but she said she'd be by to give it a try anyway. Jerry was quiet most of the evening, much as he had been on the picnic. But Jake eagerly anticipated the bits of dry wit that he shared throughout the evening.

Jake and Amy volunteered to do the dishes following the meal while Beverly and Jerry made their way to the sofa to relax. Jake washed and Amy dried the dishes as they continued their talk from earlier that day. After finishing in the kitchen, Jake and Amy joined Jerry and Bev in the sitting room. In response to Jake's question about the age of the apartment, Jerry gave a short history lesson, explaining that it had been added to the original structure in 1920 when his father opened the barber shop and needed a place to house his family. The original structure was

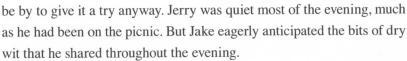

built in 1862 to be a butcher shop, then became an upholstery shop and finally the barber shop. On the same site, in 1717, the original tannery stood before being destroyed by fire.

Jerry told them about the remnants of the stone wall they had passed on the way to the river two weeks earlier—how some of the early settlers had insisted on building the wall to protect themselves from the Iroquois Indian tribes. Instead, the village elders made peace with the Iroquois by offering to trade the land for a dozen pieces of pottery, three sacks of flour and two old horses. Trading continued between the early settlers and the Iroquois for many years until the Indians disappeared.

The history lesson continued until Beverly pulled Amy into the kitchen to serve dessert. They emerged carrying large pieces of Beverly's famous carrot cake with cream cheese frosting served on plates Isaac made forty-something years earlier. Jake noticed that each of the plates bore chips on their rims. The craftsmanship on these was much different than the pots Isaac left in the showroom. Each plate was a slightly different size and the glaze was sloppily applied.

"Tell me about these plates," Jake said when Beverly had taken her seat again on the sofa.

"These were a gift from Isaac, for what was it Jerry, our tenth anniversary?"

Jerry nodded, his mouth full of cake.

"I've been curious about your relationship with Isaac. I've spent some time talking to Sam, Thomas and the Mayor and have learned a lot about Isaac from them. But I don't really know anything about your friendship with him."

Beverly nodded. "We've known Isaac for a long time. We got to know him through my best friend Lily, Isaac's wife."

"You never told me about that!" Amy said, looking surprised.

"You never asked," Beverly responded, winking at her niece. "We grew up together, Lily and I. We were quite inseparable when we were young. I spent a lot of time in her home. I guess that's your home now," she said, looking at Jake. "I was the oldest of four kids and the only girl in the Eckstein family, so when I wasn't helping my mother look after my younger brothers, I loved to escape to Lily's quieter world. Her mother passed away when she was only ten. After that, my mother treated her like one of her own. She was the closest thing I ever had to a sister and I loved her."

"She looked like a beautiful girl. I saw a picture of her last week in the Pottery," offered Amy.

"That must be the one in the gold frame, the one of her in a summer dress with her hair down."

Amy nodded.

"That was the only thing in the Pottery that Isaac always kept free of dust. She meant the world to him. If I remember right, my father took that picture of her right after we graduated."

"So when did Isaac come into the picture?" Jake asked.

"About a year before we got married. Isn't that right, honey?"

Jerry swallowed hard and spoke though his mouth was still half-full of cake. "I knew he was going to marry Lily the first time I saw them together."

Beverly chuckled. "Lily was the most precocious girl in town. She caught the eye of every young man who ever saw her, but she rarely accepted a date with anyone. A lot of the boys thought she was stuck up, but she was really just shy and reserved. Isaac often said he fell in love with her the first time he saw her. She spent the summer working the devil out of him, helping him learn the Quaker values we were raised with. Jerry was Isaac's best man and I was Lily's maid of honor at their wedding. We planned to raise our children together."

Beverly took a deep breath, wiping a tear from her eye. "Things don't always work out the way you plan. I lost a sister, but I also lost a second father. Henry was a dear man who treated me better than my own father did. Their deaths were the most tragic things I had ever experienced to that point in my life. After we were married, we invited Isaac to dinner

47

every Sunday night. We continued the tradition for many years until the boys got bigger and Isaac had to balance his time with the other folks that loved him. We used to have a full set of plates that Isaac made, but the grandkids have put an end to most of them. These four plates are the last of the original set."

Jake smiled as he glanced down again at his chipped plate. He was still full of questions about the connections between the people in this tightly knit town.

"I've also been curious about your relationship with the Mayor and Sam. Have you known them a long time too?"

"Since they were knee high to a grasshopper. I'm a few years older than they are, but when you grow up in a small town, everybody knows everyone else. They're the same age as my brother Frank so they were around the house a lot."

"In Isaac's will, he said something about them being intimidated by you, or something to that effect. What is that all about?"

Jerry started laughing, but stopped when Beverly cast him a sideways glance.

"I suppose I've always been rather tough for a girl. I think that's one of the reasons I took such a liking to Amy—poor girl with all those brothers. I grew up in a time when girls never wore pants. So when I showed up to school one day wearing a pair of pants, the boys took to teasing me. I'm ashamed to say I bloodied their noses before I left school that day. Since then, I just have to stand up straight and they still cower around me."

They all laughed out loud together. Jake tried to imagine Beverly standing up to the Mayor and Sam, both of whom stood six inches taller and outweighed her by at least a hundred pounds.

"All of our boys worked for Isaac over the years," offered Jerry. "They all thought it would be fun to be a potter until they learned how much work it takes to get good at it. They all wised up and went to college so they wouldn't have to use their hands to make a living."

"I've been wondering about that too," said Jake.

"About what?" asked Beverly.

"About how Isaac left his job and his life in New York and started over from the bottom, wedging clay for his future father-in-law and sweeping up around the shop. That had to be frustrating and humiliating for him."

"People do a lot crazier things for love," suggested Jerry.

"A lot of folks thought he was crazy when they found out where he came from," added Bev. "Back in the fifties, this was an impoverished little town. There weren't any tourists like there are today, just a whole lot of hard working folks trying to make do the best they could. We lost a lot of the folks our age to the cities, lured away by the promise of better jobs and a brighter future for themselves and their children. Isaac showed up in his little sports car, looking like a million bucks, and folks wondered if he was some kind of a fugitive, trying to hide out from the law. It just didn't add up."

"I liked him from the beginning," said Jerry. "We didn't see many out-of-towners back then and we were suspicious of anyone new. But Isaac was different. If he had a million bucks, he never showed it, other than that car of his. I met him when he stopped by for a shave and a haircut. I felt like I was his best friend in the world before he left. He was always such a sincere guy, quick to smile and to lend a hand."

"So how did this turn into a tourist destination?" Jake asked. The news that it hadn't always been surprised him a little.

"I think most folks have probably forgotten the time before the tourists came. Isaac kept pretty quiet about what he was doing, but he used some of the contacts he had back in New York and the marketing talent he had developed to start putting Niederbipp on the map," explained Bev. "He got the ball rolling after he had been here a few years. He encouraged us to embrace our uniqueness. Money was in short supply then and advertising is always expensive. Isaac was creative. I don't think there are more than a handful of folks still alive that know he spent thousands of dollars of his own money to promote the town. He used a pen name to write an article for Sunset Magazine, hiring a photographer to take pictures of the town. Not only did the magazine print the article, they paid him for it. He rolled the money back into the town, commissioning artists to fix some of the old murals. The article brought people from far and wide in search of the old world splendor he described, depicting the town as 'quaint' instead of just old. When people started showing up and folks started making money, they reinvested in the town, fixing up, painting, planting flowers. Not much had been done since the depression when the logging business declined. Isaac breathed hope into our town and inspired us to believe people would want to come here and spend their money. Many of the old logging mansions turned into bed and breakfasts and folks started talking about Niederbipp and telling their friends. He inspired our generation to stick around."

WE MAKE A LIVING BY WHAT WE GET, BUT WE MAKE A LIFE BY WHAT WE GIVE.
— WINSTON CHURCHILL —

"If she sounds like an ad for Niederbipp, it's only because she's had a lot of practice," added Jerry. "After Isaac served as the self-appointed tourism director for thirty years, he talked Bev into taking his place. Together, they've written hundreds of ads and pamphlets, trying to bring tourists here."

"So what happened to the website?" asked Jake. "I looked it up before I came here and it hasn't been updated in five years."

"It's hard to teach old dogs new tricks," suggested Jerry.

"The guy that designed that computer thingy graduated from high school and went away to college without teaching anyone how to keep it current," added Bev. "Jerry's right. Most of us are old dogs. We bought a computer years ago, but I rarely turn it on. I lived without it my whole life, and I don't think I need one now. I don't know if I have enough brain power left to learn how to use one."

Jake looked at Amy and shook his head. "I don't know that much about making websites, but I know it's not rocket science, at least not anymore. It seems like we could put some brains together and move the advertising of Niederbipp into this century at least."

"Are you volunteering?" asked Bev.

Jake looked at Amy again. "I guess I am."

"That's great! We're having our monthly meeting next Monday. I'm sure the rest of the committee will be happy to have some young blood in the group."

"How old are the rest of the people?"

Beverly looked thoughtful for a moment. "I think the youngest is 63. You might know her. She's your neighbor, Julianna. She runs the children's shop just down from you."

"Yeah, we just met a couple of weeks ago. What about Kai?"

"What about him?"

"Why isn't he on the committee? I think he knows a lot about computers. He might be able to help with the website, at least getting it updated."

"I'd like to help too," said Amy.

Jake nodded to her. "I think Brian might be able to help too. He seems to have a vested interest in making sure Niederbipp thrives. He would probably be a great sponsor if nothing else."

"I don't know why we never thought about that," said Bev. "If you're not careful, you might find yourself elected to be the newest tourism director."

The conversation continued for another hour, Jake and Amy both asking questions about the history of Niederbipp. At 10:30, Jerry excused himself and went to bed. Beverly followed him a few minutes later, leaving Jake and Amy alone.

Amy expressed her dread that she had two more days of work selling makeup. The Memorial Day Sale that had started at the store on Friday was set to run through tomorrow. As they parted, they made plans to meet again for lunch in the graveyard if Jake and Kai could get the cabinets hung in time.

As he walked past the lamp-lit stairs that rose from Hauptstrasse to the church courtyard, Jake remembered the flowers and notes left on Isaac's grave. He had hoped to pick up the notes on Monday to see what he might learn, but as he considered the rain that had already fallen and the potential crowd that might be there tomorrow, he decided it might be better to go tonight.

The dimly lit courtyard, still wet from the rain, reflected the lights from the church in long whimsical streaks that danced across the cobblestone. Jake was just about to lift the handle to the gate when he heard the soft sounds of someone sobbing. He stopped in his tracks. Unnerved by the darkness and his surroundings, he strained to listen, frozen in the moment. As his eyes adjusted to the darkness, he saw the outline of a person sitting on a bench—Isaac's bench. As quietly as he could, Jake turned and walked away.

HAVE FAITH & THE WAY WILL OPEN.
— QUAKER PROVERB

⑥
WAKE UP CALL

THERE IS BUT ONE CAUSE OF MAN'S
FAILURE AND THAT IS MAN'S LACK OF
FAITH IN HIS TRUE SELF.

—WILLIAM JAMES

Jake awoke the next morning to the sound of pounding. Stuck between the world of dreams and reality, he fumbled toward the door, tripping over his shoes and nearly crashing into the shelf filled with pottery. When he finally answered the door, Kai stood on the doorstep looking like he, too, had just stumbled out of bed.

"Hey man, sorry to wake you up. Should I come back?"

Jake shook his head, realizing he had answered the door dressed in nothing but his boxer shorts. "No, come in. I'll put some clothes on." He left the door open and turned back to the bedroom, tripping over his shoes again.

"Are you sure, man?"

"Yeah, sorry I'm not ready. I'm usually up by now. I guess I slept in."

"Late night with Amy last night, eh?" Kai asked, grinning.

"No later than usual. I just had a hard time getting to sleep." Jake pulled his shirt over his head and stepped into his shoes. "I'm ready," he said, looking sleepy.

The cool morning air coming through the open window of Kai's van chased away Jake's sleepiness. They pulled out onto the highway and picked up speed, heading north. The sun had been up for close to an hour and lit their way with sunbeams that sliced through the remaining clouds from yesterday's storm. It made Jake think about his bus ride into Niederbipp a month before. Beyond his escape on the scooter just a week ago, this was his first motorized getaway from Niederbipp since his arrival. Jake gave in to the urge to stick his arm out the window of the old van like an airplane wing. He twisted his hand up and down slightly, letting the wind raise and lower his whole arm. It was something he loved to do as a child. Jake glanced over at Kai and laughed to see him doing the same thing. They rode in companionable silence until they passed Rita's Bungee Bipp.

"Did you ever go there?" Jake asked.

"No, it was out of business before I got here. I heard it was fun though."

Jake nodded but no other words were spoken until they passed Bargain-Mart. Already there were cars in the parking lot. Jake turned to see Kai shaking his head.

"What's up?"

"Oh, I don't know. I guess it just bugs me when a store comes into a small community and tries to wipe out the competition. I know its business, but it just doesn't seem right. They offer people jobs and cheap products, but Bargain-Mart has only been open a year and already three of the shops in old town have closed. They just don't care who they hurt."

"Has your business been hurt by it?"

"Not yet, at least as far as we know. Their produce section is bigger than our whole store, but their service sucks. Did you know they pay people to smile at the customers and say hi when you walk through the door? I don't think a paid-for smile could ever be sincere, do you?"

"I never really thought about it that way."

"Yeah, well, I'm just glad there are still folks in town that care more about service and sincere smiles than they do about saving a few bucks. If it was any closer, it might be worse, but most folks walk to our store to do their shopping. I think we're safe."

Jake made a funny face, trying to stifle a yawn.

"So what kept you up?" Kai asked.

"Just thinking, I guess. Actually, I walked past the cemetery last night on my way home from Amy's and heard a woman crying. Do you know anything about that?"

Kai gave Jake a funny look. "I might."

"What do you know?"

"I've never heard it myself, but people talk about a woman that haunts the graveyard after dark. She kind of wails and whines in a high pitched voice and sometimes even screams obscenities."

"Are you serious?" Jake asked incredulously.

"No, but I had you going there didn't I?" Kai started to laugh and was still laughing when they came to a stop in front of a clapboard building on the outskirts of Warren. Kai pulled the van next to a black buggy before putting it in park. A skinny, bearded man dressed in black pants and a sky blue shirt greeted them as they got out of the van.

"Kai, good to see you my friend," he said extending his hand. "How's Molly?"

"She's good, about ready to pop any day now. Thanks for getting these done so fast. We wanted to have the kitchen put back together before the baby comes and I think we might just make it."

"Glad we could help. Who'd you bring to help you?"

"Oh, yeah, this is my friend, Jake. He's the new potter in town and the resident ghost whisperer."

Jake shot Kai a dirty look as he extended his hand to the older man. The man's firm grip caught Jake's attention and he turned to look him in the eyes.

"John Yoder," the man said.

"Nice to meet you."

"And you as well. So, they were able to find someone to take over for Isaac after all?"

"I guess so."

"That's good. I'm glad I won't have to give up one of my sons. We keep pretty busy around here."

The comment struck Jake as strange. He wondered what he meant by it, but John didn't offer any more information.

"The cabinets are just inside here," he said. He walked to the wide doors and knocked three times. There was a sound of wood sliding against wood and then the door opened, revealing a workshop filled with tools and five men of various ages dressed similarly to John.

"These are my boys," John said, talking to Jake.

Kai waved and a broad shouldered man came forward to shake Kai's hand. The man glanced at Jake but said nothing.

"Do one of you boys wanna help me with the bottles in the van?" Kai asked.

A young man stepped forward and walked out to the van. Jake watched him open the back door and pull out three boxes filled with newspaper-wrapped bottles. He carried them into the shop and disappeared into a back room. The others helped load the cabinets into the old red van. For his part, Jake tried to stay out of the way. When the doors were closed, Kai reached into his back pocket and pulled out a wad of cash. He counted it slowly into John's hand. Four thousand dollars.

John nodded and thanked Kai before signaling something to one the boys. The boy brought a small cradle that looked like it was made for a doll and handed it to Kai.

"Mrs. Yoder ordered this made for Molly. It would save me a trip if you took it with you."

"Wow," said Kai. "This is beautiful. Thank you. We haven't got around to buying a crib yet."

"Well, now you don't need to, at least until the baby gets bigger." Kai shook the older man's hand again before walking to the van to find a place for it.

"It was nice to meet you," John said, turning his attention to Jake. "Isaac was a good friend to our family. We actually named our youngest son after him. He was a true seeker, a man of great wisdom and charity. He wasn't Amish, but I think he must have been in his heart. He…he helped finance our shop when it burned down several years ago. If it wasn't for him…." He stopped for a moment, turning to look at his boys. "When I learned of the trouble he'd been having trying to find someone to take his place, I offered one of my sons to come and learn from him, but he knew I needed them too. I know you don't know us, but I want you to know that our family has been praying that you'd come for the last eight years."

John wiped his eyes with his big calloused hand.

Jake looked on, feeling the weight of what he'd just been told. *Prayers are answered in strange ways,* he thought. He extended his hand to John who looked up at Jake, trying to smile.

"I'm grateful that you've come. Any time you need a hand, please let us know. I feel as indebted to you now as I did to Isaac."

Jake watched as John wiped his tears again before turning to his boys. At his nod, they closed the doors and the sound of machines began again.

The trip home was uncomfortable, and not just because of the cradle Jake held awkwardly on his lap. The gravity of John's words and the earnestness of his tears sank like a weight in his chest. Someone had prayed that he would come. Maybe this wasn't the accident Jake had spent so much time thinking it was. Maybe he was part of a bigger picture that he couldn't even see.

⑦

A LUNCH HALF EATEN

SOMETIMES I LIE AWAKE AT NIGHT,
AND I ASK, "WHERE HAVE I GONE WRONG?"
THEN A VOICE SAYS TO ME,
"THIS IS GOING TO TAKE
MORE THAN ONE NIGHT."

—CHARLES M. SCHULZ, CHARLIE BROWN

olly's going to be psyched about this cradle!" Kai lifted the awkward burden off Jake's lap so he could escape from the van.

The van was parked on the narrow alleyway behind the store, next to the stairs that led to the apartment above. Before the new cabinets could be taken up, the old ones had to be carried down. It was back breaking work and Jake found himself wishing they had brought along a couple of the Yoder boys to help.

At eleven thirty, Molly came into the kitchen as Kai was driving the final screw into the overhead cabinets while Jake held them in place.

"You boys make good time," she said.

"That's only because Jake has lunch with Amy at noon," Kai teased. "Mrs. Yoder sent you a gift." He nodded to the corner where the cradle sat.

Molly squealed, running to the cradle and kneeling down beside it. "It's beautiful! Did she say anything?"

"No, I didn't actually see her. John said he wanted to save himself a trip."

When Molly turned back to face Kai, Jake was surprised to see tears in her eyes. "I think Mom was Mrs. Yoder's first account when she started making her jam. You remembered to take the bottles, right?"

"Bottles?" Kai asked, winking at Jake.

"Don't tell me you forgot them again." She struggled to get to her feet and rushed at him, trying to look angry. He grabbed her and hugged her, kissing her softly on the forehead.

"Of course I remembered them."

The sound of a truck horn came from the alley and Kai went to the window to see who it was.

"It's a delivery. I didn't know they were coming today."

"Oh yeah, I forgot," said Molly. "They called this morning to say they'd be bringing by some produce today."

Kai shook his head. "Do you have time to help me put the old cabinets in the van?" he asked Jake.

Jake nodded and they hurried down the stairs.

Amy was waiting for Jake when he arrived at the bench across from the department store. Haupstrasse was normally abuzz at lunchtime, but today was even busier with the weekend visitors hanging around longer than normal.

"Hey," he said, sitting down next to her.

"Hey back." She ran her fingers over his wet hair. "Did you forget your umbrella?"

Jake grinned, feeling winded and glad to have a minute to catch his breath.

"I got out of the shower and forgot I needed to make sandwiches too.

I'm sorry; I've been running late all day. But we got the cabinets in!"

"That's great! I'm sorry; I should have made us roast beef sandwiches from last night's leftovers. "

"Hey, I've got a painting to work off. You named your price and I plan to deliver."

They stood and followed the familiar path to the courtyard and then the cemetery. Amy told Jake about her hectic morning, resetting the lipstick display that was knocked over by a woman's large purse, managing the sales counter while also attempting to do makeovers. Jake laughed with her as she explained the color choices of a woman that looked more like a fancy parrot than a human.

Jake recognized the look of disappointment on Amy's face when they came to the open gate. The cemetery was filled with visitors. People milled about, stooping over graves, caring for flowers and even pulling weeds. Hand in hand, they climbed the few stairs and looked out at the place that was usually theirs alone. Jake squirmed when he saw a child standing on the bench under the crabapple tree and hoped it wouldn't be damaged.

"What are you thinking?" Amy asked, following his gaze to the mistreated bench.

"I'm thinking someone has invaded my sanctuary."

Amy nodded. "What do you want to do?"

"I want to pick up those cards on Isaac's grave and find somewhere else to sit and eat lunch."

Amy led off, pulling Jake by the hand. The mound of flowers covering Isaac's grave had grown many times over since Saturday. Jake knelt on the ground to sort through the pile of flowers and cards. He had expected some of the cards to be soggy from yesterday's rain but they were all dry. He pushed the flowers aside and took a seat on Isaac's bench.

"What's wrong," Amy asked.

"They're gone. Someone beat us to it."

"What do you mean? The cards are right there."

"Yeah, but these are dry. The ones we saw on Saturday would be wet from the rain yesterday."

Amy sat down beside him. "Who would have taken them?"

Jake looked down at the pile of cards and described the sobbing woman he had seen the night before.

"Who do you think she is?"

Jake shrugged in discouragement. "He had so many friends. It could have been any number of people."

Amy looked dubious.

"What?"

"Jake, it was after 11 when you left last night. Did you see anyone else on your way home?

"No, why?"

"Because no one is out that late around here, especially in a graveyard."

Jake smiled, "We were."

"Ok, but we were here for a good reason," she said, smiling back at him.

Jake was pleased to see some color rise in her cheeks. "Maybe she was too. Maybe it was the only time she knew no one would be around."

Amy stood up, looking around at the others in the cemetery. "Let's go. We can find a quieter place to eat." They picked their way through gravestones, flowers, and people as they exited the cemetery, looking for a quiet place.

"Have you ever prayed for someone you didn't know?" Jake asked as they reentered the courtyard.

Amy stopped walking and turned to look at him. "That's kind of a random question."

Jake nodded. "Sorry, I had a strange experience this morning that got me thinking."

"Go on," she said, pulling him over to the church stairs. They walked to the top stair and took a seat on the cool, gray-blue stone.

Jake pulled the sandwiches out of his bag, handing one to Amy before he continued. "This morning, when I went with Kai to pick up their new cabinets, I met an old Amish man who told me he and his family had been praying for me to come to Niederbipp for the last several years."

"Did he say why?"

"Not exactly. He said something about Isaac helping him fund his new woodshop when it burned down several years ago. Isaac refused to let the man pay him back. If I understood him correctly, he even offered to give Isaac one of his own sons to work as his apprentice, but Isaac never took him up on the deal. I thought that was strange enough, but then he told me that I was an answer to his prayers and the prayers of his family." Jake shook his head. "He even started crying, thanking me for coming to Niederbipp."

"What do you think about that?"

Jake shrugged. "I've had a hard time deciding what I think." Taking a deep breath and a bite of his sandwich, he leaned back on his hands and looked across the courtyard.

Amy watched, looking curious. "Have you ever prayed for someone you didn't know?"

"I've been thinking about that all morning. I remember praying with my mom for President Bush, that he'd make the right decision about going to war." Jake laughed softly, shaking his head. "I'm not sure our prayers were answered," he shrugged. "I prayed a lot for my mom and when the cancer went into remission, I felt like my prayers were answered. But when the cancer returned five years later, I really wondered if God was just playing with me. For a while there, I wondered if prayers are heard at all."

"And now?"

Jake fiddled with his sandwich bag. "Well, I'm grateful for the five years I had with my mom. It's not the way I hoped it would be, but it could have been a lot worse. Before she got cancer, I never thought about losing her. She was just always there, always Mom. I guess I needed those five years with her, so I could appreciate her more, but also to find out who I was and develop the faith I needed to make it through it all. I know my mom prayed for me too." Jake swallowed hard and looked away, not wanting his emotions to get out of control.

Amy said nothing, but Jake could feel her looking at him.

"It was a pretty humbling thing to hear my dying mother pray for me. I think those prayers, more than anything else, have helped me to keep a good attitude about life. She prayed for my happiness and success. When her nurse called to tell me she had passed away, she said my mom was praying for me as she slipped out of consciousness. She prayed that I would know she loved me and that I would find people to love me as much as she did."

Amy put her arm around Jake as tears fell down his cheek.

"I'm sorry," he said, trying to push them back up. "I haven't thought

MEN ARE WHAT THEIR
MOTHERS
MADE THEM.
- RALPH WALDO EMERSON -

about this in a long time. Meeting that guy today..." Jake breathed deeply, trying to gain control, but losing fast.

Amy pulled him closer to her as his tears fell freely. He leaned over, hiding his face from anyone who might see. The tears continued to fall for several minutes, but he couldn't utter a word. Finally, when it seemed the tears were gone, he turned to find Amy smiling at him.

"What?" he asked, returning the smile.

"It's just nice to know you're human. I was beginning to wonder if you might be from a different planet."

"Why?"

"Because you're always so calm when you talk about your mom. I wondered how you could do it. I've never lost anyone close to me, but I know I couldn't be as strong as you seem to be. You had me wondering if you already got all your tears out."

Jake shook his head. "I don't know if I've gotten any of them out. I've tried not to think too much about it."

"Jake," she said softly, "we're talking about your mom."

Jake took another deep breath, nodding. "My roommates weren't exactly the most sensitive guys in the world. I've just never had much time to think about it. And then today, this stranger tells me he and his family have been praying for me for the past eight years." He turned and looked hard at Amy. "Amy, I've only been making pots for eight years. I took my first pottery class my freshman year in high school. I never thought I'd be an answer to anyone's prayers."

The church bell tolled, marking an end to Amy's lunch break.

"I guess we need to go," Jake said, getting ready to stand.

She pulled him back. "What are they going to do, fire me?"

Jake smiled, relaxing again against the cool stone.

"I want to know how this makes you feel about Niederbipp?" The intensity in her voice hinted at the significance of her question.

"I don't know Amy. Half of me wants to give in to the idea that my being here is part of a bigger plan, that maybe it's not just a detour on my way to somewhere else."

"And the other half?"

Jake smiled. "The other half wants to run. I feel like the longer I'm here, the more I get sucked into this place. I feel like I'm beginning to forget how much I love to travel and how much of the world I still want to see. It's an amazing world out there...and the longer I stay here the less of it I'll be able to see before I die."

"You sound like you're dying already," she teased.

"I know. I know you think I'm crazy. Maybe I am. I just don't know what I should be doing with the next ten years of my life, let alone the rest of it. I've never been in a hurry to figure it out and it's worked out pretty well so far."

There was silence between them for a long moment. When he looked at her, he saw that her eyes were focused on a faraway place. Jake nudged her arm softly.

She slowly turned to him and said, thoughtfully, "Jake, what would you say if I told you that I feel like your friendship is an answer to my prayers too, that I'm grateful the heavens put us in the same place at the same time? What would you say if I told you I don't believe this is just a crazy series of coincidences?"

Her words were sobering. He had been so busy thinking about himself and his own circumstances that he hadn't considered how what he had just said might affect her. His response was slow, perhaps too slow, as he considered what he might say. After the silence had extended itself for a full minute, Amy stood and dusted off the back of her dress. "I guess I better get back to work. See you later."

She bounded down the stairs, leaving her half-eaten sandwich on the step. Jake watched her go, not sure what was happening. She had never acted this way before. Had he said something wrong? Or did he not say something he should have? He gazed across the courtyard in confusion. Had she not just been holding his hand? Had she not just listened to him cry? But now she was gone. No plans had been made for the evening. No quick kiss or even a hug. She hadn't even given him a backwards glance as she ran away across the courtyard.

Jake felt a foreboding as he gathered up the sandwiches, placing his own half-eaten sandwich on top of hers and wrapping them hastily in wax paper. He walked back to the Pottery. Puzzled. Alone. Confused.

⑧

TWINKY THERAPY

THE UNEXAMINED LIFE IS
NOT WORTH LIVING.
—SOCRATES

ake spent a solitary afternoon trying to figure out what he had said to make Amy run off after lunch.

He kept himself busy checking off things he had had on his to-do list for weeks. He opened a bank account with Mr. Smoot and deposited all of the money that had been accumulating in the old cash register since he arrived, nearly two thousand dollars. At the post office near the bus station, he finally filled out the necessary forms to have his mail forwarded to Zubergasse 12.

Returning to his apartment, he put in a load of wash and started to straighten up. Stems and bits of dried peppermint leaves were scattered on the table and floor from the tea preparation the day before. Jake swept the old linoleum floor before filling the sink with warm water. With an old rag, he scrubbed the kitchen floor, working under and around Amy's

French easel. When the washer completed its cycle, he pulled out the wet clothes and piled them on the kitchen table. He had yet to use the line hanging outside the kitchen window, but the warm and sunny day inspired him to give it a try. He swung the windows open and knelt on the bench next to the table to hang his clothes out to dry.

When he had hung the last of the clothes, Jake turned around and sat on the cushioned bench. In front of him was Isaac's sketchbook. He picked it up, flipping it over. The faded leather cover was polished and smooth, though worn thin on the edges and corners. Even with the book closed and sealed with the rubber band, Jake could see that several pages were dog eared in the corners. He held the book in his hands for a long moment, staring at the rubber band that kept it shut, wondering when or even if he would open it. He was curious, but he was also frightened of what he might learn from its pages. Not wanting to get sucked in to this place anymore than he had been, he pushed the book away.

Amy's paintings lay on the far end of the kitchen table. Those she'd completed on Thursday were nearly dry, even though the thick paint made them look wet and juicy. Jake admired the paintings anew, envious of Amy's talent and ability to find beauty and creativity in the humdrumness of lipstick tubes.

He returned to his work, stripping the sheets off his bed and putting in another load of wash. When his stomach began to growl, he returned to the kitchen and his leftover sandwich. The bread was dried from being near the open window, but he sat on the top stair and ate it anyway as he looked across the courtyard. He hoped Amy would drop by and help him understand what he had done.

When the washing machine finished and she still hadn't come, Jake draped the wet sheets over the kitchen chairs before wandering off to pick up some groceries.

Kai was alone in the grocery store, stacking apples in the produce section when Jake walked through the door.

"Dude, how's it going?"

Jake couldn't help but smile despite the questions he had in his mind. "I'm good. I just needed to pick up some groceries."

"Cool, you came to the right place."

"Where's Molly?"

"She was so psyched about the new cabinets, she left early to put everything away. Thanks again for your help this morning."

"No problem." Jake didn't have a shopping list, but he grabbed a basket and began wandering. He stopped at the snack aisle, adding Twinkies and potato chips to his basket. A dozen eggs, a six pack of Coke and a box of raisin bran followed. The basket was full before he remembered milk and peanut butter. He hobbled to the front counter with the heavy basket swinging from his arm.

"Dude, you could have used one of the carts," Kai teased.

Jake tried to laugh.

"So where's Amy tonight?" Kai asked as he rang up Jake's purchases.

"I don't know."

Kai looked at Jake for a moment, then nodded slowly. "Did you guys get in a fight?"

"I don't think so."

Kai raised his eyebrows. "So you just did something stupid then?"

"What makes you say that?"

"I'm the town grocer, remember? Nothing gets past me," he looked up from the Twinkie box to wink at Jake. "Actually, a lot probably gets past me, but in this case I know what I know because Amy came in an hour ago and was talking to Molly."

Jake's stomach somersaulted. "What'd she say?"

"I don't really know. She seemed upset though and she and Molly disappeared."

Jake shook his head. "Is she up with Molly in your apartment? I'd like to talk to her."

"I don't know if she's there or not, but if I were you, I'd give it some time before you tried to talk to her. Women tend to blow up if you try to talk to 'em before they're ready."

"Do you have any idea what I said that made her so mad?"

"No. I'd tell you if I did, but they were talkin' quietly and it was pretty obvious they didn't want me hearin' anything."

Jake let out a long breath.

"You'll hear about it soon enough. Molly used to get frustrated with me all the time because I didn't understand her. She usually let me know how big of an idiot I was within a couple of days. I'm not sure how Amy is, but Molly can't keep things inside for very long without it either spilling out or blowing out."

"What's the difference?"

"Well, if you get a choice, I'd recommend the spill-out. It's kind of blubbery and teary and you feel like an insensitive jerk afterwards, but it's a lot better than a blowout. If that happens, you better just plan on leaving town for a few days. Molly has never had the kind of blowouts my mom used to have with her boyfriends, for which I am very grateful, but I try to give her the space she needs when she clams up so it doesn't get any worse than it needs to be."

The humor of Kai's glib descriptions of complex women's emotions was not lost on Jake, but a feeling of dread was rapidly overtaking him. He looked down and shook his head again. "I don't even know what I said."

"That's ok, I'm sure Amy knows exactly what you said, and by now, so does Molly. I'm sure I'll hear about it later. If you want, I'll stop by tomorrow and give you a heads up."

"Thanks a lot," Jake said, feeling low. He trudged back to his apartment with his groceries. While putting them away, he saw Amy's sandwich wrapped partially in the wax paper. He picked it up and leaned back against the counter. The crust had nearly been eaten off, leaving what he knew was her favorite part: the center where the honey and peanut butter were the thickest. He considered Kai's words, wondering what he said that prompted Amy's response. He replayed the conversation in his mind, trying to discover his mistake. Finally, he tossed the sandwich back on the counter and walked to the window to bring in the wash.

After hanging the sheets on the line, Jake ate four Twinkies while he stared at Isaac's sketchbook and brooded. He continued to mull over the situation as he made his bed. What had he said that changed things so dramatically? Just last night he had enjoyed an evening with Amy, her Aunt Bev, and Uncle Jerry. The night before had changed his life forever; he told Amy he loved her. Whatever he did, he wanted to know so he wouldn't do it again.

9

FORGET ME NOT

SILENTLY, ONE BY ONE, IN THE
INFINITE MEADOWS OF HEAVEN,
BLOSSOMED THE LOVELY STARS,
THE FORGET-ME-NOTS OF THE ANGELS.
—HENRY WADSWORTH LONGFELLOW,
IN EVANGELINE

Sleep came slowly and didn't stay long enough to pacify Jake's troubled mind. At seven, he gave up the fight for a decent night's rest. As he ran his fingers through his hair after his shower, an idea came to him. Surely Jerry would have some insight about his favorite niece that might help Jake understand whatever it was he did. And he needed a haircut. The timing couldn't be better. If he didn't see or hear from Amy by noon, he would go for a haircut.

His first task for the day, however, was to get the kiln shelves ordered.

Like the Pottery, The Clay Palace in Pittsburgh was closed on Mondays and so Jake was forced to put off the order until this morning. The wait inspired the purchase of a few other items he didn't have on his list. The old dusty catalog on the shelf above the wedging table also gave him a few ideas. Since the delivery cost was the same if the truck was empty or full, Jake decided to order as much clay as he could imagine using by the end of the summer. Then he calculated how much clay he had already used, resolving to leave the same amount of clay for the next potter, if he moved on when the summer ended. Next, he checked the dry ingredients for the glazes. A few of these needed replenishing: silica, cobalt oxide, kaolin, feldspar and bentonite.

He rationalized the purchase of a new pyrometer though he felt quite certain the old one would still work with a new thermocouple. He added a gallon of wax resist and four new sumi brushes. He opened the kiln door and peered in as deep as he could without unloading the shelves, trying to determine how many shelves needed to be replaced. The top nine shelves, badly warped, were certainly a total loss. The six shelves below that were questionable. He decided 18 new shelves would make sense, just in case more of them came out warped or broken.

Jake was on the phone with The Clay Palace when the front door opened and Hildegard walked in. He nodded to her, pointed to the phone and motioned for her to take a seat if she liked. He nearly choked when the woman on the end of the line gave him his total: $1563. 67. He read her his credit card number, running his free hand through his hair. The delivery was scheduled for Friday morning. He had forgotten about Hildegard by the time he finished the phone call.

"I'm sorry to catch you at a bad time."

"No, you're fine," Jake said, turning his attention to her. "I was just ordering some new shelves for the kiln."

"They must be expensive." Her eyes were focused on something above Jake's head.

"They were," he said, turning around to discover what she might be looking at. When he turned back around, he found her smiling.

"I figured they must be, the way you've made your hair stand up like that."

Jake laughed in spite of himself. He combed down his hair with his fingers, remembering how Hildegard had pointed out his shoes at church when he met her. Her accent intrigued him then as it did now.

"I brought you that treat I promised," she said, pulling a brown bag from Sam's bakery out of her purse. "Have you had a chance to pull the new bowls out of the kiln yet?"

"Not yet. I was just getting to that," he lied. He had forgotten all about the bowls.

"Would you like to be the first to try my new tea recipe?" he asked, stalling.

"That's right! I heard that you and Beverly's niece were trying to duplicate Isaac's recipe. I'd be happy to be your guinea pig."

Jake moved to the sink to fill the teapot with hot water and the new tea, setting it aside to steep while he turned his attention to the kiln. He began on the bottom shelf, pulling out three mugs that stood in the way of the bowls behind them. The glazes on the mugs were shinier than they normally were, but they still looked good. Jake carried these to the front desk before returning to remove the bowls. A black and white swirl bowl was the first one out. Jake was relieved to find it in very good shape. The second was the same. He next pulled out two of the blue and green star bowls Amy had admired in the window and that had sold so quickly. Jake was pleased to see that these too were in really good shape even though the glaze was shinier than it was supposed to be. He took these to the front desk also, walking past Hildegard who oohed and awed when she saw them.

At the very back of the kiln, on the bottom shelf, four small cereal bowls remained. Jake returned with a stick to help reach these. When all four were pulled to the front of the kiln, he stacked them inside each other and set them in front of Hildegard. He was anxious to continue looking through the kiln, but he turned his attention to her as she examined each bowl.

She smiled as she ran her fingers over the bowls. Their colors were similar to the larger ones Jake had first pulled from the kiln: black on white and green on blue. She scrunched up her eyes as she looked at the pattern on one of the black and white bowls. The outside had Jake's classic swirl design, but the inside was covered with concentric black circles.

"I think this one might hypnotize my cat," she said, setting it aside.

Jake nodded. "Did you say you're one of the mug owners?" He pointed to the row of mugs.

"I am," she said, pulling her attention away from the bowls. "Mine was the first mug in Isaac's collection. It's the one on the far right."

Jake unhitched the mug from its nail and carried it to the sink to rinse it. The mug was small compared to some of the others, but its handle was disproportionately large. The sides of the mug were rough, a tell-tale sign of a beginner's pot. Rookies at the wheel tended to use too much water in the throwing process, causing the finer, smoother particles to sluff off, and leaving the coarser particles exposed. The glaze was too thin in some spots also, but on the inside it was crazed, looking like a dark spider web from years of use. Of all the mugs in the collection, it was Jake's least favorite. But he kept his opinion to himself as he filled the mug with hot tea and set it on the table in front of its owner.

"I think I'd like this one," she said, handing Jake one of the blue and green bowls. It had a star in the middle and swirls on the outside.

Jake nodded and carried it to the counter. When he returned, Hildegard was holding her mug, rubbing her thumb softly over a spot on the handle. She seemed lost in a world of her own, so Jake didn't disturb her.

"It's just like I remember it," she said, finally looking up with watery eyes. "You must have learned the secret ingredient."

"I think so."

"Isn't it amazing what a little blue flower can do?"

"You know about the secret ingredient?" Jake asked, surprised.

She nodded slightly. "But don't worry, I was sworn to secrecy. Isaac told me he needed to tell someone who could pass it on to whoever took over. I guess he underestimated his successor's sleuthing skills. How did you find out?"

"It helps to have access to the dry tea. When we discovered the tiny petals, it became a little easier."

"And you know the meaning of the flower?"

"I think so. We asked Gloria. She doesn't know it's in the tea, but she told us some stories and history."

Hildegard nodded and took a long, satisfied sip from her mug. She then pushed the bag across the table. "These are for you. As much as my mouth loves Sam's pastries, I'm afraid my body doesn't anymore. But I'd get a lot of pleasure out of seeing you eat them."

Jake thanked her before tearing open the bag.

"Now that you know the secret ingredient, perhaps you should also know the reason he included it in his tea."

Jake looked up from the pastries. "I'd like that."

"Besides myself, I know of no other living person with whom Isaac shared his secret. He began putting the flower in his tea over fifty years ago. He found it growing spontaneously on Lily's grave and saw it as a symbol of hope. At first, he put it in his tea to remember Lily, but then noticed how much it improved the flavor of the tea and continued. Isaac loved to share tea with friends who came to visit. Conversation over a mug of tea somehow helped to restore their faith and lift their spirits. It was almost like that small flower which symbolized hope grew into faith over the years that followed—an unwavering, solid faith that helped so many of us through our own hard times.

"Many people believe that his tea was magical, but I know better.

There is no magic in the tea. There was magic in the man who shared it."

Jake nodded thoughtfully. "Tell me about that magic."

Hildegard took another long sip from her mug. "Isaac had an unusual gift. Some believe it was magic, but calling it magic would deny him due credit for all the time he spent developing that gift. The tea, more than anything, served to calm the nerves. His magic, his gift, began when the troubled soul would begin to unload his burdens..." she paused for a moment, then added, "...or her burdens. Many people, including myself, believe he had the ability to solve our problems, and maybe he did for some. But the majority of us came to him simply because he had the ability and time to listen."

"So, how did that work? I can't imagine him getting much work done if all he did was listen to people."

"You're right. I'm sure there were many days when his work was put on hold for another time. But he also learned to work while people shared their tales. When he learned from Lily and Henry about consecrating one's heart to God, time became much less important to him than were the people that God led to his shop. It was actually a difficult thing for him to learn, at first. He had come to us, as I'm sure you know by now, from New York, where time was everything. An hour could mean the difference between a million dollars or nothing at all."

"So how did he change? How did he ever learn to slow down? This town is a universe away from New York."

"Your question surprises me, Jake," she said, setting her mug down. "Why did you want to become a potter?"

He thought for a long moment. "Because I love the thrill of creation," he finally uttered.

"And what lessons have you learned about creation from the clay?"

Again Jake thought for a long moment before responding. "That it takes time."

Her nod indicated to Jake that he was thinking the way she hoped he was thinking. "Jake, of all the creative arts, pottery is among the most time consuming. A painter can produce a painting in an afternoon. A glass artist rarely takes more than a day or two to complete a piece. A sculptor can shape or carve a sculpture in a week or less. If you were to attempt such speed in pottery, what would happen?"

"You'd have a big mess," Jake said, smiling.

Hildegard nodded. "I'm not a potter like you and Isaac, but I've sat here and watched Isaac work for years. From what I've learned, I know that pottery and life have many parallels. Probably the most obvious is the idea that it takes a long time for both people and clay to be shaped, glazed, and run through the refiner's fire. The pots you make today won't be done in less than two weeks, but in one form or another, they'll be around for the rest of eternity. When Isaac realized the parallels between his work with clay and  his work with people, time seemed less important. Quantity gave way to quality in every aspect of his life. To answer your question, Jake, Isaac didn't change on his own. He was shaped by a potter and his daughter before going through a lifetime of change in the refiner's fire."

Jake took a deep breath, turning to look at the kiln. "I guess I never thought about it that way."

"We're all in the process of becoming something, Jake. Isaac was a decent potter, but his work with people will outlast the finest of his vessels."

Silence fell again as Jake pondered her words. He had often been annoyed and put off by his visitors. They had come at a time when he was busy working, doing important things. All of them had been a distraction to his work of creation. He thought of Amy. Just a few days ago, she had expressed jealousy in his position—not only because of his opportunity to create art, but even more for his chance to hear great stories and meet interesting people. As he thought about her now, he realized this opportunity had been wasted on him. The stories and the people were beginning to become interesting, but he knew Amy would have found more meaning in them. He looked up to find Hildegard smiling at him.

"You remind me a lot of Isaac: determined, stubborn, driven."

He looked at her, stunned by her honesty.

"Of course, that was in the beginning. All rocks start out rough, but time and experience seem to soften even the hardest. You'll have to forgive me for being blunt. Unlike many of the German families here in town, I was born in Germany and bluntness comes naturally to us."

"I wondered about your accent. Did you come over after the war?"

"No, I was one of the lucky ones. I came over just before the war started. The rest of my family was sent to the prison camps and most likely died in the gas chambers."

"I'm sorry." As he looked at her, Thomas' words returned to him: "things aren't always the way they seem."

"Were you Jewish?" he managed.

"I was and I am. My uncle, a wood carver, immigrated to Niederbipp in 1918, after the end of World War I. My parents had just begun dating each other and were not interested in leaving their home near Stuttgart. My uncle maintained contact with my father, encouraging him to come to America, but tradition and the family business kept my parents rooted. I was born in 1923, the youngest of four children. Unlike my siblings, I was fascinated with America. While everyone else was involved in the family watch business, I spent my time day dreaming of coming to the United States. I taught myself English and began writing to my cousins. When I was thirteen, I received an invitation from my uncle to come and visit. That was the last time I saw my parents. Before my vacation was over, the threat of war had returned to Europe. Hitler and Mussolini were on the move. By the time my parents sent word that they needed help getting out of Germany, it was too late. We maintained some contact until 1941, then nothing…

"The Quakers who had embraced my uncle and his family did the same for me. They were aware of the war, but had been given the status of 'conscientious objectors' and so the war seemed distant to them. But my family was in the middle of it and I agonized over every newspaper story and radio report.

"My uncle raised me as one of his own children. When Mr. Schmelding, the clock shop owner learned I was from a watch making family in the old country, he offered me a job after school, cleaning pocket watches. Over the next few years, I fell in love with his son. Jonas was charming and always a gentleman. I had to wait until I was 18 before my uncle finally consented to let me marry him. Our

LET US TAKE THE
RISKS OF PEACE
UPON OUR LIVES,
NOT IMPOSE THE
RISKS OF WAR
UPON THE WORLD

QUAKER PROVERB

wedding was a simple affair, just two days before Pearl Harbor was attacked and the United States entered the war. Many of our friends were also recently married. Though the draft threatened to break up families in other nearby communities, my friends and I believed we were safe behind our conscientious objector status, and for a time we were.

"But things change. Our husbands grew restless as the call for support was heard on the airwaves. When pictures started coming out of Europe showing emaciated people and widespread destruction, the restlessness turned to talk. The need was so great for soldiers and supplies that even conscientious objectors were given the opportunity to serve in the Civilian Public Service. For a time, many of our boys considered joining the CPS, but they learned that many of the tasks given the CPS were little more than busy work.

"One evening, Jonas brought home a newspaper." Hildegard paused and then continued slowly, as if digging through memories she had buried deep. "The newspaper had some awful pictures on the cover— Jews, starved, naked, murdered. We had heard on the radio that things like this were happening, but these pictures made it real. I went into shock as I realized this was probably the reason I hadn't heard from my family. Within a week, my Jonas and five of his best friends relinquished their status and joined the Army. With our husbands gone, the six of us girls moved to Pittsburgh to join the war effort. We rented an apartment together and got jobs wherever we could, trying to make a difference in the war. I was a steel worker. I ran a lathe and later I became a welder. Anytime one of us received a letter from one of our husbands, it was as if we all did. We shared the good news and the bad together. Sometimes we even fell asleep at night huddled around the radio, praying and hoping for good news. The Army was good to us, and kept the boys from Niederbipp in the same company. When the letters became few and far between, we comforted each other the best we could. We kept up hope and prayed even harder..."

Jake watched her shake her head. A long silence followed until Jake spoke up.

"Did any of them come home alive?"

Hildegard shook her head. "We thought we were so blessed to have them all together and maybe we were. They lived together, fought together and died together. Now, they're all buried together, the only veterans in our cemetery."

"I'm sorry," Jake said. "That must have been tough for all of you."

"It nearly killed us. It nearly killed the whole town. They weren't only our husbands; they were the sons of Niederbipp. They had grown up here, gone to school here, fallen in love and married here. We all thought we would raise our children here. That terrible war wiped out a whole generation. We came back from Pittsburgh and tried to find ourselves. None of us remarried. None of us had children. We've done the best we can, but it wasn't the life any of us hoped it would be."

Her tale was the saddest one Jake had heard. There seemed to be no happy ending, no end to the pain and loss she and the others had experienced. He had to change the subject.

"So, how did you get to know Isaac?"

"How much time do you have?"

"How much time do you need?"

"I'd need more time than I have left in this world to tell you about Isaac. I have loved only two men with all my heart, my dear Jonas and Isaac."

Jake was surprised. Many people had expressed love for Isaac, but this was different. He was curious. "Why...?" He hesitated, wanting to continue, but not feeling comfortable enough to do so.

"Why didn't we ever marry?"

Jake nodded, feeling embarrassed.

"If it was up to me alone, we would have married fifty years ago." She smiled. "But while I loved only two men, he loved only one woman. His love for Lily was all-consuming."

"Did you ever tell him how you felt?"

"Of course not. Women in my generation weren't forward like they are today."

"But you loved him."

Hildegard took a deep breath, obviously trying to control her emotions. "I guess we all have our regrets. I was afraid I'd scare him off. We were such great friends. I would have liked to spend more time with him, but so many people needed him—loved him. I was grateful to be numbered among his friends. His undying love for Lily helped me appreciate and remember my own love for Jonas. I met him at the cemetery almost every day for more than fifty years. I spent more time with him than most married people do with their spouses. That was enough. His faith gave me hope in a better world and his friendship offered me succor in this one. We mourned our losses together, but we also laughed together. I might have married someone else and forgotten both Jonas and Isaac. I opted instead to remember them both. That connection—to touch both the living and the dead—has sustained me through my loneliness. I have lived because I have loved deeply. That is enough."

Jake listened to her words, their simple poetry filling the space between his ears. He realized he had been hoping for a happy ending, but none came. Perhaps it was happier than it could have been, but pain and sorrow were still present—a world of loss experienced by a small, humble woman. He wanted to say something to put an end to the silence, but could think of nothing to say big enough to cover the sore.

"I've been watching you," she said, peering over the rim of her mug.

Jake looked up, happy to have an end to the silence, but not sure if he should be comforted by these words.

"I watch most people who come to the cemetery. There aren't many who enter those rusty gates. Those who do are generally lost."

"Lost? I don't know about that," Jake said with a smile. "I…it's been a quiet place to eat lunch…and I've been working on Isaac's bench."

"But I'd bet there aren't many people who remember a graveyard as the location of their first kiss." She smiled wryly as Jake blushed.

He tried to laugh it off, but his color betrayed him. He wondered what else she might know. His answer came without warning.

She opened her purse and pulled out a bundle of colored envelopes held together with a rubber band. "I think you were after these the other night," she said handing them to him.

Jake looked at the bundle. The top envelope bore the name "Isaac," written in once-neat penmanship, now water stained and drooping. "I meant to get these Saturday night, before the rain came, but you and Beverly's niece made that quite impossible." She winked, obviously enjoying his discomfort at her revelation. "I heard you come on Sunday night. I hope I didn't frighten you. I saw you again yesterday as you looked for these cards among the flowers. When I found you had stacked the new ones, I thought you might be laying a trap for me so I took those as soon as you left."

Jake looked at her, surprised, then smiled. "I've known this town has eyes, but I didn't know how many. Nor did I know that they never go to bed."

"You can call me a spy, but never a liar. I've never been good at holding my tongue—which can be good or bad. When I saw that young girlfriend of yours storm off yesterday, I knew you needed these more than I did. I'm old and have many regrets in my life. But you…you have the world in front of you! And you can make of it what you will. From what I've heard, you are learning the secrets of life that most people never know until it's too late to change. If you will accept the wisdom of the past and learn from it, then I'm sure your life will be better than any of ours. The secrets of life are useless if you don't suck them in. You might say that it's none of my business what you do, and you'd be right, but I rarely mind my own business so I'm going to tell you what I think."

Jake watched her closely as she rose to her feet. She placed the straps of her purse on her elbow as if she was making to leave, but then she turned, looking quite serious.

"Jake, you don't know the treasure you have here and you may never know. But I'll tell you this; you will never know much of anything important if you believe this life is all about you. Selfishness can never be happiness. You may search the whole world over for happiness, but unless you know that truth, you will forever search in vain."

Jake stared at her, not knowing how to respond.

"I better be on my way," she said. "If you don't mind, would you wrap that bowl for me?"

Jake stood, sobered by her words, and feeling rebuked by a woman he barely knew. He walked to the counter and wrapped the bowl in brown paper. She handed him a twenty and told him to keep the change. Before she left, she smiled at him kindly. It reminded him of the day he met her and how he had imagined her to be a cute, innocent grandmother. How wrong he had been, he thought to himself as he watched her go.

THINGS BREAK

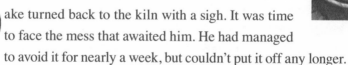

ake turned back to the kiln with a sigh. It was time to face the mess that awaited him. He had managed to avoid it for nearly a week, but couldn't put it off any longer. The small bundle of cards left by Hildegard still sat on the table. He was curious about what they would say. Hildegard implied that there was something for him to learn there, but he wasn't sure he wanted to know. Since Amy had walked down the church stairs the day before, Jake's wanderlust had flared. He wasn't sure if Hildegard had been implying that he was selfish, but he didn't like to be corrected. He was independent, always had been, and probably always would be. He didn't need her or anyone else to tell him who or what he was or wasn't.

The bowls on the top shelf were stuck fast where their glazes had run, sealing them to the shelves. He unloaded the heavy shelf carefully and set it down on the table. The high heat and weight of the bowls on top had bowed it so that it resembled a rocker on a rocking chair.

He returned again and again to the kiln, pulling out the warped shelves and broken bowls. He was glad the new shelves had been ordered, but the waste was still heartbreaking. How many hours did this mistake represent? Thirty? Forty? When he got down to the lower shelves, his mood lightened some. Like those on the bottom shelf, these pots were in fairly good shape. Their glazes had melted beyond what should have been, but they were still pretty and definitely sellable. In all, twelve bowls and six mugs had endured the high heat without succumbing to ruin. He was grateful for these. They would help pay for the new shelves and clay.

Jake carried the bowls to the front desk before arranging them on the shelves in the showroom, filling the holes where others had sold. He ran a dust rag over the pots and shelves, his thoughts turning to the other mess in his life: Amy. It was nearly noon. Amy had never called him on the phone before and he doubted she would start today. This was to be her last day at work. He knew she would want to paint, but her easel and supplies were still in the kitchen. Would she come for them?  Would she come and talk? Would she tell him what he had done to hurt her feelings?

He leaned against the front desk and looked into the studio. Twelve of the most warped shelves lay scattered about on the tables and stools. Two others leaned against the table legs, their ensnared bowls defying gravity, fused to them with glaze. "Well," he muttered, "let's get this over with." He took a deep breath then exhaled slowly before moving to the back door. The two plastic garbage cans from under the stairs were too bulky to fit in the studio, but he set them just outside the door and removed their lids. Nothing remained but the unavoidable task of throwing the mess away.

As he carried the first shelf to the garbage, he considered adding the shelf with its fused bowls to the collection in the apartment. Others would definitely know the lesson to be taught by such a sight. "Don't fall asleep and forget the kiln!" he said to himself as he let the shelf fall from his fingers and crash at the bottom of the can. Again and again, he repeated the motion. Memories of the night this disaster began returned to him: Taufer's pond, yogurt and bread, Amy painting and the conversation that had deepened their understanding of each other by light years. He smiled to himself, missing that time and the understanding they had shared.

When the first can was full of the wreckage, he slid it away from the door and pulled the other into its place. Two more shelves noisily found their way to the bottom of the can. When Jake turned back this time, he saw the bundle of cards. He picked them up, turning them over in his hand. The stack was nearly an inch thick. He guessed there were close to thirty cards. He put them back on the table, staring at them for a full minute before turning away to attend to the last two shelves.

He wanted to open the cards. He was curious about their contents and was sure he would learn a lot from them about the old man. But something held him back. It was the same feeling he had about the old man's sketchbook. The privacy issue he knew was just a lame excuse. It was fear: fear of finding something that would make him stay, that would convince him not to go to Greece. In his heart, he knew it was already happening, but refused to admit it even to himself. Amy, Gloria, Hildegard, they all were pushing him to stay, to make commitments, to accept that the universe had opened up this way for him. But he was 22 years old, a wanderer and a fool.

In a fit of rage, he picked up one of the last shelves and threw it into the garbage can. It went in, but stopped, sticking out half way. He picked up the last shelf and charged the can with his full force, slamming the shelves on top of each other.

It happened so quickly. The bowls fused to the top of the shelf shattered with the impact, but as his momentum carried him forward, the razor sharp edge of a broken bowl sliced through the flesh of his forearm.

At first, there was no pain. For a moment, Jake wondered if he might be dreaming. The broken edge of the bowl was buried deep in his arm, a few inches south of his elbow. He stared at the blood pouring from his wound. As his body recoiled, he let go of the shelf in his hand. When it fell, it pulled the shard from the wound, letting out a torrent of blood. He winced in pain, lifting his arm in front of his face. The blood was coming quickly, spurting out with each beat of his quickening heart. He knew he needed help and now.

He reached for the apron on the hook and wrapped it over the wound. He tried to push through the back door, but screamed when his left hand hit the door frame. The way was blocked by the heavy cans. He turned and bounded across the studio and showroom, out the front door and down Zubergasse as fast as he could. He elevated his arm, trying to slow the flow, but blood dripped from his elbow, painting crimson dots on the cobblestone.

As he rounded the corner of Hauptstrasse, he began to feel weak. "I need help," he said loudly.

The crowd in front of the kabob shop scattered. A woman screamed. "He's been shot!" a man yelled as another woman screamed.

Jake scanned the crowd, searching for a familiar face.

"Jake, what's going on?" It was Albert. He was already removing his blue tailor's smock. "What happened?" he asked, cradling Jake's arm in the blue cotton cloth.

"I cut myself pretty bad. I think I might need stitches. Can you help me to the hospital?"

They ran the best they could. Albert held Jake's arm as he ran backwards, stumbling toward the hospital. By the time they reached the ER, Jake could tell he was in trouble. His skin was white and he felt like fainting. A woman in scrubs met them at the doors and fired off a litany of demands to several other people dressed in scrubs behind the front desk.

Soon Jake was lying on his back on a gurney rushing into a trauma room. He tried to focus on the ceiling, but the room was spinning. He heard Albert talking to somebody about insurance and emergency contacts while the doctor pulled on gloves, strapped a tourniquet around his upper arm and began unwrapping the bloody rags from his wound. Jake strained to look, but was pushed back down by a nurse.

"It looks like he's nicked his ulnar artery," he heard someone say. He felt probing and prodding, followed by scrubbing. And then his world went black.

ICARUS

HE WHO BLINDED BY AMBITION,
RAISES HIMSELF TO A POSITION
WHENCE HE CANNOT MOUNT HIGHER,
MUST THEREAFTER FALL WITH
THE GREATEST LOSS.
—NICCOLO MACHIAVELLI

ood morning!" Jake turned his head to the sound of the voice, but was blinded by the light. Squinting, he made out the blonde hair and scrubs of a woman checking the monitors. The window behind her was aglow with the morning sun.

"Where am I?" he managed.

"Kinzua County General Hospital, Room 402 of the ICU." She smiled at him. "You're lucky you got here when you did. It could have been bad. I figure you lost at least a pint of blood on your way. Next time this happens, you might consider calling the ambulance rather than jogging to the hospital. Blood tends to flow a little faster when your heart rate is 140. At the rate you were going, your veins would have been empty in three minutes."

Jake blinked. Her words bounced off his foggy head.

"You're also lucky you just nicked your artery. If it had been severed, you could have planned on several hours of surgery and a donor implant from your leg to patch you up." She smiled as if to soften her harsh report. "You have a lot of people worried. The nurses were telling me you draw a bigger crowd than the free flu shot clinic we have in October."

Jake turned to look at his left arm. It was covered in white gauze and tape. "What happened?"

"I was just going to ask you the same thing. Thomas and the Mayor spent some time at the Pottery yesterday afternoon, trying to piece it together. You conveniently checked out before you could tell anyone what happened. They said there was a big mess by the back door: shattered pottery and blood everywhere. They couldn't make much sense of it. I was hoping you'd remember."

Jake closed his eyes again as the scene replayed itself in his mind. He winced, trying to get the image of his bleeding arm out of his mind.

"Can you remember anything?"

"I slipped," he lied. "I was taking out the trash and I slipped. It happened so fast."

"Well, you're going to have a lot of folks asking questions in the next few days. You might work on a better story." She smiled at him again. She was a pretty girl, blonde and trim. Her teeth were straight and brilliant white.

"I'm going to let you rest for a while, but I'll be back to check on you soon. My name is Dr. Johnson."

Jake nodded before leaning his head back against the pillow. He was so tired.

When he awoke again, Gloria was standing over him, her face full of concern.

"Hey," he said, blinking as though his eyelids were attached to sandbags with bungee cords.

"How are you feeling, Jake?"

"Hungry."

"That's a good sign. Would you like some lunch?"

"Lunch? What time is it?"

"Almost two," she said, turning to the clock on the wall.

"How long have you been here?"

"You mean today?"

Jake looked at her for a minute, trying to process the question. "What day is it?"

"Wednesday."

He thought about that for a minute. "How long have I been here?"

"Just over 24 hours. You had surgery yesterday afternoon and have been in this room since. Sandy said you'll be transferred out of ICU this afternoon sometime."

"Who's Sandy?"

"Oh, I thought you met her—Sandy Johnson, Dr. Johnson."

Jake grunted. "So, how long do I have to stay here?"

"Probably until Friday."

Jake grunted again. "This is so lame."

"Jake, I don't think you have any idea how lame this is. That stunt you pulled, running through the streets to the hospital…you could have bled to death. If Albert hadn't been there…it could have been really bad. You were in surgery for over an hour to stitch that artery back together. One centimeter more and you might be dead right now."

Jake closed his eyes.

"Listen Jake, a lot of people have been praying for you. Beverly, Thomas, Sam and the Mayor were here all night, keeping Joseph and me company. Albert's been calling every hour to get an update so he could let people know. The hospital finally told the Mayor he needed to do something about all the phone calls and people hanging out in the waiting room. The tailor shop has become the headquarters for 'Jake Watch.'"

Jake opened his eyes and smiled a crooked grin. "Only in Niederbipp," he said, shaking his head.

Gloria looked at him for a long moment. Her expression made her look...what was it... angry?

"Jake," she finally said. "You don't get it, do you?"

"Get what?"

"Get the fact that you nearly died. Get the fact that you lost two units of blood on the way here and another two units during surgery. You don't get that you've kept half the town up all night worrying about you. Did you even know that your blood type is O+, one of the rarest types? The hospital only had two units on hand. Over forty people came in yesterday to give blood, wanting to do anything to help. You have no idea how lucky you are that two people in town happen to share your blood type. They were scrambling for a helicopter to come from Pittsburgh and pick you up when the second donor was found. People die all the time from losing as much blood as you did. Don't you get it? You could have died! If just one of the variables had been slightly different, we wouldn't be having this conversation. A lot of folks are calling it a miracle. People have been praying for you since you got here a month ago but half the town has been praying for you for the last twenty-four hours. And you seem to be blowing it all off. Only in Niederbipp! You're absolutely right—ONLY IN NIEDERBIPP! Where else would you find people that loved you like family after one month of knowing you? Where else would you have half a town praying for you during surgery? Where else would you have people worried sick about a proud, self-centered kid who can't see the people who are trying to love him? Where else would you find a community that was busy raising funds to pay for that same proud kid's medical expenses? Jake, why can't you see these things?"

93

Jake remained frozen throughout Gloria's impassioned speech. When she stopped, he took a deep breath, then exhaled slowly. It was a lot of information to take in: the loss of blood, the scramble for donors. Had she mentioned a fundraiser for his medical expenses? And she'd called him a proud, self-centered kid. Did she mean that? His brain, still groggy from sleep, hunger, and medication struggled to sort it all out. Finally, he looked up into her face and saw the tears running down her cheeks. "I'm sorry," he uttered. "I didn't know. I…I just woke up."

"I hope that's true." She turned, wiping away her tears. "I'll go see if I can get you some lunch."

Jake watched her go, still considering her words. He hated hospitals. Since the time of his mother's first diagnosis, he had spent countless hours in rooms like this one. He felt confined—claustrophobic, even. He stared at the drab gray wallpaper and saw two long, tedious days stretching out in front him. Maybe he could get out early… There was the shipment from The Clay Palace coming on Friday. Who would be there to receive the load?

He glanced down at his bandages. A yellow stain discolored his skin around the bandage—iodine, he figured. He made a fist with his left hand and felt a dull ache in the fleshy part of his arm just below his elbow. Images of blood—his blood—returned. For the first time, he considered the fragility of his own life. He had been faced with the realities of mortality with his mother and her cancer. But this was different—this was his life. Had he really been in as much peril as Gloria described? He shuddered when he thought of "Jake Watch," imagining the tailor shop crowded with people waiting for the latest update. His time in Niederbipp had been marked by attention— attention he had never had before. Sometimes it seemed like the town had somehow begun to revolve around him: the invites to dinner, people knowing his business before he did, and now this. Hearing that John, the Amish carpenter, had been praying for him was hard enough to put his arms around. Now the town of Niederbipp was doing the same—and raising money for his medical expenses. He was grateful for the latter. He knew that the surgery, a day in ICU, four units of blood, countless other implements, and two additional hospital days wouldn't be cheap. With no insurance, he knew he would be paying for this for several years. He hoped the fundraising efforts, whatever they were, would help.

He thought again of his mother. Between doctors, hospital bills and hospice care, the last months of her life had sucked up all of her savings. She had hoped to leave some money for Jake, but by the time it was all over, there was nothing left. In a way, it was a good thing. He had become more independent and he was grateful for that. He knew how to work and save and spend his money wisely. He had to. The only other choice was starvation and homelessness.

These thoughts led him to his current circumstances. They weren't exactly what he had wanted, but they weren't all bad. For the past month, he had been doing what he hoped to do for the rest of his life, making pots and being a village potter. It was not the dream he hoped it would be, but it was reality. He recognized that postponing his decision to stay beyond the end of the summer made him feel like a visitor instead of a resident, but despite all that was good here, he couldn't make himself commit to it entirely. Images of Greece, with its whitewashed houses and lapis-colored sea still taunted him, seducing him away from reality and towards the beautiful, mysterious unknown.

Amy had changed things for him. She had weakened his resolve, causing him to sacrifice a piece of his independence. And this made him mortal. He looked down again at his bandages. He was mortal. Her kiss was the sun that had melted the wax wings of his pride and independence.

FRINGE BENEFITS

WE MOST OFTEN GO ASTRAY ON A WELL TRODDEN AND MUCH FREQUENTED ROAD.

—SENECA

y the time he moved out of ICU a few hours later, Jake had humbled himself. Once again, Gloria's words had made him think. And the more he thought, the more foolish he felt. He was proud and perhaps independent to a fault. As he thought about it, he realized these two elements were hindering his propensity for gratitude, or for seeing the big picture. In fact, his pride was keeping him from thinking clearly.

Flower arrangements, balloon bouquets, and get well cards filled his new room. He was happy to be off oxygen and connected to fewer tubes and monitors, but now that he was out of intensive care, he was soon inundated with visitors. Beverly was the first, but just as Jake was getting ready to ask about Amy, the Mayor stopped by. Sheepishly, he handed Jake a silly balloon bouquet attached to a cheap ceramic mug with a small brown teddy bear peeking out of the top. He gave his wife the credit for its selection. Beverly slipped out in the middle of the Mayor's long and rather boring account of his appendectomy. Jake had to give him credit for trying to empathize, but he was relieved when Kai and Molly showed up, putting an abrupt end to the tale. Kai brought a kabob for Jake who, already sick of hospital food, wolfed it down with relish. They didn't mention Amy, which Jake thought was odd, but he didn't bring her up either. Before they left, Jake talked to Kai about the delivery from The Clay Palace and asked him to make a phone call to see if it might be postponed until Monday.

Just before seven, Alice stopped by. She wore cut off jeans and a tank top and carried a box of Twinkies under her arm and greetings from her father. She said her dad had been to the apartment with Thomas to make sure everything was ok there and found several Twinkie wrappers. He thanked her for the thought and decided not to tell her that before Monday, it had been years since he had eaten a Twinkie, and he had done so only because he made the mistake of going shopping when he was hungry.

Alice's visit was a surprise. It had been a couple of weeks since he had seen her and, though he remembered her as attractive, she was even prettier than he remembered. Instead of sitting on the chair like his other visitors, she sat on the foot of his bed. She was much more forward than she had been the night they met, resting her arm on his leg and joking with him as if they were old friends. He was confused by the attention she was paying him and painfully aware of the onions still on his breath from the kabob. Before leaving, she leaned over to kiss him lightly on the forehead and promised to return the next day to check on him.

After she was gone, Jake's thoughts naturally turned to Amy. Where was she? Why was she staying away? Alice, the girl he had met only once, had visited, brought Twinkies and left him with a kiss. But he had yet to hear anything from Amy. He looked around at the flowers and balloons. The nurse had piled up the cards that accompanied the bouquets, but Jake hadn't had a chance to read them yet. He reached for the rolling table and pulled it closer to him. Finding it painful to open the envelopes with his left hand, he resorted to using his right hand and his teeth. There was a card from Sam's wife, June. Another was from Betty Finkel, the woman who had first invited him to dinner. Her card bore the signature of both her and her granddaughter, but Jake snickered when he noticed that both signatures looked remarkably similar and remembered that the granddaughter only came to town on the weekends. Another card was from Clea Faber. She was honest enough to only sign her own name, but he laughed when he was setting the card aside and found writing on the backside as well, inviting him to dinner the following Sunday, if he felt up to it.

There were ten cards that bore well wishes and signatures from people he had never heard of. He was surprised to find one from Sally, telling him she had heard from her mother about the accident and that she hoped he would be better by Tuesday so the girls could stop by and look at his new pots. By the time he finished reading the last card, Jake was feeling tired. The cards had offered him entertainment and a feeling of being wanted. He was surprised how they had lightened his spirits, but as he set the stack of cards aside, he remembered why he had turned to them in the first place—looking for Amy. There was nothing, not even a hint that she still cared. Even Beverly had sent a card, but it said nothing about Amy.

He laid back, feeling disappointed. He still had no answer about what he'd done to make her mad in the first place. He stared at the box of Twinkies, feeling like an imbecile. He wished he had answers and knew what he could do to change things.

Father Thomas interrupted his thoughts with a knock on his open door.

"Looks like you're deep in contemplation," he said, walking into the room. "Should I come back later?"

"No," Jake said, sitting up. "I've just been going through some cards."

"That's quite a stack of fan mail for only one day. You might consider staying a little longer and seeing what other kinds of goodies you could get out of the deal."

Jake forced a smile, sitting up a little straighter. "What brings you out so late?"

"The welfare of your soul." He smiled at Jake and pinched his big toe as he stood at the foot of his bed. "When I went to check out the shop yesterday, I noticed a stack of envelopes on the table." He pulled them from his pocket and lifted them up for Jake to see. "Since it looks like you're done with your own cards, I thought maybe you'd like to read these. I know it's late, but I thought they might offer you a diversion from your own problems." He tossed them to Jake who caught them between his right hand and chest. "I also took the liberty of stopping by your apartment and grabbing a few things you might need. They had to cut your t-shirt off of you when you arrived. I figured you might like some underwear and a toothbrush." He set a paper bag at the foot of his bed. "I better be going. I told the nurse at the counter I wouldn't be long. Visiting hours ended at nine and they all know I'm not really a priest." He winked at Jake and turned to go.

"Thanks," Jake said.

Father Thomas stopped at the door and turned. "You're welcome Jake. I hope they help."

Jake watched him go before turning to the stack of envelopes. He stared at the bundle for a full minute before looking up at the door to see if anyone was watching. Then he pulled the rubber band off with his teeth and opened the first envelope.

(13)

THE AWAKENING

ONE MAY NOT REACH THE DAWN
SAVE BY THE PATH OF NIGHT.
—KAHLIL GIBRAN

J ake awoke as the sun rose over the eastern hills. The window in his hospital room offered a commanding view of the valley. He once again remembered his first day in Niederbipp when he sat on a bench by the bus station and watched the shadows from the clouds race across the valley and the river. It seemed to him as if a decade had already passed. In the quiet of the morning, Jake thought about the notes and cards Thomas had dropped off the night before and which he had fallen asleep reading. They were compelling. Jake had felt sucked in, and read them as if they were chapters to Isaac's life story. Like the tales of the mug owners in the pottery, each card offered further insight into the man he had come to replace. Several times, he even fought back tears as people expressed love and appreciation for a man who had changed a life forever. One card especially intrigued Jake. He wondered about the details of its story. In the low light of the morning, he shuffled through the stack on the table in search of the note written on pale blue stationary. When he found it, he reread it.

Dear Isaac,

So many days have passed since that dreadful night. I have wanted so many times to write and thank you for what you did for my son. Your kindness to him at a time when he least deserved it meant the world to him, and to me. I tried so hard to raise him so he wouldn't be like his father, but Charlie always had to choose his own way. I know you wanted your generous gift of compassion to be kept a secret, but I wish I could have done something to repay you, to thank you, before you passed away. Charlie told me I could never tell a soul what you did for him. I have kept my promise, but my inability to express my gratitude for what you did for my only son has caused me much anguish and heartache. Tears of appreciation have stained my pillow over the past eight years. Your kindness, love, and generosity have inspired me to be a better person, a better mother. You have inspired me to reach out to others, to find secret ways to give, to love and to serve. You have restored my faith in the innate goodness of mankind. You have given me hope when hope was gone. You brought my son home to me and gave him his life back. He has honored your gift. He has become a man

of integrity. He has become a man like you. I am proud to be his mother. I am proud that he is working hard to continue the legacy you have given him. I thank the heavens for you and the change you wrought in him. Thank you for caring, for loving in a way no other man ever did for my son. You broke through his thick head and gave him confidence to know he could change and become a better man. We attended your funeral and wept together. Even in death, your generosity, your expectation of goodness in others was evident. Your request for Charlie to be a pallbearer brought many to tears, but none more than him. Your ability to forgive, to find goodness in the weakest of souls has inspired many. How I wish I could have shared this with you before you were gone. My prayers are full of gratitude to God who allowed you, a potter and molder of clay, to have the ability to shape the life of my son. Your funeral taught me that many share my admiration and gratitude for the life you lived and shared with each of us. I pray that these words may somehow find you, that you may know of my love and appreciation for you. I pray that I may live my life in a way that will enable me to tell you these things myself, to thank you for all you have done. I will love you forever for what you have done for me and my family.

With all the sincerity of my heart,
Thank you.
MS

Jake set the note back on the table. Outside his window, the rising sun illuminated the trees on top of the hill across the river, making them look as if they were on fire. He tried to remember the last time he had watched the sunrise. Searching his memory, he went further and further back to an early summer morning almost seven years before. His mom had woken him before the sun was up and pulled him out of bed, asking him to join her for a walk. It wasn't the first time she had done so, but it had been many years since he had agreed to go with her to her special place not far from their home. Appletree Point reached out like a thin, crooked finger into Lake Champlain. An old gazebo on its western most tip offered a 320° panorama of the lake. While the sun rose over Appletree Bay, his mother told him of her diagnosis and he cried for the first time since he was a child. His life began to change as he recognized the sometimes cruel realities that life dished out. Now, seven years later in front of another sunrise, he remembered the intense love he felt for his mother that morning in the gazebo. He had been scared, wondering how he would live without her and fearing the cancer would take her before he was ready. He shook his head, knowing he wasn't ready, wondering if anyone ever is ready to lose his mother.

His thoughts brought him around to the conversation he had with Amy just three days before on the church steps. He shared with her the sacred words his mother's nurse had shared with him, that his mother had been praying for him when she passed from consciousness. His mother had prayed that he would be able to find people who loved him as much as she did.

Tears filled his eyes now as he remembered Gloria's words to him the day before. He was being loved. People cared about him. Strangers prayed for him. Others were raising funds to help pay his medical bills—bills to pay for an accident sustained when he was kicking against the very force that brought him here. His tears poured down his cheeks as he thought about his mother's last wish.

On Jake's first visit to the graveyard, he had discovered Zebulon's bench and the words of hope written on its face, "Sweet is the peace the gospel brings." He had found peace in those words that day. Peace had remained with him the following week in the graveyard when he felt a connection to the other potters and the benches erected in their honor. But then things had changed. He gained more knowledge and understanding of who these potters were and the legacy he was continuing. He realized how much he had to live up to. He felt the pressure. And he freaked out. He didn't want the responsibility. He didn't want to be tied down to a town, or a shop, or a legacy. He was determined to set off on his own, make his own mistakes, and plow his own furrow.

And then there was Amy, that bright light that had come into his life when he needed a friend. She had changed not only his world, but his entire universe. She loved him, or at least she said she did. But she had left him sitting alone on the church steps, wondering what he had done. In a flash of memory and horror, he remembered the moments before she left. There were no words at all. Silence had filled the space between them after she had opened her soul, telling him his friendship was an answer to her prayers and challenging the possibility of all these things being merely a coincidence.

He cried again as he considered the impossibility of all these things being merely a coincidence. He had found people to love him. He had been given people to love. He had a shop and an apartment. As a stranger, he had been entrusted by Isaac's friends with intimate stories from their lives about softened hearts, changed mentalities, improved outcomes, and inspiration. These had both stirred and frightened him. He knew he could spin Isaac's wheel, fire his kiln and fill the showroom shelves with pots for the people of Niederbipp to enjoy. But he wasn't Isaac. He was a kid who lacked wisdom, patience and understanding. For the last several years, he had lived for himself and answered only to himself. He realized now that he had become proud and self-centered. Gloria was right. Part of him wanted to curse her for it, but another part, a growing part, wanted to embrace her and accept the love—albeit tough love—that she extended to him so freely.

Again his thoughts turned to Amy. It was after he began spending every day with her that he had begun to find understanding in the things he was learning from those who came to visit. Time spent with her had opened his mind and enabled him to discover his heart. She had opened new possibilities, new hopes, and new desires. She had elevated him to a better place, and made him a better person. Time spent with her inspired him to be the best him he could be. With her, he was humble, life was exciting, time had meaning and the stars shown brighter. With her, his life was better. Despite the change she brought to his agenda, he had to admit his life was fuller and more meaningful.

As the sun broke free of the hills, Jake drifted off to sleep, dreaming of the collection of flawed pots in his apartment.

14
DEATH OF AN ISLAND

NO MAN IS AN ISLAND ENTIRE
OF ITSELF; EVERY MAN IS A PIECE OF
THE CONTINENT,
A PART OF THE MAIN;
...ANY MAN'S DEATH DIMINISHES ME,
BECAUSE I AM INVOLVED IN MANKIND.
AND THEREFORE NEVER SEND TO
KNOW FOR WHOM THE BELL TOLLS;
IT TOLLS FOR THEE.

—JOHN DONNE

ake woke again to a nurse shaking him gently by his shoulder.

"Good morning. Are you ready for breakfast?"

Jake blinked several times in the bright light. "What time is it?"

"Almost nine. Dr. Johnson will be in to check on

106

you in a half hour. I thought you might want to eat first."

Jake nodded, attempting to sit up. As he did so, he put too much weight on his left arm and recoiled in pain. Looking down at the bandage, he saw a dark stain where the jagged shard entered his arm. The blood was dried now, but the pain remained. As he ate breakfast, he felt overwhelmed with gratitude for the first time since the ordeal began. He was grateful to be in Niederbipp and not in Pittsburgh, grateful for the town that supported him even when he didn't deserve it, grateful to be alive, and grateful for a chance to change. His impatience to get out of the hospital no longer centered on his discomfort of being there, nor the work he was missing. He was anxious to get out so he could fix things with Amy and apologize to Gloria. He wanted to thank the town that had supported him, prayed for him, and raised funds to pay for his brash acts of insolence. He promised himself that he'd be more thoughtful toward others, especially toward Amy. He'd try to be more sensitive and wouldn't bring up Greece, even if he was thinking about it. But he'd try not to think about it. He had already promised himself that he'd focus on the positive, but he meant it this time. He knew he had to be different.

"Good morning, Jake." Dr. Johnson stood in the open doorway. Her words pulled Jake back into the room.

"Good morning!" he replied cheerfully.

"How are you feeling?"

"I'm good. My arm is a little sore, but I guess that's probably normal. I'm sorry I didn't thank you yesterday for saving my life. I assume it was you who stitched me up."

She looked up from her charts and smiled. "Yes, and you're welcome. It's not every day we get a celebrity in the ER. I was worried about you, though. Your body was going into shock. I hate to think what would have happened if we hadn't found those donors."

"It was that bad?"

"Yeah. It's always more stressful when we get a patient in with your blood type. Did you know you were O+?"

"I've never paid that much attention. I used to give blood every once in a while during the campus blood drives, but I was always more excited about all the free cookies and juice I got afterwards."

Dr. Johnson smiled. "I had the lab make up a card for you to carry in your wallet. Heaven forbid something like this ever happens again. But if it does, I want the emergency responders to be able to move a little faster. I'd hate this town to lose another potter, especially since we just got you." She handed Jake the card. "I've been informed that you have no living relatives, is that correct?"

Jake looked up from the card and nodded.

"Is it safe to also assume that you have no insurance?"

Again Jake nodded. "I'm sorry, I just didn't ..."

"Didn't think you'd ever need it?" She smiled at him. "You're not the first twenty-something man to think he was immortal and I'm sure you won't be the last. I strongly suggest you get some insurance, at least catastrophic coverage. I hate to talk about money, but this is going to be a rather expensive stay."

Jake knew from his mother's treatments how expensive hospital stays could be. Despite his familiarity with such things, he *had* believed he was immortal. He looked at her, nodding affirmatively.

"You're a lucky man, Jake Kimball. You may have already heard about the fundraising efforts on your behalf."

"A little bit."

"Well, I don't know who you are or what you've done to deserve the admiration of so many people, but as I said before, you're a lucky man. I'd be surprised if you have much of a bill left by the time the Mayor and Mr. Smoot are done with their fundraising efforts."

"I've been wondering how long you expect me to stay. I'm feeling pretty good and I know it's expensive to be here. Can you give me any guesstimate?"

"Well, that depends a lot on your temperature. We've been monitoring it since you got out of surgery on Tuesday. Anyone who receives a blood transfusion usually runs a bit of a temperature, but we want to make sure it's not due to infection from your surgery."

Jake looked up at the monitor. His temperature was 100.8° F. "Isn't normal 96.8°?"

She smiled. "Close. Try 98.6° F. I'd like to see it drop a degree before we release you. I also came to check your incision, to see how things are healing."

Jake sat up a little straighter, offering her his arm without reservation. She set down the clipboard on the table and began unwrapping the gauze from his arm. Jake was anxious to see what lay underneath.

"It looks like you've been doing some research," she said, nodding to the table and Isaac's notes.

"I guess you could call it that."

"Did you find anything interesting?"

Jake studied her face, trying to guess what she was thinking. "I think so," he finally offered.

She nodded, peeling away the last layer of gauze.

Jake turned back to see. His arm looked bruised from the remnants of the iodine and bits of dried blood that clung to his skin. The incision was longer than he guessed, nearly three inches and crescent shaped. More than a dozen ugly black stitches held the two sides together, looking almost like long-legged ants.

"It's looking good." She let his arm down slowly and reached for several alcohol swabs which she used to clean away the stain and blood. "Another helpful hint I should give you is that if anything like this ever happens again, try wrapping your wound in something clean. The apron you used was covered with clay. We had to spend a lot of extra time making sure the incision was clean before we could sew you up. That time cost you an extra unit of blood."

"I wasn't thinking about a lot of things," Jake said, remembering his thoughts from earlier.

"So pottery must be a dangerous profession. We've had two potters, now, in the ER and both have come under dramatic circumstances. You arrived red, covered in blood. The last potter who came to us was blue."

Jake smiled a crooked smile. "Blue?"

"Yep."

"Was he a Smurf?"

Sandy laughed. "Just a crazy old man."

"Did you know Isaac very well?"

She nodded as she wrapped Jake's arm with fresh gauze. "I first noticed Isaac at church. He looked pretty out of place in his overalls, sitting on the back row with the old war widows. But it wasn't until Sam brought him to the hospital one afternoon that I officially met him. He was the sickest looking man I had ever seen. I thought for sure he must be dying. His face and hands were blue and when we made him take his shirt off to examine him, his chest and arms were also blue. Looking at him, I would have sworn he was in advanced stages of hypothermia. I had the nurses wrap him in warm blankets and ordered some blood work."

"So what was wrong?"

Sandy laughed out loud. "It was a silly thing, actually. After eliminating all of the potential causes, we found that the alcohol swab we used to prep his arm before the blood work was covered with the same blue coloring that was on his skin. I ordered a couple dozen alcohol swabs and the nurses joined me in rubbing the swabs on the old man's chest and arms. He laughed and squirmed like a child being tickled. His laughter and the silliness of the situation cracked all of us up and soon the whole emergency wing was erupting in hilarity."

"So what made him blue?" Jake asked, laughing and shaking his head in disbelief.

"That's the best part. He had been suffering from dry skin so he put on some lotion before he got out of the shower and then dried off with a new blue towel. The best we can figure, somehow the dye from the towel reacted with the lotion and caused the color to transfer to his skin. He was running late to open the Pottery and never looked in the mirror. Sam paid him a visit a few hours later and brought him to the hospital. I sent him home with a prescription to wash his towel and the problem never happened again."

Jake laughed. "You must see a lot of crazy stuff like that in the ER."

"Yeah, but that took the cake for the silliest." She took a deep breath and looked at him more seriously. "I'm sorry it took this accident for us to meet. I've been planning on stopping by for the last month, but we've been short handed and I've been working a lot of overtime. We're actually neighbors. I live just on the other side of Zubergasse: number 7. I've enjoyed seeing your new work in the window on my way to and from the hospital. I'm sure Albert isn't very happy with me. He committed me to drop by three weeks ago."

"Are you one of the mug owners, too?"

"I am. Mine is the black one, third from the left. I think I introduced myself yesterday as Dr. Johnson, but please, call me Sandy."

Jake nodded. "It seems I can't go anywhere without running into someone who knew Isaac. I'm a little curious about you though."

"Why's that?"

"Well, from what you said, Isaac came to you for help. All the others have come to him for help, friendship or both. I guess it's kind of refreshing to hear a different kind of story."

"Then maybe I should keep my mouth shut and let you think I was the hero."

"Weren't you?"

She tried to smile and shook her head. "I wish I could say the help I offered him was at least equal to the help he gave me, but I'd be lying. The truth is, like the others, Isaac came into my life when I needed a friend. He made me recognize I was headed down a long and lonely dead end road." She took a deep breath before glancing at the clock on the wall. "I normally wouldn't go into this, but a little bird told me that you're a rather independent soul who might need some help in the relationship department. If you don't mind, I feel like I need to share with you the things I learned from Isaac."

Jake smiled, feeling like he was uncovering a conspiracy. "Who have you been talking to?"

"Does it matter?"

"Maybe not."

"Let's just say you have some prominent members of the community who are worried about you. They think your independence and attitude is blinding you to the most important things in life."

Jake looked out the window. "And you think you can change me?"

"Nope, but I can at least give you a nugget of truth and let you change yourself."

"Go on then." Jake smiled. "This comes at a good time. I've been thinking about change."

"Ok. It wasn't too long ago that I was much the same way I've heard you are. I had just graduated from medical school and was matched for my residency here. I only interviewed here because it was in between two other cities where I was interviewing and I had to drive through anyway. I had never heard of Niederbipp or Kinzua County and I ranked it pretty low on my list of possible residency programs. I couldn't believe it when I matched here and was determined to do what I needed to do and get out as fast as I could. It was actually a blow to my ego; I had graduated at the top of my class and ended up at a podunk county general hospital. I started counting the days until I could leave before I even unpacked my bags."

"So what changed?"

She grinned as she looked out the window. "I've asked myself that same question a hundred times in the last few years. There was something here that I'd never experienced in my life. The people, this town…they began to feel like family. I mostly grew up in boarding schools. It gave me structure and ambition and an awesome education, but I never had much of a connection to my parents."

"Did they die?"

"No, they're still very much alive, just too busy to be bothered by a daughter. They're both professionals and have always spent a lot of time away, traveling for work. I was mostly raised by nannies before heading off to prep school. It took several years for me to realize that my ambitions were driven by my desire to be noticed by my parents. When that never really came, I tried to feed my need for attention by being better than everyone else. Just as my residency was coming to an end, I was asked to become Chief Resident of the ER."

Jake was impressed, but something wasn't adding up. "Wait a minute. You're an ER doc?"

"Yes," Sandy responded.

"Then how come you stayed with me in the ICU and here on the floor?"

Sandy paused, looking sheepish. "Well, I have to confess. Every once in a while, I take a special interest in a patient and ask to be assigned to him throughout his hospital stay. Since we're such a small operation here in Niederbipp, no one really minds. When you came in, I knew you were the new potter, and my neighbor, and I wanted to follow your case." She looked embarrassed, as if Jake had caught her spying on him. Then she got a gleam in her eye and added, "And I also wanted the media attention that comes from treating a celebrity."

Jake laughed but also felt grateful for her concern for him. "I'm sorry to interrupt your story," he said.

"Yes, well, I was made Chief Resident of the ER and felt like I was really needed, like I could make a difference. But I'm afraid it also made me pretty egocentric. Because my expectations for myself had always been high, I expected a lot from everyone I worked with. In the process, I alienated a lot of people. The nurses avoided me. The other residents walked around me. Even the full-fledged doctors chaffed at my abrasiveness. At twenty-four, I thought I had life all figured out.

I thought I was on top of the world: I had a degree; I was happy with my salary; I had a nice apartment; and I had earned the respect of my colleagues. I thought I was pretty happy."

"You make it sound like you weren't."

"I suppose it's all relative. When I think back on that time now, I realize I was trying so hard to convince myself that I was happy that I was blind to reality. After all, I had achieved all of my goals. But then one day, a blue-skinned potter showed up in my ER and threatened to shake the foundation on which I had built my fortress. In the matter of a couple of hours, my whole world seemed suddenly empty and shallow."

"That's strange. I never knew Isaac, but I've heard a lot of stories about him. It seems like they were all enlightened by Isaac. You're the first to tell me otherwise."

"Enlighten is a good word for what he did for me too. It's just that the perspective he offered me made me realize how much I still lacked. I hated that about him, but after I swallowed my pride and opened my eyes and heart to the things he had to teach me, I found meaning and happiness that I never knew I was missing. I believed I had reached my potential, but he opened my mind to a much greater potential. The incident with Isaac at the hospital was the catalyst that started all the changes in my life. When Isaac came to the ER that day, I noticed he had something I didn't have. He had something that had eluded me my whole life."

"Was it blue skin?" Jake joked.

"No!" she said, laughing. "It was much deeper than his skin. It seemed to ooze out of him from every pore. It filled the room. It was infectious and wonderful."

"You make it sound like he had a disease."

She nodded. "I've come to believe that all things have their opposites. A disease attacks the body and tries to tear it down. What I experienced that day was the exact opposite of a disease. It filled my lungs and lifted me up like helium. The ER responded not only to the laughter he inspired, but to his whole being. He came to us for help, but his medicine

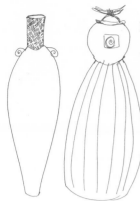

had more power than anything we could have given him. He was filled to overflowing with love."

Jake nodded, remembering similar words he had heard from the others.

"I noticed that his love and attitude affected me differently than it affected the nurses. While they were charmed by him, I remember feeling angry. I was confused by those feelings. At first I thought it was because of us all laughing together while we rubbed the blue off his skin. It was the first time I had let me guard down in front of the ER staff, and I worried they wouldn't respect me. But it was more than that. He had a peace and happiness that I had never had. A couple of days after he came to the hospital, my mind was so filled with questions and confusion that I had to leave work early to figure out what was going on. On my way home, I sat down in the shade in the church courtyard.

"I sat wondering about the secret to this old, simple man's happiness when he walked right past me. He entered the graveyard, filled a watering can at the spigot, and emptied the water on a nearby grave. Then he got on his knees to pull weeds. I walked closer to the gate to watch him work. When he finished, he sat on a bench, pulled a small book from his pocket and began reading poetry out loud. After watching him for a few minutes, I decided to take a closer look at the graveyard.

"Pretending I knew what I was doing, I went to the spigot and filled the watering can. I walked to a grave near Isaac and emptied the can on the foliage. I looked up to find him smiling. He asked if I knew I was watering weeds. Not wanting to admit my ignorance, I told him I was just getting the ground soft so I could pull them out."

Sandy laughed softly. "As it turned out, the weeds were actually very thorny vines. I winced in pain as a thorn punctured my finger.

When I turned around, Isaac had a handkerchief in his hand and was extending it to me. He seemed to be shielding a smile as he invited me to sit down next to him on the colorful bench. As I did so, he began to tell me the story of Ms. Openshaw, the woman whose grave was entangled in the vines.

"He explained that the cantankerous woman had been a loan officer at the bank for many years and had done well for herself financially. But she made some enemies by buying a home at auction when the young family that lived there failed to keep current on their payments. She moved into the large home by herself and kept all the stuff that had been left when the family was evicted. The town was appalled, but she never relented and died a lonely woman. According to Isaac, on her deathbed, she asked her only friend to plant some small seeds on her grave. The seeds sprouted and grew quickly, but no one visited her grave and before anyone noticed, the vines had developed deep roots that were sending runners throughout the entire graveyard.

"The story seemed pretty incredulous. I couldn't believe anyone would want noxious weeds adorning their final resting place. Isaac told me it was an unfortunate truth that many folks who didn't learn to love their neighbors in mortality moved on to the next life with the same disposition. He surprised me by saying that the vine's need for pruning gave him the excuse he needed to visit often and that the quiet solitude he found in the graveyard gave him a chance to think while he cared for the graves of his loved ones. He pointed to a colorful gravestone and told me his wife had been buried there for more than fifty years.

IN THE END – IT'S ONLY LOVE THAT MATTERS

"When I suggested that fifty years was a long time to be alone, he surprised me by telling me it was a long time to be without her, but that he hadn't been alone since the day he arrived in Niederbipp. Learning to love had kept him from ever feeling alone. He explained that his wife Lily taught him more about love than a hundred angels ever could have, that life was all about love—

learning to love, sharing love, being loved and teaching love.

"I remember looking at Lily's gravestone and doing the math. She was only a year older than I was when she passed away. I was impressed that someone so young could have had such a big impact on his life. When I offered my condolences, he shrugged them off, telling me that he considered himself fortunate to have had one blissful year of true love. He told me that coming to the graveyard enabled him to feel closer to her by remembering the things she taught him.

"He turned his attention to me, asking if I was married. I joked that I was married to the emergency room and wanted to keep my life simple, without wasting my time on love and dating.

"His response upset me. He told me that he felt sorry for me, and I became very defensive. He told me that if I was truly happy, I should forget he said anything, but if I wasn't, he could share with me some of the things he learned over the years. Instead, I told him to mind his own business. Then I stomped off without another word!" Sandy laughed and looked at Jake. "I'm surprised he ever spoke to me again! It was easy for me to consider him a fool when I pictured him at the hospital covered in blue dye. But his words nagged at me and made me wonder what he might know about happiness that I didn't. That was the night I had the dream…"

Jake waited for her to continue, but she seemed lost in a world of thought. "Dream?" he finally asked.

She shook herself. "It was the most awful dream I've ever had. Even now, three years later, I can still remember it. I can still feel the emptiness that it gave me."

"Tell me," he prodded.

"Ok, but it's pretty strange."

"Bring it on."

"Well, I dreamed I was watching a surgery at the hospital. Somehow I was floating over the table watching it all happen. I watched as the surgeon cut the patient's sternum, spreading the ribcage to reveal the chest cavity. Once it was opened, he and all of the nurses crowded over the patient, blocking my view.

"The doctor shook his head, telling the nurses he had never seen such a case. He expressed sorrow that the problem hadn't been discovered earlier, and lamented that it was too late to do anything now. As they pulled back from standing over the patient, I looked down into the chest cavity and saw nothing but a black hole. It was completely empty of all its vital organs. I looked at the heart monitor just in time to see it flat line. The patient was dead.

"After stapling the patient's chest back together, the surgeon removed his mask and I recognized it was Isaac. He was shaking his head and looking very sad. I stood behind the nurses as they took off their masks, all of them shaking their heads in disbelief. I flew over them to take a look at the patient. As I pulled back the sheet that was covering her head, I was startled to find it was me laying there on the table."

"Whoa!" said Jake. "You weren't kidding. That's really strange!" He smiled broadly.

"I know!" said Sandy. "Don't say I didn't warn you."

"So, did it end there?"

"No! When I saw it was me, I screamed 'Try again!' But they couldn't hear me. Isaac muttered something about it being too late just as I woke up. I was sobbing and totally wet with sweat. It took me forever to realize it was just a dream.

"I couldn't sleep the rest of the night. Every time I closed my eyes, an image from my dream would return. As soon as it started to get light, I got up and went to find Isaac. I wanted nothing more than to find the man who had performed my surgery! It was before 7:00 when I got to the Pottery. Seeing light coming from the back room, I walked around to the back door and found Isaac sitting at his wheel, hunched over an old book. He invited me in and offered me a stool while he prepared some tea.

"There was something unusual about Isaac. Knowing the impact he had on so many people in this town, I've often wondered if he put some kind of drug in that tea of his that loosened tongues and opened hearts. I had rarely confided in anyone, but never a near stranger. After just a few sips of tea, I recited my dream to him. He listened without interruption until I finished. Then he calmly asked if I knew what it meant. I wasn't sure if it meant anything at all until he explained that though his dreams were often nonsense and meaningless, whenever he remembered them as vividly as I had, he wondered what the universe might be trying to communicate to him. I tried to dismiss his comments, but in my heart, I wondered if he might be right.

"He reminded me of my words from the day before: that I didn't want to waste time on love and dating. He told me something that I've repeated to myself every day since then... 'Love is never wasted.' He explained that one of life's greatest purposes is to find joy and emphasized that it is impossible to obtain joy without love in our hearts. He said there are many different types of love, but that all love elevates us to a higher plateau and enables us to see others more clearly. He told me all varieties of love had one thing in common: unselfishness— caring more about another than you do for yourself.

"This lesson, he told me, he had learned the hard way a few years before coming to Niederbipp. He had been nearly engaged but when he went to ask his future father-in-law for his daughter's hand in marriage, her father told him he'd consent if Isaac could look him in the eye and tell him that his daughter's happiness would be more important to him than his own. Isaac said he went away, unable and unwilling to do so. As difficult as the ensuing breakup was for him, it changed him. Or, at least he started wanting to change. It began a process that eventually led him to Niederbipp and to Lily.

"The book Isaac was reading when I came in turned out to be an old Bible. He handed it to me, inviting me to read the thirteenth chapter of Paul's first epistle to the Corinthians. As I read the chapter out loud,

I began to understand the message my dream had for me—I needed to learn to love before it was too late.

"He suggested that my job put me in a unique situation where I had more intimate contact with people in one day than most folks had in a week. I tried to protest, but he seemed to read my mind, saying that professional distance was an artificial boundary that inhibited people from connecting on a human to human level. He insisted that good medicine, coupled with love, could cure all the ills in the world.

"Until his death, I stopped by nearly every week. We talked more and more about love. I learned to open my heart and share with those around me. In time, I learned to love. The more I learned, the more questions I had and I discovered that Isaac was a wealth of knowledge. We spent a lot of time talking about Lily and I became envious of the love he had for her, hoping that one day I might find someone who adored me as much as he adored her.

"Growing up in an all girls boarding school didn't give me much of a chance to fall in love. On one visit, I remember asking him what it felt like to be in love. I remember him saying that I would know love's magic when I was with someone and could feel music playing in my soul without musicians being present.

"Intrigued by that notion, I asked if that was what he had with Lily. I remember that he shook his head, explaining that theirs was true love, which he said was akin to sitting in the middle of a seventy-piece orchestra playing something from Vivaldi or Mozart with gusto. He believed that kind of love, though very rare, could last beyond the veil of death and continue in the world to come."

Sandy laughed for a moment. "True love sounded pretty good to me. I asked a lot of questions, hoping to find a way to skip the dating and move on to the good stuff. He once told me that true love was a gift from the universe, that it couldn't be found, forced or bought and that it usually came to people when they least expected it. After I stopped looking for the easy answer, he shared a few secrets with me: live the best life I could, love generously, and serve others selflessly. He taught me that when two people give more than they take, the sum of one and one is not two, but three or four—or twenty. And it grows exponentially, day by day until it fills their world. The way he spoke about love, with so much enthusiasm and passion, I had to believe that what he was telling me was true."

Jake nodded his head and pointed to Sandy's ring. "It looks like it worked out for you."

"Yeah, it did." She smiled down at her ring. "As Isaac said, it happened when I least expected it. I discovered that once I was able to set my own desires aside and get out of the way, love happened. Before I met Isaac, I NEVER would have allowed myself to fall for one of my patients. But as Isaac taught me, love knows no boundaries. A year ago, a man came into the ER with a head injury from a construction accident. He had recently moved to town to work as an architect for Briggles and Banks, the firm over on Brünnenstrasse. He was checking on the progress of one of his projects when he was hit in the head by falling debris and knocked unconscious. I assigned myself to make sure his needs were met," she smiled slyly. "I told you I sometimes follow patients throughout their stay and not just in the ER. Andrew spent a week here and, as I cared for him, I grew to love him. We went on our first date the day after he was discharged. Isaac had us to dinner several times and he was the first to know when we became engaged. He was to be the best man at our wedding next month." She looked away, tears forming in her blue eyes.

"So, why did you decide to stay here? You had big aspirations. Do you ever feel like you're settling for something less than your dreams?"

She took a deep breath and turned to him. "To be completely honest, I used to be pretty confused about that. It's not easy for me to change. I have always been stubborn, but time and this town have softened me. The quirkiness that once made me crazy now charms me. When I first got here, I spent a lot of time wishing I was somewhere else—somewhere normal. I figure I've either become quirky too or love has desensitized me to the things that bothered me."

"But do you ever feel like you're giving up on a dream?"

She looked thoughtful. "Jake, I have traded in my selfish ambitions for the opportunity to love and be loved, not only by Andrew, but by this whole town. I have traded in my team of one for a family of over 6,500. I have been a part of births and deaths. I have shared tears of joy and sorrow with people I have learned to love. Life is much different than I expected it would be even five years ago, but it's also much better than I ever imagined. I realized some time ago that I didn't give up my dream; I traded it for something infinitely better. I have sacrificed my will and in return I have received so much more than I ever could have dreamed of. From time to time, I'll hear that a classmate has been named to some prestigious position and I'll feel the pangs of jealousy flare. But what I have here, the family and community I feel here… you can't buy that. Even with all its quirks, this is still a big ol' slice of heaven. There is no place I'd rather be. Andrew and I hope to live here until the day we die."

"Aren't you afraid of that kind of commitment? I mean, you're so young. Aren't you at least a little bit afraid that you'll miss out on life?"

Sandy looked thoughtful. "No. Down the road, I may sometimes question if this is the best place for me, but I feel like the hand of providence brought me here and then provided people to love me and teach me. I've prayed my whole life for people like those I've met in Niederbipp, but until I came here—actually, until I made a commitment to stay—I never found them. I have yearned for the kind of human connection that seems so natural to these people. I have yearned to be loved, to be needed, to feel like I am an important part of the whole. Will I miss out on life because of my decision to stay here? The potential is always there, but in all honesty, I'm not sure I ever really lived until

I came here. My life is now divided into two segments: the life I lived before coming to Niederbipp and the life I've lived since. Despite my early inclinations to leave, there's simply no place I'd rather be. This town embodies all the feelings of home I've ever known." She paused before adding, "I guess I'm more scared that I'll miss out on life if I leave Niederbipp than if I stay."

Jake listened closely to her words, but couldn't quench the last ember of independence burning inside of him. "I just don't know. There are lots of things I really like about Niederbipp, but I feel like I am too young to make a decision that will affect the rest of my life. I've only seen a small part of the world. I hoped to see a lot more of it before I put down roots."

"You make it sound like a commitment to be the town potter will keep you from ever leaving."

"Sandy, you've been here long enough to know that the tradition of the potters in this town goes back almost three hundred years. It's not like I can commit to this and just decide after a year that I'd rather be in Oregon or Italy or Japan."

"I take it you haven't met Eric Schmelding yet?"

"Who?"

"He's the owner of the watch shop on Hauptstrasse. I haven't seen him for a few months. He's probably been out of town again on one of his adventures. He inherited the shop about ten years ago from his grandfather but his passion is photography and travel. I think he grew up in Florida, but he's spent time on every continent and has the pictures to prove it. Every summer during the tourist season, he entertains visitors and locals with his slide shows. He has pictures of people and places all over the world. I used to think he was rich, but I've heard he makes just enough to travel. He's a great guy. You ought to talk to him sometime. He's been around the world a dozen times or more, but he ends each of his presentations by saying, 'There's no place like Niederbipp.' Jake, it's not like if you decide to stay, you can't ever leave. Andrew and I are going on a three week tour of the fjords of Norway for our honeymoon. Eric's slide show last summer inspired us. I have a feeling this will be the first of many great vacations."

Jake nodded, imagining the fjords in his mind. He closed his eyes tightly, trying to make the images go away. "So, do you have any advice for someone like me who's trying to decide if Niederbipp is the right place to be?"

Sandy looked thoughtful for a long moment. "Maybe just two small pieces of advice: ignore reason and listen to your heart. That's the only way you'll ever know, Jake. I learned to trust the feelings of my heart a couple of years ago and things have never been better in my life. Things sometimes make sense with your heart that never do with reason alone. Reason often eliminates the potential for magic to happen, but your heart knows no boundaries, no limits to what you can become."

Jake looked at her for a long time, listening to her words echoing through the deep canyons of his soul. "Thank you," he finally said.

"It's my pleasure. I know you're not Isaac, but sharing these things with you makes me feel like the advice he gave me has now come full circle. Don't thank me, thank him. I better get back to work. If there's anything I can do, have the nurses page me."

Jake thanked her again and as he watched her go, he was reminded of a Zen proverb his professor Eric Lewis had posted on the wall of his office, "When the student is ready, the teacher will appear."

(15)
BALM

YOU CANNOT TEACH A MAN ANYTHING;
YOU CAN ONLY HELP HIM FIND IT
WITHIN HIMSELF.
—GALILEO GALILEI

 itting still had never been one of Jake's talents. Having long had an aversion to television, he looked around his room for something else to occupy his mind. He reread several of the letters on the table, both those addressed to him and several others to Isaac, then busied himself stacking them according to size. When that failed to quell his boredom, he stacked them according to color, intermixing the cards and notes according to the color spectrum. His table soon looked like the paint swatch display at Home Depot, heavy on the white end of the spectrum, but with a good representation of the other colors. He wished he had his sketchbook.

At noon, when a nurse came by to check on him, he asked if he could take a shower. She wrapped his bandages and a portion of his arm in plastic wrap and then unhooked him from his monitors. He stood under the warm water for twenty minutes, grateful to be on his feet and anxious to get out of the hospital. As he was getting dressed, however, he was struck with nausea and dizziness. He stumbled back into bed, exhausted, and quickly fell asleep.

Hushed voices awoke Jake some time later. Gloria stood in the hallway, just outside his door, talking to a nurse. Jake was curious about their furtive whispers, but he lay still, straining to make sense of what was being said. HIPAA was mentioned several times by the nurse and Gloria seemed upset. Jake knew the rules of HIPAA. Only direct family members or those authorized by a patient could be updated or given information. As he watched the women converse, an idea came into Jake's head—a chance to begin redeeming himself.

"Nurse!" He was excited, and the word came out louder than he'd intended.

She rushed to his bedside. "What is it? Are you ok?"

"Yeah, I'm fine. I've just been thinking that I never designated a next of kin for release of HIPAA information. I was hoping I might be able to do that now."

"Ahhh...sure. There is some paperwork for you to sign."

"That's fine, but in the meantime, I was hoping you could release any information to Gloria." Jake looked up. "What do you know? There she is right there!"

Gloria was standing in the doorway, beaming. His idea seemed to be working. "She's the closest thing I have to a mother. I'd appreciate it if you'd make sure she receives notification of any changes in my medication as well as regular updates about my condition."

The nurse nodded, looking flustered. "I'll get the paperwork." She walked quickly from the room, stepping around Gloria who still stood in the doorway. Gloria made room from her, but turned to kick the air after the nurse had walked by. She turned back to the room with a broad smile across her face. "Thanks," she said, walking to Jake's bedside. "I've been wrestling with this woman since you got here. The other nurses started slipping me information when they learned you had no family, but this one...she's been impossible. I don't get this whole HIPAA thing at all. How are your neighbors supposed to find out about you? I can see something like this being valuable in some cases, but not in this town. We look after each other. What if I was sick or Joseph and I were in an accident? How would anybody know? This HIPAA thing doesn't work for people like me and you." Jake grinned. "Well, would you like me to ask for another one of those papers for you and you could put my name on it? That way, if something ever happens, I'll be able to let the town know."

She looked thoughtful as she put her hands on his cheeks, holding his face like his mother often did when he was younger and wanted his full attention. "Jake, that's really thoughtful of you. Thank you." She released his face but sat down on the side of his bed. "I...I need to apologize again for getting upset with you yesterday. I need to mind my own business."

Jake shook his head, putting his hand on Gloria's shoulder. "Listen, I'm the one who needs to apologize. I've been a real jerk. And you're right; I *have* been proud and self-centered." Gloria smiled as she listened to his confession and Jake knew he was finally saying the right things. "This accident has given me a chance to think...a lot. I'm sorry for the way I've treated you and Amy and so many others who have tried to help me. I've been blind to a lot of things. I'm just not used to having people care about me. I think it's easy to become self-centered when you're an only child and an orphan. I've had to look out for myself. I've just never figured out how to do it any other way."

Gloria had a pained look on her face. "Jake, you have to let people in. We love you. You're needed and wanted here, not just because we need a potter, but because you need a family. You may not understand that yet, but we all need family. We all need a place to belong, a place where we're loved."

Jake nodded. "I'm beginning to get that."

"I understand your desire to see the world, but you've been blind to the love of a beautiful woman and a village that adores you more than you could understand." He winced at the reference to Amy.

Gloria swallowed before continuing. "Joseph and I have loved a lot of kids over the years, but we both felt a connection to you that first evening. You really endeared yourself to us. We know we're just a couple of old, childless hippies, but when we heard your story and learned that you're an orphan, I'll admit we wanted to be your family. We wanted you to be the son we never had. You couldn't be more than a year older than our son would be, had he lived."

Jake felt chills. He hadn't realized how close he was in age to their baby. It made sense why Gloria mothered him. "Every time I look at you, I try to imagine what our son would look like. I know it's unfair, but from that first day, we have pretended you are ours." She laughed at herself, then confessed, "We've had a new sense of happiness since we met you. I have to keep reminding myself that you are who you are—a strong-willed young man who has his own agenda in life."

She ran her fingers through his hair like his mother had so many times before. "Jake, I don't want to stand in your way. We just want to help you if we can. We want you to know that we love you and hope to have you around for as long as possible."

Jake met Gloria's gaze. Her dark brown eyes shone with the same kindness he had felt from her so many times before. His own eyes filled with tears. It had been years since he had allowed himself to cry. And now, in the matter of a week, tears seemed to flow freely. It wasn't that he had an aversion to tears, he just hadn't allowed himself to get started. Perhaps, unconsciously, he was trying to maintain the illusion of control. But the façade was unnecessary here where he had been accepted and embraced. The people of Niederbipp seemed eager to welcome him as one of their own. These thoughts brought on more tears that fell from his chin and splashed on his hospital gown. He felt no need to wipe them away or to hide them from Gloria. In that moment, there was clarity. Here was love—seemingly unconditional love that had been gone from his life since his mother's death. Jake had tried hard to ignore the void left at her passing. Now Gloria, with her love and kindness, was filling that void.

As Jake recalled his previous interactions with Gloria, he recognized that this love—this healing ointment—had been offered before. He recalled his first impression of her and the goodness that both engulfed her and emanated from her. It drew him in like a moth to a flame. He had basked in this light for short periods, but his future plans, independence and pride had kept him from drinking it all in.

"I'm really sorry I've wasted so much time," he finally uttered, overwhelmed by the reality of his thick head.

Gloria looked thoughtful. "You're the second person I've heard that from in the last couple of days. I…Amy…uh…I hope you'll take the chance to make things better when you get out. I'm afraid you've bruised the tender love you and Amy have been nourishing."

Jake grimaced. "Gloria, I have no idea what I'm doing. Ever since our first date, I've been waiting for her to wake up and realize how big of an idiot I am! I haven't seen her since Monday. I'm guessing that realization finally hit her. She's probably already moved on. I don't deserve her anyway."

Gloria looked away and was silent for a long moment. Jake watched her. She looked like she was hiding something, biting her tongue. Finally she turned to him.

"Jake, we all go through periods in our life when we feel unworthy of love, but believing that about ourselves is one of the worst mistakes we can ever make. We were created out of love, both spiritually and physically. If we could tap the power of love, the world itself could be propelled by it…maybe it is. There is no greater motivator or stronger force. If you've resigned yourself to the belief that you're not worthy of

Amy's love, you have already lost her."

Jake looked at Gloria, struck by her words. "So what can I do?"

"You can change!" A smile spread across her whole face. Even her eyes were smiling. "Jake, as I said, love is a motivator. It makes you want to be the best 'you' you can possibly be. It inspires you to stretch, to become more, to reach higher and farther than you ever have before. It opens your mind to new possibilities and new worlds. It fills your mind with questions and drives you to seek the answers. It teaches you, feeds you and makes you hungry for truth and understanding. If you feel you're not worthy of Amy's love, make yourself worthy."

Jake felt hope and despair at the same moment. "Gloria, that all sounds really good, but I don't know the first thing about love. I'm a fool. Amy is only the second girl I have really fallen in love with. The first one ended in a total fiasco. After not seeing Amy since Monday, I'm wondering if I've butchered any chance I had with her. I'm not good at this stuff."

"Does she know how you feel about her?"

"I thought so. I really love her. I told her that, maybe even a couple of times."

Gloria laughed. "Jake, some women—no, make that most women—need to be told that they're loved on regular basis. Daily is sufficient for some, but probably not in the beginning. It doesn't cost you anything to say those three words, but no three words have more power."

"So, I need to say 'I love you' more often?"

"Not necessarily, but if you love someone and want that love to grow and develop, those are magic words, especially when they are coupled with actions."

"Can you give me an example? Like I said, I am really dumb about this stuff."

She nodded. "When Joseph and I were dating, way back in the beginning, just hearing 'I love you' meant a lot. It still does, but Joseph put his money where his mouth was. He pursued me. In the end, if words don't accompany action, the words lose their meaning. Joseph wrote me a lot of letters after we met. I was impressed with his writing and fell in love with him through those letters. It took a lot of work and thought for him to write me at least once a week, but when he showed up on my parents' doorstep in Ft. Lauderdale, his words took flight. I knew he was serious. He invested himself, his time and his treasure in me and our relationship.

"Joseph didn't come from a family with money. He's worked hard his whole life. I will always be grateful to his parents for giving him such a great work ethic, but in addition to teaching him to work, his close knit Italian family taught him that love is a verb. The letters were wonderful in our early days, but after I fell for him, he continued to woo me. Too many folks believe the wooing is over when the knot is tied. Our love has continued to grow because we have learned the importance of constantly feeding it."

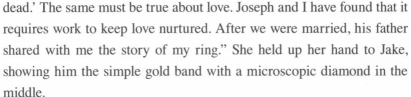

She looked away, looking thoughtful again. "I'm reminded of a small tile embedded in the floor of the church I discovered shortly after we came here. I think it gives far more understanding in fewer words than I ever could. It's a scripture from somewhere in the Bible. It says, 'Faith without works, is dead.' The same must be true about love. Joseph and I have found that it requires work to keep love nurtured. After we were married, his father shared with me the story of my ring." She held up her hand to Jake, showing him the simple gold band with a microscopic diamond in the middle.

"I liked the ring when Joseph proposed, but when I learned what Joseph had done to earn the money to buy it, I gained a whole new appreciation for both the ring and for Joseph. Through his dad, I learned that this ring represented nearly a year's worth of gas money."

"Gas money?" Jake asked, surprised.

"That's right. Joseph knew he couldn't save money for a ring without making some sacrifices, so he parked his VW bus and walked everywhere he went for almost a whole year. Every time I look at this ring, I imagine Joseph trudging through the rain, snow and heat, making plans for a life with me. He didn't buy this ring with what he could spare; he bought it with his sacrifice. He gave me the best he could give me—he gave me himself."

Her words resonated with Jake. He knew he loved Amy, but had never considered how he expressed that love. A kiss, a hug, an encouraging word—all these had been given freely, painlessly, almost effortlessly. Compared to the way Joseph had professed his love to Gloria, Jake realized his own actions lacked substance. A phrase he had heard several times sounded through his ears. "Joy, in all its glory, comes only through unselfishness," he said under his breath.

"What's that?" Gloria asked turning to face him directly.

"I said, 'Joy in all its glory comes only through unselfishness.' That's what you're trying to tell me. That's what this whole town has been trying to tell me, isn't it?"

She smiled again with her whole face, her eyes brimming with tears. "Yes," she said, reaching for his hand. "That's one of the most important lessons we can learn in life, but the problem is, we have to learn it again and again. It's one of the easiest things to forget. The very second we think of ourselves first, we turn our backs on that truth. We forget that we are part of a family, a community. If we don't change, we begin to believe we are islands."

"So what does one do if he believes he is an island?"

"You change."

Gloria and Jake turned to the doorway where Sandy stood watching them, nodding her head.

"You change," she repeated. "Take it from me, there is no joy in being an island." She walked into the room and stopped at the foot of Jake's bed.

"Hello, Sandy," Gloria said.

"Hi guys." She looked at Jake.

"I understand you requested a HIPAA release form." She smiled at the two of them.

"I did. I wanted to make sure Gloria could get any information about me that she needed."

Jake signed the paperwork attached to Sandy's clipboard and handed it back to her.

"How are you feeling?"

"Anxious to get out of here. No offense, but I have a lot of things to do. Do you think I'll be able to get out by tomorrow?"

She looked at the monitors. "Your temperature is still a little high. We might know better by this afternoon, but you're going to need to take things easy for a week or so. That artery needs to heal or you could be right back in here with internal bleeding. You probably shouldn't be lifting anything for a couple of weeks."

Jake nodded, looking disappointed.

"It sounds like you're giving Jake some good medicine," Sandy said, turning her attention to Gloria.

"I hope so. We've got to get him well. Tourist season officially started on Monday and he's got a lot of pots to make. I still haven't got my order of vases." She winked at Jake.

Sandy nodded at Jake. "Listen, I know you're anxious to get out of here. The medicine I practice will help you heal physically, but that bit about joy I heard when I came in…that medicine has far greater potency. Not only will it heal you, it will heal your love life."

Gloria winked at Sandy when her last words were spoken. To Jake, the wink communicated something between them that he didn't understand.

"What was that?" he asked looking back and forth between them.

"Nothing," said Sandy. "I uh…I need to get going. I get off in an hour and I've got a lot of paperwork to finish up before I leave. Is there anything you need, Jake?"

Jake shook his head, trying to understand what he had just missed.

"Then I'll see you tomorrow morning. Try and get some rest."

Jake and Gloria watched her go. As she left the room, she turned and winked at Gloria.

"What's going on?" Jake asked.

"What do you mean?" Gloria looked at him, wide eyed.

"I feel like the two of you just told a joke and I missed the punch line completely."

She smiled. "Well, I'll just say that you have a lot to learn about women, but there will always be a lot you'll never know. We communicate on a different level."

Jake nodded, resignedly.

"I better get going. I just stopped in to make a delivery and check on you. Joseph needs me back at the shop. I'll try to stop by again tomorrow."

As Jake watched her go, he tried to imagine what he had just missed. He couldn't remember saying anything to Sandy about his love life. He wondered if her comment about it was generic or if she knew more than she admitted.

(16)

INTENTIONS

LIFE'S GREATEST HAPPINESS IS TO BE
CONVINCED THAT WE ARE LOVED
-LOVED FOR OURSELVES, OR RATHER,
LOVED IN SPITE OF OURSELVES.
—VICTOR HUGO IN LES MISERABLES

J ake grew increasingly restless once he was alone again. Time here moved painfully slowly. He was bored and tired but his thoughts wouldn't let him sleep. He was tormented thinking about Amy. He wanted to apologize for being selfish and hoped he hadn't lost the chance to be her friend. Where was she? Why hadn't she stopped by to visit? She hadn't even sent a card or a greeting. He began to feel sorry for himself, wondering if he really deserved a card or a visit. But, remembering Gloria's words, he determined to make the first move.

The nightstand by his bed held a small note pad and a pen. An hour later, when his dinner arrived, Jake had made his way through most of the notepad. Wadded up papers covered his bed and littered the floor. When the nurse asked if she could bring him anything else, he asked for another pad of paper. His dinner was cold before he'd composed two sentences that he thought were worth keeping. Many other wads of paper had been added to the growing pile.

A knock at the door interrupted his thoughts. He looked up to see Alice's long black hair flowing over her bare shoulders and onto her pastel tank top.

"Can I come in?"

"Sure," Jake said, sitting up.

"What happened to you?"

"Uhhhh... a pottery shard gashed..."

"No, duh! I know about THAT. What happened to your mouth?! It looks like you're all bruised."

Jake touched his lips, rubbing his fingers over his stubbly cheeks. When he pulled his hand away, he saw that his fingers were blackened with ink. He shook his head. "I guess my pen broke. I have a habit of biting on my pens when I write." Embarrassed, he grabbed the napkin from his tray and tried to wipe the ink away, but it was stubborn. Alice pulled a compact mirror from her purse, sat down on the bed, and offered it to him. He dabbed the napkin in his water and his lips were soon mostly clear of the ink, but reddened from the friction of wiping it off. He stuck out his tongue in the mirror to see it too was covered with black stains.

Alice laughed. She pointed to his food tray where his dinner remained untouched. "I know hospital food is bad, but you must be pretty desperate if you're hungry enough to eat your pen. If you would have told me things were so bad, I would have brought you another box of Twinkies." They laughed together.

"What's up with all the paper?" she asked when the laughter died down.

"I've just been writing some notes."

"You didn't tell me you were a writer." She picked up one of the crumpled wads and began to open it. Before she could read it, Jake put his hand on top of hers, halting her progress.

"It's personal. I…I've been writing a note to a friend."

She looked at all the paper, nodding. "That must be some note."

Jake tried to change the subject, but the transition was painfully awkward. They talked about the weather on the outside of his small world. She talked about her day, having spent most of it outside doing yoga by the river before her ten mile run through the hills. His thoughts wandered when she spoke about the trail across the bridge on the other side of the river that climbed the steep hillside and continued for several miles. Her words were lost to him as he remembered  that evening just a week ago when Amy had taken him to the pirate lookout. From Alice's description, he knew her trail and Amy's hideout had to be nearby. The memories made Jake want to get back to his writing, get back to Amy, but Alice continued her monologue for some time before she finally noticed his mind was somewhere else.

"Are you ok?" she asked.

Jake blinked hard. "Yeah, I'm just tired. I…it's been a long day."

She leaned over and kissed him on the cheek. "I'm sorry. I'll let you rest. I'll try to stop by earlier tomorrow." She walked to the door before turning to blow Jake a kiss. He forced a smile, but was happy to see her go. He could tell she was interested in him, but if he ever had similar feelings, they had long ago evaporated. He turned back to his writing, anxious to make some progress after wasting nearly two pads of paper. A few minutes later, another knock on the door interrupted his thoughts. Thomas strode into the room with a bundle in his arms.

He nodded to Jake, holding the stack of items between his left arm and chin as he turned to close the door behind him with his free hand. "I was dropping off the mail in your apartment this afternoon. I thought maybe you could use some more clothes if you're getting out tomorrow. With tourist season started, the Mayor probably wouldn't be very keen about you walking down Hauptstrasse in your gown with your hind end hanging out."

Jake laughed. "Thanks." He sat up to receive the stack which Thomas set down on his lap.

"Sam sends his greetings and his pastries. He loaded that bag up with all your favorites and said he hopes this won't set you back too long on the tiles you're making for his floor."

Jake grimaced. He had totally forgotten about the floor. He set the paper bag next to his uneaten dinner. A pair of jeans and a t-shirt followed as he worked his way down through the stack. He set these aside, uncovering his sketchbook. He looked up at Thomas. "How did you know? I've been wishing I had this all week."

"I saw it when I picked up your clothes. I noticed that, like Isaac, you often have your sketchbook with you and wondered if you might like having it here. I'm sorry I didn't think to bring it earlier."

"Thanks." He lifted it up to reveal the last item. He recognized it immediately—its worn leather cover and wide rubber band holding it shut: Isaac's sketchbook. He looked up at Thomas, surprise in his eyes.

"I saw this on your table. Sam told me he had given it to you. I thought you might be reading it so I figured I'd bring it too."

Jake set his own sketchbook to the side, shifting his full attention to Isaac's book. The smooth cover showed signs of wear on all the edges, pieces of the leather pulling away in places. He rubbed his finger over one of the frayed edges, considering the immaturity of his previous animosity towards this book. "Thanks. I….I haven't really gotten into it yet, but maybe it's time."

Thomas nodded. "It looks like you've been keeping yourself busy," he scanned the litter of papers on the floor and bed.

Jake looked at the mess. "I guess I should clean this up."

Thomas went to the corner and moved the waste basket nearer to the bed. "I know it's none of my business, but I ran into Alice on my way in.

I don't suppose those red lips of yours have anything to do with her?"

Jake blushed and laughed nervously. "No, my pen broke in my mouth when I was writing earlier and I had to scrub it off."

Thomas raised one eyebrow and smiled. "Don't worry Jake. Your secret's safe with me."

"Thomas!" Jake said loudly, exasperated.

"I just wanted to see you blush, and wondered if you had moved on so quickly from Amy. I thought you two really had a good thing going."

"I thought so too," responded Jake, anxious to talk about her, "but I haven't seen her since Monday. I must have made her pretty mad. Were her paints in the kitchen when you were in my apartment today?"

Thomas looked at Jake for a moment before responding. "No. Beverly came and picked them up yesterday while I was there."

Jake looked away. He stared off into space for almost a full minute. "I guess that means she's painting. That's good," he turned back to Thomas. "I'm glad she's painting. She's got a lot of talent. I just wish I could do something. I wish I wasn't stuck here. I want to at least try to fix things with her. I can't tell you how bad this has been, not knowing what she's feeling."

Thomas took a deep breath and exhaled. "Jake, remember how I told you that things aren't always as they appear to be?"

Jake looked at him, processing his words. "Yes," he finally said.

"Well, I don't think you should assume that Amy's absence is due to not being worried about you."

"What else could it mean?"

"Remember Jake, things aren't always as they appear to be. I can't talk about it, but I want you to know that if you are feeling like you've lost her, you're wrong. You have some things to fix when you get out of here, but I know for a fact that Amy cares a great deal for you."

"How can you know that? I don't know that. Alice has been here twice and I haven't even heard a thing from Amy yet. How can you say that Amy even cares?"

"Jake, I wish I could tell you, but I'm going to leave that up to her. Be patient and when the opportunity to talk to her presents itself, I'd advise you to shut up and listen. You owe her that much. I've said more than I should have, but I really hope you kids can work things out. Just keep your head out of it and listen with your heart and things will work out better."

He stepped toward the door. "I need to get going, but let me give you one more bit of advice. Be careful with Alice."

Jake nodded, but felt lost. If he was confused before, he was more so now. He thanked Thomas again and watched him disappear down the hallway.

Kai dropped in a few minutes later, pulling Jake away from his thoughts. He brought greetings from Molly whose feet, he explained, were too swollen and tired to walk tonight. As they ate Sam's pastries, Jake asked Kai if he knew anything about Amy. He watched as Kai squirmed, looking uncomfortable. It seemed like he wanted to say something, but stopped. A few minutes later he excused himself, saying he needed to get back to Molly.

It was nice to see Kai and Thomas, but their visits left Jake confused about Amy. He wondered about the secrecy—something that seemed so foreign in this town where everyone knew everything about everyone. His relationship with Amy seemed to be the talk of the town just a week ago. Now, no one was talking. Why? What were they hiding? He tried to remember Thomas' advice. It didn't make much sense. He had to get out of here. He had to find Amy and talk to her. He would listen, but he also needed to talk. He needed to tell her how he really felt about her. He resolved to stop trying to be an island. He would put away his selfish desires, no matter how vulnerable it made him, and learn to share what he was feeling with her.

He gathered up the paper from his bed and tossed it into the waste basket. Then he laid his head back on his pillow, tired, but far too restless to sleep. Rolling over on his right side, he saw Isaac's sketchbook next to the bag of Sam's pastries. He looked at the book for a long time, trying to understand what had kept him from looking at it before. When he first heard of its existence, he had been excited about learning all he could from its pages. He remembered how he hoped he would be able to spend time looking at it with Amy. So much had changed in only five days. And the book remained unopened. He began feeling foolish for the way he'd acted. What was he afraid of? Why had he allowed fear to keep him from learning whatever the book had to offer? Finally, after several minutes, he adjusted his bed to sit up straight. He reached for the book, removed the wide rubber band, opened its cover and began to read.

THANKSGIVING

NO PAIN, NO PALM; NO THORNS, NO THRONE; NO GALL, NO GLORY; NO CROSS, NO CROWN.

—WILLIAM PENN

 he first yellowed page of Isaac's sketchbook stared back at Jake as he read its words.

Hand-built journey jars

These are the thoughts and ideas of a humble potter. If you are in this far, I hope you asked my permission. If I have gone to the world of spirits, read on. I hope that by writing these things down, my friends might know that the words I share with them and the feelings of my heart are one and the same. And so I dedicate this book to my God, the potters who have passed before me, the loving memory of my wife, Lily and my son who I never knew. With hope in my heart, I pray the actions of my life may prove me worthy to be with them someday.

Isaac Aaron Bingham
Started May 12, 1998
Volume 36

Jake read the words a second time, stopping to run his fingers over the final words. He wondered where the rest of the volumes might be. He hadn't seen them in the apartment or the studio, yet this implied that there were 35 other volumes somewhere. His eyes traveled a few lines up. No one had ever mentioned Isaac's son. Why? Its mention in the sketchbook piqued his curiosity. Did no one know that he had a son? Jake pictured the graveyard. There was no small grave next to Lily's, no sign of a son anywhere. Could it have been from a previous relationship? Jake asked himself. Could there be an heir out there somewhere, the son of Isaac, raised by a single mother without the knowledge of his father? The idea seemed preposterous, yet possible. Jake remembered the words of Brian and Gloria as they told him about the kind of man he had been before he came here. Even Sandy said just yesterday that he had been close to being engaged. Was it possible that Isaac could have had a love affair with this woman and broken it off? Was this the reason he had left New York and his old life, hiding out in a Quaker village where no one would ever think to look for him? Was there something dark in his past that kept him here?

The ideas were intriguing, but also troubling. Isaac was a saint. From all accounts, he had spent his life serving and loving the people of Niederbipp. He had mourned with those that mourned, comforted those in needed of comfort, lifted up the weary and downtrodden, given hope to the hopeless, and with his loving hands and big heart had shaped several generations of Niederbippians. Could such a man also be guilty of treachery and abandonment? Jake pondered this for several minutes until his eyes rested again on the dedication written in Isaac's own hand. Jake read it again. His words were vague. Was this son, whoever he was, still alive or was he dead? It could be understood either way. Still, Jake didn't want to believe the man who he had come to revere as a hero could also be capable of something dark. He tried to put it out of his head, flipping to the next page.

Like his own sketchbook, Isaac's was a jumbled collection of sketches, notes, scribbles and ideas. One page revealed a mark left by the wet foot of a mug. Jake guessed the ring was residue from peppermint tea. Another page had brown and gray splatters of glaze embedded into the paper. The book and its yellowed pages looked much older than the decade or so that had passed since the date in Isaac's inscription. Jake guessed the book must be at least fifty years old—maybe significantly older. He looked for other clues about its origin and age but found none. Its paper was high quality, thick and smooth. The bottom center of each page displayed the page number in the middle of two beautifully embellished, hand-drawn, five-petaled flowers. He smiled to himself when he recognized this flower. He had seen it on Isaac's wife's grave and later discovered it as the secret ingredient in his famous tea: myosois alpenstris—forget-me-not.

Suddenly, this book was more than a book and its pages more than a jumbled collection of doodles and scribbles. This was Isaac! It was a portion of the man himself—the secrets of his soul. Jake felt foolish for putting this off so long. This was the man he had come to replace. The presence of those simple flowers, meticulously hand drawn on every page, spoke volumes.

Jake thought back to the night he and Amy had examined the pots in the apartment. That night, he had learned the true meaning behind the collection and found the note with the John Keats quote.

> November 12, 1972
> "Don't be discouraged by failure. It can be a positive experience. Failure is, in a sense, the highway to success, inasmuch as every discovery, of what is fake leads us to seek earnestly after what is true, and every fresh experience points out some form of error which we shall afterwards carefully avoid."
> —John Keats
> I found this quote tonight in my reading and thought it applied well to the pots on the shelf.

And here he was again, wondering what bit of agony he might have avoided had he opened these pages sooner. If he had honestly sought the truth earlier, what would his circumstances be like now? The book may have opened his mind and heart to wisdom. Maybe he would be with Amy right now. Maybe their friendship would have deepened, rather than sliding backwards into obscurity. Blinking back tears, he looked at the clock on the wall. 10:15. He would be with her now. Instead, he was here, alone, his body bruised, his ego broken. He was angry with himself that just a week earlier this same lesson had been taught to him by the pots Isaac and the others left behind, yet here he was again, learning the same hard lesson. He knew he could run from these truths, but sooner or later, the truth would find him.

Jake took a deep breath, staring up at the ceiling. Isn't this what his mother had prayed for: people to love him? At this moment it seemed so clear that he was here for a reason, that he had been led here by the hand of providence. Why couldn't it always be so clear? Why did there always have to be so many questions, so much confusion? Why couldn't this clarity remain?

As soon as he had asked these questions, the answer came, filling his eyes once more with tears. There was no audible voice, but something much wiser than himself spoke to his very core. "Joy, in all its glory, comes only through unselfishness." A tingle like a warm electric current started at the crown of his head and moved slowly down his spine, exciting every cell in his body until the whole of it was reverberating. Tears poured down his cheeks. He knew in that moment that this was where he was supposed to be. This was where the gods had hand delivered him. In that moment, any residual reluctance to commit to staying faded away. This was his land of milk and honey. The spell of Niederbipp, experienced by so many before him, finally penetrated his heart and thick head—that last frontier that had kept him from it before.

As he wiped his eyes, he turned back to the book on his lap, running his finger over the forget-me-not on page 7. He flipped the page. It opened to a sketch of a tree that filled both of the pages. At the top of the left page was written in Isaac's hand, "The Crying Place."

Two low limbs jutted out from the right side of the trunk of the willow, running parallel to the ground before jumping up to mingle with the others. The sketch was nothing special. Isaac was a good potter, but was not very talented in drawing. Jake was just about to turn the page when he saw something written on the higher of the two lower branches. He held the book close to his face, straining to read what it said. "Be still and know that I am God."

Again Jake's eyes filled with tears. If he had discovered this on any other day, these words would probably have provoked thought, but today, they had extra power. It seemed timely that he find them now. He repeated the words again and again in his mind. There was something familiar about them. He wondered if they might be scripture. He opened his own sketchbook, copying the words so he wouldn't forget them.

The Crying Place

Be still and know that I am God.

une 6, 1998 —I visited the crying place today. I was
minded of something my mother taught me: " there is a
od, and it's not you!

149

At the bottom of the page under Isaac's tree was a small note Jake hadn't seen before. It had been covered by his blanket as the book rested on his lap.

June 6, 1998 –I visited the crying place today. I was reminded of something my mother taught me: "there is a God, and it's not you!"

Jake smiled through his tears. Isaac and his mother were right. Jake had wanted so badly to plough his own furrow that he hadn't allowed God to have much of an influence on his decisions. Looking at the last month of his life, however, he saw that God was extending His hand into Jake's life anyway. As he continued to flip through the pages of Isaac's sketchbook, Jake was struck again and again by the realization that his summer detour in Niederbipp was no accident; this was the place the universe wanted him to be. The book he had avoided and feared poured out the balm he needed. At midnight, emotionally drained and physically exhausted, Jake set the sketchbook aside, turned out the light, and fell asleep whispering prayers of thanksgiving.

⑱

HOMEBOUND TWICE

A KISS IS NEVER A BAD KISS UNLESS IT IS AN UNWANTED KISS.

—UNKNOWN

orning came early—too early—but when Jake saw the old leather sketchbook sitting on his table, he welcomed the day and eagerly began reading. When his breakfast tray came, he only picked at the food before pushing it aside for more important things. Sandy stopped by at 10:00 with the good news that he could check out at 2:00. Jake was surprised by the mixed feelings he had. His thoughts and attention had been so focused on Isaac's book that the thought of having to deal with other things seemed like a burden. He was actually a little sad to be leaving this peaceful cocoon. The waste basket filled with crumpled paper reminded him of the responsibilities he had ahead of him. Amy was out there, somewhere. He wanted to be near her even though he knew a lot of wrinkles needed to be ironed out before it could be as it had been. With new insight, new understanding, and new humility, he hoped it would be easier.

When Gloria stopped by at noon to check on him, he jumped out of bed and embraced her. He thanked her for not giving up on him and for helping him to see things more clearly. Most of all, he thanked her for loving him. She laughed through tears. Jake explained that things had become clearer as he studied Isaac's sketchbook. He told her he knew he needed to change and that the change had begun already in his heart. He looked forward to applying that change to his life and relationships. Gloria embraced him again and invited him to dinner at 6:30, if he didn't have other plans.

Jake was signing papers and receiving instructions just before 2:00 when Alice dropped in and insisted on walking him home. Anxious to see Amy, Jake tried to protest but Alice wouldn't take "no" for an answer. They retraced the same steps Jake had stumbled along three days earlier. This time, it seemed even longer. Alice chatted away happily while Jake's thoughts wandered anxiously to other things, especially to Amy. She grabbed his arm as they walked through the busy Hauptstrasse. Where Amy's touch had electrified him over and over again, Alice's touch felt awkward and uncomfortable. Alice was beautiful, charming, energetic and athletic, but Jake had never felt comfortable with the amount of skin she purposely kept bare. He was never sure where he should rest his eyes. It seemed that no matter where she went, she was dressed for the gym.

As they walked past one of the shop windows, Jake glanced at their reflection in the glass. His discomfort grew when he looked at Alice's reflection. Short shorts exposed all but the last inch of her thighs and were so tight that he could count the change in her pocket. Her skin tight tank top also left nothing for the imagination. He looked away, his thoughts returning to Amy. He had never considered her modesty, but now, as he walked next to her polar opposite in that department, his admiration for her grew exponentially. She had never put him in an uncomfortable situation. She, too, was playful and teasing, but her ways were different. Amy was more reserved but also more respectful of both herself and of him. One more thing to love about her, he thought to himself.

Alice insisted on walking him all the way to his apartment door and might have invited herself in if Jake hadn't said he needed to get to the shop as soon as he could. She mentioned something about her dad and other men from town being there earlier in the day, but it made little sense and Jake was so anxious to be done with her that he didn't ask any questions. She handed him the blue plastic bag from the hospital filled with his personal items, then leaned forward and surprised him by planting a kiss on his lips. He had certainly not seen that coming! In his surprised confusion, he fell back against his door. Alice smiled and stepped closer.

"Alice, uh…I'm flattered by your attention, but I think you should know that I've been dating someone."

She raised her eyebrows, disbelief in her face. "Jake, if you were dating someone, why didn't she pick you up from the hospital?"

"She must be busy."

"Uh, huh." She bit her lip then pulled her small handbag off her shoulder and scribbled her number down on the back of a receipt. "I don't want to get in the way, but call me if you change your mind. I'm going to be around a lot this summer. I know we'd have fun together." She kissed the receipt, leaving her pale lipstick behind, and handed it to Jake. "Call me," she said with a wink. "I've been looking forward to watching you work. My dad said you're very talented."

Jake nodded, but he had never felt more uncomfortable. He turned to the door before she reached the bottom stair. He reached into his pocket, looking for his keys, but he couldn't find them. His thoughts raced back to the accident and his arrival in the hospital. Had he left his keys at the hospital? Had he even taken them to the hospital? Thinking quickly, he remembered that Sam, Thomas, Beverly and the Mayor all had copies.

But how could he go looking for them with Alice hanging around? He was afraid to even turn around, for fear that she might be watching him and waiting. Without turning his head, he walked backwards to the plastic bag.

Jake's frantic search of the plastic bag yielded no keys. He tried to imagine what Thomas or Sam might think if he came looking for keys with the scantily clad Alice in tow. He cringed to think how Amy would respond if she saw them walking through town together. Closing his eyes and searching, he hoped beyond hope that he would find the keys. After emptying the bag of its contents, he leaned his head against the door, trying to calm himself down. He could feel his incision pulsing and the dull ache returning. At that moment, he wanted nothing more than to be on the other side of the door.

After several seconds, he took a deep breath and slowly turned around. To his great relief, Alice was not at the bottom of the stairs. He stooped down, looking across the courtyard. Then he slowly climbed back down the stairs, scanning the courtyard for any sign of her.

He hadn't seen which direction she'd gone, but he assumed she would head back to her parents' shop or their apartment. He strode through the courtyard to Müllerstrasse and made his way as quickly as possible up the hill and into the church courtyard. He felt like a thief in the night, sneaking across town. He knocked on Thomas' door, praying he would answer, but there was no sign of life from within. He knocked again, much louder this time, but still no one came. He closed his eyes and leaned his head against the door, wondering what to do.

In the distraction and distress Alice had caused him, he had forgotten all about his plan to drop by Amy's place on his way home from the hospital. Now, alone and close to both the hospital and Amy's apartment, he could have a do-over. Relieved, he turned around to look out from Thomas' porch and make sure he hadn't been followed. The quickest way would take him down the stairs to Hauptstrasse, but he knew he couldn't go that way. Alice might be there shopping, or worse, on the prowl for him. Instead, he went the long way around, through the narrow passage that leads to the bus station and the library. He moved quickly, as stealthily as he could. When the way ended, opening onto the street, he continued to move in stealth, hugging the walls of the buildings, scanning the crowd for anyone who looked like Alice. Anyone watching his bizarre behavior might believe he had escaped from a mental institution—deranged, paranoid, and psychotic.

The buildings ended at the corner with a view of Jerry and Beverly's porch. He stopped to scan the crowd and scout out the porch. When he saw that the coast was clear, he ran to the stairs, not stopping until he reached the front door. Safe! He felt a great sense of relief as he began to breathe again, but waited a full minute to knock on the door. He didn't want to meet Amy huffing and puffing with breathlessness.

Beverly answered his knock quickly. She stood in the doorway, an apron wrapped around her waist.

"Jake, what a nice surprise! You looked flushed. Are you feeling ok?"

"Yes, I…I just got out of the hospital and I can't find my keys. I think they might be locked in my apartment. Can I borrow yours?"

She smiled and invited him in. The apartment was filled with the scent of chocolate cake or brownies. It made Jake's mouth water. Beverly left him standing in the entryway and returned a moment later with the key ring, a ceramic bead hanging from it. ISAAC was stamped onto its surface and stained with iron oxide.

"Is Amy here?" Jake asked as she handed him the keys.

"No, I'm afraid she's not. This was her first day to paint and she was anxious to get an early start. She left this morning on her bike. I expect her for dinner though. Maybe you should stick around and wait for her. She probably won't be much longer."

Jake felt nervous. He wondered if Amy had said anything to her aunt about the current state of their relationship. He decided not to ask, but thanked her for the key and told her he hoped to see Amy soon. Beverly nodded. As he left, she encouraged him to drop by any time.

Ten paces down Hauptstrasse's cobblestone, Jake stopped, remembering why he hadn't followed this route before. His paranoia, though significantly less, drove him back the way he had come. He was distracted by thoughts of Amy and curious about what he had learned from Beverly. It was Friday. Amy's last day on the job was to have been Tuesday and she had planned to paint every day after that. So, why had today been her first day to paint? Her paints had been locked up in his apartment for a couple of days, but Thomas said Beverly had picked them up on Wednesday. He wondered why she hadn't been painting. He wondered where she could be now. Taufer's Pond? Down by the river? Up at the pirate lookout? His questions tormented him. If only he could talk to her and know what she was feeling.

Once safely at home with no sightings of Alice, he opened his door and raked the plastic bag and his other belongings into the apartment with his foot. Somehow it felt different—more cozy and welcoming.

Looking around, he assured himself that everything was just as he'd left it. Everything, except for a painting propped up against a mug in the middle of the kitchen table. Jake picked it up and stared at it for a long time before sitting down slowly at the table. It was a portrait of the green pitcher, a rolled piece of white paper sticking out above its rim and the slightest hint of a chip on its foot.

19

TOKENS OF HOPE

THE GREATEST GOOD YOU CAN DO
FOR ANOTHER IS NOT JUST TO SHARE
YOUR RICHES, BUT TO REVEAL
TO HIM, HIS OWN.
—BENJAMIN DISRAELI

 ake pulled the pitcher down from the shelf. This was the piece that had changed his understanding of the old dusty collection. He unrolled the yellowed paper for the second time in just over a week and read the words written there.

November 9, 1972 "Don't be discouraged by failure. It can be a positive experience. Failure is, in a sense, the highway to success, inasmuch as every discovery of what is false leads us to seek earnestly after what is true, and every fresh experience points out some form of error which we shall afterwards carefully avoid." --John Keats

Jake studied the pitcher, turning it over in his hands. He ran his thumb over the spot where the glaze had run then broken off, leaving several deep scars. He set the pitcher down on the table and rubbed his hands over his stubbly beard, trying to discern the meaning of Amy's visual message.

Feeling foolish, he realized he had been waiting for Amy to make a move, to seek him out and smooth things over. For his part, he had done little to try to improve things. The letter he began composing in the hospital was still only a few sentences long. Now, he wished he'd finished it and had someone drop it off to Amy. He would already be moving toward restoring what had been. Discovering the flawed pitcher after losing some of his own pots to the same runny glaze had been humbling enough. Having Amy remind him of that discovery with a portrait of that pitcher was even more poignant.

He picked the painting up again. The paint was thick and still tacky and wet in some places. He carefully turned the canvas board over, hoping to find a note, but the back was bare. He stood it back against the mug on the table and leaned back in his chair. He tried to remember that evening, just a week earlier, when they discovered the pitcher together: the bike ride, the pirate lookout, Amy's tears. Jake had been moved as she related to him her feelings of being alone in the world. She wanted so badly to paint but felt like no one in her family was behind her. He mused at the irony that, even with family, one can feel alone in the world. He remembered his feelings of helplessness and how she had taken comfort in his words of encouragement. He remembered holding her hand as they walked back to their bikes, then the cold ride home and wrapping her in the old quilt while he readied the tea. He looked again at the pitcher. That night the lesson of the ragtag collection had been so clear: maybe, if he could learn from the mistakes of others, he wouldn't have to make all of his own.

He stared at Amy's painting for another long moment before standing and walking to the door. The shop had been closed since Tuesday and he was feeling restless. He walked down the stairs feeling surprisingly grateful for Amy and the friendship she had given him so freely. He felt undeserving, and even unworthy, but also anxious to bridge the chasm that had formed between them.

As he opened the back door to the Pottery, he wondered where the two garbage cans had gone. Thomas or Beverly must have put them away. After opening the door, he stopped and stared into the darkened studio. The floor had been swept and mopped, leaving no signs of blood. The wheel had also been cleaned and his tools were organized. Who in the world had done this?! The door to the clay cellar lay open. It had been more than a week since he'd been down there. Curious, he walked toward the door and was just about to close it when he noticed a red cloth on the top step. He stooped over and picked it up. As he unfolded it, he recognized it was Kai's apron, with Braun's Market embroidered in blue lettering. Jake was even more curious. Why would Kai's apron be here? He took a few steps into the cellar, stooping low to see in as far as he could see in the low light. Again, he stopped in amazement.

His eyes, adjusting to the light, once again filled with tears. Stacked in neat piles, cardboard boxes filled with new clay packed the cellar. Jake knew he had ordered two tons of clay and each of the boxes weighed fifty pounds.

He had dreaded the thought of the work this would produce when he placed the order. But as he sat in the hospital, he knew it would be impossible to move the clay with a bandaged arm. Again, Jake was filled with gratitude. He swallowed hard, fighting back his emotions. He tried to think of the last time someone had done something like this for him. Then he tried to think of the last time he had done something like this for someone else. He had helped Kai with his cabinets, but this was different. Kai had done something Jake couldn't do for himself.

Jake climbed out of the cellar. The clock on the wall indicated it was almost 5:00. He walked through the pottery and out the front door, the strings of a red apron swinging as he made his way down Zubergasse.

(20)

MOLLY'S WISDOM

WE MUST BE WILLING TO GET RID
OF THE LIFE WE'VE PLANNED,
SO AS TO HAVE THE LIFE
THAT IS WAITING FOR US.
—JOSEPH CAMPBELL

ude, you left your apron in the cellar." Jake laid the apron down on the apples Kai was stacking.

"I wondered where I put that. I guess that kind of blew the surprise." He set down the apples and turned his attention to Jake. "Welcome home."

Jake nodded, taking a deep breath. "Kai, I don't know what to say. I owe you big time. I've been dreading moving the clay since I placed the order." He fumbled for words. "I really appreciate it. That must have taken you a couple of hours."

Kai smiled smugly, "It might have had I done it myself."

"What do you mean?"

"Well, I tried to cancel the delivery like you asked me to, but they said there would be a $50 fee—some union charge or something. So I passed the word that you needed some help and about fifteen people showed up. It was almost too many people. We were tripping over each other. We were done in less than half an hour."

Jake was amazed. "Who came?"

"Oh, Thomas, Albert, Sam and several of his employees. Josh Adams brought his kids to help before school started. Gloria and Beverly were there too, and Amy."

Jake's heart skipped a beat. "Amy came?"

Kai faked nonchalance. "Yeah, and Thomas and Albert and Sam and…" He stopped, grinning at Jake's exasperation.

"Yes, Amy came. She mopped the floor with Beverly."

"Was that this morning?"

"That's right. The truck got here around 8."

"Did she say anything?"

"Who?"

"Amy! Did she say anything?"

Kai lifted one eyebrow. "Like what?"

"I just haven't seen her all week. I just wondered if…"

"If she said something, I probably wouldn't have heard it. I was down in the cellar most of the time." He rubbed his head. "Those rafters are pretty low for a tall guy."

Jake smiled. "I know all about it. I'm sorry you had to be down there, but I'm really grateful. I don't know how I could have done this without you."

"Yeah, that's what Gloria said. No heavy lifting for two weeks. How are you going to work?"

"I haven't gotten that far yet. I need to work on Sam's tiles. I might be able to do some of that kind of work by next week. I don't know… Did she say anything at all?"

"Who?"

"Amy!"

"Dude, are you ok?"

"No, I'm going crazy. I'm in love with her and I've been such an idiot."

"You can say that again."

They turned to see Molly. She waddled to Jake and hugged him the best she could, her belly inhibiting her free movement. "Hi Jake, it's good to see you vertical."

Jake smiled. "You look like you're ready to have a baby."

"I've been hearing that all day, but Junior's taking his own sweet time." She patted her belly as if urging the baby to hurry up and come.

"I was just thanking Kai for unloading the clay."

"Oh, I thought you were asking about Amy."

Jake smiled. "So, what do you know?"

"I know she was pretty upset with you."

"You guys talked for a while last night, didn't you?" asked Kai.

"Yeah, she came over to chat while I was soaking my feet."

"That's when I came up to see you," added Kai. "I needed to get out of the apartment before my brain started to fry."

Jake smiled, remembering Kai's explanation of female communication during the rain walk on Sunday. "So…is Amy going to give me a chance to make things better?"

"I think that probably depends on you."

"Molly, I really hope this doesn't depend entirely on me because we all know how dense I am about this kind of stuff. I've been selfish, proud, and immature. I want to fix things, but I don't know how."

She put her hands on her hips and raised her eyebrows. "Well, that's a pretty good start, but you might want to throw in more adjectives."

"Help me! Molly, I love her. I want to be with her. It's terrible to go from being with someone all the time to not having her around at all. I'm not even sure what I did. This has been torture."

Molly smiled, crossing her arms across her belly. "I'm glad this has been torture for you too. It's been a really hard week for Amy. She's been sick about you in many ways."

"What does that mean?" asked Jake.

"I thought you'd know by now."

"How would I?"

"Didn't she visit you last night?"

"No, I haven't seen her since Monday."

"That's weird. She was planning on stopping by the hospital after she left here last night. I wonder why she changed her mind."

Jake thought back to the night before, sifting through his memory. When he remembered Alice's visit, he began to panic. "That wasn't around 8:00 was it?"

"Probably, why?"

Jake closed his eyes and rolled his head back.

"Why? What's up?" repeated Molly.

Jake hid his face in his hands, trying to get the idea out of his head. "I had a visitor last night while I was writing a letter to Amy. She probably stayed until about 8."

"She?" asked Molly, her eyebrows raised.

"I didn't ask her to come, she just came. What was I supposed to do?"

"So who was it?"

Jake dropped his hands from his face in resignation. "Alice," he said, under his breath.

"Alice Schreyer?" Molly and Kai asked in unison.

Jake looked at them both before nodding.

"How do you know her?" Molly asked, looking a little on edge.

"Albert invited me to dinner a few weeks ago and Alice stopped by. We met then. That was before I started hanging out with Amy."

"And…are you interested in her?" asked Molly.

"No!" Jake said, more loudly than he meant to. "I thought she was really nice when we met, but she scares me. I…she…No! She won't leave me alone. She came to the hospital when I was getting ready to check out and insisted on walking me home."

"So that's what the chatter was about today," Molly said, turning to Kai. "I told you Mrs. Schmeck and Mrs. Weinbaum were saying something about Jake when they came in this afternoon." She turned back to Jake. "What was Alice wearing this afternoon?"

Jake shook his head. "Not very much."

"That sounds like Alice," said Kai. "She's a pretty girl, but she doesn't have the greatest reputation."

"She basically attacked me on my front porch this afternoon," added Jake. "I told her I was dating someone, but she didn't believe me. She told me that if I was really dating someone, she would've been at the hospital. I spent the afternoon sneaking around town, trying to avoid running into her."

"Jake, this is really bad," said Molly. "I wonder if Amy saw you two together last night. I think she must have. When she left here, she seemed pretty excited to see you. It's hard for me to believe that she didn't try to see you. She must have found Alice there when she arrived."

"So, what do I do now?"

"Dude, this is messed up!" said Kai.

"Jake, if you really love Amy, your actions are going to have to speak louder than your words. I don't know if Amy was upset about anything you did. I think it was more about what you didn't do. I know she loves you too, but that love needs to be fed. She needs to know that you're worth her investment in time and that you want to be with her." Jake clung eagerly to Molly's words. Seeing his earnestness, Molly continued, "I shouldn't be telling you this, but because you're new at this, I'm going to help you out. Girls need to be needed. They need to know if you're serious about them, that you're going to be around, that you're making them a priority in your life."

Standing behind Molly so she couldn't see him, Kai nodded his head at Jake, exaggerating his movements. If he hadn't have been so caught up in worries over Amy, he would have laughed. Clearly Kai had learned this lesson too. Molly looked back at Kai and rolled her eyes. Her voice dropped as she continued, "That talk you had on Monday was a flop."

Jake winced.

"She felt like your travel agenda was more important to you than she was. No one likes to play second fiddle. Love has to be fed huge doses of unselfishness if it's ever going to survive. She needs to know that she's a priority in your life."

Jake's heart sank momentarily. Being in love was so much work! "You're right. I've been trying to write a letter, but I've never written a letter like this before. I suck at this."

"Jake, you don't have to be Shakespeare, just tell her how you feel. And be sure you don't say anything in a letter that you aren't willing to follow up with in person. You guys have a lot of things to figure out and only a few months to do it. She told me last night that her dad has been putting a lot of pressure on her to come home and get a real job. She knows she can't stay with Bev and Jerry forever. She feels like all of her life is in limbo."

"So why didn't she come and talk to me about this? I was a captive audience. I couldn't go anywhere. We could have figured this out days ago. Why didn't she come?"

Molly looked at Kai, then back at Jake. "You're going to have to ask her about that. She asked me not to talk about it. I will tell you that she loves you. I know this would be a lot easier on her if she didn't, but she adores you Jake. She thinks you're a jerk right now, but you can fix that. She loves you."

The front door opened and a middle aged couple walked in. Their wide and shifty eyes made it obvious that they hadn't been in the store before.

"Tourists," Molly said under her breath. "You better go see if they're lost, Honey."

Kai walked towards them as Molly turned back to Jake. "Jake, every good relationship has its challenges. I'll give you the same advice I gave Amy yesterday: Keep talking even though you don't want to and come to the table ready to eat some humble pie." She smiled and patted his shoulder. "You'll be ok. Just tell her how you feel. Too much time and love is wasted in this world. Just open your heart and the rest will follow."

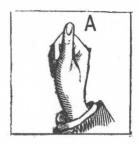  

(21)
OF WOMEN AND FIRE

LET YOUR LOVE BE LIKE THE
MISTY RAIN, COMING SOFTLY,
BUT FLOODING THE RIVER.
—MADAGASCAN PROVERB

 ake, welcome! I've been anxious to see you. Sorry I didn't make it to the hospital, but Gloria's kept me updated." Joseph stepped aside, motioning for Jake to come in. "Gloria had to make a delivery. She'll be right back."

"Do you need any help?" Jake asked, nodding at Joseph's hands covered in flour.

"Have you ever made ravioli?"

"You mean like Chef Boyardee?"

Joseph didn't even flinch. "I'll take that as a 'no.' It's one of Gloria's favorites and I thought you might like it too. Stuffing the pasta is kind of fun. I was just getting started, you can help if you want."

"I might mess it up. I'm not much of a cook."

"There's nothing to it. I learned how to make ravioli when I was six or seven. I'll show you."

They walked into the small kitchen. A marble slab was covered with flour and a thin sheet of pasta dough. Next to it sat one of Isaac's mixing bowls filled with blended cheese, artichoke hearts, spinach and mushrooms. Marinara sauce sputtered on the stovetop, filling the room with the scent of garlic and basil.

"This is way out of my league," Jake said, his stomach growling audibly.

"It's really a lot easier than it looks. This might be a good way to impress Amy, or Alice."

Jake rolled his eyes. "Hopefully Amy."

Joseph nodded, a thin smile showing through his graying beard. "If you want, I'll cut the dough and you can fill and seal."

Jake raised his eyebrows. "Are you sure? It looks like you've put a lot of work into this. I'd hate to ruin it."

"I'm sure. This is a skill every man should have if he wants to woo a woman."

Jake washed his hands and, after a short tutorial, started making his first ravioli. Joseph was right; it was relatively easy once he got the proportions right. He just had to make sure to leave enough dough to close around the filling. He was surprised at how naturally it came to him. Working with the dough felt similar to working with clay. The talk between the two men was light and easy, until they neared completion.

"So, I have to ask about your relationship with Alice. I thought you and Amy were progressing so nicely. I was surprised by the talk in the shop this afternoon. It sounded like you've moved on."

Jake sighed. "I don't have any intention of pursuing Alice. The more I get to know her, the more she scares me. I just wish I knew what was going on with Amy. I feel like the whole town knows more about her than I do, but no one's talking. Do you know anything?"

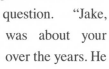

Joseph licked the wooden spoon after dipping it in the sauce. "Needs salt," he said, obviously ignoring the question. "Jake, my father taught me something when I was about your age that I've thought about many times over the years. He taught me that women are like fire."

"Because you get burned every time you get close to 'em?"

Joseph laughed. "No, not exactly. Before I met Gloria, I was dating a beautiful girl, the youngest daughter in a large Italian family. Our parents had known each other for years and I was in love with her from the time I was old enough to know the difference between boys and girls. We had a lot in common, but we also had a lot of differences. Her family was one of the richest families in our Italian community and she was treated like a princess. Anything she wanted, her father bought her. I don't remember her ever having a job. She was sophisticated and elegant and refined. But somehow, she liked me anyway. I tried to impress her, but she had insatiable tastes. Her shopping sprees cost more than I made in a month. One night I returned home from a date, feeling pretty worthless, knowing I would never be able to compete with all that her father had given her.

"My dad has always been wise. When he saw me walk through the door that night, he told me I looked like a man who had used up all his firewood but was still cold. As we sat at our humble kitchen table drinking coffee, he told me that girls are like fire. Some will consume whole forests of wood, burning hot and spreading quickly until they burn out and leave only charred remains. Others are like a fire that burns in a fireplace. It might be pretty, but all the heat escapes through the chimney. And then some women are fires whose consumption is minimal, but who keep burning through even the darkest hours, offering warmth and light to all who are near. And when the fire is gone, their coals continue to glow, radiating heat forever.

"Find a woman like that, he told me, and you will always be happy."

Jake nodded thoughtfully, thinking about Gloria and her aura that filled the world around her with loveliness. "That sounds like Gloria to me."

Joseph nodded. "I've made some good choices in my life, but I thank the heavens every day for sending Gloria into my life. We've been married thirty years and yet I wake up every day and feel like she is more beautiful and more incredible than she was the day before. The fire she has brought into my life is still burning, giving me warmth and comfort. My old girlfriend has burned through three husbands, consuming their wealth and love, growing dissatisfied, and then moving on.

"I have known Alice since she was a baby, and though she doesn't come from wealth, she has always been a raging fire, consuming all that is in her path. I'm sure most of the boys in this town have had their hearts broken by her. When she was in high school, we were delivering flowers to her a couple times a week, ordered by lovesick boys. I'm sure she broke at least as many savings accounts as she did hearts."

"I've been warned," acknowledged Jake. "I just don't know what I did to attract her attention."

"You're new in town, handsome and dating someone else. If any one of those elements was different, she probably wouldn't be interested."

"So, what do I do?"

"You concentrate on the fire that matters most. Women like Alice, if left unfed, will move on in search of fuel. I don't know Amy well, but I've been impressed with her. She seems genuine, the kind of fire that if properly treated, can offer a lifetime of warmth and happiness."

Jake nodded slowly as random memories of Amy flitted through his head—the dinner she had cooked him, drinking tea while wrapped up in his quilt, pushing her on the swing.

The front door opened and Gloria strode into the kitchen. She hugged Joseph and then Jake. Joseph continued his ravioli lesson, teaching Jake to remove them from the boiling water as they rose to the surface. Jake was a quick study and the two of them soon filled a large bowl with steaming ravioli.

The evening passed quickly. Gloria, obviously relieved that Jake's interest remained with Amy, encouraged him to mend things with her as quickly as possible and eliminate all misunderstanding between them. She told him that Amy had had a difficult week and needed his friendship and assurance of his continued love. When Jake returned home several hours later, he was anxious to resume writing his letter. He found some of the old Pottery Niederbipp letterhead on the desk in the second bedroom and sat down at the kitchen table with a mug of tea to begin his letter. He had written only one other letter in the last several years, the letter that had landed him here in Niederbipp. But the words came freely as he opened his heart.

DEAR AMY,

THIS WEEK HAS GIVEN ME A CHANCE TO THINK ABOUT MY RESPONSE TO YOU AND THE THOUGHTS YOU SHARED WITH ME ON MONDAY. I HAVE REPLAYED OUR CONVERSATION IN MY MIND A HUNDRED TIMES. THERE ARE MANY THINGS I WANT TO TELL YOU, BUT THEY ALL SEEM TO BOIL DOWN TO THIS —I AM SORRY FOR TAKING YOUR FRIENDSHIP AND LOVE FOR GRANTED. THIS WEEK HAS FORCED ME TO RECOGNIZE THE FOLLY OF MY PRIDE, SELFISHNESS AND INDEPENDENCE. I AM SORRY FOR THE PAIN I HAVE CAUSED YOU. I WOULDN'T BLAME YOU FOR FEELING LIKE YOU'VE WASTED THE LAST FEW WEEKS HANGING OUT WITH ME. BUT, NO MATTER WHAT HAPPENS, I WANT YOU TO KNOW THAT YOUR LOVE AND FRIENDSHIP HAVE MADE ME WANT TO CHANGE. I WANT TO BE A BETTER PERSON WHO IS WORTHY OF YOUR LOVE AND FRIENDSHIP.

BEFORE THIS WEEK, I NEVER CONSIDERED THAT MY INDEPENDENCE WAS A FORM OF SELFISHNESS. I SEE

NOW HOW IT HAS KEPT ME FROM OPENING MY HEART AND EYES TO A BETTER WORLD. I AM SORRY FOR HURTING YOU WITH MY LACK OF RESPONSE ON MONDAY. I AM SORRY FOR BEING INSENSITIVE, IMMATURE AND FLIPPANT. I KNOW I HAVE BEEN AN IDIOT ABOUT A LOT OF THINGS, BUT THE THING I REGRET THE MOST IS BEING AN IDIOT ABOUT YOU. I KNOW WE HAVE ONLY BEEN HANGING OUT FOR A FEW WEEKS, BUT EVERY DAY HAS BEEN AMAZING.

AMY, I AM NEW AT THIS KIND OF STUFF. MOLLY, GLORIA AND SANDY—MY DOCTOR AT THE HOSPITAL—AND SEVERAL OTHERS HAVE HELPED ME TO SEE HOW STUPID I HAVE BEEN. DESPITE EVERYTHING THAT HAS HAPPENED THIS WEEK, I AM GRATEFUL IT HAPPENED. IT HAS TAUGHT ME THINGS ABOUT MYSELF THAT I MIGHT NOT HAVE LEARNED ANY OTHER WAY. I AM SORRY FOR HURTING YOU IN THE PROCESS, BUT I HOPE YOU WILL ALLOW ME TO MAKE IT UP TO YOU. I HAVE MISSED YOU IMMENSELY. IT HAS BEEN DIFFICULT TO NOT HAVE YOU AROUND AT ALL AFTER BEING NEAR YOU EVERY DAY. I WISH WE COULD HAVE SPOKEN EARLIER IN THE WEEK, BUT I THINK I UNDERSTAND WHY YOU STAYED AWAY.

AMY, I LOVE YOU. I MISS YOU. I AM VERY SORRY TO HAVE WASTED ANOTHER WEEK OF WHATEVER TIME WE HAVE LEFT TOGETHER. PLEASE FORGIVE ME AND ALLOW ME A CHANCE TO MAKE THINGS RIGHT.

WHILE I WAS IN THE HOSPITAL, THOMAS BROUGHT ME ISAAC'S SKETCHBOOK. THERE ARE LOTS OF THINGS I'D LIKE TO SHARE WITH YOU. DISCOVERING ISAAC IN ITS PAGES HAS MADE ME REALIZE I NEED MORE TIME HERE. I HAVE DECIDED TO EXTEND MY STAY IN NIEDERBIPP INDEFINITELY. I FEEL LIKE THERE IS A LOT MORE I HAVE TO LEARN ABOUT THIS PLACE, ITS PEOPLE AND MYSELF. I'M FINALLY REALIZING THAT THIS ISN'T SUCH A BAD PLACE TO LEARN THOSE LESSONS. LIKE YOU SAID ON MONDAY, IT SEEMS THE UNIVERSE WANTS ME TO BE HERE.

POTTERY
NIEDERBIPP

I FINALLY DO TOO.

IF YOU'VE DECIDED THAT YOU HAVE ALREADY WASTED
ENOUGH TIME ON ME, I WANT TO THANK YOU FOR SHARING
THE LAST FEW WEEKS WITH ME. THEY HAVE BEEN THE
HAPPIEST WEEKS OF MY LIFE. YOU HAVE GIVEN MY LIFE A
CLARITY I'VE NEVER KNOWN BEFORE AND OPENED MY EYES
AND HEART TO LOVE.

THANK YOU. I LOVE YOU!

YOUR HUMBLE FRIEND,

JAKE KIMBALL

PS, THANKS FOR THE PAINTING AND THE MESSAGE BEHIND
IT. IT'S BEAUTIFUL. I KNOW THIS BOWL IS NOT A VERY EVEN
TRADE, BUT IT COMES WITH SANDWICHES.

It was nearly midnight when he finished his letter. He drank the last
of his cold tea and leaned back in the chair, reading the letter to himself.
Then he stood, glancing at Amy's painting before walking down to the
showroom to select a blue and green bowl from the front window.

The cool night air felt refreshing as he walked through the deserted
streets. The street lamps painted long, wiggly shadows across the
cobblestone. Jake set the bowl on the doormat, the letter inside and Mr.

Allen's black treasure on top to keep the wind from blowing the letter away. Then he turned and walked home, hoping that his offering would change the course of events for the better.

Jake climbed into bed with Isaac's sketchbook, anxious to discover all that he could about the man who was changing his life from the grave.

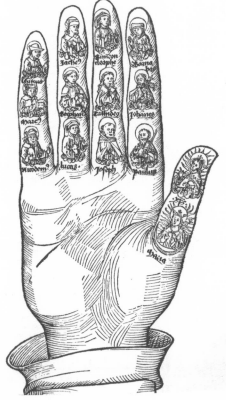

(22)
ANSWERS

IT IS NOT ENOUGH TO HELP
THE FEEBLE UP,
BUT TO SUPPORT HIM AFTER.
—WILLIAM SHAKESPEARE

ake was surprised by his feelings as he walked through the studio door on Saturday morning. The place was cleaner than he'd left it, thanks to Beverly and Amy, but it still felt like he was coming home. The day was busy with customers, mostly weekenders and out-of-towners. Hildegard also stopped by to receive a full report on Jake's recovery. Until that point, late in the afternoon, Jake had nearly forgotten about his healing arm, too busy to remember the dull pain that still remained. Sandy also stopped by just before closing to introduce Jake to Andrew, her fiancé. They placed an order for a large serving bowl and six smaller pasta bowls in Jake's blue and green glaze combination. Sandy said she had been admiring them in the window. He said he'd get started right away until she reminded Jake to take it easy for another week, giving his artery more time to heal.

Jake walked them to the door and watched as they walked down Zubergasse, hand in hand. Amy had been on his mind all day. He wondered what she thought of his letter and how she would respond—if she responded. Every time the bells on the front door rang, Jake looked up anxiously, hoping it was her. But she didn't come. He was just locking the front door when he heard a knock at the back door. Full of hope, he ran through the studio, but slowed when he recognized Thomas' black clothes. Trying not to look disappointed, he opened the door and let him in.

Thomas said he was on his way to get a kabob and asked if Jake would like to join him. They sat together on the stone benches carved into the side of the fountain, eating their kabobs and talking about the events of the week. Jake was distracted, reminded that just a week before he had been here with Amy. When Thomas asked about Alice, Jake made it clear that he planned to do all that he could to avoid her. Thomas seemed pleased with his response and shared with him some of the rumors that had been circulating around town. Thomas laughed at the silliest of them—that Jake had been injured in one of Alice's outdoor yoga classes that she taught down by the river. He added that many of the older folks were rooting for Amy, having seen the budding romance the week before.

Anxious for any information Thomas might have, Jake asked if he had seen Amy during the week. Thomas' answer was shielded. He talked around the question for several minutes, leaving Jake with more questions. Finally, when Thomas tried to change the subject, Jake couldn't take it any longer.

"Thomas, have you ever felt like the butt of a joke, like you have a sign on your back that says 'Kick Me' and you're the only one who doesn't know about it?"

Thomas smiled, but averted his eyes.

"I've been trying to piece things together all week, but I haven't done very well. No one is telling me the truth about Amy. I need to talk to her. I need to make things right, but I can't if I don't know what's going on. Everyone I ask, including you, tries to blow me off. Can you please tell me what's going on?"

Thomas sat back on the bench, folding his arms over his stomach. "I'd like to Jake, but I've been asked not to talk about it?"

"By whom? Who asked you not to talk?"

"Amy and Beverly." He looked at Jake and shrugged. "I'm not entirely sure why. Maybe it's just that this town tends to talk and she didn't want you to feel any outside pressure."

"Outside pressure?" Jake's confusion mounted. "I don't understand."

"Jake, I think you'll understand when she wants you to, but for now, please don't worry about it. I was asked not to talk about it and I'd really like to keep my word."

"But, Thomas, you gotta help me. This is making me crazy. Can't you tell me anything?"

"I'll tell you that if the letter you wrote last night is sincere, you don't have much to worry about. Amy will talk to you soon. I'll tell you that Alice has made things tough for you. Amy misunderstood some things."

"Like what?"

"Well, from the sounds of it, it was probably pretty easy to misunderstand. Amy stopped by to visit you twice this week. You happened to be busy with another visitor both times."

Jake shook his head, fuming. "Alice!"

"That's the one. Amy didn't see you walking home from the hospital yesterday, hand in hand with Alice, but a lot of other people did."

"I wasn't holding her hand!" In his excitement, Jake was practically shouting. Tourists in the square were looking his way. He lowered his voice, but still spoke earnestly. "She was holding onto my arm. She said she didn't want me to fall over. Thomas, she wouldn't leave me alone. She showed up at the hospital and insisted on taking me home. I…this is crazy. What am I going to do? How am I ever going to clear my name?"

Thomas looked at Jake and grimaced. "Jake, I've seen you with Amy and I know you have strong feelings for her. When the rumors started, I did all I could to keep people straight. Alice isn't entirely to blame either. Albert is so concerned about keeping you in town that I think he must have encouraged his daughter to do what she could to keep you here. I'm not sure he understands the reputation she has and the potential damage she could do to your reputation. We've been trying to run interference all week."

"Wait, what have you been doing?"

Thomas grinned impishly, but said sincerely, "Jake, I'm at least as interested in keeping you here as Albert is. And like I said, I've seen you and Amy together. I know you've spent most of your free time together. Anyone could see the magic you two have. A few of us have been trying to keep things on the up and up."

"Who? Who's working for you?"

"I'd rather not say."

"THOMAS!" Jake said forcefully.

Thomas took a deep breath. "The answer to that should seem pretty clear if you'll remember who visited you in the hospital."

"Gloria?"

Thomas nodded.

"And Kai and Molly? And Beverly?"

Thomas nodded again. "Don't forget Sandy."

"You had someone on the inside?" Jake asked, not believing his ears.

"She approached us after she met Amy. She said she'd wanted to visit you for a while anyway. She was our informant. When Alice tried to visit you the first night you were there, Sandy said she wanted to protect Amy's interest."

Jake considered this news for a moment, trying to tie the pieces together. "Is that why you visited me right after Alice?"

"That was Sandy's doing. She called me as soon as Alice showed up. Dressed like she was, Sandy didn't think she was up to anything good. She couldn't get a hold of me, but Beverly finally tracked me down at your apartment. I was picking up your clothes. I ran as fast as I could to the hospital. We're all quite relieved she didn't get her hooks into you."

Jake collapsed against the back of the bench and started laughing.

For his part, Thomas looked relieved. He even joined Jake in the laughter.

"So let me get this straight, half the town is in cahoots trying to steer my heart."

"You can look at it that way," Thomas said. "But it sounds better to say we were trying to protect you from a girl who tends to leave boys broken and bleeding wherever she goes. My sources tell me she actually had a date at the drive-in with someone else Thursday night after she left the hospital."

Jake looked thoughtful. "Wait a minute. How did Amy meet Sandy?"

Thomas looked away.

"Thomas!"

"That's the part I can't tell you about. Jake, you'll find out soon enough. Amy wanted to tell you herself."

"When did you talk to her last?"

"This morning. Beverly called…actually got me out of bed to tell me the good news. I had breakfast with them. Amy has had a tough week, but your letter made things a lot better."

"She shared the letter with you?"

"No. She didn't even share it with her aunt. She just said that your letter made her decide to stay."

"What does that mean?"

"Jake, you really should be talking to Amy. I only know a little bit?"

"But what does that mean? She decided to stay."

Thomas took a deep breath. "I'll tell you, but you have to act surprised whenever you finally talk to Amy. Her parents called on Tuesday. A friend of theirs was looking for an artist in his advertising agency. Apparently, he offered her a job before he even met her. She had already started packing her bags when she heard about you, but postponed her departure until she could find out how you were doing. She cares a lot about you Jake. She's a wonderful woman, but I don't think I need to tell you that. You two have a lot to talk about."

Jake shook his head. He couldn't believe how wrong he'd been. "Things aren't always as they appear to be."

Thomas nodded thoughtfully.

"Do you know where she is?"

"She said something about going painting today. I saw her ride off on her bike with an artist easel strapped to her back around ten."

"Do you know where she went?"

"Let me think…" Thomas said, itching his chin

Jake got to his feet and shook the priest by his shoulders. "Think Thomas! Think!"

"She said something about needing a quiet place to think this morning at breakfast. It sounded like crazy talk, but she said something about pirates."

"Thank you, Thomas!" Jake turned and started up Zubergasse.

"Where are you going?" Thomas hollered.

"To look for pirates!" Jake hollered back. His voice bounced off the walls and sounded in the ears of those who watched him run.

— DO NOT EXPECT MORE LIGHT UNTIL YOU FOLLOW WHAT YOU HAVE.—
— QUAKER PROVERB-

(23)

OF PIRATES AND PRAYERS

I HAVE BEEN DRIVEN MANY TIMES
TO MY KNEES BY THE OVERWHELMING
CONVICTION THAT I HAD ABSOLUTELY
NO OTHER PLACE TO GO.
—ABRAHAM LINCOLN

ake pedaled across the bridge then coasted to a stop where they had parked their bikes before. His heart raced when he recognized Aunt Bev's bike with the basket on the front, leaning up against a tree. He leaned his bike against the same tree and stumbled up the steep trail. He was nearly to the top when he tripped and, without thinking, caught himself with his left arm. A sharp shock of pain forced him to sit down, wincing. The pain continued, pulsating with every heartbeat. Jake closed his eyes tightly, rocking to the beat of the throbbing pain.

He knew he shouldn't be here. Sandy would call him a poor patient at the very least. If he had damaged something, torn open his artery or something worse, he knew he was too far away to get back in time. When the pain continued, Jake did something he hadn't done in a long time. He began to pray. Eyes closed in pain and reverence, he prayed at first for himself. Then, slowly, the words of his prayer turned from his own issues and became a prayer of thanksgiving. He thanked the heavens for leading him to a place where people loved him and cared about him. His mind filled with the faces of the people he had met, the stories they had shared and the lessons he had learned. Gloria and Joseph, Thomas, Sam, Beverly and Jerry, Mayor Jim, Kai and Molly, Brian, and even Albert with his overzealous drive to make sure Jake felt welcome and wanted. He also thought of his mother and her answered prayers. When his thoughts turned back to Amy, he felt a calm fall over him. He opened his eyes, the pain becoming more manageable, but didn't get up. Instead, he stayed where he was, looking across the river at Niederbipp rising up the hillside. The sun was still an hour from setting, but it was already beginning to paint warm colors on the walls of the buildings. The church on the hill looked like it had been carved of yellow sandstone.

Staring at Niederbipp, he realized his desire to escape to Peros Island had all but faded away. This was his home now and perhaps it would be forever. He considered being in Kai's shoes, preparing to raise the next generation of Niederbippians, and didn't feel the usual panicky claustrophobia, but an inviting sense of peace. The wanderlust that had kept him thinking about moving on now seemed shallow and unimportant. This was, after all, almost exactly what he hoped to find someday: a small, close knit community where he could be the village potter.

He sat in silence for more than thirty minutes, praying, observing his world and pondering his future in this place. The pain in his arm was gone long before he realized, forced out of his body by the most intense calm he had ever known.

His thoughts were interrupted by motion on the trail below. He watched quietly as Amy walked toward the tree where her bike stood. Stopping short, she began to look from side to side as if expecting someone to jump out of the bushes. Jake was tempted to whistle or shout, but instead he watched as she removed the easel from her back and leaned it against her bike. Turning around, she began climbing the steep trail. Their eyes met when she was still twenty feet away and a smile spread across her pretty face. Jake returned the smile, getting to his feet.

"What are you doing here?" she asked, looking up at him.

"Looking for pirates. I heard this is a good place to find them."

"How did you know I was here?"

"A little bird told me. I'm not sure, but I think it was a Niederbipp Mocking Bird."

Her smile widened as she came to a stop two feet from him.

"I can't tell you how great it is to see you," he said. "I've really missed you. I'm so sorry for being such a jerk."

She closed the gap, wrapping her arms around him. They held each other for several minutes, saying nothing.

"I was just thinking I needed to pay you a visit," she said when she finally spoke again. "You really messed me up this week."

Jake held Amy's hand and pulled her to a nearby fallen log that offered the same view he'd already been enjoying. He encouraged her to continue. As she sat down, Jake noticed her right arm looked badly bruised from her wrist to the sleeve of her t-shirt.

"What happened?" Jake asked, looking concerned. He took her arm, examining the dark purple and green skin.

"It's called a hematoma."

"It looks painful. Did you fall?"

Amy looked thoughtful. "I guess you could say that. It's happened before. I don't think my veins are very easy to find. The phlebotomist went through both sides of my vein."

Jake looked at her intently, trying to understand what she was saying. "When did this happen?"

"On Tuesday. It's looking better every day. The doctor said it should be gone in a week or so."

Understanding began to come to Jake. He knelt on the soft bed of pine needles in front of her, looking up into her eyes. "Amy, what's your blood type?"

"O+." She smiled softly as tears began to fall from Jake's eyes. He embraced her, holding her tight as he sobbed on her shoulder.

"I'm so sorry," he repeated again and again. "Why didn't you tell me?"

Amy took a deep breath, wiping away her own tears. "I was in the hospital. I passed out when I tried to stand up after giving blood and they decided to keep me overnight. I tried to visit on Wednesday and Thursday, but you had visitors."

Jake shook his head. "You have no idea how sorry I am. I don't know why she visited me. I didn't…"

"Shhhhhh."

Jake looked up at her, trying to read her expression. A smile spread across her lips.

"I know why she visited you. Gloria sat me down last night and told me all about her. If it wasn't for Gloria's visit, I don't know if I would have read your letter. I was packing my bags when she stopped by. I got offered a job at an advertising firm near my parent's home in Springfield."

Jake nodded, looking dejected. "I'm sorry I didn't offer you any reason to stay."

"No, you didn't," she said, slapping him softly on the shoulder. "But Gloria did. I was pretty upset, thinking that you had moved on so quickly when it was my blood that kept you from being life-flighted to Pittsburgh."

Jake lowered his head, still trying to comprehend the series of events. "I was on my way out the door early this morning when I found your note and the bowl. It made me realize I needed to spend some time thinking about things, so I came here. I've read your letter a dozen times today. I spent a lot of time praying, trying to know what I should do."

Jake looked up when she didn't continue. She was looking out across the river at Niederbipp. "Did you get any answers?" he asked humbly, hopefully.

"Yeah, I did."

"Can you tell me?"

She turned her attention back to him. "I've decided to extend my stay in Niederbipp indefinitely and see where my heart takes me."

(24)

GOING PUBLIC

GO CONFIDENTLY IN THE DIRECTION OF YOUR DREAMS. LIVE THE LIFE YOU'VE IMAGINED.
—HENRY DAVID THOREAU

Jake rose early, showered, shaved, and dressed in a clean pair of pants and his only button down shirt. He studied the pages of Isaac's sketchbook as he ate breakfast, drawn in by the small notes and sketches. He returned to a few pages he had seen while in the hospital: a series of pictures spread across several pages and labeled "Robert Allan's Cookie Jar—July 13, 1998."

The sketches started out looking like a traditional cookie jar, but they slowly morphed from sketch to sketch and from page to page, the opening becoming smaller, the vessel itself becoming more ornate, and the shape becoming more unusual. Isaac had written notes on the sides indicating glazes and firing processes, many of which sounded very unusual. Colored glass was mentioned several times, but there was no indication of how it was to be used.

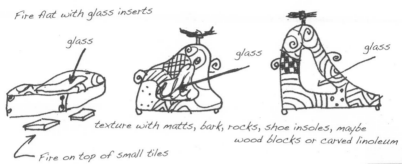

Fire flat with glass inserts
glass
glass
glass
texture with matts, bark, rocks, shoe insoles, maybe wood blocks or carved linoleum
Fire on top of small tiles

When the church bells began to chime at 9:30, Jake left his apartment with his sketchbook and Bible. Instead of taking the quickest way to the church on Muellerstrasse, Jake took the alleyway to Hauptstrasse. He knocked on the Sproodle's door, using the heavy brass knocker for the first time. Amy answered the door a moment later, dressed in a bright summer dress, a toothbrush extending from her mouth.

"Come in. I'm almost ready," she mumbled

Jake followed her into the living room where Jerry sat in his recliner reading the paper. He glanced at Jake and smiled, but kept his eyes on the paper. "Good to see you, Jake. We missed you this week."

"Thanks."

"I was rooting for you even though I didn't stop by. I hate hospitals. It's been years since I've even been to a doctor."

"Are you ready?" Amy asked.

"Sure."

Amy grabbed her sketchbook from the small table in the hallway. "Remember to save us a place," Amy called over her shoulder.

"You got it, kid," Jerry said.

They walked out the door and uphill to the back passageway leading to the courtyard. Parishioners already congregated in the courtyard as Amy and Jake walked hand in hand into the cemetery. They sat on Isaac's bench and talked quietly. Jake felt a calm that had never been there before. Their friendship had been tested to its limit, but it came out better and stronger.

Amy opened her book to the picture of Niederbipp she had drawn on the picnic down by the river. Jake talked about his ideas for Sam's floor, using the tile Isaac already made.

When the minute hand on the clock showed they had one minute left, they stood and hastily made their way to the chapel doors. Jake pulled the door open, making way for Amy to pass through. As planned, she slid her hand into his as they walked into the crowded chapel. Heads began to turn and hushed whispers followed them as they slowly walked down the center aisle and took their seats on the very front row next to Beverly and Jerry.

The prelude music stopped as Thomas took his place behind the lectern. He winked at Jake before reminding the congregation that the symbolism tour of the chapel would begin at 11:15. He then read the hymn numbers and announced a change in the morning's program. Genevieve Holtz had come down with a last minute summer cold and asked to be excused. Instead, Ron Abrams would be sharing his thoughts.

The congregation prayed and sang together before a man a few seats down from Jake and Amy stood and walked to the lectern. He removed his notes from the pocket of his camelhair jacket and slid his glasses higher onto the bridge of his nose as he looked out over the congregation. He looked nervous, and when he spoke his voice was shaky. He thanked the congregation for their prayers and friendship that had come at such a critical time in his life. He spoke of choices he had made that would have caused far better men than he to lose their families and their souls. He wept openly when he spoke of forgiveness and mercy, thankful for the grace of God that came after all he could do to change. Discretely, Jake looked around the chapel and watched members of the congregation wipe away tears with their handkerchiefs. Only a few children sat in the congregation, but even they were quiet, wrapped up in the words that were spoken and the spirit that hung from them.

As he spoke, Ron shared no details of his infractions. It seemed as though everyone already knew what they were and had been waiting—like a child waits for Christmas—for these words to come. Jake thought about his own experience in the last weeks. If the town kept tabs on where and with whom he ate his lunch, surely they would know the details of this man's life. But unlike Jake's experience, the congregation seemed to take no pride in whatever knowledge they might have of his circumstances. Instead, a spirit of compassion and love filled the hall.

Jake looked down at his fingers interlaced with Amy's. Like Ron, he had recently experienced mercy, forgiveness and change. He too felt indebted to the people of this town whose love and concern enabled him to be sitting next to Amy now. Gratitude and humility filled his heart. This wouldn't be possible without the intervention of many people who had gone out of their way to love him. Perhaps it had been the same for this man; perhaps the love and concern of a village had saved him from himself. The details were certainly different, but Jake too had been saved from himself—his future changed by the mercy and concern of those around him.

As he considered these things, an image popped into his head: a green pitcher with a cracked foot where the glaze had run, fusing it to the shelf. He squeezed Amy's hand, filled with gratitude and comprehension.

(25)
THE TOUR

THERE IS NO GREATER AGONY
THAN BEARING AN UNTOLD STORY
INSIDE YOU.
—MAYA ANGELOU

Just like the week before, as soon as "Amen" was said on the benediction, the congregation surged forward, lining up to embrace Ron Abrams. Jake and Amy stayed in place, waiting for the aisles to clear. Many of the older crowd smiled at him and Amy. He nearly laughed out loud when he saw Hildegard on the back row, her hands cupped together above her head, moving them from side to side victoriously. She winked at him and he waved, winking back. It was past eleven by the time they made it to the front doors. They stood on the landing at the top of the stairs, looking out on the bright day.

"I get the feeling everyone is watching us," Amy said under her breath.

Jake nodded. "Then it worked." He put his arm around her shoulder when he saw Gloria and Joseph watching them from the shadows of one of the courtyard trees. They both gave him a thumbs up. Jake pointed them out to Amy who smiled and waved. Kai and Molly climbed back up the stairs, embracing them both and congratulating them on working things out. As they spoke together, Ron Abrams and his entourage worked their way out into the sunlight of the courtyard. Distracted, Jake watched as many others including Gloria and Joseph moved forward to embrace him and a woman who stood at his side.

"It looks like it will be a small group today," Thomas said from behind them. The four of them turned to look at him. "Robert Allan planned on attending the tour, but phoned me this morning to tell me he's still under the weather. I guess it will just be the five of us."

"Actually, we're not staying," said Kai. "Molly had some tough Pixton Bracks last night that started again after breakfast. She needs to get off her feet."

Molly laughed. "That's Braxton Hicks," she said, rubbing her belly. "I'd love to stay, Father, but I don't think I'd make it."

Thomas nodded. They said their goodbyes and watched as Kai and Molly waddled down the stairs and across the courtyard.

"I guess it's just us then," beamed Thomas. "I was hoping for a small group."

"Do you give this tour often?"

Thomas shook his head. "Only once a year or when people ask. No one has showed up to the last several tours. You two didn't really ask, but with all the time you've been spending in the graveyard, looking at the potter's benches, I thought you could benefit from understanding some of the symbols here on the church."

"I've been curious about that," said Jake. "You mentioned one time that you didn't know much about the significance of the symbols on the benches. How is it you've come to learn so much about the church symbols?"

"I've spent a lot more time here, asking questions, looking for answers. There are symbols throughout the world whose meanings have been lost over time. Even Isaac didn't know all of the symbolism on the benches. He regretted that he didn't ask more questions before Lily and his father-in-law died. The things he did know were revealed to him by study. He looked for connections and relationships and then pieced the details together. You've heard it said that a picture is worth a thousand words, but a symbol might be worth a million or more.

"For example, Amy, your last name is symbolic in many ways."

"It is?"

"You've probably heard that the Eckstein family was one of the founding families of Niederbipp?"

Amy nodded.

"They were stone workers. They laid the cornerstones of this church and most of the buildings in old town. In fact, the name Eckstein actually means 'cornerstone.' Even though they were Quakers, they were also Masons, both professionally and fraternally." Thomas led them to the corner of the church and indicated the cornerstone. "These are the symbols of the Masons," he said, pointing to a mark just above the date, 1717.

Amy's eyes lit up. "I've seen that before! My dad has a ring that my grandfather left him with those symbols on it. What is it?"

"The compass and the square, the tools of their trade. Hollywood has made a mess of these things in recent years and caused some misunderstanding. The truth is always more simple than the lie. With a compass you can make a perfect circle. With a square you can make a perfect cube. Hundreds of other tools were needed to build this church, but these are the most basic. The cornerstone is important because it becomes the template for all the other corners. If the cornerstone is not square or is laid without precision, no stone set upon it or next to it will be square and the house, or in this case, the church, will be crooked and unstable. If the foundation isn't right, no amount of mortar will fix it."

"I guess that's kind of like centering in pottery," added Jake.

"That's a good comparison," added Thomas. "If you don't take the time to center the clay, what happens?"

Jake smiled. "Dog bowls happen."

"What does that mean?" Amy asked, looking confused.

"If the clay doesn't get centered from the beginning, it can never really grow. With every pull you make, the wobble gets worse and worse until it collapses into a heap. That might be one of the most difficult things to learn in the beginning. You want so bad to start making big things that you get tempted to move on before the clay is completely centered. The studio at school was filled with warped and crooked bowls and vases. They're good for dogs, but most people have trouble finding beauty in them."

Amy looked thoughtful. "Sounds pretty symbolic of life itself."

"And that right there is the key to understanding symbols," said Thomas. "In order to understand them, you have to be able to relate them to life. A lot of the things I'll show you today are true symbols. Many other things are phrases and scriptural passages passed down from one generation to the next. Take the words over the church doors for example," he said, pointing heavenward. They backed down the stairs slightly so they could read the writing. Jake and Amy acknowledged that neither of them had ever noticed the writing before.

DIE LIEBE UND SUCHE NACH WAHRHEIT IST WEISHEIT

Amy began reading, butchering the words written in German.

"Die Liebe und süche nach Wahrheit ist Weisheit," Thomas read aloud with a much better accent.

"What does it mean?" asked Amy.

"The translation is probably a little rough, but it says approximately 'the love of and search for truth is wisdom.' I was told that the same thing was carved above the door of the first schoolhouse in Niederbipp."

"That's right, the Quakers were also knows as 'seekers,'" offered Jake.

"Yes, but it was what they sought that set them apart."

Amy looked up from her sketchbook where she had just recorded the translation. "Truth?" she said.

"That's right Amy, they sought truth wherever they could find it. The holy scriptures offered some, but the Quakers are unique in believing that God can and will speak to all mankind. This truth, they believed, was more important, more relevant in their lives than the scriptures that were written thousands of years ago. The scriptures are still important to them, but were not as valuable as the voice of God in their own lives."

Jake snickered. "I bet that went over well."

"You guessed it. George Fox and William Penn, the main founders of Quakerism spent a lot of time in jail. They were branded as heretics and blasphemers."

"But didn't William Penn have something to do with Pennsylvania?" asked Amy. "I guess things worked out for him in the end."

"If you consider being banished from England a good thing. You need to remember that America was a penal colony, receiving many of England's outlaws. Some of the land was purchased by the Quakers, but much more of it was given to Penn to settle the debt King Charles II and England owed his father for military service. And so William Penn's Holy Experiment began, to see if religious toleration, democracy and equality could produce a better life. Penn called it the Frame of Government and much of it later became a cornerstone for the constitution."

"Why don't they teach us this stuff in school?" Jake asked.

"Because William Penn was a religious fanatic who encouraged pacifism among his followers. He paid the Indians for their land and was a terrible business man, losing all of his wealth by opening his land to anyone who needed a home. He was never given a dime by those who settled here and he died a pauper. History isn't written by people like that. What mattered to Penn was that he serve God by serving mankind. He knew that the Golden Rule was better when it was lived instead of just talked about. That brings us to the next symbol." He pointed high above the door to the center stone of the archway. "What is that?"

Jake squinted. "It looks like an 'A' and an upside down 'U.'"

"And you know from your time around the Greek fraternities and sororities that those letters are what?"

"Alpha and Omega," Amy offered.

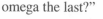

"Very good. Where in the Greek alphabet do those letters fall?"

They looked at each other to see who would answer.

"I know alpha is first," Jake said. "Is omega the last?"

"Yes. Christ referred to himself in the book of Revelation as the beginning and the end, the first and the last and our advocate with the father. What can you tell me about the placement of those symbols?"

They turned together and looked at the top of the arch before turning back to Thomas without an answer.

"That stone is the keystone. Without it, the arch would crumble. If the arch crumbles, the church literally falls apart. Do you see the meaning?"

Jake nodded slowly and spoke thoughtfully, "Christ called himself Alpha and Omega. So those symbols on the keystone indicate him. That means that…"

He fumbled, but Amy continued his thought. "Christ is the keystone. If he were removed, the church would crumble!"

Thomas beamed and clapped his hands. "You two will be giving the tour next time!"

"Isn't Pennsylvania the Keystone State?" asked Amy.

"It sure is. You don't have to look very far to find examples of it. You'll see a keystone on every state highway sign. The next time you have fries, look at the ketchup bottle. If it's Heinz, you'll see the keystone in their logo. Heinz actually got their start just down the road in Pittsburgh."

"So why is it the keystone state?" asked Jake.

"There are probably a lot of reasons; its central location in the 13 colonies was as good a reason as any, but a lot of good things have come out of Pennsylvania that have shaped America. The Liberty Bell was forged here. The constitution, the very document on which our liberty hangs, was written and signed in Philadelphia. The Quakers laid a cornerstone for this country, but their beliefs in God also formed a keystone to keep this country together. The founders of this country wanted freedom from a tyrannical state religion, but never desired a nation devoid of faith in God. They believed the hand of providence had preserved this land as a promised land where mankind could worship God according to the dictates of their own souls. I believe this symbol, carved in the keystone, is one of the most powerful symbols in the church. If we try to apply it to ourselves, well, then we learn something else, don't we?"

Thomas paused, watching as Jake and Amy recorded these things in their sketchbooks.

Amy looked up. "So, this seems to suggest that having Christ at the center of our lives can help us keep our lives together, too."

Thomas smiled and nodded, then turned to Jake with a wink. "It sounds like she's ready to give the Sunday sermon, doesn't it?"

Amy shook her head, looking frightened.

"One of my favorite quotes from William Penn is 'if men will not be governed by God, they will be ruled by tyrants.'" Without another word, he pulled the door open and pulled back the braided grass matt that covered the tile floor, revealing a large five-petaled flower carved into the clay tiles.

"If you're a Dan Brown fan, you might get excited about this. I know I did when I first discovered it. I decided to keep it covered so people don't think this is some missing link to a crazy treasure or secret. I think this is a German Wild Rose. There are a bunch of them growing wild down by the river. I've heard that the founders of Niederbipp brought rose bushes with them, but I haven't been able to figure out what this one means or why it's here. I actually just discovered it a few years ago when I was cleaning the floor. It's kind of a sad place for a rose if you ask me. You can't walk through here without walking on top of it."

Jake looked at Amy and raised his eyebrow. She nodded. They both knew this five-petaled flower was no rose. When Thomas turned his back on them, moving into the chapel, Jake looked at Amy and chills ran up his spine as she mouthed the words, "Forget-me-not."

MEANING

YE SHALL KNOW THE TRUTH,
AND THE TRUTH SHALL
MAKE YOU FREE.
—JOHN 8:32

The tour continued with Thomas marching to the front of the chapel.

"You might be curious about our Christus."

Jake and Amy both nodded.

"I grew up with a crucifix over my bed, over my kitchen table and at the front of every church I ever attended. This was really new for me to see a live Jesus at the front of a church. I've learned a lot about it over the years. It was carved by an immigrant to Niderbipp, a Jewish woodcarver."

"Was that Hildegard's uncle?" asked Jake

"Very good," said Thomas, looking surprised. "What else do you know?"

"Nothing. Just a lucky guess. Hildegard told me she lived with her uncle when she first came here. I knew he was a wood carver."

"There were lots of woodcarvers back then, but he was one of the best. He gave this as a gift to the town of Niederbipp a few years after he got here. He wanted to show his gratitude for the way the town had taken him in and treated him like one of their own. His message, I've been told, was that Jesus was not dead for these people, but rather a living, breathing God who compassionately sought out the lost sheep and brought them into the fold. I'm not certain why it was placed among the organ pipes, but I'm sure it became the visual centerpiece."

Jake looked at the rounded structure of the organ. Then he turned around, looking down the walls of the chapel. "The whole church is like a long arch, coming together at the ceiling. But if you were to lay the arch down, that statue would be the keystone."

Thomas nodded. "Very good, Jake. I've never considered that, but you're right. I guess I've always paid more attention to the two trees behind the organ pipes."

"The trees?" asked Amy.

"Yeah." He motioned for them to follow him behind the pipes. "I've only been in a few Quaker churches, but this is the only one with an organ, let alone a big pipe organ like this. Quakers are generally minimalists, but old habits are hard to break. One of the founders of the town was Johann Schneider, a Swiss organ maker who converted from his Lutheran roots shortly before the exodus from Niederbipp, Switzerland. He wanted to leave his mark on the church as he had in churches throughout Switzerland, but your great-great grandfather wouldn't have it. Fortunately for us, Johann Schneider outlived Mr. Eckstein, so he got to build his organ. From what I understand, Mr. Eckstein always planned for two trees to adorn the front of this church, but he fell from the scaffolding and never recovered. His sons decided against completing the trees and so no one complained when the organ covered up his unfinished work."

The space behind the pipes was cramped but it was clear to see that the columns on the foremost arch in the chapel had been carved to look like they were covered in thick bark.

"Trees have a lot of symbolism that is fitting for a church: the cycles of life that a tree faces each year can be symbolic of our own spiritual and physical journey. It seems we all go through cycles where our faith that was once strong and vibrant fades away from neglect, but is often reborn, becoming stronger and vibrant again."

Jake and Amy both nodded, recognizing the occurrence of this cycle in their own lives.

"Nearly every culture around the world uses the symbol of the tree of life in one form or another."

"Jake has one on his sketchbook," Amy added.

Thomas looked at Jake, moving closer.

"It's just a tree with some Celtic knot work," Jake said, lifting the book for Thomas to see.

Thomas ran his fingers over the cover, rubbing his thumb over the corner where white clay was permanently engrained in the leather. "Where did you get this?" he asked.

"My mom gave it to me just before she died."

"Did she say anything about it?"

"No, why?"

"Because you may have underestimated the meaning here."

Jake and Amy moved next to Thomas, curious what he would have to say. "What do you mean?" asked Jake.

"I see at least three major symbols here that you ought to know something about. This is definitely a tree of life. That itself is a symbol of eternal life, but this tree is different than many I have seen before. There is fruit on it. Many stories from around the world talk of men searching their whole lives for the tree of life, believing that if they eat of the fruit of this tree, they will never die. It's almost a Holy Grail story."

Jake ran his fingers over the cover, stopping at the fruit. He had never noticed this before.

"The next two symbols are fairly simple," Thomas continued. "First, the circle. This is perhaps the simplest of eternal symbols. The circle has no beginning and no end. The same is true of the Celtic knots." Thomas smiled proudly. "These were first created by my ancestors, thousands of years ago. The druids who became the Celts were mostly pagan, worshippers of the sun and nature, but believers in the eternal nature of the soul. And look, there's one of those five-petaled flowers on that button. I'm guessing whoever made this book was probably a fan of the DaVinci Code and the Cult of the Rose."

Jake looked at the button in disbelief. Thomas moved on to the next symbol, but Jake and Amy stood, transfixed by the shiny pewter toggle. They had seen it a thousand times before, but had never really seen it. "My roommate told me it was a pansy," he said softly.

Amy shook her head.

Jake had carried this book with him nearly every day for the last eighteen months, yet he had never truly seen it. He rubbed his thumb over the toggle, feeling emotions swell within him. When he thought of it as a pansy, Jake had been embarrassed by it. But as he looked at it now, he knew this was no pansy. If his mother had known what this was, she had never spoken of it. Yet, as he stared at it, really seeing it for the first time, there was something in his heart that told him she knew what she was doing. He looked at Amy who looked as if she could see his thoughts. She smiled softly, her eyes filling with tears. Jake's roommate couldn't have been more wrong. A pansy is a symbol of weakness. But the flower on his sketchbook was a symbol of love, a symbol of the greatest strength he had ever known.

(27)

ONE OF THE HIVE

A SINGLE DAY IS ENOUGH TO MAKE US A LITTLE LARGER.

—PAUL KLEE

Thomas cleared his throat and the echo sounded throughout the church. "Shall we continue?" he asked when Jake and Amy looked up. They nodded, moving forward. The next symbol was also at the front of the church, off to the right of the organ. A small wooden box, about twelve inches cubed sat atop a stone shelf built into the wall of the church.

"This is the treasury box of the church," Thomas said.

"So is the box the symbol or is it the beehive on the front?" asked Amy, peering closely at the box.

Thomas smiled. "Both. Can you see what the beehive is resting on?"

Amy and Jake bent over to take a closer look.

"It looks like two round balls," Amy offered.

"Or possibly two coins," suggested Thomas. "Do you remember the story of the widow's mite?"

Jake and Amy looked at each other blankly.

"In the Gospel of Mark, Jesus teaches his disciples the meaning of sacrifice and true charity. At a synagogue, they watched as many rich worshippers put a lot of money into the treasury. Then a poor widow dropped in two mites which were equal to a farthing, the smallest denominations in circulation. Jesus taught his disciples that this widow's offering was more substantial than the offerings made by the rich."

"I don't get it," said Amy, her left eyebrow raised, looking confused.

Jake jumped in. "Because the rich people didn't sacrifice. They just basically gave their spare change. But the widow gave everything she had. Right?"

"That's right!" Thomas said.

"I think I might be catching up." Jake nudged Amy.

"Oh, does that mean you're ready to give a sermon?" Thomas asked with a teasing grin.

Jake's short-lived confidence melted, fading back into his fear of public speaking and humiliation.

Thomas winked kindly at Jake before he continued, pointing to the two circles below the beehive. "The law of sacrifice and tithing has been in effect since the beginning of time and the founders of this town continued the tradition. I've learned that the original treasury was kept by the doors, but it was stolen a hundred years ago by a lumberjack who pawned it off down river."

"So this is where people pay their tithes?" Jake asked.

"Yes. It was moved here to the front of the church for peace of mind, but I'm not sure it would be any more difficult to steal. In keeping with tradition, the church doors have no locks. People can come and go all hours of the day and night. Some have suggested it would be a good idea to protect the church and get some locks. Others have suggested that we move the treasury to another part of the church where it can be locked up and hidden away from public view."

"Are people worried about it being stolen again?" asked Amy.

"That's the most serious concern, but this box represents more than just the money inside. Though the design of this box is much simpler than its predecessor, its symbolism is similar to the original, at least as far at the beehive and widow's mites go. The founders of Niederbipp recognized the responsibility they had to use these funds according to the dictates of God."

"So it's kind of like the offering baskets that are passed around in other churches?" asked Amy.

"In some ways, yes, but Malachi didn't say anything about offering baskets."

"Who?" asked Amy and Jake together.

Thomas rolled his eyes in mock exasperation. "The last prophet in the Old Testament. He taught that tithing, a term which literally means one tenth or ten percent, would bless the lives of those who made the sacrifice and commitment to pay it. He promised that the blessings of heaven would be poured out beyond one's ability to receive, that evil would be kept at bay and that the tithe payer and his family would be protected. The giving of tithing was to be kept secret. Christ himself taught that alms were to be given quietly. For these reasons, the church has never had a basket."

Amy turned to Jake. "Didn't one of the benches in the graveyard say something about tithing?"

Jake nodded. "'Rob not God, the source of all good gifts.' I think that's on Abraham's grave, isn't it?"

"I'm impressed," said Thomas. "You've been doing your homework."

"We've been trying," said Amy, reaching for Jake's hand. "We've been anxious to learn everything we could about this place."

"Brian also told me a lot about tithing," Jake added. "He seemed convinced that much of his success was due to keeping the law of the tithe."

Thomas nodded. "He was a good student. There aren't many young people any more who keep the traditions of the past. Brian is a great example of paying tithing. And he's received blessings that are beyond his ability to receive. He's a good man—built his life on a solid foundation and he's been blessed for it."

Jake nodded.

"So what is the tithing used for?" inquired Amy.

"Well, because we have no paid ministry, moneys collected from this box are used to care for the poor and needy. All of these donations are made in secret and were historically distributed by the village elders who sought out the poor, the widowed and the fatherless to make sure their needs were met. The funds are also used to maintain the church. Left over money has traditionally been given to the hospital. That's probably the main reason why the hospital is still here."

"What do you mean? Still here?" asked Amy.

"Niederbipp isn't exactly a booming metropolis. It's not the center of the county anymore, at least not as far as population goes. The hospital was built during the logging boom, when Niederbipp's population was twice what it is today. There are dozens of communities in the county that are bigger than ours, but the hospital remains here because of the generosity of the people of Niederbipp. Somehow, there is always enough in this box to take care of all the needs of the community's poor and still have enough to share with the hospital."

"I remember you saying something about the beehive when we were in the graveyard," Jake said, rubbing his fingers over the lines carved deep into the front of the box. "You said it was a symbol of community, didn't you?"

"That's right. Isaac explained that to me not long after I got here.

As a bee keeper himself, he taught me that bees were the perfect model of community: industrious, hard-working and protective of each other

and the hive as they work together to make something sweet. Like the compass and square, the beehive was also a Masonic symbol, but its use as a symbol of community is used in cultures throughout the world."

Amy ran her fingers over the beehive. "It seems like Niederbipp is more than just a community. It seems like it's more of a big family."

"That's true on several levels. The blood of the earliest settlers still runs in the veins of many of Niederbipp's citizens. But unlike many small towns, Niederbipp has always been welcoming to those who come here. Jake, you mentioned earlier that Quakers are sometimes called Seekers. This village and its people have never been satisfied that they had all the truths. Like that German phrase on the front of the church, they sought truth wherever it could be found. Congregations throughout the world are dying out because their people are starving for truth. Much of this, I believe, is because many churches teach that the heavens are sealed, that God finished speaking with his apostles and that the Bible contains all the words He will ever speak. William Penn and other Quakers bucked those beliefs, teaching instead that God still speaks to mankind through personal revelation. Niederbipp's settlers were hungry for truth and wisdom. They sought direction from the heavens, but also adopted truths from many who joined them permanently, and many more who passed through. Missionaries and other Seekers of different traditions have shared their truths with the people of Niederbipp, making them stronger in their faith, and have added pieces to the great puzzle of life. To those who come without faith, Niederbippians share their faith. To those who come with more faith, Niederbippians ask and answer questions and everyone's understanding is increased."

Jake thought about how the townspeople had shared their faith with him.

"But there are lots of crazy ideas out there! How did they separate the truth from random ramblings and silly ideas?" asked Amy.

"The same way the people of Christ's time were taught to do."

Jake raised his eyebrows, waiting on his words.

"It boils down to the fruits," said Thomas, pointing to Jake's sketchbook. "We learn to know a tree by its fruits; if the fruit is good, the tree must also be good. Jesus taught his followers to look at the fruits of those around them. By their fruits we can know who they are and the truth they might have."

Jake looked confused. "What do you mean by 'their fruits'?"

Thomas thought for a moment. "The goodness of their lives." He thought for a moment longer. "Their works, the way they treat others."

"I get it," said Jake. "If someone is evil, the things he teaches are probably also evil."

Thomas nodded, continuing. "The Quakers believed that Jesus placed the burden of finding truth on all people, instructing them that when they asked, answers would be given and when they knocked, doors would be opened to them. They believed that a personal witness of God's grace and spirit was available to everyone, regardless of his lot in life. This environment became a fertile ground for the seeds of faith to grow and expand. Communities are shaped and built on the ideals and values of its people. Niederbipp is no different. When the love of and search for truth is the motto of the town, people tend to be focused, driven and inspired."

Jake nodded thoughtfully. "So is that why everyone looks out for everyone else? Is it because they are trying to find the truth others might have?"

Thomas nodded, "That's probably part of it. But I'm sure the main reason is because these people believe brotherly kindness is part of our responsibility as Christians. I know it can be overwhelming at times, having your neighbor know everything about you, but we're all just people. We're trying to live the best lives we can and build and protect the hive and each other."

Thomas pointed at the beehive. "The thing that inspires me most about this town is that the majority of its people are really trying to be the best people they can be. They look out for their neighbor, they care for the widowed and fatherless, and they love each other and treat each other with kindness and respect. I'm sure you could find some of those attributes in other communities, but I've never been to a place where so many people are trying so hard to do the right things. It's like a slice of heaven on earth. If it weren't for people like me, the town might be lifted up into heaven like the city of Enoch in the Old Testament." Jake and Amy laughed.

"That actually brings us to the next symbol," Thomas said, pointing to the top of the organ.

Jake and Amy turned their attention to the wooden frame of the old organ. Near the top, with only a few organ pipes poking out above, they saw the words carved into the dark wood. Jake squinted, trying to read the words, carved in an old script. "Veela stimmy, ein geesong?"

"Not bad," said Thomas, but it's pronounced a little different. Viele Stimme, ein Gesang."

VIELE STIMME
EIN GESANG ~
(MANY VOICES, ONE SONG)

"What does it mean?" asked Amy.

"Literally translated, it says, 'Many voices, one song.'"

Amy looked thoughtful. "Sounds a bit like a beehive," she said turning to the offering box.

"Very good. And do you see anything else on the organ?"

They focused their attention back on the organ. On both sides of the ancient organ, sitting atop the wooden frame surrounding the largest pipes, were two tall wooden domes very similar to the beehive on the offering box. When they turned back to Thomas, they found him smiling.

"Things aren't always as they appear to be," he said, winking at Jake. "You two have sat in this church several times now and have missed a lot of really important stuff. There are dozens more symbols in this church. Shall we continue?"

Thomas walked them around the church, pointing out other symbols on the floor and ceiling. The all-seeing eye of God was carved in the top of one of the arches as well as a sun, a moon and lots of stars. The church was a veritable treasure trove of symbols, most of which Jake and Amy had never really seen. They filled their sketchbooks with notes and drawings, drinking in all that Thomas had to say. He stopped at several places along the way, pointing out things the potters of the past had contributed to the church. Many of Alvin's tiles, similar to those on his bench, but in much better condition, had been laid into the floor or mounted on the walls. There were also many tiles they hadn't seen before. They copied these down too, even though Jake thought he'd seen rubbings of many of them in Isaac's sketchbook.

Jake paused before one tile, set into the floor right in front of the lectern. It was a scripture from Ecclesiastes 4: 9-10. Amy read the words aloud.

"Two are better than one…If one falls down, his friend can help him up. But pity the man who falls and has no one to help him up!"

The words sank into Jake's humbled heart. Many people had tried to lift him up since he'd arrived here, but Thomas and Amy had been among the most important. He openly expressed his gratitude for their friendship and for sticking by him even when he'd been so undeserving. Thomas tried to shrug it off, but Jake persisted until he felt Thomas knew how grateful he was. As for Amy, he blamed her blood which now coursed through his veins for his change of heart. Thomas suggested dryly that perhaps Amy's blood would bring about other desirable changes in Jake.

As they worked their way to the doors, Jake confided in Thomas that he'd decided to stay in Niederbipp indefinitely. The priest let out a whoop, sending a flock of startled pigeons into the air. He didn't ask any questions. Maybe he didn't need to.

There was a long pause in the conversation as they sat together on the front steps of the church, watching the pigeons strut across the courtyard. Finally, Thomas broke the silence. "I can't tell you how good it feels to share these things with the two of you. The older folks don't talk about them anymore and so few of the younger generation have interest in learning the old ways. There is a very real potential of these things sliding away into history."

"Aren't they written down anywhere?" asked Amy.

"They are in part, but if only two people show up for a tour given once a year, you might imagine the books in which these things are recorded could get a little dusty. People tend to be so concerned about the future that they forget about the past. In native cultures with oral traditions, people are selected to memorize the history for hundreds and even thousands of years so they can share it with future generations. When I came here and began to learn the stories, I felt it was my calling to remember them so I could pass them on. I fear that if I don't, things will be lost."

"So, why use symbols at all? I mean, if there's a potential that the meaning be lost forever, why would the founders of this town use so many symbols in the church?" Jake asked.

"Because they get people thinking and asking questions—and questions are the beginning of knowledge. Ignorance only comes when people stop asking questions."

Amy shook her head. "But so few people know the answers to all of this. Won't the truth eventually be lost?"

"That depends on you," Thomas said. "Your actions will determine if these things will continue to be taught and understood."

"Sounds like a lot of responsibility," said Amy.

"Now you know how I feel," said Jake, letting out a little laugh. "I thought I was just here to be a potter, but making pots has turned out to be the easy part. The longer I'm here and the more I learn about Isaac, the more I realize that turning his wheel is only the tip of the iceberg. I feel like I've been given the only map to a buried treasure."

"And you only have one volume of Isaac's sketchbooks," Thomas said with a wink.

"That's right," said Amy, poking Jake in the ribs. "We were going to read that together."

Thomas' eyes twinkled as he turned his head to watch them. "Then your journey has just begun. I need to shut up now and get out of your way."

"But what if we have questions?" asked Jake.

"Then your journey will be long indeed," he replied, getting to his feet. "Just remember that all questions have their answers, but you must be patient. Some answers will come to you when you're not even looking, but most of those are worth little. Sometimes you may have to look at a question upside down and backwards before it makes sense. There is no such thing as a bad question, but some are much better than others. If you ask the right questions of the right people, you'll get the right answers—eventually. But remember this; things are often not as they appear to be. If you run into trouble, you know where to find me."

Jake and Amy nodded, looking up at the priest who cast a shadow across them. They thanked him for his time and the things he shared with them. They watched him in silence as he crossed the yard and entered the small white cottage adjacent to the church. Amy turned to look at Jake. Without words he knew what she was thinking. He stood, offering her his hand, and the two friends walked off to begin discovering Isaac together.

(28)

QUESTIONS

MOST OF THE CHANGE WE THINK
WE SEE IN LIFE IS DUE TO TRUTHS
BEING IN AND OUT OF FAVOR.
—ROBERT FROST

S o what do you make of this?" Amy asked. They were sitting at Jake's kitchen table sharing a loaf of Sam's sunflower bread with honey and some chilled peppermint tea. A note from Alice greeted them when they'd arrived. She'd stuck it to the door with a piece of chewing gum, and embossed it with a red lipstick kiss. Jake had handed the note to Amy and teased, "Do you want to write her back for me?" Now, huddled over Isaac's sketchbook, Alice and her note were forgotten.

Amy read Isaac's dedication aloud, looking up again

when it spoke of his son. "I don't understand. This could mean at least a dozen different things."

"I know. I wondered about it too."

"Did he write anything more about it?"

"No. Not yet. I haven't gotten too far. I've been distracted by his sketches and some of his other notes. My first thought was that he had an illegitimate child that he never knew, but I'm having second thoughts, especially after what Thomas said."

"About what?"

"You know, that bit about things not being as they appear. I've made the mistake of misjudging a lot of things by going with my first impression. I feel like I need to look a little deeper, maybe ask some questions."

"But who would you ask? Do you think Thomas knows about this?"

"If he does, he hasn't said. I'm not sure if he's holding back or just waiting for me to ask. The way he talked about questions being the beginning of learning makes me wonder how much I've missed."

"What are you thinking?"

"I don't know for sure, but I know I need to think more about it. Like he said, some questions are better than others. Maybe in our quest to learn, it would be wise to develop some good questions. As eager as people have been to share their stories with us, I have to wonder what else we could learn if we asked the right questions. Thomas might know something about this, but if he doesn't, I'm sure there's got to be someone here who does. It's just a matter of finding the right person and asking the right question. We have to remember that Isaac was very respected. I'm pretty sure if we went snooping around, asking people if Isaac had an illegitimate son, we'd make a lot of people wonder if we were trying to smear his name. I don't think we'd get any cooperation."

"So what do you suggest?"

"I think we have to be patient. Everyone seems to know everything about everyone else in this town. If we're patient, I think things will come out."

Amy nodded, looking thoughtful. "Gloria had a baby who died. Do you think she might know something? Didn't Isaac spend a lot of time with her and Joseph?"

"Yeah, but she's never said anything about Isaac having a son. He also spent a lot of time with your aunt and uncle, but they've never offered anything either. It's curious to me that he so openly speaks of him here, but there's no mention of a son anywhere in his will, or anywhere else for that matter. I'm at a loss."

Amy flipped open her own sketchbook to a blank page and wrote "Good Questions" on the top in bold lettering. Then she wrote: #1 What can you tell me about Isaac's family?

Jake laughed. "That sounds like a question from the tabloids."

She raised her eyebrows. "Do you have a better idea?"

His smile faded. "Not yet, but there has to be a better question. We just haven't gotten to it yet."

Amy nodded, flipping the page in Isaac's book.

Jake leaned next to her, turning the page back to the dedication. "There's something else there that makes me curious."

"What's that?" She looked up, their noses nearly touching.

"That!" He pointed to "Volume 36."

"Does that mean he has 35 more volumes somewhere?"

"It seems to, but the date is also curious. He started this volume more than ten years ago and was still working on it when he died. If he has 35 more volumes somewhere, he must have been pretty prolific in his early days. I think he was here about 55 years, so there was plenty of time to fill that many volumes, but I can't figure out why he slowed down. At the rate he was going with this book, it would have taken him twelve years to fill it."

"Maybe he ran out of things to say?"

"Maybe, but if you're used to filling a book every 18 months, why would you all of a sudden slow down to a snail's pace?"

Amy responded by turning to her questions: #2 Why did Isaac slow down his writing? #3 Where are the other 35 volumes?

"I don't know much about books, but I'm sure this paper is handmade and its cover is leather—looks like buckskin. Did you see the binding? Those ridges on the spine are where it was sewn. It would probably take someone several days to make a book like this, if they even could. I've only seen books like these in museums and in the special collections at the library on campus. I had to wear special white gloves to even touch those books."

"Didn't those ladies at church last week say he carried it with him all the time?"

"That's right! I forgot about that. They made it sound like he was never without it. Didn't they say something about him having all his secrets in it?"

"Yeah," she said. She added another question to her list: #4 Where did the sketchbook come from? "So, have you found any secrets yet?"

Jake reached over, turning the page and pointing to the flower at the bottom. "There's two of those on every page."

"Hey, those are forget-me-nots."

"I know."

"I wish we could have seen this before. It might have helped us figure out what the secret ingredient was."

"I'm not so sure it would have. I don't usually equate flowers drawn at the bottoms of pages in an old book with the secret ingredient in anything. I think this might be what Thomas was talking about."

"Huh?"

"We found the secret ingredient because we were asking questions. Lots of people have tried, including Thomas, to replicate Isaac's tea. Sam had this book for a whole month and I'm sure Thomas has had access to it too. You heard Thomas talking about the five-petaled flower under that rug in the church. He thought it was a rose. It's almost like he's been asking the wrong question. Or maybe it's the right question, but the wrong source."

"Do you think we should straighten him out?"

"I don't know. It seems like Isaac wanted to keep it a secret, even though it's right here. Thomas told me that Isaac knew he was trying to copy his tea. He kept the secret ingredient a secret. I feel like we need to honor that."

Amy nodded, looking thoughtful. She ran her finger over the flowered number before turning the page. She stopped when she reached the page with the tree. She ran her fingers over the ink drawing as if she were reading Braille, stopping when her fingers came to the limb with the words written on them. "I feel like I know this tree," she said, turning to face Jake. "I think its down by the river."

Jake looked at the drawing. "What are you doing this afternoon?"

"I was hoping I could spend some time with you, that is if you don't have a date with Alice."

Jake laughed. "Do you think we could find this tree?"

"I'm pretty sure we could, but it might take the rest of the afternoon."

"Promise?" He wrapped his arms around her shoulder and kissed her softly. "I'll get my bag."

He packed the bag with the old quilt, a water bottle, Isaac's sketchbook and the rest of the sunflower bread. As they walked out the door, Amy's eyes fell on her painting of a green pitcher hanging on the wall near the door. Jake smiled, grateful he'd found a place for it.

THE DEAL

EVERY ARTIST DIPS HIS BRUSH IN
HIS OWN SOUL, AND PAINTS HIS OWN
NATURE INTO HIS PICTURES.
—HENRY WARD BEECHER

obblestone gave way to blacktop and then to fields of alfalfa and sunflowers. Jake and Amy spoke of how things had changed since Mother's Day. They promised each other not to waste any more time trying to guess what the other was feeling. They shared expressions of love in ways that couldn't be misunderstood. By the time they reached the banks of the river, they had decided that the last week, full of apprehension and confusion, could never be repeated. They promised each other they'd learn from it so they could move forward.

The afternoon was warm and muggy. Mayflies and mosquitoes

buzzed about them as they walked hand in hand along the path that paralleled the river. It was otherwise quiet here, though the well worn path suggested it was not always so. When they came to a graying weathered bench, hand hewn from a giant log, they stopped to rest in the shade. They watched a lonely canoe float slowly in the current of the Allegheny, its rider making long, graceful arcs with his bright fly line, casting it toward the shallows. The water was significantly lower than it had been a month before, exposing more beach and several rocky islands. They watched in silence until the canoe floated around a bend in the river. Then Amy stood, pulling Jake with her and they scrambled down the steep banks to the rocky beach.

"I want to swing," she said, giving him a smile that made his heart gallop. Jake stopped to pick up a stick, polished and gray from the water. He tossed it into the water and watched as it floated by. When he turned around, he saw that Amy was bent over, her hands full of rocks. She stood, skipping one across the water. It bounced four, five, six times before sinking into the green water. Jake joined her, giving the stones back to the river. They laughed together as several of his first throws resulted in splashes, but no skips. He blamed his balance, thrown off by

the dull ache in his arm. But Amy teased him, mimicking his clumsy throws until it turned into just throwing rocks into the drink. They laughed again like children, trying to make the biggest splash.

When Amy found an old water bottle among a pile of driftwood, she sat down. Ripping a page from her sketchbook, she began a note.

Help me.

I'm stranded on an island with a handsome potter and we have nothing to eat but sunflower bread and nothing to do but throw rocks in the river and kiss. He's getting better at both, but he still needs some practice.

If you find this note, know that I am happy on my island. I'm in love.

Amy Eckstein

Jake laughed, kneeling on the gravel next to her.

She twisted the cap off the water bottle and rolled up the note, sliding it inside. Then she replaced the lid and tossed the bottle back into the river. They watched until it disappeared around the same bend as the canoe. Jake pulled Amy to her feet and embraced her tightly. "I don't deserve you," he whispered in her ear.

"You're right," she said, tickling his ribs, but not letting go enough for him to squirm. She turned her face until their lips met. "It's time for your practice." She smiled and Jake kissed her nose, laughing. They held each other for a long time. Finally a pesky mosquito buzzed in Amy's ear and sent a chill down her spine that quaked her whole frame. She broke away, grabbed her sketchbook and ran upstream across the rocky beach. Jake followed, laughing.

She was resting on the old swing when he finally caught up to her. The light breaking through the canopy above made her hair glow in the shadows. He stepped behind her, bending over to grab onto the ropes. He took them in his hands, but paused, inhaling the scent of her hair. The scent triggered an avalanche of memories from the last month and flooded his mind with the things that had endeared her to him. He pulled her back, wrapping his arms around her waist, and giving her a gentle squeeze before letting her go. He pushed her again and again and soon she was soaring high above the rocky floor. He sat down on the gravel to watch her, wondering why a girl like her would be interested in spending time with a guy like him. Whatever the reason, he was grateful.

She sat down next to him, leaning against his shoulder. As they talked together, enjoying the lazy afternoon, Amy began stacking the round rocks on top of each other. When Jake pulled her to her feet an hour later, they had several small stacks of rocks precariously balanced on top of each other.

They continued their walk upstream along the rocky banks, stopping from time to time to skip rocks and sort through piles of drift wood. Their progress was slow and aimless, having no real agenda or time line. After walking around several bends in the river, Jake pulled Amy by the hand up the steep bank to the well worn path. He felt fatigued in the lazy afternoon. They laid out the old quilt on a shadowy patch of grass and sat down. Billowy clouds drifted through the window of blue sky, framed by the branches of the giant elm trees. They ate more sunflower bread before lying back to concentrate on the clouds.

Without a watch to know the exact time, Jake knew it was

several hours later when he awoke. Amy's hair had tickled his nose as he slept. She was curled up against his side, her back towards him. He ran his fingers gently through her amber hair before rolling onto his side to get closer to her. He couldn't think of anything as wonderful as the closeness he felt right then. She stirred, snuggling against him and pulling his arm tighter around her stomach. His arm ached as she pulled against his stitches, but he bit his lip and waited for the pain to subside. He didn't want to protest or move it away.

"I'd be getting home right about now if you hadn't written that letter," she whispered.

The reality of her words startled Jake. "Then I'm glad I did," he said, leaning up on the elbow of his good arm.

She turned to face him. "I'm glad too. I really don't like riding the bus."

Jake started laughing and laid back down, their shoulders and heads touching.

Amy pointed to huge white cloud. "That one looks like a pterodactyl eating a duck."

They laughed together for a moment before Jake turned his head and spoke. "I've been meaning to ask you about your paintings. I was wondering if you got any done last week."

Amy turned her head so their noses touched. "Yeah. I finished six small ones. I had some long days, but it was nice to finally be painting. I feel like a few of them were the best pictures I've ever painted."

"I'm sorry I wasn't there to watch. Where'd you go?"

"I painted one in my room—just a still life of an old chest at the foot of my bed. I used to imagine it was a pirate's chest, but Aunt Bev just uses it to store quilts. The rest I did plein air."

"What does that mean again?"

Amy smiled. "I guess potters don't do plein air. It's a French term, it means something like 'in the open air.' In non-painters terms, it just means 'outside' or 'on location.' Like what we did last week. I actually went back to Taufer's Pond on Friday to finish the painting I started there with you. It was going to be my last painting, something to take home with me to remind me of the beauty of this place. It almost killed me to think about leaving before I really had the chance to paint."

Jake nodded thoughtfully. "Tell me about that job you were going to take."

"My mom said I'd be painting for an advertising firm, doing stuff their digital design people didn't want to mess with. I guess the painter they've had took a job teaching at a college or something."

"It sounds like a good job."

"They were going to start me out at $40,000.00 a year after only having seen my senior portfolio."

"That sounds pretty tempting. That's a lot of money."

"Yeah, it is," she said, pursing her lips. "I don't think they'll be too happy when I don't show up for work tomorrow."

"What! You didn't tell them you're not coming?"

"Nope."

"Why?"

"It's complicated, Jake. It's probably a pride issue, but the simple answer is I don't want to give my father the satisfaction of shaping my life anymore. He thinks I've wasted the last four years, majoring in art instead of business. I told you he had a fit when he found out how I planned to spend my summer. My mom gave me a ride to the bus station when he was at a baseball game; otherwise I'd probably still be stuck working for one of his business buddies. He thinks the only way for me to redeem myself is to get a good job and use the skills he paid for me to develop. If I had a hundred thousand dollars, I'd pay him back today and be done with him. I'm afraid he'll hound me for the rest of my life. When I got the answer I needed, I decided it would be easier to just let it go and deal with the consequences rather than try to explain."

"What do you mean?"

She turned her head, looking back at the sky and took a deep breath. "I needed to know what God wanted me to do with my life. That's what

I was doing yesterday when you found me. I went looking for answers."

"Is that why you took your paints?" Jake asked, remembering the night at Taufer's Pond when she explained the spiritual connection she had with painting.

She nodded. "I'd made the decision to leave, but I didn't feel good about it. When I got your note, I felt sick inside, thinking about all the things you told me… all the things we've talked about. I didn't want to give up, but I also knew I needed to know—really know what I was supposed to be doing. I knew I needed to come here this summer. I knew that as well as I know my own name. So, yesterday I went searching for the same feelings of confirmation I had when I came here. I'd made the decision to leave, to go to work for Daddy's friend, but as I began painting in the woods, the resolve I had vanished away and was replaced with a strong feeling that I needed to stay and paint here, even if it means living a life of poverty."

She turned to Jake, resting her nose on his. "I know this is where I am supposed to be. Finding your bike next to mine last night only added to the confirmation I had already received. Being with you today, the tour of the church with Thomas…I know there's probably going to be hell to pay when my dad finds out I'm not on that bus, but everything in my heart tells me that I need to be here."

Jake smiled at her. "So is this an act of disobedience?"

"No, it's an act of following my heart and my conscience. I'm not sure I could be any happier working for that advertising firm than I was selling makeup." She sat up, folding her arms across her knees. "I can't do it Jake. I've only been here five weeks, but already my heart beat is synced with the vibrations of this place. I feel like I'm home."

Jake sat up. He put his hand on her arm, waiting for her to look at him. "Amy, I know this is where I'm supposed to be, too. I'm sorry it took me so long to see that. I don't know if it's your fault because of the blood you gave me, or if it's because of all the humble pie I've been eating lately, but my heart has changed. I feel like I'm finally hearing the voice of God. Looking back, I know I've heard it all along, but I'm finally listening. I wish I could start over. I wish I could have come here with the same mentality I have today. Things are so much clearer."

Amy nodded.

"So what are you going to do about your parents?"

"Hide!" she said, laughing. "I'll just plan on being gone a lot. There's a reason I don't have a cell phone. I feel like I'm just getting in the groove with my painting. I'll just plan on busying myself with that. If they can't reach me, they can't hurt me. It'll be fine."

Jake watched her. He was inspired by her resolve, but knew it was at least partially over inflated. Somehow he knew she was still vulnerable. An idea came to him in the silence that followed, one he wished he'd thought of earlier. "Do you have a plan for your paintings?"

"What do you mean?"

"Well, I was just thinking that you could show them at the Pottery. It's always dusty and the lighting isn't great, but I have a whole lot of wall space that's not being used. I think they'd be a nice addition."

"Are you serious?"

"Of course. Unless you think the studio isn't good enough. It's not a real gallery, but it could work. Your paintings would be seen by a lot more people than are seeing them now."

Amy laughed. "I don't know what to say."

"I'd like it if you said yes."

"But that's not really fair to you. You'd need to get a commission. Most galleries take fifty percent."

Jake nodded, smiling. "Ok, but since it's not a real gallery, I'll settle for a gift wrapping tutorial and lunch with you everyday. Oh, and maybe you could clean up around the shop after hours. Kai did that for Isaac for a while."

She laughed. "Then I think I have some credit coming to me. You left the studio a mess when you went to the hospital."

"I'm sorry I forgot to thank you. Kai and Molly said you and Bev cleaned it up. I was shocked at how clean it was. Maybe if you were around more, I wouldn't let it get so bad. Oh, and I told you before that I'm a pretty good model. There's not a ton of space, but you could set up your easel in the studio if you wanted, at least on the rainy days when you can't do that plein air stuff."

"Would you mind if I gave the showroom a fresh coat of paint?"

"Of course not. I might be as much help as a one armed paper hanger, but I'll help if I can."

"And we should plant flowers in the flower box in front. I've been meaning to help you with that since our first date. There've just been so many distractions," she said with a wink.

"So is it a deal then?"

"It's a deal!" She wrapped her arms around his neck.

Jake got to his feet, reaching down for Amy. "Come on. Let's go find that tree."

WE MUST BE LOVERS, AND AT ONCE THE IMPOSSIBLE BECOMES POSSIBLE.

– RALPH WALDO EMERSON –

(30)

OLD MAN WILLOW

I WENT OUT FOR A WALK
AND FINALLY CONCLUDED TO
STAY OUT TILL SUNDOWN,
FOR GOING OUT, I FOUND,
WAS REALLY GOING IN.

—JOHN MUIR

hey followed the meandering path around the next bend where the banks were not nearly as high as they were downstream. Amy took the lead, clipping along at a quick pace like she suddenly had an agenda. Jake rushed to keep up, keeping his eyes on her ginger hair as it bounced off her flowered summer dress and reflected the waning light. Suddenly, she stopped and pointed. Jake nearly ran into her, not paying attention.

"I think that's it." She pointed to a broad willow tree fifty yards away. "I knew I had seen it before when I saw Isaac's drawing. My brothers used to swing on the low branches."

The weeping willow's branches reached out toward the water, falling like the waters of a huge green fountain. Even from this distance, they could see that its lowest branches danced on top of the river's surface. They kept walking along the path that straightened out in front of them, leading right to the tree. Amy stopped again, ten feet from it.

"Hello there," said an old man, somewhat hidden in the shadows. He was stooped over, leaning heavily on his cane as he shuffled out into the sunlight. Something about him seemed familiar and when he removed his gray hound's-tooth hat, Jake recognized him.

"Hello, Mr. Allan," Amy said.

"Ahh, Amy, Jake. What a pleasure to see you. I understand I missed our tour this afternoon. Thomas visited me a few hours ago and told me you all had a lovely time."

"We did," said Amy. "Thomas said you've been sick. Are you doing better?"

"I'm feeling well enough to keep my appointment with old man willow." He took a few steps toward them before reaching into his pocket. "I've got a treasure for you both," he said, reaching his hand out to them.

They stepped forward to receive whatever it was he had.

The old man smiled a toothless grin before dropping his cane and putting both hands behind his back. When he pulled them forward again, both hands were made into fists, covering whatever it was he had inside. "Choose," he said with a twinkle in his eye.

Amy stepped forward and pointed to his right hand. He turned it over and opened his fist to reveal a rusty bottle cap. "One of my favorites," he said, flashing another smile and handing it to her.

"And you, young potter, what'll it be?"

Jake tried to keep from laughing. "I guess I'll go with your left hand."

"Oooh, that's a good choice, especially considering that my other hand is empty. Smart boy, smart boy." He opened his hand to reveal a small piece of broken mirror. "It was sharp when I found it. I had to sand the edges off with a rock." He lifted it higher for Jake to examine.

"Gee, thanks Mr. Allan. This is really nice."

"You're right. It's small, but I discovered it's just the right size to look at my eyeball. I've probably spent the better part of a full day discovering my own eyeball. I never knew how beautiful it was until I found this piece of mirror. Sometimes I look into it when I walk around and I almost fall over. Did you know when you look in the mirror, everything's backward? I might have known that when I was younger, but I forgot."

"Are you sure you want to give it to me?" asked Jake, trying hard to keep a straight face.

"Yes, of course I'm sure. It's one of my favorites, but maybe it can be one of yours too. I almost forgot. It has magical powers. Let me show you." He took the small mirror back from Jake and walked to a point on the trail where the last sunbeam of the day found its way through the trees. He held the mirror to the sun, angling it so that a sunbeam shot back at Jake and Amy. As the light flitted on Amy's hair, he began giggling like school boy. "See, I told you its magic. It's a sunbeam maker." He held the mirror close to his eye as he walked back to them. Then he smiled at it and stopped walking. "Oopsy Daisy, it looks like I forgot to put my teeth in again. Mom would be awful angry with me if she knew. You won't tell her, will you?"

Jake and Amy shook their heads, charmed but confused by this strange little man. He gave Jake the mirror once again and hobbled over to his cane. As he stooped over to pick it up, a passage of gas escaped his backside. "Did you say something, dear?" he asked, turning to Amy.

"Uh…Thank you." It was Amy now who was trying hard not to laugh, but failing. She looked away, biting her cheeks.

"Ahh, you're welcome. I better run along and find my teeth. The tree is all yours now. It's such a nice tree isn't it? Yes, I better find my teeth. You two love birds have a nice evening."

"Are you sure you're ok getting home by yourself?" Amy asked.

"Of course. I've been there a million times. I almost never get lost." He waved his cane at them as he scampered clumsily down the path.

When he was out of earshot, they turned to each other and laughed.

"Did you say something, dear?" Jake repeated, laughing with full abandon.

"He's a really nice old man," Amy countered. "This is the first time he's given me anything but a rock."

"Yeah, that's a really nice rusty bottle cap." Jake continued to laugh, but stopped when he saw that Amy's face was growing serious.

"I have no doubt that he's a bit crazy, but I've never known a crazy person to walk around handing out treasures. It makes me curious. He's got to have an unusual story."

"Ya think?"

"We need to ask Thomas more about him. I bet my aunt might know something too. I noticed she has a broken bowl on a shelf that's full of river rocks. I have a hunch some of them are from him."

As she spoke, Jake took off his backpack and bent over to remove Isaac's sketchbook. When he rose to his feet, he found Amy looking after the old man as he made his way slowly up the well worn path. Jake stood next to her, watching her.

"There's something special about that man, something innocent and childlike. He makes me smile. He has ever since I first met him. He must be getting crazier, but he's so cute."

Jake nodded, trying to be serious. When the man's grey hat disappeared in the willows and grasses, he opened the book to page seven and eight: the sketch of the tree that stood before them. In fact, they seemed to be standing near the very spot where Isaac had stood when he made the sketch. One of the lower limbs stretched out like a long park bench before its end jutted heavenward and cascaded back

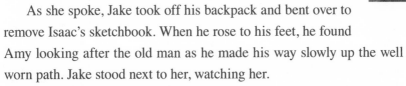

down in vine-like branches and leaves. Jake and Amy walked toward the tree and gave in to the urge to climb the low branch.

"The drawing has some notes here, written on the upper limb. Do you see anything carved on that branch?"

The light was fading fast, and under the canopy of the willow, it was nearly dark. "There's something here," Amy said, rubbing her hand over the scarred bark.

"Can you read it?"

She squinted, putting her nose next to the limb. "Something like… 'Be still and know that I…' I can't read the rest."

"Be still and know that I am God, maybe?"

"I think so. Does it say that on Isaac's drawing?"

"Yeah. Hmmm…" Jake pondered the inscription on the branch, duplicated in the sketchbook. "Isaac calls this 'the crying place.' I've been curious about that. One of my mom's co-workers, a guy named Mr. Williams wrote that in a card he gave me at my mom's funeral. He was the one that got us going to church and looking for answers." He paused again, thoughtfully. "I think it might be from Proverbs or somewhere in the Bible. I can't say I thought much about it before I found it written here in Isaac's book. I wondered if it was really carved on the tree or if Isaac just wrote it on the sketch."

Amy nodded, but even in the dim light, she looked distracted. "Do you know what Mr. Allan meant? Something about his appointment with, what'd he call it, 'Old Man Willow?' Did you get any of that?"

"No, I'm not sure I got much of anything that he said. But judging by the well worn path, this tree must be pretty special to a lot of people. Maybe we need to ask around," Jake suggested.

They packed up their things and began their walk back to town, their minds swelling with more and more questions. As they rounded a bend in the path, Jake stopped suddenly and held his breath. A bush on the bank of the river was glowing a strange yellow-green, pulsing erratically.

"Fireflies!" said Amy, stopping beside him.

"I've never seen so many!"

"Don't you have them in Vermont?"

"We did when I was a kid. I used to collect them with my mom, but I haven't seen any in a long time. Did you have them in Springfield?"

"Yeah. I used to catch them in mayonnaise jars with my brothers. Sometimes they'd smear them onto their faces so their faces would glow."

"Yuck, you can do that?"

"My brothers thought of everything. I guess I never really thought about how gross it is when I was a kid."

Jake took off his pack. He offered Amy a last drink of water before pouring out the rest of it. Amy walked to the bush and shook it softly. A thousand flashing lights took flight. For the next ten minutes they chased bugs, catching them in their hands and feeding them gently into the water bottle. When the bottle was filled with a dozen flashing lights, they continued home, giddy as children on a summer's night.

Jake walked Amy to her door and gave her a long hug, thanking her for loving him. He lingered over a goodnight kiss before reluctantly handing her the blinking lantern. He smiled to himself as he walked home, feeling content and filled with peace about his decision to stay.

㉛

A DELAYED BEGINNING

WORK WHILE YOU HAVE THE LIGHT.
YOU ARE RESPONSIBLE FOR THE
TALENT THAT HAS BEEN
ENTRUSTED TO YOU.
—HENRI-FREDERIC AMIEL

Jake awoke to a dull ache in his arm, but by the time he'd showered and shaved, the pain was nearly gone and his thoughts were on to other things. He looked around the kitchen in search of food. He and Amy had finished off the bread yesterday. He considered making pancakes, but knew his recipe made far more than he could eat alone. Feeling a little sheepish, he left his apartment, following his nose and the well worn path to Sam's bakery. The line of customers stopped at the unfinished floor in the bakery's entryway and Jake felt a pang of guilt as he remembered his commitment to Sam. He considered walking away, but hunger and the scent of fresh bread and pastries kept him moving forward. He was nearly drooling by the time he reached the counter.

"Well, Jake. It's good to see you on your feet. You look well."

"Thank you," he said, smiling as he looked up at Sam. "I'm feeling pretty good. Sandy told me I should be back to work in a week or two."

"Great to hear!" said Sam.

Jake swallowed. "I'm awful sorry about the floor. I was hoping to be ready to start laying tile in a week. Now it looks like…" Jake felt a hand on his shoulder and turned to see Amy. She looked ready to work with her hair wrapped into a knot on the back of her head, secured with a yellow pencil.

"Hi, Sam. Jake was just saying that he's sorry for the delay, but he—I mean we—we plan to get started on your tiles today. Depending on how gimpy he really is, we should only be a week to ten days behind schedule."

Sam smiled through his handlebar mustache. "That's even better news! Are you going to be helping him then?"

"Yes. I heard about the arrangements you made with Jake and I decided I want in." She turned to wink at Jake.

"And you think you can motivate this boy to finally do something?"

"If I can't, I'll do it myself. I don't like the idea of free bread being left on the bargaining table. He already told me he'd split it with me if I helped him."

"Well, well," Sam said, crossing his arms over his chest. "Maybe I should have hired you in the first place. You sound like a woman of action. I like that."

Jake was smiling, but remained silent, watching the interaction with interest.

"Oh, I am that, but before we cut Jake out of the deal, maybe we should give him one more chance to redeem himself. I think he already owes you for five weeks worth of bread, doesn't he?"

"Indeed he does," said Sam, his voice strong and deep.

They didn't notice that everyone in the bakery had stopped to watch the interaction. Thomas, who had been busy helping another customer, turned his full attention to Amy and Jake.

"Well, Sam," continued Amy. "I have shared much of that bread and feel it would be quite dishonest of me to not accept my share in that debt." She straightened herself to her full height and placed her hand over her heart. "I pledge to do all I can to help this poor, clumsy potter make good on his promise to you."

Sam smiled heartily, stifling a laugh as he shifted his attention back to Jake. "It sounds like Amy has you on a pretty short leash."

Many of the customers began laughing, but Sam raised his hands to calm them. "Because you'll be working with a clumsy potter, I'll give you kids 'til the end of the month to have the floor completed. But I'll warn you—if I catch you slacking off, I'll have to send my posse to break your knees." He nodded toward Thomas and a woman behind the counter, who simultaneously bared their teeth and growled through lips that quickly turned to smiles. Again the customers laughed and turned back to their business. Soon the bakery buzzed again with chatter from both sides of the counter as business resumed. Jake felt his face flush.

Sam grabbed a brown paper sack and filled it with a fresh loaf of sunflower bread. Then, looking up at Amy, he slid a second loaf into the sack before handing the bundle to Jake. "I'm glad you're back," he said, leaning over the counter and motioning for Jake to come closer. "You better take care of her," he whispered, "or I'll break your knees myself." He smiled warmly before turning to the next customer.

Amy tugged Jake by the hand, pulling him out the door and into the street. They laughed together for a moment.

"What are you doing?" asked Jake.

"I was looking for you. When you didn't answer your door, I figured you wouldn't be far. Aunt Bev wanted me to remind you about the Visitor Bureau meeting today. It's in the Mayor's office at noon."

"Oh, that's right. I totally forgot about it. What are you doing today?"

"I'm making tiles," she said, taking the bag from him and ripping off the end of one of the loaves.

"I thought you said you've never worked with clay."

"I haven't," she mumbled, her mouth full of bread. "But it can't be that hard. I figured we could make tile until noon, go to that meeting and then go pick out some paint later on."

"It sounds like you've been thinking."

"Some people get out of bed before nine," she said, tousling his still-wet hair. "I already started a painting but realized we hadn't made any plans for the day."

"You mean we get to hang out all day?" Jake asked, looking surprised.

"Did you have plans to hang out with anyone else?"

He shook his head before grabbing the piece of bread from Amy's hand and sprinting away. She chased him all the way up Zubergasse where he stopped at the Pottery's door, fumbling for the key in his pocket. She grabbed his ribs, tickling him until he gave up and relinquished the bread he'd stolen.

A few minutes later, they were sharing bread and peppermint tea as they studied the notes Jake had made for the bakery floor. Amy pulled the pencil from her hair and made several sketches before they decided on one. Jake had made some tiles at school, but most of these were small and used for mosaics rather than something like this. The bakery floor would be walked on for many decades to come. He wished he had time to experiment with thickness and design, but knew Sam was anxious to get the floor done. In college, he had learned a trick for keeping tiles from warping as they dried. If the clay was dried slowly on top of drywall, the effects would be much better than if they were left out in the open air. When he told Amy about his need for drywall, she said she thought she'd seen some scrap pieces at Kai and Molly's the week before.

Kai and Molly looked up as Jake and Amy entered the grocery store. Molly greeted them halfheartedly, looking tired and uncomfortable in her last week of pregnancy. Jake left Amy with Molly and went in search of Kai. He found him near the back, restocking shelves. He learned that Kai had purchased several sheets of drywall to cover the crack in the kitchen ceiling, but opted to repair the old plaster instead when he couldn't find anyone to help hang it. He had used a few smaller pieces to make some other repairs, but was anxious to find a place for the rest of it before the baby came. They left the girls in the store while they ran up to the apartment and returned a few minutes later with two stacks of drywall that had been cut into manageable two foot square pieces.

Kai accompanied Jake and Amy back to the Pottery, insisting that he help Jake with the heavy load so he wouldn't put undue strain on his arm. After Kai left, they cleared the Pottery floor. With the stools and furniture stacked to one side, they had room to lay out the drywall. To account for the shrinkage of the clay and grout lines, the design had to be increased by fifteen percent. Jake crunched the numbers on a calculator while Amy rendered the design in pencil. When they left, just before noon, a pattern for each tile had been created with paper, filling both of them with anticipation and excitement for the final product.

WHEN ALL THAT YOU RETAIN
IS LOVEABLE,
THERE IS NO REASON
FOR FEAR TO REMAIN
WITH YOU.
— A COURSE IN MIRACLES —

(32)
THE ADVOCATE

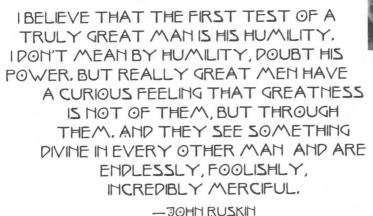

I BELIEVE THAT THE FIRST TEST OF A
TRULY GREAT MAN IS HIS HUMILITY.
I DON'T MEAN BY HUMILITY, DOUBT HIS
POWER. BUT REALLY GREAT MEN HAVE
A CURIOUS FEELING THAT GREATNESS
IS NOT OF THEM, BUT THROUGH
THEM. AND THEY SEE SOMETHING
DIVINE IN EVERY OTHER MAN AND ARE
ENDLESSLY, FOOLISHLY,
INCREDIBLY MERCIFUL.

—JOHN RUSKIN

They arrived at the Mayor's office five minutes late to find the council room filled mostly with gray-haired people repeating the pledge of allegiance. They found two empty seats toward

the back, right behind Kai—the only other participant within three decades of their age.

The Mayor was positioned at the front of the room, but everyone knew who was really running the meeting. Beverly was in fine form. As soon as everyone was seated, she asked Jake to stand, welcoming him as the newest business owner in Niederbipp. Jake smiled as those in the room applauded and turned to face him. He was relieved to recognize faces in the room. Gloria and Joseph winked at him while Roberta Mancini turned her nose up at him and looked away. Albert, Sam, Thomas and another woman Jake recognized but couldn't say from where, sat at the front table, flanking Beverly on either side.

The next item of business was to review the minutes of the last meeting. Beverly called for a motion of approval, which was offered by the Mayor and seconded by a blue-haired woman on the front row.

Beverly quickly proceeded: "As the president of the Niederbipp Travel Council, I asked you all in the last meeting to put together a marketing campaign for Niederbipp. Since then, I have been made aware that we have overlooked some of our younger, more…how do I put this…more techno savvy residents." A small chuckle rippled throughout the room. "Many of you may not even be aware that Niederbipp has a website on the world wide web internet, though I've been told that it's outdated. Let's face it, we have an aging population with few young people to take over for us when we want to retire. Isaac Bingham, the first president of this council went to great trouble and personal expense to put Niederbipp on the map. He was concerned about legacy. And his death—I'm sure—has caused all of us to worry about our own. I want us to keep things moving forward, if for nothing else, then to honor Isaac and his efforts to keep Niederbipp on the tourist map. It's those tourist dollars that set us apart from towns like Codham and Hickory. We need those tourist dollars to stay alive. We need to continue to set ourselves apart from the other towns in this area. That being said, I would like to open the floor for the sharing of ideas."

A gray haired man on the front row raised his hand and spoke before he was called on. "I think this town needs a new museum," he said in a squeaky voice. "I propose we build it in the old fire station."

"But that's Mona's antique shop," a woman on the second row said loudly.

"When was the last time it was open?" the man asked.

"She's sick. She can't very well have her shop open if she's sick in bed, now can she?"

"No." The man stood and turned to face the council. He blinked a couple of times and hiked his pants up to the middle of his chest before he spoke. "Hauptstrasse is prime real estate. An antiques store is just fine, if it's open, but if it's closed 99% of the time, it's an eyesore to our community."

"So, are you proposing that we pack up Mona's stuff and close the shop so you can have a place for your silly museum?" the woman asked testily.

"I've been looking for space on Hauptstrasse for ten years. I don't think that antique store has been open more than five days in that length of time."

A hushed murmur filled the room. The Mayor raised his hand to silence the assembly.

"Lamar, you're forgetting the lease. I agree, Hauptstrasse is prime real estate, but Mona has a lease, a signed document with the town of Niederbipp to care for that space. That lease won't expire for another..."

"Another week. I have a copy of the lease right here," Lamar said, pulling the paper from his back pocket. "The lease is set to expire one week from tomorrow. I would like to sign a fifty-year lease and open a museum to showcase my extensive collection. It will be the first museum in the world dedicated to nothing but pudding molds."

He continued to speak, but his words were drowned out by the voice of the people. Jake looked at Amy and found her smiling.

"Is that the guy you were telling me about?" she asked.

Jake nodded as the noise in the room escalated.

Beverly responded by pulling a kazoo from her pocket and humming into it as loudly as she could. Jake looked at Amy again and they burst into laughter. But within a minute, the kazoo had silenced the people and they slowly quieted down.

"Listen," Beverly said. "We have a lot to accomplish in this meeting. We don't have time for this. Lamar, you know the rules of this assembly. In order to make a change to Hauptstrasse, you need at least one advocate. Have you brought an advocate with you?"

Lamar looked away, appearing dejected. At that moment, Jake, despite his better judgment, spoke up. "I'd like to hear more about this museum idea."

All eyes in the room turned to stare at him.

"I know I'm new here," he continued, "but I've been a little curious about this since I first heard about it. It sounds kind of interesting."

"You can't be serious," said Roberta Mancini, sliding her glasses higher onto her nose, her eyes full of rage.

"Have any of you ever seen such a museum?" Jake asked, standing his ground.

A wave of silence quieted the room.

"Listen, I don't mean to ruffle your feathers. This idea seems pretty crazy to me too, but good things begin with crazy ideas all the time. You and I have never seen a museum dedicated to pudding molds, but that alone shouldn't stop us from supporting this. There are all sorts of unusual collections that draw thousands of people every year. I've heard that the world's biggest ball of string in Missouri draws 20,000 people a year. Those people have to stay somewhere and eat something. They might buy t-shirts and post cards and go home and tell their friends. Minnesota has the world's biggest pile of burlap bags. Tennessee has the world's biggest mound of bowling pins. Compared with some of those things, the world's biggest collection of pudding molds seems pretty tame."

"But what about the curse? That collection has already caused one fire," said an older man on the third row.

"Oh my, can you imagine? We'd lose the whole town of Niederbipp!" said a small woman whose purple hat and cat eye glasses almost hid her entire face.

"Didn't you say you wanted to build this museum in the old firehouse?" asked Jake.

"That's right."

"It seems like a firehouse, even an old one, would have plenty of quick access to water, *if* there ever was a fire. Am I the only one who thinks it's probably impossible for a pudding mold to spontaneously combust?"

Jake's words were met with laughter and a low murmur of comments.

"Gadzooks, boy, whose side are you on anyway?" asked Roberta Mancini.

"Do you have a better idea?" asked Jake. "From all that I've heard about your mother and the farm for neglected and unwanted snails she sponsored, I have to believe she would have given this a chance. If that snail farm helped put Niederbipp on the map, maybe the world's first and biggest pudding mold museum would help keep it on the map."

"I was thinking more like a zoo or maybe an amusement park," said a different woman, looking up from a pad of paper.

Jake nodded and slowly walked down the aisle. When he reached the front table, he turned around to look at the assembly. "Hey, I don't understand all the politics or know all the history, but I do know a little about marketing. The things I learned in my marketing classes are still only theory, but I think having something as unusual as a pudding mold museum might be helpful to our town. I don't know much about pudding molds, but I imagine some people would feel nostalgic if they saw a mold like their mother used when they were kids. I could imagine a café inside serving pudding and a gift shop selling t-shirts and miniature souvenir key chains. If the town of Niederbipp had a few million dollars to spend, a zoo might be the right thing, but I'm guessing we don't have that kind of money. We do, however, have an idea, albeit a little wacky. We probably have the world's foremost pudding mold aficionado who wants to share his collection with the world. And we have prime space on Hauptstrasse that has been used as a storage unit for antiques for the past ten years. I'm not sure what we have to lose."

"So tell us, Mr. Smartee Pants. Why would anyone come here to see something like that?" asked a balding man wearing a red bow tie.

"Yeah, this is a stupid idea," added a woman who Jake recognized from the pottery shop.

He nodded thoughtfully. "A lot of crazy ideas get tossed because people think they're stupid, but this man has a passion. It may be passion for something none of us understands, but passion, given a chance, usually turns into something great."

"So let me get this straight," said the man with the bow tie. "You think Lamar's crazy passion for pudding molds is going to bring people to Niederbipp?"

"I don't know, but it might just be quirky enough to work. People go out of their way to see strange things. That giant ball of string out in the middle of Missouri somewhere is totally off the beaten path, yet people still flock to it. We may even know someone who has been there."

"I saw the world's tallest tower made from elk antlers when I was a boy. It was out in Wyoming somewhere," said an older man, beaming with pride. Several people turned to look at him.

"And did you have to go out of your way to get there?" asked Jake

"Isn't Wyoming out of everybody's way?"

The crowd responded with laughter.

"What if I wanted to make a museum for all my dental floss?" asked a woman, obviously not convinced.

"Do you have a dental floss collection?"

"Well, no, but I could if I wanted to."

"Yes, and that's my point. You don't have a collection because you don't have a passion for dental floss. No one would come to your museum because you lack that passion."

"But how will the museum be funded?" someone asked.

Jake turned to Lamar for answers.

"It will pay for itself," he responded shrilly. "People will come and pay a few bucks to see my collection. I never considered a café or a gift shop, but that could bring in money too."

"What about also selling post cards and t-shirts for Niederbipp?" asked Jake. "T-shirts would be great advertising for our town."

"We could sell those on the website too," added Kai. "I'd be willing to update the website if you think it could help bring people here."

"I think it would," said Jake. "The site, old as it is, got me excited enough to go out of my way to come here."

The Mayor stood and walked next to Jake, putting his arm on his shoulder. "Do you really think this could work?" he asked.

Jake shrugged. "I don't know, but I guess I'm willing to be Lamar's advocate and give it a try. Like I said, we don't have anything to lose."

"But what are people going to do once they get here?" asked a middle aged man. He was dressed smartly in a blue polo shirt with embroidery over the chest. "This isn't exactly a fun place. Once they find out you don't have high speed internet or cable TV and only substandard cell phone service, do you really think they'll stay for long?"

"If you're coming to Niederbipp to watch TV, maybe you're coming for the wrong reasons," offered Amy.

The man turned to Amy, surprised. "Don't you miss HBO, Discovery Channel and Food Network?"

Amy shrugged. "I never watched TV before I came here, why do I need it now?"

"And how do you keep in touch without decent cell service?"

"That's one thing I'll never miss. Being disconnected from electronics may not appeal to some people, but not having those things makes you connect with people in a different way, a way you can't through phone or high speed email."

The man shook his head and stood to leave.

"I hate to say I told you so," said the Mayor.

"I'll be back," said the man. "Your town won't always want to be in the dark ages. You might as well be Amish."

"Thank you," said the Mayor. "We consider that a compliment."

(33)

VIVA NIEDERBIPP!

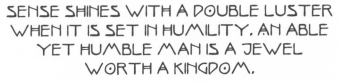

SENSE SHINES WITH A DOUBLE LUSTER
WHEN IT IS SET IN HUMILITY. AN ABLE
YET HUMBLE MAN IS A JEWEL
WORTH A KINGDOM.
—WILLIAM PENN

 he committee chewed on Lamar's museum idea for another few minutes and finally decided to grant him the chance to try his museum idea in the old firehouse in exchange for his dropping his case against those involved in losing his prized German pudding mold.

A brainstorming session followed for ideas that might give the tourists something to do while in town. Most of the proposed activities were fairly sedentary—nature walks and hikes, canoe rides, fishing, camping, cross country skiing in the winter. Then someone mentioned the legend of an exotic strain of genetically mutated, one legged, river carp. According to the legend, which had originated in the logging days, these carp would dam up the river with the timbers and capsize canoes, leaving boaters covered in purple hickeys. The old timers in the room said they still heard the mating calls of these strange beasts while they took their summer walks along the banks of the river. The idea conjured up all sorts of ideas in Jake's head, many relating to the legend of Nessie, Scotland's Loch Ness monster. He wondered how, in a town without alcohol, such a legend could be perpetuated until the modern day. Amy seemed to be thinking on the same wave length as she began writing what looked like ideas for a story in Jake's sketchbook. He wondered if regular sightings of these exotic animals might bring more tourists. He imagined t-shirts boasting, "I saw the Niederbipp River Monster" or something more poetic.

– I SAW THE LEGENDARY ONE-LEGGED, RIVER CARP –
VIVA NIEDERBIPP !
– ONLY IN NIEDERBIPP, PA –

The council also discussed ideas about catchy slogans that might help people remember Niederbipp. Jake had always considered the slogan of his home state "Vermont, naturally" a rather silly slogan. But when someone brought up Philadelphia's slogan: "The city of brotherly love," he had to wonder if a slogan might help. He and Amy were taking turns scribbling down ideas that came to them when Beverly, as the last order of business, reminded the group that the position of vice president of The Niederbipp Travel Council remained unfilled and asked if anyone wished to accept the position or nominate someone else. During the long pause that followed, Amy winked at Jake and nodded towards her aunt.

"You should do that," she whispered.

"Me?"

"Yeah. You've got some good ideas. This council needs at least one

representative from the younger generation. I'll help you. It could be fun."

"Is there a volunteer from the back," Aunt Bev asked, looking eager.

All eyes turned toward Jake and Amy.

Jake stood slowly, pulling Amy to her feet also.

"Uh, Amy was just suggesting we fill this position together, that is if there can be two vice presidents."

Beverly looked pleased, but the Mayor stood and cleared his throat before she could respond. All eyes in the room turned to him.

"I'm glad you kids want to be involved, but this position requires a minimum two-year commitment. It was Isaac's desire, God rest his soul, that the vice president serve for two years and then move up to be the president for another two years."

Jake nodded, looking thoughtful. "In that case, I would like to nominate myself, Jake Kimball, and my friend Amy Eckstein to serve on this committee for the next four years."

There was an audible gasp as every person in the room turned again to stare at Jake and Amy.

The Mayor cleared his throat. "Maybe I didn't make myself clear. You have to be here for…"

He was interrupted by Thomas who stood next to him grinning from ear to ear, his arm around his shoulder. "I think what these kids are trying to say, Mayor, is that they're ready to make that commitment."

The Mayor blinked a couple of times, visibly processing Thomas' words. "Wait…you mean…Jake are you telling me you plan to stay in Niederbipp?"

"That's right."

"For how long?"

"As long as I can."

"He told me he was planning on staying here indefinitely," Amy said, a smile spreading across her face. "And I plan on sticking around as long as my Aunt and Uncle let me stay," she added.

Albert whooped loudly.

"I would like to second the nomination," Gloria said loudly over the din of the crowd. She turned to look at Jake and Amy, beaming.

Gloria's proposal turned the din to heavy chatter which was quickly subdued by the refrain of Beverly's kazoo. "Does anyone have an objection to having two vice presidents?" she asked.

The assembly was quiet except for Roberta Mancini whose hand shot up and began waving feverishly.

Beverly looked right at her. "Is there anyone else who objects?"

The assembly remained quiet.

"Then I propose we elect Amy Eckstein and Jake Kimball, co-vice presidents of the Niederbipp Travel Council. All in favor?"

Hands shot up all over the room.

"Any opposed?"

One hand, that of Roberta Mancini rose above her red beehive-do.

"Mayor, the voting appears to be unanimous," Beverly said without giving Roberta a second glance.

"Very well," said the Mayor. Clumsily, he rose to his feet and started towards them, but the aisle was clogged with others who rushed Jake and Amy. Council members pumped their hands, offered them congratulations and patted their backs.

"When did you make this decision?" the Mayor asked when he finally reached Jake.

"Last week, in the hospital. I realized this town needs a potter and it might as well be me. Besides that, I have a debt to pay this town for making sure I was taken care of after my accident. I'm sorry I didn't tell you sooner."

"This is great news," he gushed. "Thomas bet me dinner at Robintino's that you'd stay. I'm sorry I bet against you but that is one bet I'm happy to lose."

The Mayor smiled, wrapping his arms around Jake in the tightest bear hug Jake had ever received. "Thank you. You won't regret this."

"No. I don't think I will," said Jake, taking Amy's hand.

"We've got some ideas for a new slogan," Amy said, reaching for Jake's sketchbook with her free hand. "Our favorite so far was inspired by Elvis. How do you like 'Viva Niederbipp!'?"

They watched as the Mayor repeated the slogan several times before breaking into a wide smile. "I like it!" he said laughing.

"Viva Niederbipp!" Gloria shouted, raising her fist in the air. "I think we could get a lot of mileage out of a slogan like that…t-shirts, bumper stickers, hats, aprons, postcards. I think it's brilliant."

"You kids better be careful. I might just have to resign from the council so I don't get in your way," Beverly said, patting them both on the back. "I've been carrying

around a spare kazoo for the last couple of years, waiting for someone to assist me. We'll make sure to get you another one, but you can share this for now?" She handed Jake a lanyard with a red kazoo dangling from a hook. He let go of Amy's hand to accept it, then slid it over her head.

"The kazoo was Isaac's way of maintaining order in the meetings while keeping things light hearted," Thomas interjected.

"I offered him a gavel, but he always declined," said the Mayor.

Sam started laughing and moved forward to shake the co-vice presidents' hands. "I think he must have been getting us ready for two creative kids to take over. I think he'd be pleased to know his legacy is being perpetuated by you two. I was just thinking I'd like your slogan to be part of the floor you're working on for me, if you don't mind."

"I think we could work that in," Amy said, winking at Jake.

The rest of the committee dispersed as the clock tolled one. Back in the Pottery, Jake and Amy spent the afternoon rolling out clay with a giant rolling pin they found in the cellar. They added "Viva Niederbipp" to the design, directly under Isaac's portion. They painstakingly cut out pieces of clay and laid them out on the drywall matching the pattern they made earlier.

It was Amy's first experience working with clay. Her fingernails had never been very long; nevertheless, they were too long to work with the clay without gouging it and she ended up cutting them.

As they worked, Jake told Amy about some of the things he'd learned from Isaac's sketchbook. They continued to wonder out loud about Isaac's son and where the other 35 volumes might be hiding. During a quiet moment, Jake reflected on how much better life was when he and Amy were understanding each other. Even so, he didn't mind so much that they'd had a misunderstanding. Working through it seemed to have brought them closer. When Jake's arm ached and he didn't feel like he could continue to roll out the clay, Amy took over the rolling pin and quickly proved to be at least as efficient as he was.

Evening came and then twilight as they continued to work, stopping only to eat Sam's bread. When they finally finished, it was nearly eleven. They stacked the sheets of drywall on top of each other, sandwiching the tiles in between, hoping this technique would provide flat, evenly dried tiles.

As Jake walked Amy home, they made plans for the next day. They had forgotten about painting the showroom, so Amy agreed to visit the hardware store in the morning and return with paint swatches so they could make a decision together. On the doorstep, Jake held Amy for longer than usual before the co-vice presidents of the Niederbipp Travel Council parted ways with a kiss.

(34)

THE PROFESSOR'S TALE

WE SHALL NOT CEASE FROM
EXPLORATION, AND THE END OF ALL
OUR EXPLORING WILL BE
TO ARRIVE WHERE WE STARTED AND
KNOW THE PLACE FOR THE FIRST TIME.

—T. S. ELIOT

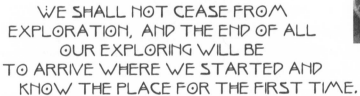

homas tells me these are your favorites." A woman, vaguely familiar, climbed the stairs to the showroom. "He also said you would have company, so I brought three marzipan slices. Where's Amy?"

Jake tried to hide the fact that he'd been startled by the woman, and had spilled wax resist on the old table. He looked up, forcing a smile, but was inwardly disappointed it wasn't Amy. At least the woman had brought marzipan slice.

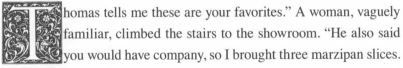

"Good Morning," he said, turning his attention away from the mess. "I'm sorry to come unannounced. Am I disturbing you?"

"Uh, no. I was just doing some glazing."

"Do you remember me? Susan Rosenthal. I met you a week ago at church?"

"Sure." Jake was grateful she'd given him her name again. He remembered very well listening to her speak in church, but her name had slipped his mind.

"I probably should have called, but I was so happy to be able to get out of the house, I just came right over. I don't suppose it's too late for tea, is it? I've been dying to try your new recipe after hearing you and Amy talk about it last week. How'd it turn out?"

"I'll let you decide," Jake said, rising from the stool to get the tea going. When he turned around he found Susan sitting on his stool, spinning the bowl he had resting on the banding wheel.

"Is this a new tool?" she asked. "I don't remember Isaac ever using one of these."

"My professor gave it to me as a graduation gift. I use it when I glaze. It helps me get the lines straight."

"Is that how you decorated those bowls in the window?"

Jake nodded. "I've been teaching myself a new technique, layering the glazes and using wax resist to create the designs."

Susan spun the wheel again, watching the half finished design whirl into a blur. She stared at the bowl even after the momentum slowed and the bowl came to rest. "It's strange being here without Isaac. I keep thinking he's going to come from around the corner and give me a big hug…pour me a cup of tea and ask me how my life is going. I bet you've had a lot of people stop by to blubber."

Jake nodded. "I've met a lot of his friends. Albert sent a bunch of them, but lots of other people have been stopping by to visit. Almost every day I meet someone new who loved him."

"How do you feel about that? It must get kind of old."

"It did at first, but I've learned to enjoy it. I didn't realize when I accepted this job how many strings are attached to it, but it's given me a lot to think about. To be honest, I don't think it was until my accident that I really began to open my eyes and see what a great place this is."

"That's right. I stopped by last week to see you but found the shop closed. Hildegard told me you were in the hospital. It sounded pretty serious, but you look like you bounced back pretty well."

"I feel like I did." He turned his arm to her, exposing his stitches. "I'm lucky to have good friends and a town that wants to keep me here."

The back door opened and Amy walked in. She wore cut-off blue jeans and an old t-shirt with a rainbow of paint splatters. "Oh, hi," she said, looking surprised. "Am I interrupting something?"

"No, Amy. I was hoping you'd be here too so I won't have to eat two of Sam's Marzipan Slices," Susan said.

"Mmmm." She took off her backpack. "That would probably be even better with tea."

Jake smiled. "We're one step ahead of you." He pointed to the steeping teapot. "I was just about to ask Susan if she had her own mug."

"As a matter of fact I do," she said, turning to the beam. "But I'm sure I can't reach it. It's the yellow and blue one." She pointed to the mug and Jake stretched to retrieve it. He was surprised to find its top side covered in a thick layer of dust. He rinsed it in the sink before filling it with warm tea and handing it to Susan.

"Do you have a mug?" Susan asked Amy.

"No, I don't." She raised her eyebrows and looked at Jake.

"I haven't made one that's worthy of her yet," he responded and turned away to pull two house mugs from the shelf above the sink. When he turned back, they were both staring at him, apparently unconvinced. "I just haven't made a lot of mugs yet and I wanted hers to be special.

I'll work on it."

The women looked at each other and winked.

"So what's the occasion for Marzipan Slice? I thought that was only for therapy sessions." Amy looked from Jake to Susan.

The comment led to a review of the past few weeks—the kiln meltdown and the Marzipan Therapy administered by Father Thomas. "I was lucky, it could have been a lot worse," Jake said, ending his report.

Susan looked thoughtful for a moment before she spoke. "That's an interesting word to use, 'lucky'. I heard you use it twice in the past couple of minutes."

"I did?"

"Yeah. I know I'm probably OCD, but I've begun taking notice of that word since my last visit to this shop. I've been surprised at how often it gets used to explain unusual phenomena." She laughed a little but continued looking thoughtful. "Over the years, I'm sure I've written off all sorts of minor miracles as mere luck, but Isaac always had a way of making me open my eyes a little wider. He had more faith in God than anyone I've ever known." She picked up her mug, cradling it with her hands. "What most people call good luck, he called blessings. That was easy enough to swallow, but when I learned that he called bad luck 'blessings' too, I had to wonder if he wasn't a masochist. I spent a lot of time over the years trying to psychoanalyze him." She gave a small laugh. "I wanted to figure out what made him tick, what was the source of his goodness. Looking back on it now, I realize I spent too much time trying to dissect the goose that laid the golden eggs instead of just enjoying the golden eggs for what they were." She sipped from her mug, then set it back down. "By the time I stopped fighting the eternal truths he lived and taught, I was wrapped up in a tenured position and couldn't pull myself away to learn more from him. It was always going to be 'next summer' or 'during my sabbatical' that I would get back here and take the time to learn wisdom. After several years' worth of delays, this was going to be the summer I would spend with him. I was planning on bringing recording devices and spending every spare minute with him, tapping into his brain and learning all I could."

"What exactly did you hope to learn?" Amy asked.

Susan looked very thoughtful, as if she were considering her words carefully before answering. "That's a difficult question for me to answer, but it's the very question I've been asking myself since I learned of his death. There was something Isaac had that I've never found in another human being."

"How long did you know him?" asked Jake.

"I'm sure I knew of him since I was born. My parents collected his work. My mom must have forty pieces: mugs, bowls, plates and platters. My dad, who passed away several years ago, knew Isaac's pottery was the one gift he could give my mother that she'd always like. Most of my older siblings collected his work too. He gave each of them bowls for their weddings. I always looked forward to getting one for my wedding, but..." She smiled at Amy and Jake and shrugged good-naturedly.

"So, you grew up here in Niederbipp?" Amy asked.

"Just south of town. But I went to school here."

"You're probably about Brian's age. Did you know him?" Jake asked.

"Yeah, I wondered if you might have met him. He's a year older than I am. He's a good egg—always knew his place in the universe. It took me a little longer to discover who I was and decide what I want to be when I grew up. Isaac helped me with that a lot. I've probably spent less than a hundred cumulative hours with him over the years, but the impact that time has had on my life is enormous. If it weren't for him, I'm not sure I would have found my faith."

Jake looked at Amy, remembering their discussion of faith at Taufer's Pond just two weeks before. "Did you grow up Quaker?" he asked.

Susan burst into laughter. "Sorry," she said as she regained composure. "No, my parents were hippies! They met in the Peace Corps and I grew up with a pinch of Christianity and a dash of Eastern religions including Buddhism, Islam and Hinduism. It wasn't until my senior year that I began to consider myself a Christian."

"What brought on that change?" Jake asked.

"A series of visits with a local potter. I used to write for the school newspaper and decided I wanted to do a series of articles highlighting influential people in our community. I interviewed the Mayor and several business owners before I recognized that each of their lives shared a common element: Isaac. The deeper I dug, the more I learned that he had had an impact on several generations of people. On one of my first visits to Isaac, I asked him what motivated him to treat people the way he did. I was surprised by his answer. Faith and love, he said were the purest motivators he knew. I knew a little bit about love, but faith had always been an enigma to me. To him, faith was always real, almost to the point that it somehow seemed tangible. But Isaac never forced his faith on me. He answered my questions and always invited more. He told me that faith is a journey, that there would be many guides and gatekeepers along the way, but that if the final destination would ever be worthwhile, it had to be my journey."

Jake and Amy nodded. That sounded so…Isaac.

"That journey has taken me around the world on the roller coaster ride of my life. The funny thing is—I realized a year ago that after almost twenty years and a zillion miles, my faith journey has brought me home, to the very place I started. As Isaac promised, there were many guides along the way. Even so, I might have made it back sooner if I had learned the difference between truth and its counterfeits earlier on. Not seeing those differences sooner has cost me a lot. I will probably never be a mother. The likelihood of finding a husband is less than encouraging. I have missed out on some of the most important things in life, listening instead to a selfish muse and bogus truth. But coming home, being here in this shop, I feel like my life has more purpose and hope than I've had in years."

Jake watched as Amy helped herself to one of the marzipan slices that Susan had put out on a plate. He tried to remember the feelings he first had when people started showing up, telling him their life's stories. Even though they often came at inopportune times, he had grown to enjoy these visits and even look forward to them. This was partly because of the things he had learned about Isaac, the individuals who shared their stories and the history of this unique town. The events of the previous week, however, had given him a deeper understanding and appreciation for these people's tales. Though his was different from those he'd heard, he realized that many of their stories helped him to understand his own. They offered a different perspective, opening his eyes and mind. As he watched Amy eating her treat, he noticed something in her facial expressions that intrigued him. It seemed she was hungry to hear, to learn, to understand—as if she were an eager student, excited by the potential lessons that awaited her. Her attitude was inspiring, even contagious.

"With that kind of story, you must be an incredible teacher. What do you teach?" Amy asked.

"I teach in the College of Humanities: mostly philosophy and some religion. Did either of you study much of the Humanities?"

"Only to get the generals out of the way," responded Jake. "I mostly focused on art and business classes."

"Yes, but not the from the Philosophy department. I had Art History classes as part of my major," Amy added.

"Then I suppose I'm the odd man out in this crowd," Susan said. "I don't have an artistic bone in my body. I've always been the analytical type, trying to make sense of the way things are. My parents gave me a love for books and learning which led to a life-long interest in science. I got to know Roberta Mancini pretty well during the thousands of trips I made to the library in my younger years. She always told me that if I read more romance and less science, I might learn how to attract men. She might have been right, but it didn't seem to work all that well for her."

Jake and Amy laughed.

"So, why philosophy? Amy asked.

"I was looking for answers to all of life's questions. My talks with Isaac gave me a lot of those answers, but a lot of questions too. Until I left for college, I had Isaac to help me work through those questions, but a college campus isn't a very fertile ground for the seeds of faith. When I began studying philosophy, I felt like it answered a lot of questions I'd had since my childhood. It gave my life purpose. I read all I could find about Socrates, Aristotle and Plato before moving on to James, Nietzsche, Sartre and Marx. In the beginning, the things I learned gave me understanding. I believed I was gaining wisdom and the ability to reason. Like I said last Sunday, I believed I was filling my lamp and vessel with truth.

"Shortly before I finished my undergraduate work, I came home to visit my parents. I stopped by to visit Isaac and thank him for the direction he had given me in my life. I told him about my studies and shared with him some of the things I was learning. I was surprised to find he knew a lot about philosophy, but was much less enthusiastic about it than I hoped. Instead, he turned the discussion toward faith and God and what he called eternal truths. My analytic mind questioned him. Proof and scientific process had consumed my thoughts for four years, crowding out my faith.

"I remember leaving the Pottery that day, feeling sorry for him and his foolish life. He knew so much about philosophy, yet he dismissed the reasoning behind it. There have been hundreds of times over the past fifteen years that I wished I would have spent more time listening to him that day instead of excusing myself and ending the conversation. I believe that decision cost me many aimless years.

"I finished school and spent several months roaming Europe, following the paths of the great philosophers. I was still young and knew I wanted to make a difference in the world so I followed my parents'

—THE ALLEGHENY ARGYLE TROUT— (VERY RARE)

example and joined the Peace Corps. I spent two years in Western Africa teaching school in refugee camps. Witnessing first hand the hardship and carnage of war gave me reason to embrace Nietzsche's philosophy of Nihilism: the idea that life is without meaning, purpose or inherent value.

"I returned home a cynic and started my doctorate work so I could eventually share what I had learned with others. Nihilists believe that morality is weak, if it exists at all, so I found it easy to participate in activities I would have previously considered immoral. It was a fun way to live. I felt free from obligations to anyone else, free to do whatever I wanted to do, free of consequences—or so I thought. In that world, there was no right or wrong, no black or white—it was all gray and the world was free. I made a lot of friends in the department who shared my philosophy of life.

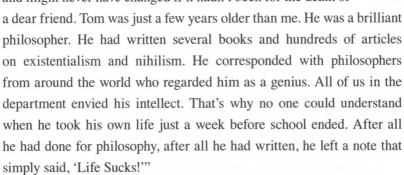

"When I finished my PhD, I started teaching and then got caught up in working towards tenure. My visits home became increasingly less frequent as I found fewer and fewer people who understood me here. Isaac continued to reach out to me. He sent me postcards from time to time, but I considered him a misguided simpleton and rarely returned the tokens of his friendship. Life continued along that course for almost a decade and might never have changed if it hadn't been for the death of a dear friend. Tom was just a few years older than me. He was a brilliant philosopher. He had written several books and hundreds of articles on existentialism and nihilism. He corresponded with philosophers from around the world who regarded him as a genius. All of us in the department envied his intellect. That's why no one could understand when he took his own life just a week before school ended. After all he had done for philosophy, after all he had written, he left a note that simply said, 'Life Sucks!'"

Jake heard Amy gasp and looked over to see the concern on her face.

"I was devastated. For two years, Tom and I had been much more than friends. My devastation only increased when I learned over the following weeks that several other women, even some of his students, had also been more than his friends. The lack of moral laws our brand of philosophy embraced dictated that I couldn't be angry, and yet I was. For the first time since I'd started my studies, I began to see the cracks in my foundation. In cutting God and faith out of my life, I'd gone looking for something else that was transcendent. But, for the first time, I realized my life and career had perhaps been misguided at best.

"I had never felt so lost. I even considered taking my life…it seemed so meaningless and worthless. I actually went so far as to buy a bottle of aspirin and write a note to my folks."

"Oh no!" cried Amy. She reached out to squeeze Susan's small wrist.

"My plan was to mail the letter and then put an end to my misery. I walked to the post office and was about to drop my letter in the slot when I remembered it had been a week since I'd checked my box. Among the bills and advertisements, I found a postcard from Isaac. Out of respect for our past friendship, I read it. He told me he'd been thinking about me and that he looked forward to the time when we could chat again. I'd ignored most of his previous postcards, or read them bemusedly as relics from my distant past, but the timing of this one caused me to stop. I sat down on the curb in front of the post office. Hours later, I knew what I needed to do. First, I crumpled the note I had written to my parents and tossed it in the trash. Next, I walked home, packed a bag, and drove to Niederbipp."

Susan paused and laughed as Jake and Amy cheered. "When all else fails, return to Niederbipp!" quipped Amy.

"Exactly! I spent that whole summer here, trying to put my life back together. This shop became a haven for me as I sorted through the bits and pieces of my old life, trying to determine what to keep and what to toss. Isaac showered me with love as my search for meaning recommenced. Over time, that long dormant seed of faith awoke and began to grow again. I was fragile, but Isaac encouraged me. He taught me about God's love and assured me of its unconditional nature. He taught me that truth—real truth—never changes. It is, was, and ever will be. He compared this to the philosophies of men that are as changing and shifting as sand in the wind.

"His words and his love gave me the strength to begin a new foundation, built on the rock of faith. Where I had previously turned to the philosophies of men for answers, he taught me to seek the wisdom of God, both from the scriptures and from the Bible. One passage in particular spoke to my soul: 2 Timothy chapter 3. As I studied Paul's words, I realized he was speaking to me. To that point, I had been 'ever learning but never able to come to a knowledge of the truth.' In an effort to live a free life and gain all the education I could, I had traded the truth I once knew for an ever-changing imitation. Isaac helped me open my heart to truth...and it was that truth that set me free, just like it says in the book of John chapter 8 verse 32.

"When I returned to school in the fall, my life had a new direction and meaning. Tom's death had caused our whole department to fall apart and I soon found myself in the driver's seat, serving as the Chair of the Philosophy Department. I knew that the faith Isaac resuscitated in me and the ideas of nihilism could not coexist. I enlisted the help of several of my classes, looking for philosophies that could work with faith. We also spent time examining the lives of philosophers whose ways of thinking had become popular over the years. This exercise proved to be very insightful. So many who had renounced God went on to live lonely and tragic lives. Many committed suicide. Several others spent time in mental institutions. We found a strong correlation between the Godless and the tragic. The fact that nature abhors a vacuum seems relevant in the realms of human spirituality as well. If we remove God from our lives, we seek a substitute, trying to fill that void with something meaningful or transcendent. The problem, though, is that only truth transcends time and fashion. Everything else—the world's imitations and man's philosophies—fades into history. Time has given me a chance to see the fruits of these philosophies. So many who buy into them are left comfortless, lonely and in the end, pitiful."

"Then why do people continue to study Philosophy?" Amy asked.

"Because humans are thirsty for understanding. Like so many other counterfeits, portions of truth are mingled with their theories. Some truth is better than none at all. Many people become satisfied with the truth they find. Others believe they can create their own truth. But as I've come to understand, truth can neither be created nor destroyed by man. Truth is eternal, but the knowledge of man is fluid and ever-changing. Isaac taught me that a big part of wisdom is knowing the difference. I have been in the presence of amazing minds over the course of my life, but none have had as much wisdom and understanding as the humble potter who taught me the most important lessons I have ever learned."

Susan looked away, tears filling her eyes. She took a long drink from her mug before looking up at Jake and Amy. "Isaac and I spent many hours on the phone over the years before he died. He continued to nourish my soul from a distance: giving me hope, encouraging me in my work, answering questions, and inspiring my learning. Sometimes I wonder what might have happened if Isaac had not loved me. He loved me when I didn't even love myself. Because of his influence, the Department of Philosophy has made room for God and spirituality."

"So just like that, you were able to make a change?" asked Jake, looking surprised.

"Well, to be fair, the whole department didn't suddenly accept faith, but many became more tolerant of those who do accept it. And I hope it will continue to become a fertile ground where seeds of faith and truth can flourish. Since the time I was a child, I wanted to change the world. With the gifts of truth Isaac shared with me, that desire has been magnified."

"So, you plan to continue teaching?" Jake asked.

Susan nodded, swallowing a mouthful of marzipan slice. "From personal experience, I know I have something to share that the world needs. Only the light of truth can shatter the darkness of this world. I feel a responsibility to carry on Isaac's legacy, wherever that light directs me."

"But don't you get a lot of opposition from the university? Don't they ridicule faith as small-minded, as the 'opiate of the masses?'" Amy asked.

Susan rolled her eyes. "Yes, I hear that lovely phrase from Karl Marx quite often. It doesn't hurt to be the department chair, though. I have to be careful, but they can't argue with the enrollment for my program. I've had to expand the size of my classes every semester and there's still a waiting list. Like I said before, people are thirsty for truth. They know it when they see it. It burns in their hearts. Ours is a world of confusion. The fact that maybe there is a right and a wrong is comforting to many in a world of existential obscurity. People, whether they admit it or not, are looking for anchors, something honest and real they can hold on to while the whirlwind of life breeds chaos. I encourage my students to open their minds to the possibility of a higher power and develop their own hypothesis based not only on their observations, but also on what they feel in their hearts. It makes for some fun dialog."

"I think I might have spent more time outside the studio if that kind of class would have been available to me," Amy said.

Jake nodded in agreement. "I know you're right. People are hungry for truth. It's too bad it's not more readily available."

"Oh, it's not hiding very deep. You just have to know how to look for it, and you have to be ready to accept it when it arrives," Susan responded.

"How do you mean?" asked Jake.

"One of the truths Isaac taught me is that truth is everywhere?"

"Then why is it so hard to see?" asked Jake.

"Because we're not ready. There's an old Zen proverb that says 'When the student is ready...'"

"...the teacher will appear," Jake said, finishing her sentence. "I remembered that last week when I was in the hospital." He looked pensive. "That idea came to me when I finally started making sense of why I was here in Niederbipp."

"And if you think back to just before that, I'm willing to bet you went through a pretty humbling experience."

Jake laughed. "To say the least."

"Isn't it interesting that we have to be brought low before we are allowed to soar?" Susan asked.

"I'm just remembering, I went through a humbling process before I had my first spiritual experience. Do you think some humbling event is necessary for us to be ready to listen?" Amy asked.

"Sometimes I wish it wasn't, but I think it is for most. It seems we're either naturally humble or compelled to humility before any window becomes open to us." She laughed, looking thoughtful. "The problem with that statement is that mankind is not naturally humble. One of my classes focused on this idea a few years ago. I believe the requirement of humility before the conveyance of understanding is one of those universal truths. The Bible is full of these examples, but so are the sacred writings of every other religion. Jesus taught that we must become as children before we can learn."

Jake looked up at the mugs hanging overhead. "I think I'm finally beginning to understand what these are all about. Every one of these people, at least those that I've met so far...."

"Came here in search of truth," Susan said, finishing his sentence.

"Yes! I never thought about it that way until now, but you're right. It's like they were somehow washed up on this island in the thick of their problems and found all the balm they needed to soothe their wounds."

"Arise and go down to the potter's house, and there I will cause thee to hear my words," Susan said.

"Where does that come from?" asked Amy.

"From the Old Testament, Jeremiah 16... or maybe 18. I found it a couple of years ago. It blew me away how it seemed to be talking about Isaac."

Jake reached for his sketchbook and flipped to the page where he'd written down the words on the tiles from Alvin's bench. 'Behold, as the clay is in the potter's hands, so are ye in mine hand.' I think that might be from the same chapter!" He looked excited.

"That sounds about right. I never paid too much attention to the rest of the chapter. Do you know what it means?"

Jake looked back at his book, reading the passage again. "It seems to suggest that God is shaping our lives, or at least he could if we're willing."

"And if we're not willing?"

"Then I guess he has to wait until we are." Jake looked thoughtful.

"What are you thinking?" asked Amy.

"I buy my clay from a manufacturer. I've never had to dig clay out of the ground like the potters had to two thousand plus years ago when this was written. When I was in New Mexico a few years ago, I watched a Hopi potter prepare his clay and I think he must have done it the same way it's been done for thousands of years. He told me he digs it out of a river bank and then spends the next two weeks cleaning it and refining it before he can begin to mold it. I was amazed at the patience he had for that process. I could never be a potter if I had to mix my own clay. Recycling good clay scraps was hard enough. I can't imagine starting from scratch. And I guess my point is that…God must be pretty patient with us, knowing what we can become, waiting for us to ask for help."

"I think that's one of the eternal truths, Jake," Susan said, wide eyed.

"Mixing clay?" Jake asked, looking confused.

Susan laughed. "Maybe, but I was thinking about what you just said about God waiting for us to ask for help. If humility is not part of our nature, then neither is prayer. Babies, on the other hand are

I'll lift thee, and thee lift me, and we'll ascend together.
— Quaker Proverb

dependent on a parent for all they have. When they need to be changed, they cry. When they are hungry, they cry even louder. Maybe that process of asking evokes humility. It connotes dependence. I've spent the last few years studying the sacred texts of all the major religions and I've been surprised by the repeated admonition to ask if we desire to receive. One of my favorites is from James, 'If any of ye lack wisdom, let him ask of God, that giveth to all men liberally.' Like any parent, it seems God is anxious to give to his children, but He's waiting for us to say the magic word."

They looked at each other, waiting for someone to reply, but the silence remained for a long moment as they digested Susan's words.

"So how do you maintain humility so you can continue to receive?" Amy asked.

"That's the million dollar question, Amy. The fact that the Bible is replete with the admonition to ask suggests to me that God expects that our nature will pull us away from Him. We begin to believe we can do it on our own. The problem is, it's like trying to direct air traffic from the ground without the advantage of a bird's eye view or radar. You may be ok for a while, but it eventually leads to some form of turmoil. If God bids us to invite him in by asking for his help, we have to believe He'll respond."

"Do you believe God answers all prayers?" Amy asked.

Susan took a deep breath. "I want to believe he does answer all sincere prayers, but I know it's not always in the way we desire."

"Isn't that a bit of a cop out?" asked Jake, playing the devil's advocate.

"I'm still working on this one. It seems we often don't appeal to Him until we're in crisis mode. Part of that is because of our lack of humility. We feel like we can take the reins for a while when the trail is smooth. The problem is, when the trail is smooth for too long, we fall asleep and forget the horse and buggy belong to someone else. We usually don't ask for instructions or directions until the horse is hanging over a hundred foot cliff and the buggy is dangling on the edge. I think the response we get at those times is often very different than if we'd remained alert during the whole journey and asked for directions every mile or so. Humility again seems to be the key to our answers and the timing in which they're received.

"And then there are the prayers that seem to never get answered. We don't recognize it in the moment, but sometimes those are the best answers of all. It just requires hindsight and earned understanding to recognize that, had our prayers been answered the way we wished, disaster would have been the result. By the time I knew him, Isaac had the patience of Job and sage wisdom, but I know for a fact he didn't start out that way. He learned who he was along the way, as we all have the opportunity to do. It took me a lot longer than it has apparently taken you both, but I am grateful for the journey and the calling I feel I've been given to serve as a guide for others."

She finished her last bite of marzipan slice. "I better get back to my mom," she said getting to her feet. "I hope I haven't overstayed my welcome."

"Not at all," said Jake. "I really enjoyed your story. If you don't mind stopping back in from time to time, Amy and I will probably have more questions. We've been trying to learn all we can about Isaac."

"Then next time, I'll bring questions for you. From the stories you've heard from others, you might be able to answer some of my questions."

"We'll do our best," responded Amy. "And I hope you'll teach in church again. I really enjoyed what you had to say."

"Well, that makes one of us," she said, reaching out to embrace Amy. She then turned to Jake and embraced him also. "You're probably tired of hearing it, but I'm really glad you're here, both of you. You breathe life into this town. I expect great things from you. Oh, and thank you for the Marzipan Therapy. That's always been my favorite treat too."

"I have just one more question, if you don't mind," Jake said, feeling nervous.

"Sure, what is it?"

"To your knowledge, did Isaac ever have any children?"

"Probably at least fifty, including me. So many of us who grew up here considered him a father figure. I think he always had a soft spot for kids, but no, he never had any children of his own, at least as far as I know. Why do you ask?"

Jake looked at Amy, searching for words.

"Since he decided to stay here, Jake just wants to make sure no one is going to show up and vie for ownership of the Pottery."

"I don't think you'll have any trouble with that. I've been home less than two weeks and I've heard nothing but praise for the new potter. Just take time to heal. I understand Sam's been pushing you to finish that floor of his. I'd hate to see you be set back by not giving yourself time to heal."

"Thanks for your concern, but I'll be ok. I've got some good help. Amy and I finally got started on that yesterday. By the time it's ready to install, I'll be fully mended, I'm sure."

"Then I'll be excited to see it. I'll drop by in a week or so to see if you've learned anything amazing. Oh, and I'll see you at church," she said with a wink.

With that, she bid them farewell once again and left them to talk about all the new things they had learned.

35

THE DISCOVERY

HAVE COURAGE FOR THE GREAT
SORROWS OF LIFE AND PATIENCE FOR
THE SMALL ONES; AND WHEN
YOU HAVE LABORIOUSLY
ACCOMPLISHED YOUR DAILY TASK, GO
TO SLEEP IN PEACE. GOD IS AWAKE."
—VICTOR HUGO

Celery Green and Dandelion Yellow. After nearly an hour of sorting through the paint swatches Amy picked up at the hardware store, they reached a decision. The colors they chose would brighten the walls far better than the drab, dirty white paint that had hung in the studio for an unknown numbers of years. The old plaster was in fairly good repair, so while Amy walked to the store to pick up the paint, Jake unloaded the old shelves, stacking the pots in piles on the front counter and throughout the studio. After the pots were removed, there was no space for the shelves and pedestals to be moved anywhere but to the middle of the room.

He was covering the floor with newspaper when the front door opened and Hildegard poked her head in to say hello. After Jake assured her he was feeling fine, she informed him that her cat had already broken the bowl she'd bought the week before. She asked if he had any more then looked about at the pots piled up everywhere and said she'd be back in a couple of days to check on him.

Amy returned with four cans of paint—two more than she had set out to purchase. She explained that in route to the store, she'd had a crazy idea come to her that she couldn't shake. The third and fourth cans were a pale blue and a powder white which she thought could be used on the ceiling to look like the sky with fluffy white clouds. She was so animated and excited about it that Jake couldn't argue, even though he wasn't entirely sure about it. She'd also picked up a couple of brushes, rollers, packs of tape and paint trays. They washed the spider webs and dust off the walls before opening the can of Celery Green and pouring the liquid color into the paint tray. In this quantity, it seemed much brighter than the small swatch, but they dove their rollers into it anyway, quickly covering the wall adjacent to the front door.

Standing back, they admired their work before moving on to the wall across from the big showroom window. The Dandelion Yellow also seemed brighter than they'd imagined, but that didn't stop them. As they finished the wall, they turned to see several of the war widows peering in at them, their noses pressed to the glass. Jake waved his paint-covered hand at the women who returned the gesture before moving on.

By closing time, the shop looked entirely different. The light reflected off the new paint, filling the room with an aura that was playful and exciting. They stopped their work to visit the kabob shop on Hauptstrasse, but their desire to complete the job before sundown brought them back before their food had settled.

While Amy worked on the ceiling, Jake turned his attention to the brushwork in the corners where the rollers couldn't reach. Their conversation roamed from art, to food, to personal interests, to marketing ideas for the new space they were refurbishing to share. Having never had a sibling, the notion of sharing was new to Jake, but he was comfortable with the idea of sharing with Amy. In the short time they'd been hanging out, they'd learned a lot about each other. Their friendship had grown and been graced by the addition of love that grew every hour they spent together. Even though the decision they'd each made to stay in Niederbipp made their friendship feel more permanent, there were still many questions that were awkward. These, they avoided. There was a part of Jake that looked forward to the chance to talk about these things, but another part, a larger part, was happy to let those things remain unspoken for the time being.

Jake was surprised when he turned around and saw what Amy had done to the ceiling. The blue paint gave the ceiling depth, as if it continued upward a dozen feet higher than it actually did. Standing on top of a glaze bucket, she was using the very tip of her brush to dab on the last of the white, billowing clouds that looked like they floated in on the wind of a summer afternoon.

"What do you think?" she asked as she dabbed on the last bit of paint.

"I love it! It reminds me of lying on a blanket with my mom on the beach at Lake Champlain, watching the clouds."

"I think I would have liked your mom."

"I know you would have. She would have liked you too." He reached for her hand and helped her off the bucket. "I've got an idea." He took the brush and cup of paint from her and quickly pushed the shelves out of the middle of the room.

"What are you doing?"

"I was just wondering if you would like to lie down and watch the clouds with me."

The sun had already set and the only light came from the lamps in the window. They lay down in the middle of the room on the newspaper Jake had lain to cover the wooden floor. Their heads and shoulders touched each other as they stared up into the sky Amy created.

"I really like this! It was a great idea." Jake turned his head to look at Amy.

"Thanks," replied Amy, obviously pleased with her handiwork. "I was worried the blue might be too dark, but from this angle at least, it looks pretty good."

"Those clouds are amazing. How'd you do it?"

"Well, I am an artist you know." She poked him in the ribs, but he grabbed her hand and held it until she stopped. "I love you," she said, turning her head 'til their noses touched. "Thanks for letting me follow my crazy ideas."

"Hey, if it weren't for you, this shop would have been drab and colorless for another twenty years or more. Guys don't usually fuss too much about details like this. Thanks for adding some color to my life."

She squeezed his hand and turned back to look at the ceiling. A moment later, a knock came from the big front window and they turned to see Kai and Molly peering in at them. Jake motioned for them to come in and a minute later the four friends were sprawled out on the floor together, staring up into the beautiful sky.

"Do you have any paint left?" asked Molly.

"Yeah, why?" asked Amy.

"We just painted the nursery a few weeks ago, but I think our baby needs a sky like this. Do you hire out?"

"I think we could make some arrangements."

"That would be awesome," said Kai. "Then we wouldn't even have to go outside to see the clouds."

They laughed together until Molly asked them all to stop. "I don't want to have a baby right here," she said, gasping to catch her breath.

"Molly thinks the baby is coming in the next couple of days," reported Kai. "Our Lamaze teacher says going on walks can make the baby come faster."

"Are you ready for that?" asked Amy.

"I guess I better be. I've invested nine months of my life and sacrificed my size six figure for this baby. I'm anxious to see if it will be worth the investment."

They laughed again.

"Have you decided on a name?" asked Amy.

"If it's a boy, we're thinking Isaac. If it weren't for him, we would have never met," said Molly.

"And if it's a girl, we'll call her Eve," added Kai. "That was Molly's grandmother's name. But both names are subject to change if the little squirt comes out looking like someone else. I'm kind of partial to Bubba."

"You can't do that to our son," Molly shrieked. "It may be ok in the south, but we live north of the Mason Dixon line and probably always will."

"I was actually thinking about that name for our daughter," Kai teased.

After Molly once again insisted they stop laughing, they spent the next twenty minutes watching the baby within her move about. Amy had seen this many times with her sisters-in-law, but for Jake, it was something entirely new. When Molly learned this, she took his hand and held it tight against her belly. At first he blushed awkwardly, but then he felt it: the unmistakable movement of something inside Molly's belly. It was some unseen appendage, maybe a knee or a shoulder. Feeling life move through a thin wall of skin shocked and amazed him. The impression it made on him remained long after he had removed his hand

and Kai and Molly had left. He knew it was something he would always remember.

It was already past eleven, but they decided it would be best to put the shop back together that night, rather than wait until morning. They picked up the paper and swept the floor before moving the shelves back into place. Amy asked if she could work on the display window and left the rest of the showroom to Jake. He watched her work, admiring the eye she had for design and the care she took in displaying each piece. It took her much longer than he would have spent, but he was pleased with the way it looked and even more pleased to see the joy she had in doing it.

It wasn't until they were almost finished that Jake noticed the rack he was filling was wobbly. With a piece of cardboard, he made a shim and was slipping it under the lowest leg when he noticed the floorboard beneath it was loose. Upon closer inspection, he noticed several adjacent floorboards were also loose. He went to the shelf behind the counter and pulled out the old toolbox, returning with a hammer and nails. It seemed simple enough to fix, but as the hammer hit the nail the floorboard gave way and disappeared into a dark hole.

"Dang it!"

"What is it?" Amy asked, turning her attention from the window.

"I'm not sure, but I think I just knocked a piece of the floor into the cellar."

She knelt down next to Jake, looking into the blackness below. "Do you have a flash light?" she asked.

"No, and I don't really feel like going down into the cellar tonight. I'll fix it tomorrow."

"Are you sure? I could help."

Jake looked at Amy, his eyebrows raised. "Do you want to go down into the cellar tonight?"

She laughed a nervous laugh. "No, I guess I don't. I hate spiders."

"Good, so do I." He stood and reached for Amy's hand. As he lifted her up, her foot kicked the hammer. It teetered on the edge of the hole for a second before falling in.

"I'm sorry," she said, bending down to look into the hole again. "Wait, the handle is still sticking out."

Jake bent down and saw the last two inches of the handle sticking out of the hole. He reached for it and pulled it up. The adjacent board came with it, one end lifting up and then falling into the blackness. But now the hole wasn't so black. He looked at Amy, confused.

"I don't think that goes to the cellar," she said, moving her head closer to the hole. The next three adjacent boards, each three inches by about fifteen inches were also loose. Amy lifted these away, revealing a small wooden box built below the floor. They peered into the box slowly, as if anticipating a spider might jump out at any minute. This combined movement toward the hole blocked the already small amount of light that found its way under the lowest shelf on the rack.

"Let's move this," Jake said, scrambling to his feet.

With the shelf out of the way, the light fell into the box. At first, it looked empty except for the floorboards that had fallen in, but when he reached in to retrieve them, his fingers touched something soft and smooth. It felt like cloth. He lifted the boards out so he could see clearly. Then he peered in again, squinting, hoping to see whatever it was he'd touched.

As he fumbled around inside, his fingers found a loop of twine which he clutched and lifted.

"What is it?" Amy asked, looking over his shoulder.

"It looks like a bundle of some sort. It's so dusty, I…I'm not sure." He set the bundle on the floor and brushed away the dust from the faded blue rag. He unwrapped the twine from the bundle and began unfolding the cloth that had been wrapped tightly around whatever was inside. As he pulled back the last layer, Amy gasped. It was a book: a leather bound sketchbook, identical to the one Sam had given Jake just ten days before.

275

"That looks just like Isaac's sketchbook, doesn't it?" Amy asked, her chin now resting on Jake's shoulder.

"Yeah. Maybe this is where he kept the other thirty five volumes." He leaned over to look back into the hole, expecting to see more bundles, but the hole was empty. "Why do you think this is here?" He turned to Amy, searching her face.

"I have no idea. Why don't you open it?"

"I've got a feeling this is going to take a while. Are you sure you want to do this tonight?"

"Do you honestly think I could sleep? I'd be up all night trying to imagine why a book would be buried in the floor."

Jake nodded. "You're right. I'll make some tea." He stood and walked to the studio, taking the unwrapped bundle with him.

"Let's go upstairs," she said, pulling his arm. "I want to sit down where it's comfortable."

They locked the doors and turned off the lights before climbing the stairs to see what they could discover in the old book.

BE STILL
AND
KNOW THAT
I AM
GOD.

(36)

VOLUME 31

THE LIFE OF EVERY MAN IS A DIARY IN WHICH HE MEANS TO WRITE ONE STORY, AND WRITES ANOTHER.
—J.M. BARRIE

he unwrapped bundle lay on the table next to Isaac's other sketchbook as Amy sat patiently, waiting for Jake to finish the tea. The warm and muggy night inspired him to try something he'd never done before. After steeping the tea in hot water, he poured the amber liquid into a pitcher filled with ice cubes. As he worked, he felt Amy's gaze on his back and turned to find her smiling.

"What's up?" he asked, returning the smile.

"I'm just thinking how grateful I am that I didn't leave last week."

"Why's that?"

"Because, I would have missed this. You'd probably be sitting here learning all sorts of cool things about Isaac and I'd be back in my childhood bedroom, wondering about you."

"You think I would have found this book without you?"

She answered with a blank look.

"I never would have found it if we hadn't painted the showroom, and that would have been years in the future, if at all."

Amy nodded her understanding.

"I don't know what's in this book, but I'm guessing it must be pretty special for it to be hidden away like it was. If you'd left last weekend, I'm sure I wouldn't be sitting here now. I'm really glad you stayed, Amy. I can't imagine Niederbipp without you."

She squeezed his hand and pulled him to the chair next to hers. He poured the iced tea into two of Isaac's mugs before turning his attention to the book.

"You can open it," he said as he scooted his chair next to hers until their shoulders touched.

"Are you sure? It's kind of late. We could do this tomorrow." She said in a teasing voice. She laid her hand on top of the sketchbook's buff-colored leather cover. A faded yellow ribbon, tied in a bow, kept the book closed. She didn't wait for his answer, but tugged at the end of the ribbon and untied the bow. She laid the ribbon out on top of the blue rag then opened the leather cover and read aloud the inscription.

Volume 31

To Isaac, my new son.
May you be inspired as you fill these pages
with the wisdom and learning you gain in
your new role as the seventh potter of Niederbipp.

I have given you that which is of most value to me
and I pray you will cherish my Lily as I have.

God bless you in your efforts now and forever.
With love and admiration,
Your new father, Henry Jakob Engelhart
On the occasion of your wedding,

March 20, 1953

Amy was teary as she finished reading the last words. "This was his wedding gift."

Jake looked at her and nodded before running his fingers over the inscription. "I never realized Henry's middle name was Jakob. What a strange coincidence that his middle name is my first name and vice versa."

"Where's your sketchbook?" she asked. "Didn't you do a rubbing of Lily's gravestone in your book?"

"Yeah. It's downstairs. I'll be right back."

Jake returned with his sketchbook already open to the grave rubbing.

"She passed away on March 14, 1954."

"They were married less than a year," Amy lamented. "What a tragedy. How did you say she died?"

"Pneumonia, or influenza...I'm not sure. If I remember right, she was taking care of her dad until he died and her health was weakened in the process. They died within only a week of each other."

"That's a lot of loss in such a short period of time. That must have been devastating to Isaac."

Jake looked thoughtful. "I think I have a pretty good idea of what that was like." He swallowed hard as Amy put her arm around his shoulder.

"I'm sorry," she said. "I didn't...I..."

"It's ok, Amy. I just didn't expect this."

"There might be some pretty sad stuff ahead in this book. Are you sure you want to go on?"

Jake took a deep breath, exhaling slowly. "I'm sure. This is a wedding gift and I know his love for Lily, even though they were only married for a year, kept him going through his whole life. I'm sure there are some sad things, but there has to be some great stuff ahead too. Let's keep reading."

Amy was in the process of turning the page when she stopped, turning it back.

"What?" Jake asked.

"I just realized something curious."

Jake looked at it again and saw it too. "Volume 31?"

"Yeah, that's weird, huh? Maybe Isaac never filled 35 volumes of sketchbook."

Jake nodded. "Do you think that Henry could have filled that many?"

"I guess he could have, but what if these went back even further than that? What if they went back to the first potter of Niederbipp? What was his name?"

"I think it was Abraham. That was almost three hundred years ago. I can't imagine that…"

"What?"

"I was going to say I can't imagine the tradition going back that far, but there are lots of traditions in this town that are at least that old. I…." He got up and walked to the bedroom, returning with several sheets of paper.

"What's that?" Amy asked.

"It's Isaac's will. I seem to remember something about Isaac studying the notes of the potters… yes, here it is. It says, 'Time passed slowly as I fumbled around town, looking for answers. In time, the answers came as I got back to work. I studied the notes and the pots of the potters before me. From their notes, pots and a lot of work, I developed the skills I needed.'" Jake looked up from the papers. "Doesn't this suggest that he had access to something the other potters left behind?"

"Yeah, it does. Where do you think the other volumes would be?"

Jake bit his lip. "Maybe in the cellar?"

"Have you seen any books when you've been down there before?"

"No, but its pretty dark down there. Maybe there's another secret compartment in the studio somewhere."

"Maybe Thomas or Sam know something," Amy suggested

"That's too many maybes to solve tonight. We better move on."

Amy nodded and turned back to the book. Flipping the page, she began to read aloud.

March 22, 1953

I begin this book in Warren, Penn—On the banks of the Allegheny River, under a beautiful weeping willow as my wife slumbers at my side.

Two days ago, I married the only woman I have ever truly loved, Lily Engelhart. I believed that would be the happiest day of my life, but I was wrong. Yesterday was even better and today tops them both. After the ceremony, a traditional Quaker wedding, we spent the night in Sharon at the Buhl Mansion, a charming old estate that has been transformed into a bed and breakfast. It made me wonder why some of the old logging mansions in Niederbipp couldn't serve the same purpose.

I knew I was marrying a beautiful woman, but seeing Lily in all her radiance redefines beauty. I woke yesterday before she did and watched her sleep for nearly an hour. I had never dreamed of the happiness I feel being near her. The most amazing thing of it all is that she loves me too.

I am so sorry that my parents never knew her. I felt their absence stronger than ever at the wedding. I miss them both, but the faith I have found here and the things I have learned from the Engelharts give me hope that one day I will be able to introduce my bride to my mother and father, and that I will be able to meet Lily's mother.

I hoped to spend a week away on honeymoon, but I have a lot to learn in the pottery and Henry is anxious to teach me all he knows. When I accepted the job as his apprentice, Henry told me I'd be doing nothing but preparing clay during my first year. I have been here only nine months, but Henry started me on the wheel three weeks ago. After watching him work over the past months, I anticipated the work to be as easy as it looks. I was wrong. I should have known, for I am learning that many things are different than they first appear. I was growing tired of mixing clay, but after these weeks at the wheel, I wonder if I should not have been more satisfied mixing clay. I have done many difficult things over my lifetime, but working on the wheel is proving to be one of my biggest challenges yet. Maybe there is no easy part of the pottery process. If it weren't for the prize of marrying the potter's daughter, I might have left Niederbipp months ago.

I know I have much to learn and I look forward to the adventure of it all. Still, I wish for a week of this bliss before we return to work. Lily consoles me by saying as long as we're together, our honeymoon will continue. We moved most of her things into my apartment on Müllerstrasse before the wedding and so tonight we will come home to our apartment for the first time. Even so, I wish for a thousand days like yesterday. We strolled around the gardens and lounged about. I have waited my whole life for this moment and I feel intoxicated with my love for her.

This morning, we left Sharon before noon and drove to Erie to enjoy a picnic at the lake. I bought Lily a strand of freshwater pearls from a shop there. Despite her protest, I think she must like them. The Engelharts are a simple people. After living in New York, it has taken me some time to remember the joy that can be found in simple things. They have very little and none of the luxuries I have grown accustomed to, yet they want for nothing and consider themselves rich because of it. While I was in the city, I was earning more in a month than Henry makes in a year, yet his apparent happiness and that of Lily's seems beyond anything I experienced before I came here. I would love to shower her with gifts, but her deep seeded modesty and piety prevent her from standing out among her friends. Jerry Sproodle, the beau of Lily's best friend, Beverly, has also been helpful in teaching me about the Quaker ways. I have found it a challenge to live the simple life, but I recognize the virtue of the lifestyle and my life has already been blessed by it. I believe I am a better man than I ever have been and I have felt the love of God in my heart and mind for the first time since my childhood. I feel at home. The community of Friends has welcomed me in and made me feel like one of them. I hope to raise our children in Niederbipp and remain there for the rest of my life.

We were on our way home when Lily asked if we could stop here in Warren to rest. We have driven from Erie with the top down on the Porsche, and as Lily lies on the blanket next to me, I see that her beautiful face has been kissed by the sun. As I look at her, I feel unworthy of her, but I also feel inspired to do all I can, that one day I might be worthy of her love.

Amy turned to Jake, looking somber. "I wish I didn't know how this would end. It makes me sad. I feel like we're reading the story of the Titanic and there's nothing we can do to change the outcome."

Jake paused before answering, trying to control his emotions. "I was thinking the same thing. I think I might understand why we found this book hidden away. I can't imagine how difficult it would be to read this just a year later when everything he felt that day had changed."

"Did you notice where he was when he wrote this?" Amy asked.

Jake looked again at the top of the page and his eyes filled with tears. He opened Isaac's other sketchbook to page seven. "Be still, and know that I am God," he read, his voice choked with emotion. Through teary eyes he looked at Amy. "I don't know how he did it, how he went on."

"I only have a small idea, but from the tree we saw down by the river on Sunday and the things you told me up at Taufer's Pond, it seems there's a lot to be gained by faith." She pulled the newer sketchbook closer and pointed to the date in the upper corner. "This was drawn forty-four years after his wedding day. It makes me think he never got over her."

Jake shook his head before standing and walking out the door. He returned a minute later with the golden framed photograph of Lily that Isaac had kept in the studio all those years.

Amy took the picture from him and cradled it in her hands as she had two weeks before. "I'm trying to figure out why, if he never forgot her over all those years, he would want to forget this portion."

"Isn't it obvious?" Jake asked. "She died less than a year after this book was started."

"Yeah, I get that, but something tells me there has to be more. There has to be something darker. He had almost a year of something incredible enough to keep him going for fifty-something years. You'd think he'd want to read about those days more often, not hide them away."

Jake nodded, looking thoughtful. "Maybe there's only one way to find out." He turned back to the book and flipped the page.

Sketches of bowls and vases filled the margins of the next several pages; the majority of each page covered the events of Isaac's days. He spoke of his frustrations with the clay, his love for Lily and the growing respect he had for her and his father-in-law. He recorded little things that mattered to him: walks by the river with Lily, working with her and Henry in the studio, attending church, meeting different people in town, and talks he'd had with a variety of people—many of whom Jake and Amy already knew and many others they did not. But the things that seemed most important and most oft repeated were the words of praise and affection Isaac had for his wife.

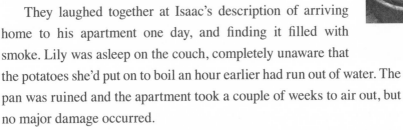

They laughed together at Isaac's description of arriving home to his apartment one day, and finding it filled with smoke. Lily was asleep on the couch, completely unaware that the potatoes she'd put on to boil an hour earlier had run out of water. The pan was ruined and the apartment took a couple of weeks to air out, but no major damage occurred.

On another occasion, Lily surprised him for his birthday with the gift of a beautiful sweater she'd been knitting for months. The only problem was that his head didn't fit through the neck hole. He wrote how he laughed about the problem until he saw that she was crying. The next entry reported that the sweater was made into a v-neck to accommodate his big noggin. Many of the following entries recorded that he wore the sweater often, writing of the love he felt for her every time he did.

Jake and Amy took turns reading Isaac's words as he wrote about digging clay from the river banks with Henry before the year's first frost and using a borrowed pickup truck to cart the clay back to the studio where they cached it in the cellar. Jake chuckled as Isaac lamented that there had to be an easier way. He was grateful Isaac had begun ordering premixed, predug clay sometime before he passed away.

Throughout it all, Isaac praised his wife, writing like a love-struck teenager. His words were always poetic and complimentary when he wrote about her. On several occasions he wrote how his love for her was constantly growing and maturing, his appreciation for her becoming deeper and stronger. Jake watched Amy carefully as they read each entry and learned more about him. He listened to the emotion rise in her throat as she read sections about how Isaac felt about Lily. Theirs was a story that was filled with love, mutual respect and selflessness.

Time passed quickly as they continued to read, lost in the story of Isaac and his young bride. The weariness and fatigue they'd felt in the studio faded away as they became emotionally entangled in the potter's story. One entry in early October recorded the sad events of the demise of his Porsche. And even though the story Jake had heard was told decades later and passed on through someone else, the details shared by Brian were remarkably similar. The loss of the car was troubling for Isaac until, as he recorded, Lily told him, "I married you in spite of your car, not because of it." From that point on, he seemed to be settled about it and never mentioned it again.

Thanksgiving was a joyous time. Isaac recorded spending the day with Lily and Henry at the Eckstein home where the announcement was made that Beverly and Jerry Sproodle would be married the following spring. After writing many complimentary things about both Beverly and Jerry, Isaac used the better part of three pages to record things he was grateful for. The top of the list included Lily, being led to Niederbipp and his discovery of many eternal truths. Among other blessings, he included health, happiness, piece of mind, learning to be satisfied with very little, fresh German bread with raw honey, a new career and a loving family. As Amy finished reading this section, she repeated the last line slowly.

Before coming to Niederbipp, I never would have believed
I could be happy with so little, but I see now that I
have never had more of what truly matters and have never
been happier.

She smiled at Jake before wrapping her arms around him. "I think I must be under the same spell," she said softly in his ear.

"What do you mean?"

"It's hard to put it into words, but maybe that's the essence of what I've always found in Niederbipp. Somehow, when I'm here, it's easier for me to recognize the things that matter most. I've felt that way every time I've come here, but this time, having found love and friendship…I don't know…I guess I feel like I could be happy here for the rest of my life."

These words had been said in different ways many times, but the honest clarity they carried with them now caused Jake to smile. He pulled her closer and held her tight. "I love you," he whispered.

"I know. And I love you back."

"It's almost 1:00," Jake said, pulling back to face her. "I should walk you home. I'd hate to worry Bev and Jerry."

"I'm sure they're sound asleep and I know there's no way I could sleep until I figure out why this book was hidden away."

"I was hoping you'd say that."

They began reading again, moving into the Holiday season. Isaac wrote of his joy in finally making pottery that he felt good about and, even though it was still not as nice as the things Henry made, he felt he was improving quickly. He wrote about the satisfaction he felt, selling pottery that he'd made with his own hands. He wrote about his worries that Lily had been sleeping a lot, requiring a nap every day and often falling asleep before dinner. He used these extra quiet hours at night to read and write. He wrote of the snow and cold north wind that blew off

Lake Erie. And he continued to write about Lily and the love that grew in his heart for her day by day.

On Christmas Eve, Isaac wrote about the joy he felt when he unloaded the new set of dishes he'd spent the previous weeks making for Lily. He described them as the most meaningful thing he'd ever made. It was only a setting for four, two of the bowls were warped, and none of them were exactly the same size. But he felt it was the best work he'd ever made and expressed pride in being able to give her something of himself.

The entry for Christmas Day, 1953 was jubilant. They awoke early to surprise Henry by making breakfast in his apartment. Isaac set the table with the new dishes, which Lily doted on for several hours. The three of them spent the morning together, telling stories and making memories. Lily made a zopf—a traditional Swiss braided bread that they consumed with some unusual peppermint tea that Henry had been given by some neighbors. Isaac reported that the day would have been complete as it was, but Lily had been holding back a surprise. Just before they were set to leave for home, she pulled a small package from a hiding place and handed it to Isaac. He unwrapped it to find a soft blue flannel cloth. It looked like a blanket but was only big enough to cover his head and shoulders. He wrote that he was surprised when he looked up to find Lily smiling and Henry's eyes brimming with tears. At that moment, he said he knew that the blue cloth was not intended to adorn the head and shoulders. He knew he was going to be a father.

Jake and Amy turned to each other, but said nothing. The ink on the page was smeared in places where it looked like Isaac's tears had dampened the paper. Lily's gift had been the first mention to anyone of her pregnancy and they decided they'd try to keep it a secret for a few more months since it was still early. But the joy Isaac expressed was beyond anything he'd written to that point. Lily felt certain it would be a boy, but no explanation was given why. They spent the rest of the afternoon and evening talking about hopes and dreams and plans for their expanding family. Then, after putting Lily to bed early, Isaac retired to the kitchen to record his thoughts and feelings.

Subsequent entries recorded aspects of Isaac's fears associated with the responsibilities he would have as a father. Here, he spoke of his own parents, the relationship they had had and the way he'd been raised. Isaac had been given his name because of the age of his parents when they'd conceived him: his mother was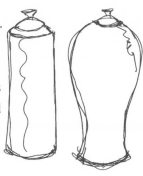

nearly fifty and his father, fifty-three. They had completely given up hope of having children of their own and considered him a miracle. As an only child being raised by parents old enough to be his grandparents, Isaac expressed sadness in not knowing his parents better. They were hard working farmers who were tired and perpetually poor, but they'd given him a great gift that he hadn't recognized as such until they had passed away: they taught him how to work. With that gift, the world had become his oyster.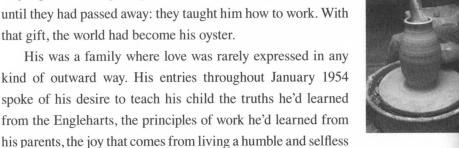

His was a family where love was rarely expressed in any kind of outward way. His entries throughout January 1954 spoke of his desire to teach his child the truths he'd learned from the Engleharts, the principles of work he'd learned from his parents, the joy that comes from living a humble and selfless life and, most certainly, that his parents love him.

He reported that Lily's fatigue continued, but he was grateful for the opportunity to dote on her. He learned how to cook simple meals and care for all her needs. When she was nauseated, he would read to her from Shakespeare, Thoreau, Keats and other writers. They made plans for the nursery and Isaac wrote of commissioning an Amish woodworker to make a special rocker. The recognition of the responsibilities that would soon be his inspired him in the Pottery too. He wrote of the continual progress he was making, learning how to fire the kiln and being entrusted by Henry with the ancestral glaze book, written in Swiss German.

Jake rubbed his tired eyes and passed the book to Amy to continue. She flipped the page and began to read.

February 10, 1954

Just before I awoke this morning I dreamt I was walking down Zubergasse when a young boy, not more than three, reached up and grabbed my hand, halting my progress. I stopped to look at him and tousle his straight blonde hair. His blue eyes drew me in and I knelt down on the street to embrace him. In that moment, I knew him. I knew he was my son. And I knew his name even before Lily called for him.

'Jakob, come here' She called from the Pottery's doorway and we turned to look at her as we laughed together."

"What did you say?" Jake asked, suddenly very alert.

Amy pointed to the name written in Isaac's own hand.

Jake stared at it for a long moment. "Am I awake?" he asked, turning to face Amy.

She laughed. "I think so, but maybe we're in the same dream together. Should I keep reading?"

"Yeah! If I'm awake, I want to know more."

"Let's see…umm, oh yeah," she said pointing to the place where she'd left off.

"Lily hurried to catch up to us. She kissed us both and then took Jakob's other hand and the three of us continued down the street. As we neared Hauptstrasse, the street magically turned into the meadow near the river where Lily and I often visited. I turned to look at her just as the sun came out from behind a cloud, illuminating her golden hair like she was on fire. She smiled at me and I felt a strange sensation, almost like she was filling my body with warmth just by looking at me. Her skin looked pale, but it glowed as if light

was coming from within. My eyes followed hers as she looked down at our son. He was surrounded by the same glow as his mother. The warmth I was feeling also filled me with happiness. I looked into the palm of my free hand, expecting to find the same glow, but my hand didn't look any different than it normally did.

I looked at Lily again, searching for understanding, but she only smiled at me. Confused, I lifted my hand to the sky, blotting out the sun. While the sun was behind me, I believed I was glowing too, but when I lowered my hand, the light was gone. I looked again at Lily and Jakob and saw that they had wandered closer to the river. I called after them and they both turned to look at me, but continued walking under the softly swaying branches of the weeping willow tree.

I followed them under the green canopy, but they weren't there. I found only glowing footprints in the tall grass where they'd been. I heard their laughter in the branches above me and turned, looking for them. But though I heard their voices, they were nowhere to be found. I woke up before I could find them. I've thought about the dream many times today. And when I've thought about this unusually vivid dream, I have heard the same gentle laughter rolling through the chambers of my mind. I can't think what it might mean.

I told Lily about the dream tonight. She said she told me so about our baby being a boy. The vivid nature of the dream has erased any hesitation I had about painting the second bedroom blue. We've been debating names every *evening. Jakob has been one our favorites, but after our talk tonight, we are both at peace about it. It is, of course, Henry's middle name and a strong name. After telling Henry about my dream today, he told me about another Jakob from the Old Testament. He was the son of Isaac, the grandson of Abraham. Henry said his name was later changed to Israel and his twelve sons became the leaders of the twelve tribes of Israel. He told me that the traditions of faith had been passed down from father to son through that family line until a portion of the blood and faith of those men beat in the hearts of all mankind. I like the idea of my son being named Jakob. I hope this strong name will inspire him to become a man of character and faith.*

Amy stopped reading and slid the yellow ribbon into the book to mark her place. Tears were in her eyes as she turned to look at him. "I don't know if I want to go on."

Jake swallowed hard, trying to hold back his own emotions. "I think I know how you feel. It makes me want to wrap this back up and put it back where we found it."

"If it would change the outcome..." She shook her head. "If this wasn't so sad...I...Jake, do you realize the things we've discovered tonight?"

Jake nodded thoughtfully. "You mean like the tree?"

"That's part of it, but there's so much more. When we read the dedication in the other book, we wondered if he had an illegitimate child out there in the world somewhere. We couldn't have been more wrong."

Jake nodded again. He looked down at the bundle on the table. "Things aren't always as they appear to be."

Amy sighed. "What else have we missed?"

"At least one thing right in front of us."

"What's that?"

"That's not a rag that was wrapped up around the book."

There was a long pause as Amy looked at the small bundle. "It's the blanket Lily gave Isaac, isn't it?"

"It has to be. Can you imagine the pain that would have caused him to see that around the house after Lily passed away? It would have been a constant reminder of everything he'd lost." Jake shook his head. "I feel awful that I believed Isaac could have been guilty of some form of treachery."

"Is the truth any less tragic?"

Jake took another deep breath. "No, but I feel like we're discovering who he really was. Lots of folks have had a portion of his story. Maybe they picked up bits and pieces because of his sensitivity or empathy to their struggles. I don't know for sure, but I'm guessing from the way he kept this hidden away all these years, that most people never had a clue of who he really was…of the pain he hid beneath his smile. If Gloria ever knew that he lost more than just his wife when she passed away, she never said anything to me. I doubt she ever considered that the advice he gave her was gained from personal experience. His words were full of truth and understanding because he'd been there."

"Which brings us back to this collection of pottery and that Keats quote, doesn't it?"

Jake blinked several times, trying to figure out what Amy had already discovered. "Let's see, the Keats quote suggests that every failure can bring about an even greater success. Even our mistakes give us experience and teach us." He gazed at Amy, the connection between the quote and Isaac's tragedy still not clear.

"It's not just mistakes, though," Amy explained. "It's also the bad things that happen to us. They're not pleasant—sometimes they're horrible—but we can learn from them."

Jake's tired brain began to understand. He turned to look at the green pitcher. "You're right. Maybe the lessons we have to learn from this collection run far deeper than we can even imagine. Maybe everything is connected…maybe it's just a matter of discovering those connections and putting the pieces together."

(37)

SIMPLE GIFTS

THE WISE MAN IN THE STORM
PRAYS TO GOD, NOT FOR SAFETY
FROM DANGER, BUT FOR
DELIVERANCE FROM FEAR.
—RALPH WALDO EMERSON

Amy poured the rest of the tea into their mugs. The ice had melted while they were discovering Isaac. The clock on the wall indicated it was after four. They were both exhausted, but their desire to know kept them planted in their chairs. They continued to read, taking turns and stopping often to discuss what they were learning.

In the entry for February 20, 1954, Isaac wrote that he'd worked alone that day in the pottery for the first time since he'd arrived in Niederbipp. Henry was feeling under the weather and Lily, the ever-devoted daughter, was caring for him even though she was tired and weak herself. The next several entries, not more than two days apart, continued the tale of working alone while Henry struggled to fight influenza. They moved into Lily's old bedroom in his apartment so they could be closer to him. He wrote of sitting with Henry late at night, listening to the heavy sounds of his labored breathing. He held his hand, which ranged from cold and clammy to sweltering hot. He helped bathe him in hot and cold baths to try and regulate his temperature. And he closed the Pottery so he could help Lily more with the care of her father.

Another entry, on March 1, told how he'd gone to the hospital to visit several friends who were there with the same symptoms. Beverly Eckstein was among them. He described the exhausted nurses who'd been working around the clock to care for the sick. He'd returned home, scared, after hearing that many had already passed away, their beds not even cool before they were needed by someone else.

Henry rallied on the morning of March 5, rising from his bed to eat breakfast for the first time in many days. But by noon, he seemed much worse than before. His labored breathing became inconsistent and his temperature spiked. As he lay in bed, he reached out to squeeze Isaac's wrist. Then he reached for Lily's hand and placed hers on top of Isaac's. "Always love each other," he whispered before falling back on his pillow.

Isaac ran to the hospital, looking for help but returned home after finding the nurses already overwhelmed with the dead and dying. Without medicine that had any measurable effect, he and Lily knelt to pray at the side of Henry's bed as he slipped into unconsciousness. They sat with him all night, speaking softly of the reality and probability of death. Despite the feelings of loss, Isaac wrote of the unexpected peace they both felt as they watched and listened to Henry take his final breaths and pass away quietly in the early hours of March 6.

Isaac wrote next on March 8. He spoke of the need to forgo the normal Quaker funeral services because of the warning to avoid gathering in groups out of fear of spreading sickness. This news, Isaac wrote, was very troubling to Lily who explained her mother's funeral service as "a time of hope, memories and music that brought peace to her soul when she needed it most."

Isaac wrote of feeling helpless, trying to console his wife while struggling to make sense of their future. With so many in town either sick or involved in the care of those who were, Isaac went to the graveyard to dig a grave himself for Henry in the still-frozen ground. Henry was buried the following day, March 9, as a small gathering of friends looked on. Some shared words of peace and hope with the couple. But, according to Isaac, the thing that most comforted Lily was the organ music that emanated from the chapel and filled the small graveyard with peace. They sat together on her grandfather's bench, holding each other as Mrs. Meier played a medley of hymns including Simple Gifts, Nearer my God to Thee, and Amazing Grace. He recalled that the chill on the wind was no match for the warmth they felt as the music played, but Lily asked Isaac to take her home after the music ended, saying she was tired.

After making sure she was comfortable, Isaac returned to the cemetery to bury Henry. He lingered there for an hour afterward, pouring out his soul in thought and prayer, seeking direction and comfort.

Amy passed the book to Jake and moved to the padded bench under the window, across from him. He smiled weakly at her tired face before he continued.

I returned home this evening feeling tired and weak. Lily was asleep in her father's bed and I watched her for several minutes, knowing this had to be difficult for her. For the past fifteen years, Henry was her best friend and only parent. Now, like me, she is an orphan, having

lost both parents long before she was ready. I have
spent the day searching for understanding. So many have
passed away this season. I counted six fresh graves
in our small cemetery alone, but I know many others
have fallen and many more are struggling. Jerry Sproodle
attended the services today. Beverly was sorely missed,
but is still in the hospital. Jerry did not look well. With
influenza claiming so many, I can imagine his worries
about Beverly. I pray all will be well with her. They have
been such great friends to me and Lily. I can't imagine
our future without them in it.

As I stood near my sleeping wife, I thought
of Henry. He was without his wife for nearly
sixteen years. I know I have not yet been married
a year, but I can't imagine the loneliness he must
have felt at losing his wife. The faith he and Lily
have nurtured in me offers me hope that even
now they are enjoying a happy reunion with each
other.

As for our future, it seems to have changed in
the past few days. I am grateful for the progress I
have made in learning the potter's art, but I'm not sure I
know enough. I know Lily can help me with some things,
but I fear that many of the things I need to know have
been lost forever. Lily and I have a lot to think about.
I don't know if my skills as a potter are sufficient to
support us. I know there would be more opportunities
somewhere else, yet I feel compelled by some unseen
power to stay here.

I am grateful to Henry. He has given me a new life.
Beyond the sharing of eternal truths that have softened

my heart and mind, he has given me more love than any man ever has. These things alone would endear him to me forever, but to be given the trust of taking his only daughter's hand in marriage—well that is something quite remarkable. I feel tonight that if I were to spend my whole life living the best I could, it would not be enough to repay him for his kindness. I pray he rests in peace in the arms of his loving wife and his Savior."

Jake looked up to see tears flowing down Amy's cheeks. "Should I keep reading?" he asked.

She nodded, reaching for a napkin to wipe her eyes and nose. "We know how this ends, but we have to continue."

Jake swallowed and turned the page.

March 11, 1954

I am worried about Lily. She didn't get out of bed yesterday, saying she was tired and felt weak. She's also developed a terrible cough. I trudged through the heavy snow today to visit the hospital to seek advice, but the nurses and doctors were stressed and suggested I keep Lily home. There are no beds available, and with so many sick people, she'd be better off at home. They gave me some medication to administer to her. I returned home nearly frozen. It has done nothing but snow since yesterday and the streets are nearly impassable. Even if I had a car, I know I could get anywhere faster by walking. I am comforted by fact that her symptoms seem much different than Henry's. She has only a slight fever. This afternoon, though, her cough was very severe. She spoke of her fear of losing the baby. I am worried, but with nowhere to take her and the roads being clogged with snow anyway, we have no option but to stay where we are and try to keep warm. I am feeling lonely. She sleeps most of the time and starts to cough every time she speaks. Mrs. Schmidt knocked on the door this evening with a pot of hot soup and a basket of fresh rolls. She wouldn't come in for fear of catching whatever it is Lily has, but her gift of food was a godsend. Lily ate for the first time in two days and has slept peacefully since.

This has been a difficult day. The phone lines are down with the snow and I feel isolated, maybe even stir-crazy. I've tried reading. I've tried going to the Pottery to work, but the water pipes are frozen and I don't want to be away from Lily if she needs me. So I wait, and as I do, my mind fills with worry. Having lost Henry, the reality of death still burns hot inside me. I don't know what I would do if things turned worse for Lily and so I have set my mind on thinking about Jakob. I have read and reread my entry from February 10. I turned there looking for comfort, but there is something unsettling about that dream. Oh, how I wish I might have slept longer that morning and could have found them. Why did I not? I hate to consider the answer to that question. I have spent the afternoon praying for a miracle. I have never felt so helpless. Prayer, it seems is my only option.

Jake didn't look up at Amy. He could hear her sobbing softly. He turned the page.

March 12, 1954,

Help! I am so tired. I was up with Lily all night as her coughing returned with such force that she vomited continually. Still, her coughing has continued and is now producing blood. I left in search of help before sunrise. The snow has continued to fall and is now above my waist. The whole town seems to be in hibernation. I knocked on the doors of my neighbors, looking for someone to help me carry Lily to the hospital. Mr. Schneider said he would help, but suggested we wait for the snow to stop. His wife and children are also weak with fever and the snow seems to have no end in sight. I returned a few hours ago just in time for the power to go out. Our firewood is nearly gone and Lily's coughing continues to produce blood. With the power out and the deep snow impeding our way, I can't imagine the hospital being a better choice than what we have here. I am so tired and feel my mind beginning to swim.

Lily has said very little since yesterday. She seems to be lost in a world of sleep. I have given her only water, fearing that any more than that would cause her vomiting to return. If I carried her to the hospital, I fear she would die of exposure and I would die of exhaustion. If I stay here, I fear she will die anyway. I do not know how many days it has been since she began to cough. It seems like a thousand years. I am so tired.

Jake looked up this time. Amy's tears were still present, but her sobbing had stopped.

"Just finish it," she said softly.

Jake nodded and began again.

March 14, 1954

My world is broken. I held Lily in my arms all day yesterday, trying to keep her warm, trying to hold her quivering body still as she coughed and gasped for life. I prayed all day for a miracle, but when the night came, my prayers began to change. I prayed to know God's will. I have no peace in the answer he gave me.

This morning I woke with Lily in my arms. She was still. At first I thought her coughing had finally ended, that God had answered my prayers. But then I realized she was cold. Mr. Schneider knocked on the door a few hours later. He lost one of his sons last night and said he'd heard many others died at the hospital. We cried together in the kitchen before he left. He apologized he hadn't come sooner.

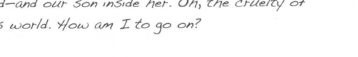

I feel numb. What has happened to my family? In the matter of a week full of days that lasted a hundred years, I have lost everything I love. I feel lost in a terrible dream. My sweet Lily is dead—and our son inside her. Oh, the cruelty of this world. How am I to go on?

Amy let out a long breath. "I need some fresh air."

"Me too," said Jake. He closed the book and stood, stretching his arms above his head. Amy stood also and embraced him. They held each other for a long time. Jake listened to Amy's heart beat as she continued to sob quietly.

The sound of someone climbing the stairs behind them caused them to stir and Jake turned to open the door.

"Thomas?"

"Ah, Jake, good morning. I was on my way home from the bakery and saw your light on. Is everything ok?"

Jake nodded, opening the door wider to invite him in.

Thomas took a step inside before looking up. He looked at Amy, a startled expression filling his face. "I'm sorry," he said, taking a step back. "I didn't know I was interrupting something."

Amy forced a smile. "You're fine, father. It's been a long night. We found something in the Pottery." She pointed to the table.

Thomas turned his head before nodding softly. "I shouldn't jump to conclusions. You two had me worried there for a minute. When I saw your teary eyes at this early hour, I thought…well, never mind. It looks like you found Volume 31."

"How did you know that?" Jake asked.

Thomas' smile broadened. "It's the lost book. It's the only one I haven't read. I asked Isaac about it several times, but he always managed to change the subject. Judging from your faces, it looks like you've discovered why."

Amy nodded.

"Where did you find it? I searched this whole apartment and the Pottery after he died, looking for it. I finally concluded that it had been destroyed."

"Wait a second," Jake said. "Let's back up. You know the location of the other sketchbooks?"

"Of course. Isaac left them to my keeping a few years ago."

"Did he ever tell you why Volume 31 was missing?" Jake asked.

"No, never directly. He told me it was his first one, though. I put two and two together and figured it contained a lot about Lily's death. Am I right?"

"Yeah," said Amy, visibly holding back her tears. "It's pretty sad stuff."

Thomas took a deep breath and exhaled slowly. "I've been waiting a long time. Do you mind if I take a look?"

Jake moved aside, extending his hand. "Help yourself. If Isaac gave you access to the others, you might as well know about this one. But tell me, where are the other ones?"

Thomas laughed. "Where do most people keep books?"

"In a bookcase?" Jake asked.

"Yep, and where is my other job?"

"The bakery?" Amy asked.

"The library!?" Jake answered.

Thomas raised one eyebrow. "I can't think of a better place for books, can you?"

"Well no, but are you telling me they're just on a shelf for anyone to check out?"

"Are you kidding? Those books are almost three hundred years old! They're locked up in a climate-controlled shelf in the special collections area. And I'm the only one who holds the key." He pulled a chain from under his black shirt and flourished a silver cross hanging next to a brass-colored key.

"How long have they been in your custody?" Jake asked.

"Almost ten years. I learned about them after Isaac found me in the river. He used to keep them in the bookcase in the second bedroom. I discovered them the night he took me in. He loaned them to me over the years when I began asking questions. When I realized the value they had from an historical context, I convinced him that they needed to be preserved in a better way than gathering dust and mold on an old shelf."

"But you know there's much more than the historical value, don't you?" asked Amy.

"Of course and so did Isaac, but it was the historical content that enabled me to get the grant I needed for the special shelf. Do you think a government grant would ever be given to preserve some dusty old books that talked about faith and eternal truths? That would be a conflict of interest, mixing church and state. I convinced all the right people of their historic value and that was enough."

"So why did Sam have Volume 36?" Jake asked.

"He was adamant that Isaac had a sketch in there that would make it easy for him to complete his floor. I had already read the book so I put it in Isaac's room where Sam would find it."

"But if it's so valuable, why did he just give it to me without much explanation? You brought it to me at the hospital and didn't say much either. Why?"

Thomas smiled. "Value is an interesting concept. What is priceless to some is worthless to others. There are many amazing things in each of the books, but unless you're hungry to find out what they are, you might as well just be perusing a magazine. So many of the truths are subtle and tied to other things. Even though I knew Sam wouldn't find what he was looking for, I also knew he respected Isaac enough to keep it safe."

"And what about me? I could have thrown the book away or spilled something on it."

"I wasn't worried," Thomas replied. "I saw the way you treated your own sketchbook. You always carry it with you, care for it, and make good use of it. I knew Sam would be suspicious of me if I asked him for it, so when I saw it in the bakery a few weeks ago, I suggested he give it to you to see what you might learn."

Amy laughed. "You knew that book would change Jake's mind about staying, didn't you?"

"Well, not exactly, but I knew if it ever could, it would be when he was most humble and capable of understanding its message. That's why I brought it to you at the hospital, Jake. I knew you needed to be here the moment I met you. I was just waiting for the time to be right for you to discover that yourself."

"But—how did you know I was ready?"

"Because I've been there, Jake. The book I read was different than the one you got. It was volume 33. Isaac left it on my bed one night, shortly after he'd found me. It was the truth I needed to hear, but I had to discover it for myself. Most people don't respond well to truth being thrust upon them. If, however, it whispers softly in our ears, and we tune our ears to listen, we tend to develop within ourselves the desire to know the truth of all things."

Jake and Amy looked at each other and smiled through tears of understanding. "Can we read the others?" Amy asked.

"Not today," Thomas said, smiling. "You kids look like you've been up for weeks. Why don't you get some sleep? I'll be working at the library tomorrow afternoon. If you'd like, you could visit me during your lunch break. We can talk more then."

Jake nodded, winking at Amy. "Can I hang on to volume 36? I haven't finished it yet."

"Sure. Are you done with volume 31?"

"Yes, we just finished. You can take it if you would like."

"I'd like that."

"This one comes with some accessories," Amy said. "It might be best understood if we gave it to you as we found it." She tied the yellow ribbon around the cover before Jake wrapped the book in the faded blue blanket, wrapping the bundle loosely with the twine. He turned and handed the book to Thomas.

"There's a lot here that might surprise you."

Thomas winked at them. "Don't spoil it, Jacob. I've been looking for the missing links for many years."

IF THEE LIVES UP TO THE LIGHT THEE IS GIVEN, MORE WILL BE GIVEN THEE.
— QUAKER PROVERB

(38)
THIRTY-SEVEN

TWO ROADS DIVERGED IN A WOOD,
AND I--I TOOK THE ONE LESS
TRAVELED BY,
AND THAT HAS MADE ALL THE DIFFERENCE.
—ROBERT FROST

Dreams often have a strange way of setting the tone for the waking hours that follow. After walking Amy home, Jake's sleep was short, but filled with vivid dreams inspired by the things he'd learned from Isaac's sketchbooks. There were so many things to take from the potter's records, but the feeling that remained with him was one of appreciation and gratitude. As he finished putting the showroom back together, he quietly counted the events of the past month as the blessings they truly were.

When Amy arrived, just after noon, Jake took her in his arms and

held her for a very long time. Still filled with the emotions from his dream, he thanked her—humbly and contritely—for loving him. He asked her again to forgive him for being pigheaded and blind. She offered her forgiveness freely, thanking him for loving her enough to change and open his heart and mind.

They spoke openly with each other as they worked on the tiles they'd made for Sam's floor. The drywall had absorbed much of the moisture from the clay, making most of the tiles ready to be sanded. They scratched numbers into the back of each one according to the patterns they'd made on paper.

Sally, Marge, Mary, and Emily stopped by in the afternoon to check on Jake. They examined his healing arm and seemed delighted to meet Amy. Each of them purchased one of Jake's new pieces, complimenting him on his work and the changes he and Amy were making to the showroom. Before they left, Sally pulled Jake aside and whispered in a tone loud enough for the others to hear that she was happy he'd found such a pleasant girl. As they bid farewell, they promised to be back soon to check out Amy's new work.

By closing time, the tiles had all been sanded. Those that were dry were stacked carefully in the kiln on the new shelves. In the four years he'd spent working in the busy campus ceramics studio, filling the kilns had always been a lonely and solitary job. He often performed it late at night when his other work was done and the studio was quiet. He had never really enjoyed this part of the work, but it was different with Amy helping him. As he thought about it, everything was different when she was with him. Even the most mundane activities were somehow fun. Only a few weeks before, he might have kept these thoughts to himself, but now, after the accident and his time in the hospital, things had changed. He no longer felt any hesitation to share his feelings with her. The vulnerability that dogged him before was gone, replaced with confidence and understanding.

They left the Pottery and walked to Hauptstrasse in search of food to satisfy their empty stomachs. They enjoyed kabobs on the bench at the fountain. Still exhausted from their late night, they lingered lazily until it was nearly dark, then walked to Mancini's Ice Café. They found seats at a table on the cobblestone patio under the string of lights. They had only just sat down when they heard their names and turned to see Kai and Molly walking towards them. Walking, in this case is a generous word. While Kai walked, Molly waddled.

"Hey guys!" Kai said, helping Molly move.

Jake stood to offer Molly his chair, which she fell in to, exhausted. "Have you been out walking again?" he asked.

"Yeah, Kai wanted to see if there were any fireflies down by the river, but I got tired before we got that far."

"I think she just wanted some ice cream," Kai offered. "She's developed a craving for Mancini's lemon sherbet that seems to strike every day about this time. Not that I'm complaining. Fireflies are awesome, but they don't taste anywhere near as good as Mancini's ice cream."

They laughed together as they placed their orders with the dark haired waiter. While they waited for their ice cream to arrive, Molly reported on her visit to the doctor that morning. Her Braxton-Hicks contractions had grown increasingly uncomfortable in the last couple of nights and her doctor suggested that walking might help alleviate some of the pain while encouraging the baby to come.

"I feel like a four-hundred pound duck," she mused.

They laughed together again, but the conversation never drifted far from the pregnancy and impending changes that would come to their family. Molly rested her ice cream bowl on her stomach and they watched as the baby kicked and punched, moving the bowl up and down and from side to side. He seemed to grow more active with each spoonful of lemon sherbet.

After their bowls were empty, they continued chatting for nearly an hour. Jake watched as Molly's face contorted in pain when the contractions began again. This was still new for Jake. Molly was the first pregnant woman he'd ever known well. His thoughts unavoidably turned to Isaac and Lily and the things he and Amy had read the night before. Worry filled his mind. He looked at Kai, wondering what he would do without Molly. She seemed like such an anchor in his life. Like Lily was for Isaac, Molly was one of the main reasons Kai had stayed here. What would happen if she died? Jake tried to shake the idea, but the fears lingered. He was lost in his own world of thought when Amy touched his arm, telling him it was time to go. He was just standing when he felt a splash of water on his shoes and turned to see Molly's face flush with color.

"What'd ya do, pee your pants?" Kai whispered loud enough for them all to hear. He looked embarrassed.

Molly shook her head and sat back down. "I think my water just broke." Another gush of water fell through the wicker seat and splashed on the cobblestones.

"What should we do?" Kai looked panicked.

"I think we better get to the hospital."

"I'll go get the van," The expectant father started to run off.

"Kai, we're only two blocks away from the hospital. Don't freak out. We could walk there faster than it would take you to get back here with the van." Jake was amazed at how cool Molly was. She tried to stand again but her face writhed in pain. She grabbed Kai's shoulder. "I don't think those were Braxton-Hicks I was feeling earlier. Those were real contractions. We need to get to the hospital!"

Kai's eyes lit up wildly as he looked at Amy and Jake. "Jake, if we're going to walk, I'm going to need your help."

Jake nodded, moving closer.

"What can I do?" asked Amy.

"You can run to the hospital and tell them we're coming," Molly responded calmly, then winced as another contraction hit. "Tell them the contractions are coming every two minutes."

"Is that bad?" Jake asked. His fears ratcheted up several notches. He watched as Amy disappeared up the street.

"No, it's good," Molly said, standing again. "It means the baby is finally coming. We better hurry."

Another contraction hit as Jake pulled her arm over his shoulder.

"Breathe!" Kai yelled as Molly gripped Jake's shoulder. They were walking as quickly as they could, but the next contraction came as they reached the top of Haupstrasse and Molly screamed out in pain. Her feet stopped moving and the trio halted.

"Can you help me carry her?" Kai asked.

Jake nodded. Forgetting the pain he already felt in his arm, he stooped and linked arms with Kai underneath her knees. Her jeans were wet from the amniotic fluid, but he barely noticed as they raced across the street. They stumbled over the curb, but caught themselves, propelled forward by the deadweight in their arms and the urgency of their mission. Jake's left arm was pulsating with pain emanating from his scar, but he knew he had to keep moving. Molly screamed out several more times before they saw the lights of the emergency entrance. A wheeled gurney awaited them as they walked through the automatic doors. Several of the nurses looked at Jake and smiled as they laid Molly down.

"I thought you weren't supposed to lift anything over twenty pounds," Sandy said, flashing Jake a wink. "We'll take it from here" she said. "We've called Dr. Wilkinson, but he lives north of Warren. It might take him a while to get here. Do I understand that your contractions are coming fast?"

Molly nodded, biting her lower lip.

"I need to check how far you're dilated. Gina, Abby, take her to room one and get those jeans off. Kai, are you coming with me?"

Kai nodded, but his pale face seemed to say he wasn't so sure he wanted to be there.

"We'll be in the waiting room," Amy said, her face registering both concern and excitement. "We'll be excited to hear."

Kai nodded, but still looked like a deer in the headlights. Another scream from Molly turned him around and sent him running down the hallway in pursuit of the nurses and his wife.

Amy and Jake stood there, watching him go. "This is amazing!" Amy exclaimed. "I get the impression Kai has no idea how much his life is about to change."

Jake laughed. "That's funny you say that. I was just thinking that he understands that more now than he ever has. I'd be freaking out right now if it were me."

"So you're not ready to be a father yet, huh?"

Jake paused at the baited question, considering his response. He took a deep breath. "I think I ought to figure out who I am before I have a child. Besides that, I probably ought to have a wife first. I hear its best not to put the cart before the horse. I think it might be fun to be a dad someday, like maybe when I'm forty."

"Will it take you that long to figure out who you are?"

Jake looked thoughtful. "I don't know. I feel like I'm light years ahead of where I was just six weeks ago. I might be able to move that date up a couple of years. Thirty-seven, thirty-eight…that wouldn't be so bad."

Amy smiled. "That's funny. I always thought I'd wait until I was thirty-seven too. What do you say if…well, if we're still single when we turn thirty-seven, we get married and have a few kids."

Jake laughed nervously. It wasn't an idea he hadn't had a hundred times before, but the thought of waiting fifteen years to marry and have children seemed like cruel and unusual punishment. "Ya know…" He took a deep breath, exhaling slowly. "I've learned a few things about life since I came here. Probably the most important one is that selfishness can never produce joy. If I was to remain single for fifteen years, it would only be because no woman would have me or because I'm too selfish to open my heart to other possibilities."

Amy grabbed his arm as she often did and pulled him toward the waiting room. "What are you saying?" she asked when they reached the black vinyl sofa in the corner.

He turned and looked into her green eyes, smiling softly. "Amy, I love you. I've known you for…what, one month? And a whole week of that, you weren't even talking to me. And yet, if I'm allowed to say how I really feel, I can't imagine not hanging out with you."

Amy shook her head, flashing a broad, flirty smile. "Jake you're so romantic. Are you telling me you want to hang out with me until we're thirty-seven?"

"Yes, I mean no, I mean…" he took another deep breath, looking away.

She rested her palm softly on top of his hand. "I'm sorry to agitate you…please go on."

He shook his head. "I want to marry you, Amy. I want to be with you when we're thirty-seven and fifty-seven and ninety-seven. I want to fall asleep next to you under the clouds and wake up next to you in the morning and bring you pancakes in bed. I want to share the same air with you for the rest of our lives. I want to have the kind of love Isaac had with Lily, the kind of love that kept him going more than fifty years, even after losing her. The idea of waiting until we're thirty seven to get married makes me crazy. I know marriage is kind of an old fashioned idea, especially for kids our age, but hanging out with you, even living in the same apartment as you would never be enough. If I lived a hundred years, I don't think it would be long enough to be with you."

His honesty scared him. He hadn't looked at her while he spoke, focusing instead on their rippled reflection in the dark window twenty feet away. When the silence spanned several seconds, he began to wonder if his words had been somehow offensive or unwelcome.

She put her hand on his chin and turned his face to meet hers. Her serious face alarmed him. "So, does that mean we still have to wait until were thirty-seven to have kids?" A smile raced across her mouth. She pulled him in, wrapping her arms tightly around his neck, burying his face in her amber hair.

> NEITHER IS THE MAN WITHOUT THE WOMAN, NEITHER THE WOMAN WITHOUT THE MAN IN THE LORD.
> — 1 CORINTHIANS 11:11 —

He breathed deeply, relieved. He hadn't noticed he'd been holding his breath, but his breathing became regular as he inhaled the familiar scent of her hair.

"I love you," she whispered. "And I think I'd like to marry you too."

"You think?" he asked, pulling back to look at her.

She laughed softly. "Ok, maybe I'm sure."

"Maybe you're sure?" He raised one eyebrow. "Do you want some time to think about it?"

"No. I don't. I mean I do want to marry you. I've been thinking about it now for the last three weeks. I just didn't expect this conversation tonight...I...I didn't imagine it happening for a few months."

"Hey, you're the one who brought it up," he said, poking her softly in the ribs.

She laughed and kissed the end of his nose. "I guess I did."

"I'm glad you did. I've spent my whole life playing my cards close to my chest. It's pretty amazing to be able to speak as freely as I want." He pulled her close again in a jubilant kiss. They held each other for several minutes, enjoying the comfortable silence.

"My parents are going to freak out!" she said, pulling back to look at him. "My dad's been telling me since I was a little girl that he plans to be pretty tough on the guy that comes to ask to marry me."

Jake bit the side of his lip. "I think I can handle it."

She raised her eyebrows. "You don't know my dad. He's really tough.

Maybe we should just elope."

"Do you really think that would help?"

She let out a long breath. "No. I'd really like to make things better with my dad. He's already convinced I'm wasting my time trying to be an artist. He'd really have a cow if he knew I was going to marry one."

"I could pretend to be a business man until after the wedding."

"Jake, get real. Business men usually wear ties. Do you even own one?"

"Well, no. But I could get a few."

"Jake, do you even know how to tie a tie?"

"Uh, nope. I could learn."

"Forget it. I don't think it would be a good idea to try and mend my relationship with my parents by lying."

Jake nodded thoughtfully. "So should we elope?"

"Can you believe we're even talking about this? I mean, I was heading home last Sunday. I was madder than...I was just really mad at you for kissing that girl and... and now we're talking about marriage! What are we doing?"

"So, I guess we're not going to elope either."

She laughed, wrapping her arms around him again. "I don't know, Jake. I've never gotten married before. This seems like the most important decision we'll ever make and it kind of feels like we're treating it like a trip to the senior prom, like I'm trying to sneak out the backdoor with the kid my parents have grounded me from seeing. Maybe we're not really ready for it if we're thinking about eloping or talking about trying to con my parents into believing you're a business man. I've never imagined my wedding that way."

"How did you imagine it?"

"I've tried to forget. I don't know. Even though I haven't been on the same page as my parents, especially my dad, for a few years, I still want to have their approval and blessings. I don't know if that will ever come, but I'd like to hope that we could change their minds. I need them to know that the road I've chosen, even though it's not their road, is still one that leads to happiness."

"So how do we do that?"

"I think you need to meet them."

"When?"

"My family has always come here during the week of July 4. Niederbipp is magic on the 4th. They're probably coming then.

"But that's like a month away. Maybe we should go visit them."

"I don't think that's such a good idea. If they found out we rode the bus home, they'd really have a cow. You should have seen my mom crying when she dropped me off at the bus station to come here. She cried, telling me I was going to be drugged and kidnapped by strangers and I'd never be seen alive again. I don't think my parents have ever taken a bus anywhere."

"They probably wouldn't be very impressed if we drove up on the scooter either."

Amy shook her head, but smiled. "Jake, this makes me sound really shallow. I'm not like my parents. I like simplicity. I love you and the simple life you've made for yourself. It's the life I've craved. I like the fact that you don't have a car and that you don't know how to tie a tie, but those things would make my parents even crazier than they already are. Cars and houses are symbols of success and stability to them. My brothers all drive expensive cars and live in big houses. More than anything else, I think it was my father's drive for stuff that made him leave Niederbipp and pursue his fortune."

Jake nodded, looking very disappointed. "That's a big dose of reality. What are we going to do?"

"I don't know, Jake. I think the Quaker principle of simplicity must have skipped a generation. I've been embarrassed by my family's outward expressions of their wealth ever since I was a kid. It wasn't just that, but also the way they looked down on people who didn't have what we had."

"Amy, it's doubtful that I'll ever have that kind of wealth. I've never wanted it."

"I know," she said, cutting him off. She put her arm around his back and gave him a reassuring squeeze. "Jake, you have to believe me when I say I don't need any of those things to make me happy. I've been the odd ball in the family ever since I was a little girl. My brothers teased me, telling me I was adopted when I turned down my parents' offer of a big screen TV for my bedroom and asked for paints instead."

Jake nodded. "So, what should we do, Amy?"

She looked away and was silent for a long moment. "I don't know, Jake. I want to marry you, but despite my current frustrations with my parents, I don't want to hurt them by eloping and cutting them out of our lives forever. They're the only family I've got. And I guess that means they're the only family we've got."

These words struck Jake. Since becoming an orphan, 'family' had been a word that fostered mixed emotions. "What if we choose our own 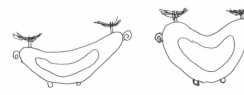 family?" he asked after a long silence.

"What do you mean?"

"I'm talking about the people here, Beverly and Jerry, Gloria and Joseph, Thomas, Kai and Molly. Isn't that enough? Gloria has already taken upon herself the role of mothering me. Kai and Molly are the closest things I've ever had to a brother and sister. Couldn't they be our family?"

"I think they will be, Jake, but there's something different about your own flesh and blood. Despite all the trouble they've given me, I still crave their support and approval. Sometimes I wish I didn't care, but I do and I probably always will." She took a deep breath. "There's got to be a way to have our cake and eat it too. We just have to be creative. We have to find a way for my parents to see you for who you are."

"And not for what I don't have?" He looked disappointed, dejected.

"I guess you could see it that way, but I hope you won't, Jake."

"How am I supposed to see it? You've been raised with a bunch of money on the right side of town. I'm an orphan kid with no money who wants to play in the mud for the rest of my life. How am I supposed to react? I feel like I'm just waking up to the reality that our two worlds may not be compatible."

"I'd rather see this as a chance to challenge them, like I said, to show my parents that there's more than one road to happiness."

Jake nodded, feeling the fire of disappointment in his heart begin to calm down. "Albert told me about how Isaac taught him something very similar to that idea. I've never been good at patience, Amy. And I have a difficult time pretending to be someone I'm not."

"I know. That's one of the many reasons I love you." She embraced him again. "Jake, there may be a few big obstacles in front of us, but the way I see it, providence has brought us together. There have been way too many coincidences over the past few weeks for this to simply be a random twist of fate. I didn't come here to fall in love, but the universe obviously had something else in mind. Some things may still not be easy, but it seems like there are a million things going our way. We just need to stay focused on the things that make sense and pray that the loose ends will work themselves out."

"That sounds like you're leaving a lot of this to faith."

"I guess I am. I don't know what else to do. I know there are some things I can control, but there are a zillion more I know I can't. It's hard for me to believe that anything that feels as right as our relationship could go anywhere but in a positive direction."

"Why do you have so much faith in us?"

She turned away, looking thoughtful. "Jake, since that night at Taufer's Pond, I've been praying for direction. When things went bad last week, I got really confused because what was happening seemed so contrary to what I was feeling. The night I saw that girl kiss you, I went home really angry. I was angry at you and, sadly, I was angry at God for allowing me to be in love with someone I didn't think felt the same way about me."

"But Amy, you know…"

"I know that now, Jake, but I didn't know then. I only knew what I saw and from that I imagined up a whole jumbled mess. I was really angry. It wasn't until I spoke to Gloria and got your letter that I realized I might have been wrong."

"Things aren't always as they first appear," Jake mused.

"I get that now. I also learned that my faith is still pretty weak. I didn't realize until I got your letter that I hadn't prayed since the morning I left you on the church steps. My feelings of anger and frustration kept me from wanting to know God's direction for my life. But when I got your letter, I prayed. I didn't get an immediate answer, but I knew that if I was praying, God would make it turn out okay. And here we are. That's why I have so much faith in us."

"I'm really sorry, Amy."

"I know you are, Jake, and I am too. Things would have been a lot better if I'd just been more…I don't know, humble I guess. If I'd just swallowed some pride and tried to talk to you rather than trying to ignore you, we might have avoided the whole hospital thing."

Jake shook his head. "And if we would have avoided that, Amy, I'm pretty sure I'd still be trying to figure out how to get out of Niederbipp. I needed that experience to teach me, to help me figure out who I am. I needed to discover Isaac in the pages of his sketchbook. If it weren't for you, I might never have even opened it. All the understanding and wisdom might have been lost to me, closed in a book my pride wouldn't even allow me to open. If we'd never had that conversation on the church steps— if you hadn't told me then how you felt about me—I might have never…I probably would be counting down the days until my commitment here was over. Like Susan said, we're either humble or compelled to become humble. Amy, I never thought I'd be saying this, but thank you for walking away from me. It made me angry, but the result—the change that it inspired in me—has made it all worth it. If you hadn't helped me see the changes I needed to make, we wouldn't be having this conversation."

Amy looked deeply into his eyes as her own eyes began to swell with tears.

"Thank you for saving my life, Amy. And thank you for giving me the best reason I've ever had to live."

He wrapped his arms around her tightly and held her as she shook with emotion. "I love you," he whispered. "And I know you're right—somehow, everything is going to work out."

A WINDOW TO ETERNITY

INFANCY IS THE PERPETUAL MESSIAH,
WHICH COMES INTO THE ARMS OF
FALLEN MEN, AND PLEADS WITH THEM
TO RETURN TO PARADISE.
—RALPH WALDO EMERSON

"It's A Boy!" Kai burst into the waiting room. Jake and Amy were slouching on the vinyl sofa, half asleep in each other's arms. They jumped up quickly at Kai's announcement and fought to be the first to hug and congratulate the new father. Molly's father, Bob Braun, had been waiting on the other side of the room. He joined them in congratulating Kai and laughing at his boyish excitement.

"Seven pounds, five ounces! He looks like a big, red wrinkly raisin. I'm not sure if he looks like either of us yet, but he screams like Molly and he's got more hair than you, Dad."

Bob smiled, running his hand over his shiny scalp. "Congratulations, Kai. When can we see them?"

"Right now. He was born a half hour ago. Molly sent me to get you guys. The nurses got the mess all cleaned up and the baby's trying to figure out how to nurse. She wants you to come and meet Baby Zane."

"Baby Zane? Did you decide on a name then?" Amy asked.

"Yep," Kai said, flashing his signature goofy grin. "We're going to call him Zane Isaac. He looks like a Zane and if it weren't for Isaac, he never would have been. Come and see him."

They followed him swiftly down the tiled hallway. Sandy was briefing Dr. Wilkenson who had obviously just arrived, at least a half hour too late for the baby's debut performance. She looked up and winked at them, pulling the doctor out of the room to make space for the three visitors.

Amy rushed to Molly's side and pulled back the blanket that covered the baby's tiny orange face. Bob, Kai and Jake followed her, looking over her shoulder at the sleeping baby.

"He's so tiny," Amy said, touching his cheek with the top of her finger.

Jake stared at the baby, trying to pull the sleep from his own eyes. He had never seen such a fresh baby, so small and orange. Molly carefully passed the small bundle to Amy. As Bob moved in to hug his only daughter, Jake and Kai looked over Amy's shoulder.

"I think he looks like you, Kai," Amy said softly.

"Maybe like me with a sunburn," Kai said, laughing.

For his part, Jake was silent as he looked into the baby's small, round face. He was swaddled tightly in the hospital-issued flannel blanket, only his face protruding from the beneath the cloth. The rest of the room echoed with congratulatory words, but Jake was still, his attention focused entirely on the child in Amy's arms. It was the strangest thing he'd ever seen. Here, in a bundle no bigger than a shoebox, was a human soul—a small seed that would grow up reflecting the microscopic contributions his parents had given him. And yet beneath his skin, beneath even his genes, there was something else there—something amazing and incredible. Jake looked at the tiny bundle of life and saw… no he felt…the presence of a soul as tangible and vibrant as his own. While part of his mind contemplated the significance of this observation, another part wondered what he was feeling. Had he felt this before? It seemed somehow familiar, but he couldn't remember when or why. He thought hard, trying to understand exactly what his emotions were. It was as if the curtain that separated this life from the heavens had been pulled back and a portion of pure joy had come in through the window. The feeling was so intense, so profound that Jake found himself smiling uncontrollably.

"Are you ok, Jake?" Kai asked.

He looked up and nodded, but realized the others were looking at him too. "What's up?"

"You looked like you were crying," Kai said.

It was then he felt the dampness on his cheeks. The joy he had tasted in that moment was so real it left no room for sorrow, yet his cheeks were wet with his own tears. He turned and looked at Amy who smiled a knowing smile. She winked at him as he placed his hand softly on the baby's head. "This is an amazing child. I hope you know that. I hope you'll remember that."

Kai smiled and nodded, turning to look at Molly. "We know," he said softly.

Bob stood from the chair and the old grocer, in two easy steps, stood next to his grandson. Amy gently surrendered the baby to his grandfather and stepped away.

Bob's eyes too filled with tears. "I wish your mother was here, Molly. She'd be so proud of you…"

"I know, dad," Molly replied. "I miss her too."

"You felt it too, didn't you?" Amy asked as they stepped out into the night air.

Jake looked up into the dark sky illuminated with a million stars. "I did," he said, tears flooding his eyes again. "But I'm not sure what it was."

"I'm not sure either," Amy said. "But there was definitely something in that room."

"I thought it was the baby." Jake turned to look at her. "I've never spent much time around little kids and I've never been around a baby. It was the strangest thing to look at him and realize he's a human being, just a real teeny one. But…"

"But what?"

"There was something else there. Just as I was getting over how small he was, I had this feeling come over me that there's something inside of him that's bigger than the entire universe. I don't know…I can't really explain what I was feeling. It seems like I've always believed a part of every person is immortal, a part that lived before we were born and will continue to live after we die. I guess I've just never felt so strongly about that as I did tonight. Is that what you were feeling, too?"

"Yeah, but there was something else, too. I found myself thinking about Isaac and Lily and their son. There was obviously a deep connection between Isaac and his unborn son. Fifty years later he was still dedicating his sketchbooks to his family. As I felt that…whatever it was in the room, I found myself thinking that Isaac must have felt it too. At some point during the pregnancy, or maybe after their deaths, he had to have had some sense of that immortal somethingness. Otherwise, how would he have kept going? Why would his love for Lily and Jakob remain constant so long after they were gone?"

"Maybe that's what true love is," Jake mused.

"What do you mean?"

"Maybe true love is recognizing, knowing, and loving that part of a person that is immortal."

Amy took looked away to ponder Jake's answer. "That's pretty deep, Jake. I don't suppose you know how one can accomplish that."

Jake shook his head. "No, I don't think I do. After learning what we've learned about Isaac and his love for Lily, it seems the world would be a better place if every husband could share a love with his wife that was immortal…or at least know his wife and his children well enough to love that part of them that is immortal."

"That's a beautiful thought. Do you think that's the way it was for Isaac?"

"I don't know. But Molly, Kai and Bob seemed to have felt something tonight, too. I think we all witnessed a small piece of eternity, even though none of us knows what to call it, or even how to describe it. But it was there and it was real, as understandable as anything else. It was something so foreign…"

"And yet there was something so familiar about it," Amy said, finishing his sentence.

"Yeah."

"If we know what it feels like, it seems we ought to be able to recognize it if it happens again."

"So, do you just want to hang out in the maternity ward for a couple of weeks until we figure it out?"

Amy laughed. "I think they'd take us for baby snatchers and call the cops."

"So how are we going to learn more about…whatever that eternal something is?"

There was silence for a long moment as they walked slowly back to Amy's. "I think the answer to your question lies in your sketchbook, Jake."

"It does? Where?"

"I'm thinking about what you wrote down from one of the tiles we saw in the church. Wasn't there something about when we lack wisdom, we should ask God?"

"That's right! Come to think of it, there was another one that said something about knocking and asking if we want doors to be opened."

"I remember that too. Hmmm…"

"What?"

"Do you remember the translation of that German saying carved in the church façade?"

"I wrote it down so I wouldn't have to remember it. Do you?"

"Not exactly, but it was something about how loving and seeking for truth is wisdom."

"Oh yeah, that one. I just saw it yesterday in my sketchbook. I think it's the love of and seeking after truth is wisdom. Does that sound right?"

"Yeah, it does. It sounds pretty simple, but maybe that's the recipe, Jake—to love truth enough to seek it. Isn't that what Susan was trying to teach us—the difference between the oil of truth and its counterfeits?"

"It seems to all tie together, doesn't it? This reminds me of the night I finally decided to open Isaac's book. I felt like when the student is ready to learn, the teacher will appear."

"Well, maybe we've just received a lesson from Zane, the youngest teacher ever."

Jake nodded. They approached Amy's front steps, but didn't stop until they reached the front door. She wrapped her arms around his neck and started laughing.

"What?" Jake asked.

"I was just thinking how nice it will be someday, hopefully before we're thirty-seven, to not have to go to our separate homes. I'll just fall asleep talking to you and pick up in the morning where we left off."

"Yeah," Jake said, too exhausted to expound or pontificate. "For now, I'll take heart in your promise that you'll maybe marry me sometime in the next fifteen years."

㊵

THE CORONATION

YES, I HAVE DOUBTED. I HAVE WANDERED
OFF THE PATH. I HAVE BEEN LOST. BUT I
ALWAYS RETURNED. IT IS BEYOND THE
LOGIC I SEEK. IT IS INTUITIVE—
AN INTRINSIC, BUILT-IN SENSE OF
DIRECTION. I SEEM TO FIND MY WAY
HOME. MY FAITH HAS WAVERED BUT
HAS SAVED ME.

—HELEN HAYES

Aren't you a sight for tired eyes," Jake looked up from Sam's tiles. "Did you just get up?"

Amy stood in the open doorway, smiling. "No, I'm sorry. I should have called this morning, but I didn't want to wake you. I just got back from Warren where I met someone you know."

"Really?"

"Yeah, John Yoder, the Amish woodworker who made Kai and

Molly's cabinets. He said to say hi."

"He remembered me?"

"Yeah, you must have made some kind of an impression on him. He actually started crying when he talked about you."

"But why did you go up there?"

"Aunt Bev woke me up this morning and told me she was going up that way. Did you know John makes picture frames too?"

"No, I had no idea."

"Yeah, they're the prettiest frames I've ever seen, and the prices were really reasonable. When I told him I was going to be hanging my pictures in the Pottery, he asked if I knew you. Beverly went on and on about us like we were as good as married. I picked out fifteen frames that fit the canvases I already have and ordered a dozen more. When I went to pay, he gave me a huge discount. He said something about being indebted to Isaac and anyone who was working in his shop. Do you know anything about that?"

"Only what he told me when we picked up the cabinets. Something about his shop burning down and Isaac helping him rebuild it. I don't know any more than that, but that's great that you got some frames. Where are they?"

"There at Jerry and Bev's. I've been putting the canvases in the frames ever since we got home, but thought I'd come down and see how many would fit on the walls before I schlepped them all down here."

"I was just getting ready to take a break. Do you want a sandwich? I picked up some fresh bread this morning."

"I'd love a sandwich. Can I make them while you clean up?"

When Amy returned to the shop, she found Jake struggling to gift wrap a bowl for a well-dressed middle aged woman. She relieved Jake of the duty and took the liberty of starting over, producing something much more attractive. The woman seemed very pleased and tipped Amy $5 for her troubles. When she found out Amy was a painter and that her painting would be adorning the walls of the pottery that afternoon, she promised to return later to have the pick of the litter. Jake watched the interaction with interest. It was far more animated than his interaction with the woman had been, reminding him of Kai's commentary on female to female communication. He knew he was going to enjoy having Amy around the shop more.

They ate their sandwiches en route to the hospital to visit Molly and Baby Zane before their appointment with Thomas at the library. After scrubbing his hands, Jake held the sleeping Zane. His orange skin had morphed into a handsome shade of pink. The feelings Jake had had the night before returned, but to a lesser degree and he found himself yearning for the feelings he'd had before. As the girls talked he examined the boy's tiny fingers and finger nails, intrigued by the miniature human. Jake ran his hand over the boy's shiny brown hair, stopping at his little ear. Zane stretched and whimpered before settling back into a ball, sucking on his exposed wrist.

They left Molly alone, promising to be back after work. Jake was surprised to realize that he didn't want to leave. He wanted to stay there and watch the baby. When he thought of Kai, he considered how difficult it must have been that morning to leave his wife and new child to go to work. Though Jake didn't know the first thing about the grocery business, he considered the idea of taking Kai's place at work so he could be with his family. He talked to Amy about it as they walked to the library and she loved the idea, even offering to run the Pottery while Jake was out.

After an icy greeting from Roberta Mancini at the front desk, they found their way to the back room where Thomas had told them to meet him. Hanging from the door with yellowing scotch tape was a simple paper sign: Special Collections.

"I was just beginning to wonder if you forgot," Thomas said as he swung the door open and stood aside for them to enter. It was a small room, not bigger than twelve feet squared, but the old shelves lining the walls and running down the center of the room sagged under the capacity load of old books. The air was cool inside the room, but smelled like old leather and dust. A small desk in one corner held an old green glass library lamp. Piles of old books covered all but a small section of the desk's surface where the pages of an open book sat glowing in the light of the lamp.

"Welcome to my office," Thomas said, removing his clean, white gloves. He set the gloves on a shelf and reached outside the door for two metal folding chairs. "I don't often have visitors. I'm sorry this isn't a more comfortable space."

"No, it's fine," Jake said. "It's pretty much what I expected, just smaller."

Amy took a seat, but her eyes wandered over the shelves and books. "How many books do you have here, Father?"

"Over four thousand," Thomas said, removing the small reading glasses that had been perched on the end of his nose. "But this is the one I've been most looking forward to reading." He pointed to the book lying under the light. "I resigned myself to believe I'd never see Volume 31. Thank you for sharing it with me. It has been most enlightening."

"How far into it are you?" Amy asked.

"I just finished reading about Thanksgiving with the Ecksteins."

Amy smiled. "It's been good to come back to my roots, to discover where my people came from. I've learned more about my family in the past month than I've learned in the past 22 years combined. My dad rarely spoke of his family. I'm grateful for Bev. Without her, I probably wouldn't know much of anything about my roots."

Thomas nodded, taking a seat on the dark wooden chair at the desk. "This is an interesting town. If it weren't for the deep religious roots and the value those early settlers placed on tradition, it would probably be like the rest of America."

"In what way?" asked Jake.

"In almost every way. America is about progress, moving forward, overcoming the past and looking to the future."

"Isn't that good?" asked Jake.

"Yes and no. Unfortunately, when you throw out the past, you often throw away a lot of wisdom that has been gained from experience. America is an infant compared to most countries around the world. In Europe, Asia and especially Africa, you don't have to look very hard to find evidence of ancient peoples and their culture. For the most part, those evidences are revered and preserved. Museums are built up around them and people pride themselves on being descendents of this king or that duke."

Jake shifted in his chair, thinking about the ancient culture in Greece. But his thoughts were different now. He imagined walking along the beautiful shore with Amy's hand in his. His thoughts were interrupted by Thomas' words.

"America, at least as far as the white man goes, has a very shallow history. Its earliest settlements, those of Jamestown and Plymouth are scarcely more than 400 years old. Throughout Europe and Asia, there are cities and villages, even inns that are thousands of years old. The past is preserved, offering a link between the modern day and the ancient. In cities like Jerusalem, you can see structures that Jesus and his disciples walked past two thousand years ago. There is history, and with that history comes the potential for understanding."

"But doesn't it also bring the potential of getting stuck in a rut that you can never get out of?" Amy asked.

"Indeed. It sounds like you've been to Europe."

They both nodded.

"You make a good point. Tradition can be both a blessing and a curse. I'm sure you've noticed how important it is for many Europeans to keep things consistent. I remember a trip I made to my ancestral village in Ireland. I watched as several homes were being built on the hillside overlooking the town. Instead of choosing a building design that was new, they were simply building a newer version of every other home in the village. When they were finished, it was nearly impossible to distinguish the new gray homes from the old gray homes."